NOUMENA  CLAS
THE HUMAN COMED
A Start in Life and Ot
by Honoré de B

A Start in Life

On a coach ride between towns, a callow young man gets caught up in a round of tale-telling with his fellow passengers and ends up committing an indiscretion that will take a lifetime to undo . . .

Albert Savarus

In the town of Besançon, a cloistered young girl reads a romance penned by a mysterious newcomer and schemes to take the place of the story's real-life inspiration: a beautiful Italian duchess . . .

The Vendetta

Two lovers stand in defiance of the age-old feud that has decimated their families: a *vendetta* that even Napoléon Bonaparte himself may be powerless to stop . . .

Beginning again in life, whether in one's profession, or, to a lesser extent, for the purpose of concealing one's identity, is the theme that unifies the three stories in this volume of *The Human Comedy*.

Left unfinished at the time of Balzac's death, *La Comédie Humaine* is a vast literary undertaking composed of nearly one hundred short stories, novellas, and novels set in the shadow of the Napoleonic Wars during the Bourbon Restoration and the July Monarchy. Throughout, Balzac utilizes nineteenth century French society to examine humanity and the human experience with all its attendant virtues, vices, and peculiarities.

Honoré de Balzac (1799-1850) was one of France's most prolific and influential authors. In his lifetime, he worked as a legal clerk, publisher, printer, businessman, and even ran for political office. Failing in all these endeavors, he was nonetheless able to make use of these experiences in his writing to create some of the most memorable stories and characters in French literature.

de Balzac

THE HUMAN COMEDY, VOL. III:
A Start in Life and Other Works
by Honoré de Balzac

Translated from the French by Clara Bell
with Illustrations by Bertall, Eugène Lampsonius,
Alcide-Joseph Lorentz, & Others

Noumena Press
Whately, Massachusetts
www.noumenapress.com

Noumena Classics are published by Noumena Press
Cover design, front matter, textual revisions, appendix I, and
endnotes © 2012 Noumena Press. All rights reserved.
www.noumenapress.com

Version 1.0

ISBN-13   978-0-9767062-4-3 (paperback)
LCCN   2008943784

Printed on acid-free paper

Text: edited and annotated by R.J. Allinson, BA, MLIS
Cover: detail of *Oscar Husson* by Alcide-Joseph Lorentz
Cover design & interior layout: Rachel Thern

Noumena Press makes every effort to publish books of
the highest possible quality. Please help us to improve our
editions by reporting any errors, omissions, or other problems
to editor@noumenapress.com.

Table of Contents

The Human Comedy
Studies of Manners
Scenes From Private Life

Addenda that follow each story provide cross-references to character appearances in other works of *The Human Comedy*.

Appendices

List of Plates

A Start in Life
(*Un début dans la vie*)
February 1842

To Laure
To whose bright and modest wit I owe the idea of this Scene.
Hers be the honour!

Her brother,
De Balzac

PIERROBIN.

...... Pendant l'exercice de ses fonctions il portait une
blouse bleue, etc., etc.

UN DÉBUT DANS LA VIE.

Plate I

Railroads, in a future now not far distant, must lead to the disappearance of certain industries and modify others, especially such as are concerned in the various modes of transport commonly used in the neighbourhood of Paris. In fact, the persons and the things which form the accessories of this little Scene will ere long give it the dignity of an archaeological study. Will not our grandchildren be glad to know something of a time which they will speak of as the old days? For instance, the picturesque vehicles known as *coucous* which used to stand on the Place de la Concorde and crowd the Cours-la-Reine,* which flourished so greatly during one century, and still survived in 1830, exist no more. Even on the occasion of the most attractive rural festivity, hardly one is to be seen on the road in this year 1842. In 1820 not all the places famous for their situation, and designated as the Environs of Paris, had any regular service of coaches. The Touchards, father and son, had however a monopoly of conveyances to and from the largest towns within a radius of fifteen leagues, and their establishment occupied splendid premises in the Rue du Faubourg Saint-Denis.* In spite of their old standing and their strenuous efforts, in spite of their large capital and all the advantages of strong centralisation, Touchards' service had formidable rivals in the *coucous* of the Faubourg Saint-Denis for distances of seven or eight leagues out of Paris. The Parisian has indeed such a passion for the country, that local establishments also held their own in many cases against the Petites Messageries, a name given to Touchards' short distance coaches, to distinguish them from the Grandes Messageries, the general conveyance company, in the Rue Montmartre. At that time the success of the Touchards stimulated speculation; conveyances were put on the road to and from the smallest towns—handsome, quick, and commodious vehicles, starting and returning at fixed hours, and these, in a circuit of ten leagues or so, gave rise to vehement competition. Beaten on the longer distances, the *coucou* fell back on short runs, and survived a few years longer. It finally succumbed when the omnibus had proved the possibility of packing eighteen persons into a vehicle drawn by two horses. Nowadays the *coucou*, if a bird of such heavy flight is by chance still to be found in the recesses of some store for dilapidated vehicles, would, from its structure and arrangement, be the subject of learned investigations, like Cuvier's researches on the animals discovered in the lime quarries of Montmartre.*

These smaller companies, being threatened by larger speculations competing, after 1822, with the Touchards, had nevertheless a fulcrum of support in the sympathies of the residents in the places they plied to. The master of the concern, who was both owner and driver of the vehicle, was usually an innkeeper of the district, to whom its inhabitants were as familiar as were their common objects and interests. He was intelligent in fulfilling commissions; he asked less for his little services, and therefore obtained more, than the employees of the Touchards. He was clever at evading the necessity for an excise pass. At a pinch he would infringe the rules as to the number of passengers he might carry. In fact, he was master of the affections of the people. Hence, when a rival appeared in the field, if the old established conveyance ran on alternate days of the week, there were persons who would postpone their journey to take it in the company of the original driver, even though his vehicle and horses were none of the safest and best.

One of the lines which the Touchards, father and son, tried hard to monopolise, but which was hotly disputed—nay, which is still a subject of dispute with their successors the Toulouses—was that between Paris and Beaumont-sur-Oise,* a highly profitable district, since in 1822 three lines of conveyances worked it at once. The Touchards lowered their prices, but in vain, and in vain increased the number of services; in vain they put superior vehicles on the road, the competitors held their own, so profitable is a line running through little towns like Saint-Denis and Saint-Brice, and such a string of villages as Pierrefitte, Groslay, Écouen, Poncelles, Moisselles, Baillet, Montsoult, Maffliers, Franconville, Presles, Nointel, Nerville, and others. The Touchards at last extended their line of service as far as to Chambly;* the rivals ran to Chambly. And at the present day the Toulouses go as far as Beauvais.

On this road, the high road to England, there is a place which is not ill-named La Cave,* a hollow way leading down into one of the most delightful nooks of the Oise valley, and to the little town of L'Isle-Adam, doubly famous as the native place of the now extinct family de L'Isle-Adam, and as the splendid residence of the Princes of Bourbon-Conti.* L'Isle-Adam is a charming little town, flanked by two large hamlets, that of Nogent and that of Parmain,* both remarkable for the immense quarries which have furnished the materials for the finest edifices of Paris, and indeed abroad too, for the base and capitals of the theatre at Brussels are of Nogent stone. Though remarkable for its beautiful points of view, and for famous châteaux built by princes, abbots, or famous architects, as at Cassan, Stors, Le Val, Nointel, Persan,* etc., this district, in 1822, had as yet escaped competition, and was served by two coach owners, who agreed to work it between them. This exceptional state of things was based on causes easily explained. From La Cave, where, on the high road, begins the fine paved way due to the magnificence of the Princes of Conti, to L'Isle-Adam, is a distance of two leagues: no main line coach could diverge so far from the high road, especially as L'Isle-Adam was at that time the end of things in that direction. The road led thither, and ended there. Of late, a high road joins the valley of Montmorency to that of L'Isle-Adam. Leaving Saint-Denis, it passes through Saint-Leu-Taverny,* Méru, L'Isle-Adam, and along by the Oise as far as Beaumont. But in 1822 the only road to L'Isle-Adam was that made by the Princes de Conti. Consequently Pierrotin and his colleague reigned supreme from Paris to L'Isle-Adam, beloved of all the district. Pierrotin's coach and his friend's ran by Stors, Le Val, Parmain, Champagne, Mours, Prérolles,* Nogent, Nerville, and Maffliers. Pierrotin was so well known that the residents at Montsoult, Moisselles, Baillet, and Saint-Brice, though living on the high road, made use of his coach, in which there was more often a chance of a seat than in the Beaumont *diligence,* which was always full. Pierrotin and his friendly rival agreed to admiration. When Pierrotin started from L'Isle-Adam, the other set out from Paris, and vice versa. Of the opposition driver, nothing need be said. Pierrotin was the favourite in the line. And of the two, he alone appears on the scene in this veracious history. So it will suffice to say that the two coach drivers lived on excellent terms, competing in honest warfare, and contending for customers without sharp practice. In Paris, out of economy, they put up at the same inn, using the same yard, the same stable, the same coach shed, the same office, the same booking clerk. And this fact is enough to show that Pierrotin and his opponent were, as the common folks say, of *a very good sort.*

That inn, at the corner of the Rue d'Enghien, exists to this day and is called the Lion-d'Argent.* The proprietor of this hostelry—a hostelry from time immemorial for coach drivers—himself managed a line of vehicles to Dammartin on so sound a basis that his neighbours the Touchards, of the *Petites Messageries* opposite, never thought of starting a conveyance on that road.

Though the coaches for L'Isle-Adam were supposed to set out punctually, Pierrotin and his friend displayed a degree of indulgence on this point which, while it won them the affections of the natives, brought down severe remonstrances from strangers who were accustomed to the exactitude of the larger public companies; but the two drivers of these vehicles, half *diligence* half *coucou*, always found partisans among their regular customers. In the afternoon the start fixed for four o'clock always dragged on till half-past, and in the morning, though eight was the hour named, the coach never got off before nine. This system was, however, very elastic. In summer, the golden season for coaches, the time of departure, rigorously punctual as concerned strangers, gave way for natives of the district. This method afforded Pierrotin the chance of pocketing the price of two places for one when a resident in the town came early to secure a place already booked by a *bird of passage*, who, by ill luck, was behind time. Such elastic rules would certainly not be approved by a puritan moralist, but Pierrotin and his colleague justified it by the *hard times*, by their losses during the winter season, by the necessity they would presently be under of purchasing better carriages, and finally, by an exact application of the rules printed on their tickets, copies of which were of the greatest rarity, and never given but to those travellers who were so perverse as to insist.

Pierrotin, a man of forty, was already the father of a family. He had left the cavalry in 1815 when the army was disbanded, and then this very good fellow had succeeded his father, who drove a *coucou* between L'Isle-Adam and Paris on somewhat erratic principles. After marrying the daughter of a small innkeeper, he extended and regulated the business, and was noted for his intelligence and military punctuality. Brisk and decisive, Pierrotin (a nickname, no doubt) had a mobile countenance which gave an amusing expression and a semblance of intelligence to a face reddened by exposure to the weather. Nor did he lack the "gift of the gab," which is caught by intercourse with the world, and by seeing different parts of it. His voice, by dint of talking to his horses, and shouting to others to get out of the way, was somewhat harsh, but he could soften it to a customer. His costume, that of coach drivers of the superior class, consisted of stout, strong boots, heavy with nails, and made at L'Isle-Adam; trousers of bottle green velveteen; and a jacket of the same, over which, in the exercise of his functions, he wore a blue blouse, embroidered in colours on the collar, shoulder pieces, and wristbands. On his head was a cap with a peak. His experience of military service had stamped on Pierrotin the greatest respect for social superiority, and a habit of obedience to people of the upper ranks; but while he was ready to be on familiar terms with the modest citizen, he was always respectful to women, of whatever class. At the same time, the habit of *carting folks about*, to use his own expression, had led him to regard his travellers as parcels, though, being on feet, they demanded less care than the other merchandise, which was the aim and end of the service.

Alerted to the general trend, which since the peace had begun to tell on his business, Pierrotin was determined not to be beaten by the progress of the world. Ever since the last summer season he had talked a great deal of a certain large conveyance he had ordered of Farry, Breilmann and Co., the best diligence builders, as being needed by the constant increase of travellers. Pierrotin's equipment at that time consisted of two vehicles. One, which did duty for the winter, and the only one he ever showed to the tax collector, was of the *coucou* species. The bulging sides of this vehicle allowed it to carry six passengers on two seats as hard as iron, though covered with yellow worsted velvet. These seats were divided by a wooden bar, which could be removed at pleasure or refixed in two grooves in the sides, at the height of a man's back. This bar, perfidiously covered by Pierrotin with yellow velvet, and called by him a back to the seat, was the cause of much despair to the travellers from the difficulty of moving and readjusting it. If the board was painful to fix, it was far more so to the shoulder blades when it was fitted; on the other hand, if it was not unshipped, it made entrance and egress equally perilous, especially to women. Though each seat of this vehicle, which bulged at the sides like a woman before childbirth, was licensed to hold no more than three passengers, it was not unusual to see eight packed in it like herrings in a barrel. Pierrotin declared that they were all the more comfortable, since they formed a compact and immovable mass, whereas three were constantly thrown against each other, and often ran the risk of spoiling their hats against the roof of the vehicle by reason of the violent jolting on the road. In front of the body of this carriage there was a wooden box seat, Pierrotin's driving seat, which could also carry three passengers, who were designated, as all the world knows, as *lapins*.* Occasionally, Pierrotin would accommodate four *lapins* and then sat askew on a sort of box below the front seat for the *lapins* to rest their feet on; this was filled with straw or such parcels as could not be injured. The body of the vehicle, painted yellow, was ornamented by a band of bright blue on which might be read in white letters, on each side, *L'Isle-Adam—Paris*, and on the back, *Service de L'Isle-Adam*. Our descendants will be under a mistake if they imagine that this conveyance could carry no more than thirteen persons, including Pierrotin. On great occasions three more could be seated in a square compartment covered with tarpaulin in which trunks, boxes, and parcels were generally piled, but Pierrotin was too prudent to let any but regular customers sit there, and only took them up three or four hundred yards outside the barrier. These passengers in the *poulailler*,* the name given by the conductors to this part of a coach, were required to get out before reaching any village on the road where there was a station of gendarmerie, for the overloading, forbidden by the regulations *for the greater safety of travellers*, was in these cases so excessive that the gendarme—always Pierrotin's very good friend—could not have excused himself from reporting such a flagrant breach of rules. But thus Pierrotin's vehicle, on certain Saturday evenings and Monday mornings, carted out fifteen passengers, and then to help pull it, he gave his large but aged horse, named Rougeot, the assistance of a second nag about as big as a pony, which he could never sufficiently praise. This little steed was a mare called Bichette, and she ate little, she was full of spirit, nothing could tire her, she was worth her weight in gold! "My wife would not exchange her for that great lazy beast Rougeot!" Pierrotin would exclaim, when a traveller laughed at him about this concentrated *extract of horse*.

The difference between this carriage and the other was that the second had four wheels. This vehicle, a remarkable structure always spoken of as *the four-wheeled coach*, could hold seventeen passengers, being intended to carry fourteen. It rattled so preposterously that the folks in L'Isle-Adam would say, "Here comes Pierrotin!" when he had but just come out of the wood that hangs on the slope to the valley. It was divided into two lobes, one of which, called the *intérieur*, the body of the coach, carried six passengers on two seats, and the other, a sort of cab stuck on in front, was styled the coupé. This coupé could be closed by an inconvenient and eccentric arrangement of glass windows which would take too long to describe in this place. The four-wheeled coach also had at top a sort of gig with a hood into which Pierrotin packed six travellers; it closed with leather curtains. Pierrotin himself had an almost invisible perch below the glass windows of the coupé.

The coach to L'Isle-Adam only paid the taxes levied on public vehicles, for the *coucou* represented to carry six travellers, and whenever Pierrotin turned out the four-wheeled coach he took out a special license. This may seem strange indeed in these days, but at first the tax on vehicles, imposed somewhat timidly, allowed the owners of coaches to play these little tricks, which gave them the pleasure of *putting their thumbs to their noses* behind the collector's back, as they phrased it. By degrees, however, the hungry tax office grew strict: it allowed no vehicle to take the road without displaying the two plates which now certify that their capacity is registered and the tax paid. Everything, even a tax, has its age of innocence, and towards the end of 1822 that age was not yet over. Very often, in summer, the four-wheeled coach and the covered chaise made the journey in company, carrying in all thirty passengers, while Pierrotin paid only for six. On these golden days the convoy started from the Faubourg Saint-Denis at half-past four and arrived in style at L'Isle-Adam by ten o'clock at night. And then Pierrotin, proud of his run, which necessitated the hire of extra horses, would say, "We have made a good pace today!" To enable him to do nine leagues in five hours with this machinery, he did not stop, as the coaches usually do on this road, at Saint-Brice, Moisselles, and La Cave.

The Lion-d'Argent occupied a plot of ground running very far back. Though the front to the Rue Saint-Denis* has no more than three or four windows, there was at that time, on one side of the long yard with the stables at the bottom, a large house backing on the wall of the adjoining property. The entrance was through an arched way under the first floor, and there was standing room here for two or three coaches. In 1822, the booking office

11

for all the lines that put up at the Lion-d'Argent was kept by the innkeeper's wife who had a book for each line; she took the money, wrote down the names, and good-naturedly accommodated passengers' luggage in her vast kitchen. The travellers were quite satisfied with this patriarchally free-and-easy mode of business. If they came too early, they sat down by the fire within the immense chimney place, or lounged in the passage, or went to the Café de l'Échiquier at the corner of the street of that name,* parallel to the Rue d'Enghien, from which it is divided by only a few houses.

Quite early in the autumn of that year, one Saturday morning, Pierrotin, his hands stuffed through holes in his blouse and into his pockets, was standing at the front gate of the Lion-d'Argent whence he had a perspective view of the inn kitchen, and beyond it of the long yard and the stables at the end, like black caverns. The Dammartin diligence had just started, and was lumbering after Touchard's coaches. It was past eight o'clock. Under the wide archway, over which was inscribed on a long board, Hôtel du Lion-d'Argent, the stablemen and coach porters were watching the vehicles start at the brisk pace which deludes the traveller into the belief that the horses will continue to keep it up.

"Shall I bring out the horses, Master?" said Pierrotin's stableboy when there was nothing more to be seen.

"A quarter past eight and I see no passengers," said Pierrotin. "What the deuce is become of them? Put the horses to, all the same. No parcels neither. Bless us and save us! This afternoon, now, *he* won't know how to stow his passengers, as it is so fine, and I have only four booked. There's a pretty lookout for a Saturday! That's always the way when you're wanting for money! It's dog's work and work for a dog!"

"And if you had any, where would you stow 'em? You have nothing but your two-wheel cab," said the luggage porter, trying to smooth down Pierrotin.

"And what about my new coach?"

"Then there is such a thing as your new coach?" asked the sturdy Auvergnat,* grinning and showing his front teeth, as white and as broad as almonds.

"You old good-for-nothing! Why, she will take the road tomorrow, Sunday, and we want eighteen passengers to fill her!"

"Oh, ho! A fine turn-out; that'll make the folks stare!" said the Auvergnat.

"A coach like the one that runs to Beaumont, I can tell you! Brand new, painted in red and gold, enough to make the Touchards burst with envy! It will take three horses. I have found a fellow to Rougeot, and Bichette will trot unicorn like a good 'un. Come, harness up," said Pierrotin, who was looking towards the Porte Saint-Denis* while cramming his short pipe with tobacco, "I see a lady out there, and a little man with bundles under his arm. They are looking for the Lion-d'Argent for they would have nothing to say to the *coucous* on the stand. Aha! I seem to know the lady for a customer."

"You often get home filled up after starting empty," said his man.

"But no parcels!" replied Pierrotin. "By the Mass! What devil's luck!"

And Pierrotin sat down on one of the enormous curb-stones which protected the base of the walls from being bumped by the axles, but he wore an anxious and thoughtful look that was not usual with him. This dialogue, apparently so trivial, had stirred up serious anxieties at the bottom of Pierrotin's heart. And what could trouble Pierrotin's heart but the thought of a handsome coach? To cut a dash on the road, to rival the Touchards, extend his service, carry passengers who might congratulate him on the increased convenience due to the improvements in coach building instead of hearing constant complaints of his drags: this was Pierrotin's laudable ambition. Now the worthy man, carried away by his desire to triumph over his colleague, and to induce him some day perhaps to leave him without a competitor on the road to L'Isle-Adam, had overstrained his resources. He had ordered his coach from Farry, Breilmann, and Co., the makers who had lately introduced English coach springs in the place of the swan's neck and other old-fashioned French springs, but these hardhearted and mistrustful makers would only deliver the vehicle for ready cash. Not caring, indeed, to build a conveyance so unsaleable if it were left on their hands, these shrewd tradesmen had not undertaken the job till Pierrotin had paid them two thousand francs on account. To satisfy their justifiable requirements, Pierrotin had exhausted his savings and his credit. He had bled his wife, his father-in-law, and his friends. He had been to look at the superb vehicle the day before in the painter's shop; it was ready, and waiting to take the road, but in order to see it there on the following day he must pay up. Hence Pierrotin was in need of a thousand francs! Being in debt to the innkeeper for stable room, he dared not borrow the sum from him. For lack of this thousand francs, he risked losing the two thousand already paid in advance, to say nothing of five hundred, the cost of Rougeot the second, and three hundred for new harness, for which, however, he had three months' credit. And yet, urged by the wrath of despair and the folly of vanity, he had just declared that his coach would start on the morrow, Sunday. In paying the fifteen hundred francs on account of the two thousand five hundred, he had hoped that the coachmakers' feelings might be touched so far that they would let him have the vehicle, but, after three minutes' reflection, he exclaimed—"No, no! They are sharks, perfect skinflints. Supposing I were to apply to Monsieur Moreau, the steward at Presles—he is such a good fellow, that he would, perhaps, take my note of hand at six months' date," thought he, struck by a new idea.

At that moment, a servant out of livery carrying a leather trunk, coming across from the Touchards' office where he had failed to find a place vacant on the Chambly coach starting at one o'clock, said to the driver—"Pierrotin? Is that you?"

"What then?" said Pierrotin.

"If you can wait less than a quarter of an hour, you can carry my master; if not, I will take his portmanteau back again, and he must make the best of a chaise off the stand."

"I will wait two—three quarters of an hour, and five minutes more to that, my lad," said Pierrotin, with a glance at the smart little leather trunk, neatly strapped, and fastened with a brass lock engraved with a coat of arms.

"Very good, then, there you are," said the man, relieving his shoulder of the trunk, which Pierrotin lifted, weighed in his hand, and scrutinised.

"Here," said he to his stableboy, "pack it round with soft hay and put it in the boot at the back. There is no name on it," said he.

"It has Monseigneur's arms on it," replied the servant.

"Monseigneur? Worth his weight in gold! Come and have a short drink," said Pierrotin, with a wink, as he led the way to the Café de l'Échiquier. "Two of absinthe," cried he to the waiter as they went in. "But who is your master, and where is he bound? I never saw you before," said Pierrotin to the servant as they clinked glasses.

"And for very good reasons," replied the footman. "My master does not go your way but once a year, and always in his own carriage. He prefers the road by the Orge valley* where he has the finest park near Paris, a perfect Versailles, a family estate, from which he takes his name. Don't you know Monsieur Moreau?"

"The steward at Presles?" said Pierrotin.

"Well, Monsieur le Comte is going to spend two days at Presles."

"Oh, ho, then my passenger is the Comte de Sérisy!" cried Pierrotin.

"Yes, my man, no less. But, mind, he sends strict orders. If you have any of the people belonging to your parts in your chaise, do not mention the Comte's name; he wants to travel *incognito* and desired me to tell you so, and promise you a handsome tip."

"Hah! And has this hide-and-seek journey anything to do, by any chance, with the bargain that old Léger, the farmer at Les Moulineaux, wants to make?"

"I don't know," replied the man, "but the fat is in the fire. Last evening I was sent to the stables to order the chaise *à la Daumont* by seven this morning to drive to Presles, but at seven my master countermanded it. Augustin, his valet, ascribes this change of plan to the visit of a lady who seemed to have come from the country."

"Can anyone have had anything to say against Monsieur Moreau? The best of men, the most honest, the king of men, I say! He could have made far more money than he did had he wanted to, take my word for it!"

"Then he was very foolish," said the servant tersely.

"Then Monsieur de Sérisy is going to live at Presles at last? The château has been refurnished and done up," said Pierrotin after a pause. "Is it true that two hundred thousand francs have been spent on it already?"

"If you or I had the money that has been spent there, we could set up in the world. If Madame la Comtesse goes down there, the Moreaus' fun *will* be over," added the man, with mysterious significance.

"A good man is Monsieur Moreau," repeated Pierrotin, who was still thinking of borrowing the thousand francs from the steward, "a man that makes his men work and does not spare them, who gets all the profit out of the land, and for his master's benefit too. A good man! He often comes to Paris, and always by my coach; he gives me something handsome for myself, and always has a lot of parcels to and fro. Three or four a day, some-times for Monsieur and sometimes for Madame, a bill of fifty francs a month say, only on the carrier's score. Though Madame holds her head *a little above her place*, she is fond of her children; I take them to school for her and bring them home again. Each time she gives me five francs, and your biggest pot would not do more. And whenever I have anyone from them or to them, I always drive right up to the gates of the house—I could not do less, now, could I?"

"They say that Monsieur Moreau had no more than a thousand écus in the world when Monsieur le Comte put him in as land steward at Presles," said the servant.

"But in seventeen years' time—since 1806—the man must have made something," replied Pierrotin.

"To be sure," said the servant, shaking his head. "And masters are queer too. I hope, for Moreau's sake, that he has feathered his nest."

"I often deliver hampers at your house in the Chaussée-d'Antin,"* said Pierrotin, "but I have never had the privilege of seeing either the master or his lady."

"Monsieur le Comte is a very good sort," said the man confidentially, "but if he wants you to hold your tongue about his *cognito*, there must be trouble; at least, that is what we think at home. For why else should he coun-terorder the travelling carriage? Why ride in a public chaise? A Peer of France* might take a hired chaise, you would think."

"A hired chaise might cost him as much as forty francs for the double journey, for, I can tell, if you don't know our road, it is fit for squirrels to climb. Everlastingly up and down!" said Pierrotin. "Peer of France or trades-man, *everybody looks at both sides of a five franc piece*. If this trip means mischief to Monsieur Moreau—dear, dear, I should be vexed indeed if any harm came to him. By the Mass! Can no way be found of warning him? For he is a real good 'un, an honest sort, the king of men, I say——"

"Bah! Monsieur le Comte is much attached to Monsieur Moreau," said the other. "But if you will take a bit of good advice from me, mind your own business and let him mind his. We all have quite enough to do to take care of ourselves. You just do what you are asked to do; all the more because it does not pay to play fast and loose with Monseigneur. Add to that, the Comte is generous. If you oblige him that much," said the man, measuring off the nail of one finger, "he will reward you that much," and he stretched out his arm.

This judicious hint, and yet more the illustrative figure, coming from a man so high in office as the Comte de Sérisy's second footman, had the effect of cooling Pierrotin's zeal for the steward of Presles.

"Well, good day, Monsieur Pierrotin," said the man.

A short sketch of the previous history of the Comte de Sérisy and his steward is here necessary to explain the little drama about to be played in Pierrotin's coach.

Monsieur Hugret de Sérisy is descended in a direct line from the famous President Hugret, ennobled by Francis I. They bear as arms *party per pale or and sable, an orle and two lozenges counterchanged*. Motto, I, SEMPER MELIUS ERIS,* which, like the two winders assumed as supporters, shows the modest pretence of the citizen class at a time when each rank of society had its own place in the State, and also the artlessness of the age in the punning motto, where ERIS with the I at the beginning, and the final S of *Melius*, represent the name (*Sérisy*) of the estate, whence the title. The present Comte's father was a Premier President of Parlement before the Revolution. He himself, already Councillor of State in the Grand Council in 1787* at the age of twenty-two, had been noted for his careful handling of sensitive matters. He did not emigrate during the Revolution, but remained on his lands of Sérisy, near Arpajon,*

where the respect felt for his father protected him from
molestation. After spending a few years nursing the
old President, whom he lost in 1794, he was elected to
the Council of Five Hundred, and took up his legislative functions as a distraction from his grief. After the
eighteenth Brumaire,* Monsieur de Sérisy became the
object—as did all the families connected with the old
parlements—of the First Consul's attentions, and by him
he was appointed to the Council of State to reorganise
one of the most disorganised branches of the administration. Thus this scion of a great historical family became
one of the most important wheels in the vast and admirable machinery due to Napoléon. The Councillor of
State ere long left his department to be made a minister. The Emperor created him count and senator, and
he was proconsul to two different kingdoms in succession. In 1806, at the age of forty, he married the sister
of the ci-devant Marquis de Ronquerolles, and widow,
at the age of twenty, of Gaubert, one of the most distinguished of the Republican generals, who left her all his
wealth. This match, suitable in point of rank, doubled
the Comte de Sérisy's already considerable fortune; he
was now the brother-in-law of the ci-devant Marquis de
Rouvre, whom Napoléon created count and appointed
to be his chamberlain. In 1814, worn out with incessant
work, Monsieur de Sérisy, whose broken health needed rest, gave up all his appointments, left the district of
which Napoléon had made him governor, and came to
Paris where the Emperor was compelled by ocular evidence to concede his claims. This indefatigable master,
who could not believe in fatigue in other people, had at
first supposed the necessity that prompted the Comte de
Sérisy to be simple defection. Though the Senator was
not in disgrace, it was said that he had cause for complaint of Napoléon. Consequently, when the Bourbons
came back,* Louis XVIII, whom Monsieur de Sérisy acknowledged as his legitimate sovereign, entrusted the

Senator, now a Peer of France, with the management of his private affairs, and made him a Minister of State. On the 20th of March, Monsieur de Sérisy did not follow the King to Ghent; he made it known to Napoléon that he remained faithful to the House of Bourbon and accepted no peerage during the Hundred Days, but spent that brief reign on his estate of Sérisy. After the Emperor's second fall,* the Comte naturally resumed his seat in the Privy Council, was named Vice President of the Council of State,* and liquidator on behalf of France in the settlement of the indemnities demanded by foreign powers. He had no love of personal magnificence, no ambition even, but exerted great influence in public affairs. No important political step was ever taken without his being consulted, but he never went to court and was seldom seen in his own drawing room. His noble life, devoted to work from the first, ended by being perpetual work and nothing else. The Comte rose at four in the morning in all seasons, worked till midday, then took up his duties as a peer or as Vice President of the Council of State, and went to bed at nine. Monsieur de Sérisy had long worn the Grand Cross of the Legion of Honour; he also had the Orders of the Golden Fleece, of Saint Andrew of Russia, of the Prussian Eagle;* in short, almost every order of the European courts. No one was less conspicuous or more valuable than he in the world of politics. As may be supposed, to a man of his temper the flourish of court favour and worldly success were a matter of indifference. But no man, unless he is a priest, can live such a life without some strong motive, and his mysterious conduct had its key—a cruel one. The Comte had loved his wife before he married her, and in him this passion had withstood all the domestic discomforts of matrimony with a widow who remained mistress of herself, after as well as before her second marriage, and who took all the more advantage of her liberty because Monsieur de Sérisy indulged her as a mother indulges a spoilt child. Incessant work served him as a shield against his heartfelt woes, buried with the care that a man engaged in politics takes to hide such secrets. And he fully understood how ridiculous jealousy would be in the eyes of the world, which would certainly never have admitted the possibility of conjugal passion in a timeworn official. How was it that his wife had thus bewitched him from the first days of marriage? Why had he suffered in those early days without taking his revenge? Why did he no longer dare to be revenged? And why, deluded by hope, had he allowed time to slip away? By what means had his young, pretty, clever wife reduced him to subjection? The answer to these questions would require a long story, out of place in this Scene, and women, if not men, may be able to guess it. At the same time, it may be observed that the Comte's incessant work and many sorrows had unfortunately done much to deprive him of the advantages indispensable to a man who has to compete with unfavourable comparisons. The saddest perhaps of all the Comte's secrets was the fact that his wife's repulsion was partly justified by ailments which he owed entirely to overwork. Kind, nay, more than kind to his wife, he made her mistress in her own house; she received all Paris, she went into the country, or she came back again, precisely as though she were still a widow; he took care of her money and supplied her luxuries as if he had been her agent. The Comtesse held her husband in the highest esteem, indeed, she liked his turn of wit. Her approbation could give him pleasure, and thus she could do what she liked with the poor man by sitting and chatting with him for an hour. Like the great nobles of former days, the Comte so effectually protected his wife that he would have regarded any slur cast on her reputation as an unpardonable insult to himself. The world greatly admired his character, and Madame de Sérisy owed much to her husband. Any other woman, even though she belonged to so distinguished a family as that of Ronquerolles, might have found herself disgraced forever. The Comtesse was very ungrateful—but charming in her ingratitude. And from time to time she would pour balm on the Comte's wounds.

We must now explain the cause of the minister's hurried journey and wish to remain unknown.

A rich farmer of Beaumont-sur-Oise, named Léger, held a farm of which the various portions were all fractions of the estate owned by the Comte, thus impairing the splendid property of Presles. The farmlands belonged to a townsman of Beaumont-sur-Oise, one Margueron. The lease he had granted to Léger in 1799, at a time when the advance since made in agriculture could not be foreseen, was nearly run out, and the owner had refused Léger's terms for renewing it. Long since, Monsieur de Sérisy, wanting to be quit of the worry and squabbling that come of such enclosed plots, had hoped to be able to buy the farm, having heard that Monsieur Margueron's sole ambition was to see his only son, a modest official, promoted to be collector of the revenue at Senlis. Moreau had hinted to his master that he had a dangerous rival in the person of old Léger. The farmer, knowing that he could run up the land to a high price by selling it piecemeal to the Comte, was capable of paying a sum so high as to outbid the profit derivable from the collectorship to be bestowed on the younger Margueron. Two days since, the Comte, who wanted to have done with the matter, had sent for his notary Alexandre Crottat and Derville his soliciter to inquire into the state of the affair. Though Crottat and Derville cast doubts on the steward's zeal—and, indeed, it was a puzzling letter from him that gave rise to this consultation—the Comte defended Moreau who had, he said, served him faithfully for seventeen years. "Well," Derville replied, "I can only advise your Lordship to go in person to Presles and ask this Margueron to dinner.

Crottat will send down his head clerk with a form of sale ready drawn out, leaving blank pages or lines for the insertion of descriptions of the plots and the necessary titles. Your Excellency will do well to go provided with a cheque for part of the purchase money in case of need, and not to forget the letter appointing the son to the collectorship at Senlis. If you do not strike on the nail, the farm will slip through your fingers. You have no idea, Monsieur le Comte, of peasant cunning. Given a peasant on one side and a diplomate on the other, the peasant will win the day." Crottat confirmed this advice, which, from the footman's report to Pierrotin, the Comte had evidently adopted. On the day before, the Comte had sent a note to Moreau by the Beaumont diligence, desiring him to invite Margueron to dinner, as he meant to come to some conclusion concerning the Moulineaux farmlands. Before all this, the Comte had given orders for the restoration of the living rooms at Presles, and Monsieur Grindot, a fashionable architect, went down there once a week. So, while treating for his acquisition, Monsieur de Sérisy proposed inspecting the works at the same time and the effect of the new decorations. He intended to give his wife a surprise by taking her to Presles, and the restoration of the château was a matter of pride to him. What event, then, could have happened that the Comte, who, only the day before, was intending to go overtly to Presles, should now wish to travel thither *incognito* in Pierrotin's chaise?

Here a few words are necessary as to the antecedent history of the steward at Presles.

This man, Moreau, was the son of a proctor in a provincial town who at the time of the Revolution had been made a magistrate at Versailles. In this position the elder Moreau had been largely instrumental in saving the property and life of the Sérisys, father and son. Citizen Moreau had belonged to the party of Danton;* Robespierre, implacable in revenge, hunted him down, caught him, and had him executed at Versailles. The younger Moreau, inheriting his father's doctrines and attachments, got mixed up in one of the conspiracies plotted against the First Consul on his accession to power. Then Monsieur de Sérisy, anxious to pay a debt of gratitude, succeeded in effecting Moreau's escape after he was condemned to death; in 1804 he asked and obtained his pardon; he at first found him a place in his office, and afterwards made him his secretary and manager of his private affairs. Some time after his patron's marriage, Moreau fell in love with the Comtesse's maid and married her. To avoid the unpleasantly false position in which he was placed by this union—and there were many such at the Imperial Court—he asked to be appointed land steward at Presles where his wife could play the lady, and where, in a neighbourhood of small folks, they would neither of them be hurt in their own conceits. The Comte needed a faithful agent at Presles because his wife preferred to reside at Sérisy, which is no more than five leagues from Paris. Moreau was familiar with all his affairs and he was intelligent; before the Revolution he had studied law under his father. So Monsieur de Sérisy said to him—"You will not make a fortune, for you have tied a millstone round your neck, but you will be well off, for I will provide for that." And, in fact, the Comte gave Moreau a fixed salary of a thousand écus and a pretty little lodge to live in beyond the outbuildings; he also allowed him so many cords of wood a year out of the plantations for fuel, so much straw, oats, hay for two horses, and a certain proportion of the payments in kind. A sub-prefect is less well off. During the first eight years of his stewardship, Moreau managed the estate conscientiously and took an interest in his work. The Comte, when he came down to inspect the domain to decide on purchases or sanction improvements, was struck by Moreau's faithful service and showed his approbation by handsome presents. But when Moreau found himself the father of a girl—his third child—he was so completely established at his ease at Presles, that he forgot how greatly he was indebted to Monsieur de Sérisy for such unusually liberal advantages. Thus in 1816, the steward, who had hitherto done no more than help himself freely, accepted from a wood merchant a bonus of twenty-five thousand francs with the promise of a rise, for signing an agreement for twelve years allowing the contractor to cut fire logs in the woods of Presles. Moreau argued thus: he had no promise of a pension; he was the father of a family; the Comte certainly owed him so much by way of premium on nearly ten years' service. He was already lawfully possessed of sixty thousand francs in savings; with this sum added to it he could purchase for a hundred and twenty thousand a farm in the vicinity of Champagne, a commune on the right bank of the Oise a little way above L'Isle-Adam. The stir of politics hindered the Comte and the countryfolks from taking cognisance of this investment; the business was indeed transacted in the name of Madame Moreau, who was supposed to have come into some money from an old great-aunt in her own part of the country, at Saint-Lô.* When once the steward had tasted the delicious fruits of ownership, though his conduct was still apparently honesty itself, he never missed an opportunity of adding to his clandestine wealth; the interests of his three children served as an emollient to quench the ardours of his honesty, and we must do him the justice to say that while he was open to a bribe, took care of himself in concluding a bargain, and strained his rights to the last point, he was still honest in the eye of the law; no proof could have been brought in support of any accusation. According to the jurisprudence of the least dishonest of Paris cooks, he shared with his master the profits due to his sharp practice. This way of making a fortune was a matter of conscience—nothing more. Energetic and fully alive to the Comte's interests, Moreau looked out all the more keenly for good opportunities of driving a bargain since he was sure of a handsome tip. Presles was worth sixty-two thousand francs in cash rents, and throughout the district, for ten leagues round, the saying was, "Monsieur de Sérisy has a second self in Moreau!" Moreau, like a prudent man, had, since 1817, invested his salary and his profits year by year in the funds, feathering his nest in absolute secrecy. He had refused various business speculations on the plea of want of money, and affected poverty so well to the Comte that he had obtained two scholarships for his boys at the Collège Henri IV.* And, at this moment, Moreau owned a hundred and twenty thousand francs in the *tiers consolidé*,* then paying five percent, and quoted at eighty. These unacknowledged hundred and twenty thousand francs and his farm at Champagne, to which he had made additions, amounted to a fortune of about two hundred and eighty thousand francs, yielding an income of sixteen thousand francs a year.

This, then, was the steward's position at the time when the Comte wished to purchase the farm of Les Moulineaux, of which the possession had become indispensable to his comfort. This farm comprehended ninety-six plots of land adjoining, bordering, and marching with the estate of Presles, in many cases indeed completely surrounded by the Comte's property like a square in the middle of a chessboard, to say nothing of the dividing hedges and ditches, which gave rise to constant disputes when a tree was to be cut down if it stood on debatable ground. Any other Minister of State would have fought twenty lawsuits a year over the lands of Les Moulineaux. Old Léger wanted to buy them only to sell to the Comte, and to make the thirty or forty thousand francs of profit he hoped for; he had long been endeavouring to come to terms with Moreau. Only three days before this critical Saturday, farmer Léger, driven by press of circumstances, had, standing out in the fields, clearly demonstrated to the steward how he could invest the Comte de Sérisy's money at two and a half percent in purchasing other plots, that is to say, could, as usual, seem to be serving the Comte's interests while pocketing the bonus of forty thousand francs offered him on the transaction. "And on my honour," said the steward to his wife as they went to bed that evening, "if I can make fifty thousand francs on the purchase of Les Moulineaux—for the Comte will give me ten thousand at least—we will retire to L'Isle-Adam to the Pavillon de Nogent." This *pavillon* is a charming little house built for a lady by the Prince de Conti in a style of prodigal elegance. "I should like that," said his wife. "The Dutchman who has been living there has done it up very handsomely, and he will let us have it for thirty thousand francs since he is obliged to go back to the Indies. It is but a stone's throw from Champagne," Moreau went on. "I have hopes of being able to buy the farm and mill at Mours for a hundred thousand francs. We should thus have ten thousand francs a year out of land, one of the prettiest places in all the valley, close to our farm lands, and six thousand francs a year still in the funds."

"And why should you not apply to be appointed Justice of the Peace at L'Isle-Adam? It would give us importance and fifteen hundred francs a year more."

"Yes, I have thought of that." In this frame of mind, on learning that his patron was coming to Presles and wished him to invite Margueron to dinner on Saturday, Moreau at once sent off a messenger, who delivered a note to the Comte's valet too late in the evening for it to be delivered to Monsieur de Sérisy; but Augustin laid it, as was usual, on his master's desk. In this letter Moreau begged the Comte not to take so much trouble: to leave the matter to his management. By his account Margueron no longer wished to sell the lands in one lot, but talked of dividing the farm into ninety-six plots. This, at any rate, he must be persuaded to give up, and perhaps, said the steward, it might be necessary to find someone to lend his name as a screen.

Now, everybody has enemies. The steward of Presles and his wife had given offence to a retired officer named de Reybert and his wife. From stinging words and pin-pricks they had come to daggers drawn. Monsieur de Reybert breathed nothing but vengeance; he aimed at getting Moreau deposed from his place and filling it himself. These two ideas are twins. Hence the agent's conduct, narrowly watched for two years past, had no secrets from the Reyberts. At the very time when Moreau was despatching his letter to Monsieur de Sérisy, Reybert had sent his wife to Paris. Madame de Reybert so strongly insisted on seeing the Comte, that, being refused at nine in the evening when he was going to bed, she was shown into his study by seven o'clock next morning.

"Monseigneur," said she to the minister, "my husband and I are incapable of writing an anonymous letter. I am Madame de Reybert, *née* de Corroy. My husband has a pension of no more than six hundred francs a year, and we live at Presles where your land steward expos-es us to insult upon insult though we are gentlefolks. Monsieur de Reybert, who has no love of intrigue—far from it!—retired as a Captain of Artillery in 1816 af-ter twenty years' service, but he never came under the Emperor's eye, Monsieur le Comte, and you must know how slowly promotion came to those who did not serve under the Master himself, and besides, my husband's honesty and plain speaking did not please his supe-riors. For three years my husband has been watching your steward for the purpose of depriving him of his place. We are outspoken, you see. Moreau has made us his enemies, and we have kept our eyes open. I have come therefore to tell you that you are being tricked in this business of the Moulineaux farm lands. You are to be cheated of a hundred thousand francs, which will be shared between the notary, Léger, and Moreau. You have given orders that Margueron is to be asked to dinner, and you intend to go to Presles tomorrow, but Margueron will be ill, and Léger is so confident of getting the farm that he is in Paris realising enough capital. As we have enlightened you, if you want an honest agent, engage my husband. Though of noble birth, he will serve you as he served his country. Your steward has made and saved two hundred and fifty thousand francs, so he is not to be pitied." The Comte thanked Madame de Reybert very coldly and answered her with empty speeches, for he detested an informer; still, as he remembered Derville's suspicions he was shaken in his mind, and then his eye fell on Moreau's letter; he read it, and in those assurances of devotion and the respectful remonstrances as to the want of confidence implied by his intention of conducting this business himself, he saw the truth about Moreau.

"Corruption has come with wealth, as usual," said he to himself. He had questioned Madame de Reybert less to ascertain the details than to give himself time to study her, and he had then written a line to his notary to desire him not to send his clerk to Presles, but to go there himself and meet him at dinner.

"If you should have formed a bad opinion of me, Monsieur le Comte, for the step I have taken unknown to my husband," said Madame Reybert in conclusion, "you must at least be convinced that we have obtained our knowledge as concerning your steward by perfectly natural means; the most sensitive conscience can find nothing to blame us for." Madame de Reybert *née* de Corroy held herself as straight as a pikestaff. The Comte's rapid survey took in a face pitted by smallpox till it looked like a colander, a lean, flat figure, a pair of eager, light-coloured eyes, fair curls flattened on an anxious brow, a faded green silk bonnet lined with pink, a white stuff dress with lilac spots, and kid shoes. Monsieur de Sérisy discerned in her the wife of the poor gentleman: some puritanical soul subscribing to the *Courrier Français** glowing with virtue, but very well aware of the advantages of a fixed place, and coveting it.

"A pension of six hundred francs, you said?" replied the Comte, answering himself rather than Madame de Reybert's communication.

"Yes, Monsieur le Comte."

"You were a de Corroy?"

"Yes, Monsieur, of a noble family of the Messin country,* my husband's country."

"And in what regiment was Monsieur de Reybert?"

"In the 7th Artillery."

"Good!" said the Comte, writing down the number. He thought he might very well place the management of the estate in the hands of a retired officer, concerning whom he could get the fullest information at the War Office.

"Madame," he went on, ringing for his valet, "return to Presles with my notary, who is to arrange to dine there tonight, and to whom I have written a line of introduction; this is his address, I am going to Presles myself, but secretly, and will let Monsieur de Reybert know when to call on me." So it was not a false alarm that had startled Pierrotin with the news of Monsieur de Sérisy's journey in a public chaise and the warning to keep his name a secret; he foresaw imminent danger about to fall on one of his best customers.

On coming out of the Café de l'Echiquier, Pierrotin perceived, at the gate of the Lion-d'Argent, the woman and youth whom his acumen had recognised as travellers, for the lady, with outstretched neck and an anxious face, was evidently looking for him. This lady, in a re-dyed black silk, a grey bonnet, and an old French cashmere shawl, shod in openwork silk stockings and kid shoes, held a flat straw basket and a bright blue umbrella. She had once been handsome and now looked about forty, and her blue eyes, bereft of the sparkle that happiness might have given them, showed that she had long since renounced the world. Her dress no less than her person betrayed a mother entirely given up to her housekeeping and her son. If the bonnet strings were shabby, the shape of it dated from three years back. Her shawl was fastened with a large broken needle converted into a pin by means of a head of sealing wax. This person was impatiently awaiting Pierrotin to commend her son to his care; the lad was probably travelling alone for the first time, and she had accompanied him as far as the coach office, as much out of mistrust as out of motherly devotion. The son was in a way supplementary to his mother, and without the mother the son would have seemed less comprehensible. While the mother was content to display darned gloves, the son wore an olive-green overcoat with sleeves rather short at the wrists, showing that he was still growing as lads do between eighteen and nineteen. And his blue trousers, mended by the mother, showed that they had been newly seated whenever the tails of his coat parted maliciously behind.

"Do not twist your gloves up in that way," she was saying when Pierrotin appeared, "you will wear them out. Are you the driver? Ah! It is you, Pierrotin!" she went on, leaving her son for a moment and taking the coachman aside.

"All is well, Madame Clapart?" said Pierrotin, with an expression on his face of mingled respect and familiarity.

"Yes, Pierrotin. Take good care of my Oscar; he is travelling alone for the first time."

"Oh! He is going alone to Monsieur Moreau's then?" said Pierrotin, so as to see if the young man was actually going there.

"Yes," said the mother.

"Has Madame Moreau a liking for him, then?" said the man with a knowing look.

"Oh! It will not be all roses for the poor boy, but his future prospects make it absolutely necessary that he should go."

Pierrotin was struck by this remark, and he did not like to confide his doubts concerning the steward to Madame Clapart while she, on her part, dared not offend her son by giving Pierrotin such instructions as would put the coachman in the position of a mentor. During this brief hesitation on both sides, under cover of a few remarks on the weather, the roads, the stopping places on the way, it will not be superfluous to explain the circumstances which had thrown Pierrotin and Madame Clapart together and given rise to their few words of confidential talk. Frequently—that is to say, three or four times a month—Pierrotin, on his way to Paris, found the steward waiting at La Cave, and as the coach came up he beckoned to a gardener, who then helped Pierrotin to place on the coach one or two baskets full of such fruit and vegetables as were in season, with fowls, eggs, butter, or game. Moreau always paid the carriage himself, and gave him money enough to pay the excise duties at the barrier if the baskets contained anything subject to the octroi. These hampers and baskets never bore any label. The first time, and once for all, the steward had given the shrewd driver Madame Clapart's address by word of mouth, desiring him never to trust anybody else with these precious parcels. Pierrotin, dreaming of an intrigue between some pretty girl and the agent, had gone as directed to No. 7 Rue de la Cerisaie, near the Arsenal,* where he had seen the Madame Clapart above described instead of the fair young creature he had expected to find. Carriers, in the course of their day's work, are initiated into many homes and trusted with many secrets, but due to the chances of the social system—a sort of deputy providence having ordained that they should have no education or be unendowed with the gift of observation—it follows that they are not dangerous. Nevertheless, after many months Pierrotin could not account to himself for the friendship between Madame Clapart and Monsieur Moreau from what little he saw of the household in the Rue de la Cerisaie. Though rents were not at that time high in the neighbourhood of the Arsenal, Madame Clapart lived on the third floor on the inner side of a courtyard, in a house which had been in its day the residence of some magnate, at a period when the highest nobility in the kingdom lived on what had been the site of the Palais des Tournelles* and the Hôtel Saint-Paul. Towards the close of the sixteenth century, the great families spread themselves over vast plots previously occupied by the royal palace gardens, of which the record survives in the names of the streets: Rue de la Cerisaie, Rue Beautreillis, Rue des Lions,* and so on. This apartment, of which every room was panelled with old wainscot, consisted of three rooms in a row—a dining room, a drawing room, and a bedroom. Above were the kitchen and Oscar's room. Fronting the door that opened on to the landing was the door of another room at an angle to these, in a sort of square tower of massive stone built out all the way up, and containing besides a wooden staircase. This tower room was where Moreau slept whenever he spent a night in Paris. Pierrotin deposited the baskets in the first room where he could see six straw bottomed, walnut wood chairs, a table, and a sideboard; narrow russet-brown curtains screened the windows. Afterwards, when he was admitted to the drawing room, he found it fitted with old furniture of the time of the Empire, much worn, and there was no more of it at all than the landlord would insist upon as a guarantee for the rent. The carved panels, painted coarsely in distemper of a dull pinkish white and in such a way as to fill up the mouldings and thicken the scrolls and figures, far from being ornamental, were positively depressing. The floor, which was never waxed, was as dingy as the boards of a schoolroom. If the carrier by chance disturbed Monsieur and Madame Clapart at a meal, the plates, the glasses, the most trifling things revealed miserable poverty; they had silver plate, it is true, but the dishes and tureen, chipped and riveted like those of the very poor, were truly pitiable. Monsieur Clapart, dressed in a dirty little frock coat, a squalid pair of slippers, and, as always, wearing green spectacles over his eyes, displayed, after removing an ugly old cap, a high pointed skull with a few dirty slender filaments hanging about it which a poet would have refused to call hair. This colourless creature looked a coward, and was probably a tyrant. In this dismal apartment, facing north, with no outlook but on a vine nailed out on the opposite wall and a well in the corner of the yard, Madame Clapart gave herself the airs of a queen and trod like a woman who could not go out on foot. Often, as she thanked Pierrotin, she would give him a look that might have touched the heart of an onlooker; now and again she would slip a twelve sou piece into his hand. Her voice in speech was very sweet. Oscar was unknown to Pierrotin, for the boy had but just left school and he had never seen him at home.

This was the sad story which Pierrotin never could have guessed, not even after questioning the gatekeeper's wife as he sometimes did—for the woman knew nothing beyond the fact that the Claparts' rent was but two hundred and fifty francs, that they only had a woman in to help for a few hours in the morning, that Madame would sometimes do her own little bit of washing, and paid for every letter as it came as if she were afraid to let the account stand.

There is no such thing—or rather, there is very rarely such a thing—as a criminal who is bad all through.

How much more rare it must be to find a man who is dishonest all through! He may make up his accounts to his own advantage rather than his master's, or pull as much hay as possible to his end of the manger, but even while making a little fortune by illicit means, few men deny themselves the luxury of some good action. If only out of curiosity, as a contrast, or perhaps by chance, every man has known his hour of generosity; he may speak of it as a mistake and never repeat it; still, once or twice in his life, he will have sacrificed to welldoing as the veriest lout will sacrifice to the Graces.

If Moreau's sins can be forgiven him, will it not be for the sake of his constancy in helping a poor woman of whose favours he had once been proud, and under whose roof he had found refuge in danger? This woman, famous at the time of the Directory for her connection with one of the five kings of the day,* married, under this powerful patronage, a contractor who made millions and then was ruined by Napoléon in 1802. This man, named Husson, was driven mad by his sudden fall from opulence to poverty; he threw himself into the Seine, leaving his handsome wife expecting a child. Moreau, who was on very intimate terms with Madame Husson, was at the time under sentence of death, so he could not marry the widow, and was in fact obliged to leave France for a time. Madame Husson, only twenty-two, in her utter poverty married an official named Clapart, a young man of twenty-seven—a man of promise, it was said. Heaven preserve women from handsome men of promise! In those days officials rose rapidly from humble beginnings, for the Emperor had an eye for capable men. But Clapart, vulgarly handsome indeed, had no brains. Believing Madame Husson to be very rich, he had affected a great passion; he was simply a burden to her, never able, either then or later, to satisfy the habits she had acquired in her days of opulence. Clapart filled—badly enough—a small place in the Bureau of

Finance at a salary of not more than eighteen hundred francs a year. When Moreau came back to be with the Comte de Sérisy and heard of Madame Husson's desperate plight, he succeeded, before his own marriage, in getting her a place as woman of the bedchamber in attendance on MADAME, the Emperor's mother.* But in spite of such powerful patronage, Clapart could never get on; his incapacity was too immediately obvious. In 1815 the brilliant Aspasia of the Directory, ruined by the Emperor's overthrow, was left with nothing to live on but the salary of twelve hundred francs attached to a clerkship in the municipal offices which the Comte de Sérisy's influence secured for Clapart. Moreau, now the only friend of a woman whom he had known as the possessor of millions, obtained for Oscar Husson a half-scholarship held by the Municipality of Paris in the Collège Henri IV, and he sent to the Rue de la Cerisaie, by Pierrotin, all he could decently offer to the impoverished lady. Oscar was his mother's one hope, her very life. The only fault to be found with the poor woman was her excessive fondness for this boy—his stepfather's utter aversion. Oscar was, unluckily, gifted with a depth of silliness which his mother could never suspect in spite of Clapart's ironical remarks. This silliness—or, to be accurate, this bumptiousness—disturbed Monsieur Moreau so greatly that he had begged Madame Clapart to send the lad to him for a month that he might judge for himself what line of life he would prove fit for. The steward had some thought of introducing Oscar one day to the Comte as his successor. But, to give God and the Devil their due, it may here be observed as an excuse for Oscar's preposterous conceit that he had been born under the roof of the Emperor's mother; in his earliest years his eyes had been dazzled by Imperial splendour. His impressible imagination had no doubt retained the memory of those magnificent spectacles, and an image of that golden time of festivities, with a dream of seeing them again. The boastfulness common to schoolboys, all possessed by desire to shine at the expense of their fellows, had in him been exaggerated by these memories of his childhood, and at home perhaps his mother was rather too apt to recall with complacency the days when she had been a queen of Paris under the Directory. Oscar, who had just finished his studies, had, no doubt, often been obliged to assert himself as superior to the humiliations which the pupils who pay are always ready to inflict on the "charity boys" when the scholars are not physically strong enough to impress them with their superiority. This mixture of departed splendour and faded beauty, of affection resigned to poverty, of hope founded on this son and maternal blindness, with the heroic endurance of suffering, made this mother one of the sublime figures which in Paris deserve the notice of the observer.

Pierrotin, who, of course, could not know how truly Moreau was attached to this woman, and she, on her part, to the man who had protected her in 1797 and was now her only friend, would not mention to her the suspicion that had dawned in his brain as to the danger which threatened Moreau. The manservant's ominous speech, "We have all enough to do to take care of ourselves," recurred to his mind with the instinct of obedience to those whom he designated as *first in the ranks*. Also, at this moment Pierrotin felt as many darts stinging his brain as there are five franc pieces in a thousand francs. A journey of seven leagues seemed, no doubt, quite an undertaking to this poor mother, who in all her fine lady existence had hardly ever been beyond the barrier, for Pierrotin's replies, "Yes, Madame; no, Madame——" again and again, plainly showed that the man was only anxious to escape from her too numerous and useless instructions.

"You will put the luggage where it cannot get wet if the weather should change?"

"I have a tarpaulin," said Pierrotin, "and, you see, Madame, it is carefully packed away."

"Oscar, do not stay more than a fortnight, even if you are pressed," Madame Clapart went on, coming back to her son. "Do what you will, Madame Moreau will never take to you; besides, you must get home by the end of September. We are going to Belleville,* you know, to your Uncle Cardot's."

"Yes, Mama."

"Above all," she added in a low tone, "never talk about servants. Always remember that Madame Moreau was a lady's maid——"

"Yes, Mama."

Oscar, like all young people whose conceit is touchy, seemed much put out by these admonitions delivered in the gateway of the Lion-d'Argent.

"Well, good-bye, Mama; we shall soon be off, the horse is put in."

The mother, forgetting that she was in the open street, hugged her Oscar, and taking a nice little roll out of her bag—"Here," said she, "you were forgetting your bread and chocolate. Once more, my dear boy, do not eat anything at the inns; you have to pay ten times the value for the smallest morsel."

Oscar wished his mother further away as she stuffed the roll and the chocolate into his pocket. There were two witnesses to the scene, two young men a few years older than the newly-fledged schoolboy, better dressed than he, and come without their mothers; their demeanour, dress, and manner proclaiming the entire independence which is the end of every lad's desire while still under direct maternal government. To Oscar, at this moment, these two young fellows epitomised the world.

"*Mama!* says he," cried one of these strangers, with a laugh.

The words reached Oscar's ears, and in an impulse of intense irritation he shouted out—"Good-bye, Mother!"

It must be owned that Madame Clapart spoke rather too loud, and seemed to admit the passersby to bear witness to her affectionate care.

"What on earth ails you, Oscar?" said the poor woman, much hurt. "I do not understand you," she added severely, fancying she could thus inspire him with respect—a common mistake with women who spoil their children. "Listen, dear Oscar," she went on, resuming her coaxing gentleness, "you have a propensity for talking to everybody, telling everything you know and everything you don't know—out of brag and a young man's foolish self-conceit. I beg you once more to bridle your tongue. You have not seen enough of life, my dearest treasure, to gauge the people you may meet, and there is nothing more dangerous than talking at random in a public conveyance. In a diligence well-bred persons keep silence."

Cette scène eut deux témoins.

Plate II

The two young men, who had, no doubt, walked to the end of the yard and back, now made the sound of their boots heard once more under the gateway; they might have heard this little lecture, and so, to be quit of his mother, Oscar took heroic measures, showing how much self-esteem can stimulate the inventive powers.

"Mama," said he, "you are standing in a draft, you will catch cold. Besides, I must take my place."

The lad had touched some tender chord, for his mother clasped him in her arms as if he were starting on some long voyage, and saw him into the chaise with tears in her eyes.

"Do not forget to give five francs to the servants," said she. "And write to me at least three times in the course of the fortnight. Behave discreetly and remember all my instructions. You have enough linen to need none washed. And, above all, remember all Monsieur Moreau's kindness; listen to him as to a father, and follow his advice."

As he got into the chaise Oscar displayed a pair of blue stockings as his trousers slipped up and the new seat to his trousers as his coattails parted. And the smile on the faces of the two young men, who did not fail to see these evidences of honourable poverty, was a fresh blow to Oscar's self-esteem.

"Oscar's place is number 1," said Madame Clapart to Pierrotin. "Settle yourself in the corner," she went on, still gazing at her son with tender affection.

Oh! how much Oscar regretted his mother's beauty, spoilt by misfortune and sorrow, and the poverty and self-sacrifice that hindered her from being nicely dressed. One of the youngsters—the one who wore boots and spurs—nudged the other with his elbow to point out Oscar's mother, and the other twirled his moustache with an air as much as to say, "A neat figure!"

"How am I to get rid of my mother?" thought Oscar, looking quite anxious.

"What is the matter?" said Madame Clapart.

Oscar pretended not to hear, the wretch! And perhaps, under the circumstances, Madame Clapart showed want of tact, but an absorbing passion is so selfish!

"Georges, do you like travelling with children?" asked one of the young men of his friend.

"Yes, if they are weaned, and are called Oscar, and have chocolate to eat, my dear Amaury."

These remarks were exchanged in an undertone, leaving Oscar free to hear or not to hear them. His manner would show the young man what he might venture on with the lad to amuse himself in the course of the journey. Oscar would not hear. He looked round to see whether his mother, who weighed on him like a nightmare, was still waiting, but, indeed, he knew she was too fond of him to have deserted him yet. He not only involuntarily compared his travelling companion's dress with his own, but he also felt that his mother's costume counted for something as provoking the young men's mocking smile. "If only they would go!" thought he.

Alas! Amaury had just said to Georges as he struck the wheel of the chaise with his cane—"And you are prepared to trust your future career on board this frail vessel?"

"Need must!" replied Georges in a fateful tone.

Oscar heaved a sigh as he noted the youth's hat, cocked cavalierly over one ear to show a fine head of fair hair elaborately curled, while he, by his stepfather's orders, wore his black hair in a brush above his forehead, cut quite short like a soldier's. The vain boy's face was round and chubby, bright with the colour of vigorous health; that of "Georges" was long, delicate, and pale. This young man had a broad brow, and his chest filled out a shawl pattern waistcoat. As Oscar admired his tightly fitting iron-grey trousers and his overcoat, sitting closely to the figure, with Brandenburg braiding and oval buttons, he felt as if the romantic stranger, blessed with so many advantages, were making an unfair display of his superiority, just as an ugly woman is offended by the mere sight of a beauty. The ring of his spurred boot heels, which the young man accentuated rather too much for Oscar's liking, went to the boy's heart. In short, Oscar was as uncomfortable in his clothes, homemade perhaps out of his stepfather's old ones, as the other enviable youth was satisfied in his.

"That fellow must have ten francs at least in his pocket," thought Oscar. The young man turned. One can imagine Oscar's feelings when he discerned a gold chain about his neck with a gold watch, no doubt, at the end of it. Living in the Rue de la Cerisaie since 1815, taken to and from school on his holidays by his stepfather Clapart, Oscar had never had any standard of comparison but his mother's poverty-stricken household. Kept very strictly, by Moreau's advice, he rarely went to the play, and then aspired no higher than to the Ambigu Comique* where little elegance met his gaze, even if the absorbed attention a boy devotes to the stage had allowed him to study the house. His stepfather still wore his watch in a fob in the fashion of the Empire, with a heavy gold chain hanging over his stomach and ending in a bunch of miscellaneous objects—seals and a watch key with a flat round top in which was set a landscape in mosaic. Oscar, who looked on this out-of-date splendour as the ne plus ultra of luxury, was quite bewildered by this revelation of superior and less ponderous elegance. The young man also made an insolent display of a pair of good gloves, and seemed bent on blinding Oscar by his graceful handling of a smart cane with a gold knob. Oscar had just reached the final stage of boyhood in which trifles are the cause of great joys and great anguish, when a real misfortune seems preferable to a ridiculous costume, and vanity, having no great interests in life to absorb it, centres in frivolities, and dress, and the anxiety to be thought a man. The youth magnifies himself, and his self-assertion is all the more marked because it turns on trifles; still, though he envies a well-dressed noodle, he can be also fired with enthusiasm for talent, and admire a man of genius. His faults, when they are not rooted in his heart, only show the exuberance of vitality and a lavish imagination. When a boy of nineteen, an only son, austerely brought up at home as a result of the poverty that weighs so cruelly on a clerk with twelve hundred francs' salary, but worshipped by a mother, who for his sake endures the bitterest privations—when such a boy is dazzled by a youth of twenty-two, envies him his frogged coat lined with silk, his sham cashmere waistcoat, and a tie slipped through a vulgar ring, is not this a mere peccadillo such as may be seen in every class of life in the inferior who envies his betters? Even a man of genius yields to this primitive passion. Did not Rousseau of Geneva envy Venture and Bâcle?* But Oscar went on from the peccadillo to the real fault; he felt humiliated; he owed his travelling companion a grudge, and a secret desire surged up in his heart to show him that he was as good a man as he. The two young bucks walked to and fro from the gateway to the stables and back, going out to the street, and as they turned on their heel, they each time looked at Oscar ensconced in his corner. Oscar, convinced that whenever they laughed it was at him, affected profound indifference. He began to hum the tune of a song then in fashion among the Liberals, "*C'est la faute à Voltaire, c'est la faute à Rousseau.*"* This assumption, no doubt, made them take him for some underling lawyer's clerk.

"Why, perhaps he sings in the chorus at the opera!" said Amaury.

Exasperated this time, Oscar bounded into his seat; raising the back curtain, he said to Pierrotin—"When are we to be off?"

"Directly," said the man, who had his whip in his hand, but his eyes fixed on the Rue d'Enghien.

OSCAR HUSSON.

Et quand ils retournaient, ils regardaient toujours Oscar,
tapi dans son coin:

UN DÉBUT DANS LA VIE.

Plate III

The scene was now enlivened by the arrival of a young man escorted by a perfect pickle of a boy, who appeared with a porter at their heels hauling a barrow by a strap. The young man spoke confidentially to Pierrotin, who wagged his head and hailed his stableman. The man hurried up to help unload the barrow, which contained, besides two trunks, pails, brushes, and boxes of strange shape, a mass of packets and utensils which the younger of the two newcomers who had climbed to the box seat stowed and packed away with such expedition that Oscar, smiling at his mother, who was now watching him from the other side of the street, failed to see any of the paraphernalia which might have explained to him in what profession his travelling companions were employed. This boy, about sixteen years of age, wore a holland blouse with a patent leather belt; his cap, knowingly stuck on one side, proclaimed him a merry youth as did the picturesque disorder of his curly brown hair tumbling about his shoulders. A black silk tie marked a black line on a very white neck and seemed to heighten the brightness of his grey eyes. The restless vivacity of a sunburnt, rosy face, the shape of his full lips, his prominent ears, and his turned up nose—every feature of his face showed the bantering wit of a Figaro* and the recklessness of youth, while the quickness of his gestures and saucy glances revealed a keen intelligence, early developed by the practice of a profession taken up in boyhood. As though he were conscious of some intrinsic moral worth, this boy, already made a man either by Art or Vocation, seemed indifferent to the question of his dress, for he looked at his unpolished boots as if he thought them rather a joke, and at his plain drill trousers less to make the stains on them disappear than to study their effect.

"I have acquired a fine tone!" said he, giving himself a shake and addressing his companion.

The expression of the senior showed some authority over this youngster, in whom experienced eyes would

MISTIGRIS.

...... Ce joyeux élève en peinture, qu'en style d'atelier
on appelle un *rapin*.

UN DÉBUT DANS LA VIE.

Plate IV

at once have discerned the jolly art student, known in French studio slang as a *rapin*.*

"Behave, Mistigris!"* replied the master, calling him no doubt by a nickname bestowed on him in the studio.

The elder traveller was a slight and pallid young fellow with immensely thick black hair in quite fantastic disorder, but this abundant hair seemed naturally necessary to a very large head with a powerful forehead that spoke of precocious intelligence. His curiously puckered face, too peculiar to be called ugly, was as hollow as though this singular young man were suffering either from some chronic malady or from the privations of extreme poverty—which is indeed a terrible chronic malady—or from sorrows too recent to have been forgotten. His clothes, almost in keeping with those of Mistigris in proportion to his age and dignity, consisted of a much worn coat of a dull green colour, shabby, but quite clean and well brushed, a black waistcoat buttoned to the neck, as the coat was too, only just showing a red handkerchief round his throat. Black trousers, as shabby as the coat, hung loosely round his lean legs. His boots were muddy, showing that he had come far, and on foot. With one swift glance the artist took in the depths of the hostelry of the Lion-d'Argent, the stables, the tones of colour, and every detail, and he looked at Mistigris, who had imitated him, with an ironical twinkle.

"Rather nice!" said Mistigris.

"Yes, very nice," replied the other.

"We are still too early," said Mistigris. "Couldn't we snatch a toothful? My stomach, like nature, abhors a vacuum!"

"Have we time to get a cup of coffee?" said the artist, in a pleasant voice, to Pierrotin.

"Well, don't be long," said Pierrotin.

"We have a quarter of an hour," added Mistigris, thus revealing the genius for inference which is characteristic of the Paris art student.

The couple disappeared. Just then nine o'clock struck in the inn kitchen. Georges thought it only fair and reasonable to appeal to Pierrotin.

"I say, my good friend, when you are the proud possessor of an old contraption such as this," and he rapped the wheel with his cane, "you should at least make a merit of punctuality. The deuce is in it! We do not ride in that machine for our pleasure, and business must be devilish pressing before we trust our precious selves in it! And that old hack you call Rougeot will certainly not pick up lost time!"

"We will harness on Bichette while those two gentlemen are drinking their coffee," replied Pierrotin. "Go on, you," he added to the stableman, "and see if old Léger means to come with us——"

"Where is your old Léger?" asked Georges.

"Just opposite at number 50; he couldn't find room in the Beaumont coach," said Pierrotin to his man, paying no heed to Georges, and going off himself in search of Bichette.

Georges shook hands with his friend and got into the chaise, after tossing in a large portfolio with an air of much importance; this he placed under the cushion. He took the opposite corner to Oscar.

"This 'Old Léger' bothers me," said he.

"They cannot deprive us of our places," said Oscar. "Mine is number 1."

"And mine number 2," replied Georges.

Just as Pierrotin reappeared, leading Bichette, the stableman returned, having in tow a huge man weighing nearly seventeen stone at least. Old Léger was of the class of farmer who, with an enormous stomach and broad shoulders, wears a powdered queue and a light coat of blue linen. His white gaiters were tightly strapped above the knee over corduroy breeches and finished off with silver buckles. His hobnailed shoes weighed each a couple of pounds. In his hand he carried a little knotted red switch, very shiny, and with a heavy knob, secured round his wrist by a leather cord.

"And is it you who are known as old Léger?"* said Georges gravely as the farmer tried to lift his foot to the step of the chaise.

"At your service," said the farmer, showing him a face rather like that of Louis XVIII, with a fat, red jowl, while above it rose a nose which in any other face would have seemed enormous. His twinkling eyes were deep set in rolls of fat. "Come, lend a hand, my boy," said he to Pierrotin.

The farmer was hoisted in by the driver and the stableman to a shout of "Yo, heave ho!"* from Georges.

"Oh! I am not going far; I am only going to La Cave!" said the farmer, answering a jest with good humour.

In France everybody understands a joke.

"Get into the corner," said Pierrotin. "There will be six of you."

"And your other horse?" asked Georges. "Is it as fabulous as *the third* horse of a post chaise?"

"There it is, Master," said Pierrotin, pointing to the little mare that had come up without calling.

"He calls that insect a horse!" said Georges, astonished.

"Oh, she is a good one to go, is that little mare," said the farmer, who had taken his seat. "Good morning, Messieurs. Are we going to weigh anchor, Pierrotin?"

"Two of my travellers are getting a cup of coffee," said the driver.

The young man with the hollow cheeks and his follower now reappeared.

"Come, let us get off," was now the universal cry.

"We are off—we are off!" replied Pierrotin. "Let her go," he added to his man, who kicked away the stones that scotched the wheels.

Pierrotin took hold of Rougeot's bridle with an encouraging *kit! kit!* to warn the two steeds to pull themselves together, and, torpid as they evidently were, they started the vehicle, which Pierrotin brought to a standstill in front of the gate of the Lion-d'Argent. After this purely preliminary manoeuvre, he again looked down the Rue d'Enghien and vanished, leaving the conveyance in the care of the stableman.

"Well! Is your governor subject to these attacks?" Mistigris asked of the man.

"He is gone to fetch his oats away from the stable," replied the Auvergnat, who was up to all the arts in use to pacify the impatience of travellers.

"After all," said Mistigris, "*time is a great plaster.*"*

At that time there was in the Paris studios a mania for distorting proverbs. It was considered a triumph to hit on some change of letters or some rhyming word which should suggest an absurd meaning, or even make it absolute nonsense.

"And *Paris was not gilt in a play*,"* replied his comrade.

Pierrotin now returned, accompanied by the Comte de Sérisy, round the corner of the Rue de l'Échiquier; they had no doubt had a short conversation.

"Père Léger, would you mind giving your place up to Monsieur le Comte? It will trim the chaise better."

"And we shall not be off for an hour yet if you go on like this," said Georges. "You will have to take out that infernal bar we have had so much trouble fitting in, and everybody will have to get out for the latecomer. Each of us has a right to the place he booked. What number is Monsieur's? Come, call them over. Have you a way-bill? Do you keep a book? Which is Monsieur le Comte's place? Count of what?"

"Monsieur le Comte," said Pierrotin, visibly disturbed, "you will not be comfortable."

"Can't you count?" said Mistigris. "*Short counts make tall friends.*"*

"Mistigris, behave!" said his master quite seriously.

Monsieur de Sérisy was supposed by his fellow travellers to be some respectable citizen called Lecomte.

"Do not disturb anybody," said the Comte to Pierrotin; "I will sit in front by you."

"Now, Mistigris," said the young artist, "remember the respect due to age. You don't know how dreadfully old you may live to be. *Manners take the van.** Give your place up to Monsieur."

Mistigris opened the front of the chaise and jumped out as nimbly as a frog into the water.

"You cannot sit as *lapin*, august old man!" said he to Monsieur de Sérisy.

"Mistigris, *tarts are the end of man,"** said his master.

"Thank you, Monsieur," said the Comte to the artist, by whose side he now took his seat.

And the statesman looked with a sagacious eye at the possessors of the back seat in a way that deeply aggrieved Oscar and Georges.

"We are an hour and a quarter behind time," remarked Oscar.

"People who want a chaise to themselves should book all the places," added Georges.

The Comte de Sérisy, quite sure now that he was not recognised, made no reply, but sat with the expression of a good-natured tradesman.

"And if you had been late, you would have liked us to wait for you, I suppose?" said the farmer to the two young fellows.

Pierrotin was looking out towards the Porte Saint-Denis, and paused for a moment before mounting to the hard box seat where Mistigris was kicking his heels.

"If you are still waiting for somebody, I am not the last," remarked the Comte.

"That is sound reasoning," said Mistigris.

Georges and Oscar laughed very rudely.

"The old gentleman is not strikingly original," said Georges to Oscar, who was enchanted with this apparent alliance.

When Pierrotin had settled himself in his place, he again looked back, but failed to discern in the crowd the two travellers who were wanting to fill up his cargo.

"*Parbleu!* A couple more passengers would not come amiss," said he.

"Look here, I have not paid; I shall get out," said Georges in alarm.

"Why, whom do you expect, Pierrotin?" said Léger.

Pierrotin cried *hi!* in a particular tone which Rougeot and Bichette knew to mean business at last, and they trotted off towards the hill at a brisk pace, which, however, soon grew slack.

The Comte had a very red face, quite scarlet indeed, with an inflamed spot here and there, and set off all the more by his perfectly white hair. By any but quite young men this complexion would have been understood as the inflammatory effect on the blood of incessant work. And, indeed, these angry pimples so much disfigured his really noble face that only close inspection could discern in his greenish eyes all the acumen of the judge, the subtlety of the statesman, and the learning of the legislator. His face was somewhat flat; the nose especially looked as if it had been flattened. His hat hid the breadth and beauty of his brow, and, in fact, there was some justification for the laughter of these heedless lads, in the strange contrast between hair as white as silver and thick, bushy eyebrows still quite black. The Comte, who wore a long, blue overcoat, buttoned to the chin in military fashion, had a white handkerchief round his neck, cotton wool in his ears, and a high shirt collar, showing a square white corner on each check. His black trousers covered his boots, of which the tip scarcely showed; he had no ribbon at his buttonhole, and his hands were hidden by his doeskin gloves. Certainly there was nothing in this man which could betray to the lads that he was a Peer of France, and one of the most useful men living to his country. Old Père Léger had never seen the Comte, who, on the other hand, knew him only by name. Though the Comte, as he got into the chaise, cast about him the inquiring glance which had so much annoyed Oscar and Georges, it was because he was looking for his notary's clerk, intending to impress on him the need for the greatest secrecy in case he should have been compelled to travel, like himself, by Pierrotin's conveyance. But he was reassured by Oscar's appearance and by that of the old farmer, and, above all, by the air of aping the military, with his moustache and his style generally, which stamped Georges an adventurer, and he concluded that his note had reached Master Alexandre Crottat in good time.

"Père Léger," said Pierrotin as they came to the steep hill in the Faubourg Saint-Denis at the Rue de la Fidélité,* "suppose we were to walk a bit, heh?" On hearing the name, the Comte observed—

"I will get out too; we must ease the horses."

"Oh! If you go on at this rate, we shall do fourteen leagues in a fortnight!" exclaimed Georges.

"Well, is it any fault of mine," said Pierrotin, "if a passenger wishes to get out?"

"I will give you ten louis if you keep my secret as I bid you," said the Comte, taking Pierrotin by the arm.

"Oh, ho! My thousand francs!" thought Pierrotin, after giving Monsieur de Sérisy a wink, conveying: Trust me!

Oscar and Georges remained in the chaise.

"Look here, Pierrotin—since Pierrotin you are," cried Georges, when the travellers had got into the chaise again at the top of the hill, "if you are going no faster than this, say so. I will pay my fare to Saint-Denis and hire a nag there, for I have important business on hand which will suffer from delay."

"Oh! he will get on, never fear," replied the farmer.

"And the road is not a wide one."

"I am never more than half an hour late," answered Pierrotin.

"Well, well, you are not carting the Pope, I suppose," said Georges, "so hurry up a little."

"You ought not to show any favour," said Mistigris, "and if you are afraid of jolting Monsieur—" and he indicated the Comte "—that is not fair."

"All men are equal in the eye of the *coucou*," said Georges, "as all Frenchmen are in the eye of the Charter."*

"Be quite easy," said old Léger, "we shall be at La Chapelle yet before noon."

La Chapelle is a village close to the Barrière Saint-Denis.*

Those who have travelled know that persons thrown together in a public conveyance do not immediately amalgamate; unless under exceptional circumstances, they do not converse till they are well on their way. This silent interval is spent partly in reciprocal examination, and partly in finding each his own place and taking possession of it. The soul, as much as the body, needs to find its balance. When each, severally, supposes that he has made an accurate guess at his companion's age, profession, and temper, the most talkative first opens a conversation, which is taken up all the more eagerly, because all feel the need for cheering the way and dispelling the dullness. This, at least, is what happens in a French coach. In other countries manners are different. The English pride themselves on never opening their lips, a German is dull in a coach, Italians are too cautious to chat, the Spaniards have almost ceased to have any coaches, and the Russians have no roads. So it is only in the ponderous French diligence that the passengers amuse each other, in the gay and gossiping nation where each one is eager to laugh and display his humour, where everything is enlivened by raillery, from the misery of the poorest to the solid interests of the upper middle class. The police do little to check the license of speech, and the Tribune has made discussion fashionable. When a youngster of twenty-two, like the young gentleman who was known so far by the name of Georges, has a ready wit, he is strongly tempted, especially in such circumstances as these, to be reckless in the use of it. In the first place, Georges was not slow to come to the conclusion that he was the superior man of the party. He decided that the Comte was a manufacturer of the second class, setting him down as a cutler; the shabby looking youth attended by Mistigris he thought but a greenhorn, Oscar a perfect simpleton, and the farmer a capital butt for a practical joke. Having thus taken the measure of all his travelling companions, he determined to amuse himself at their expense.

"Now," thought he, as the *coucou* rolled down the hill from La Chapelle towards the plain of Saint-Denis, "shall I pass myself off as Étienne, or as Béranger?* No, these bumpkins have never heard of either. A Carbonaro? The Devil! I might be nabbed. One of Marshal Ney's sons?* Bah! What could I make of that? Tell them the story of my father's death? That would hardly be funny. Suppose I were to have come back from the government colony in America?* They might take me for a spy and regard me with suspicion. I will be a Russian prince in disguise; I will cram them with fine stories about the Emperor Alexander! Or if I pretended to be Cousin, the Professor of Philosophy? How I could mystify them! No, that limp creature with the tousled hair looks as if he might have kicked his heels at lecture at the Sorbonne. Oh, why didn't I think sooner of trotting them out? I can imitate an Englishman so well, I might have been Lord Byron travelling *incognito*. Hang it! I have missed my chance. The executioner's son? Not a bad way of clearing a space at breakfast. Oh! I know! I will have been in command of the troops under Ali, the Pasha of Janina."*

While he was lost in these meditations, the chaise was making its way through the clouds of dust which constantly blow up from the side paths of this much trodden road.

"What a dust!" said Mistigris.

"Henri IV is dead," retorted his comrade. "If you said it smelt of vanilla now, you would hit on a new idea!"

"You think that funny," said Mistigris. "Well, but it does now and then remind me of vanilla."

"In the East——" Georges began, meaning to concoct a story.

"*In the least——*"* said Mistigris's master, taking up Georges.

"In the East, I said, from whence I have just returned," Georges repeated, "the dust smells very sweet. But here it smells of nothing unless it is wafted up from such a manure heap as this."

"You have just returned from the East?" said Mistigris, with a sly twinkle.

"And you see, Mistigwis, Monsieur is so tired that what he now wequires is west," drawled his master.

"You are not much sunburnt," said Mistigris.

"Oh! I am but just out of bed after three months' illness, caused, the doctors say, by an attack of suppressed plague."

"You have had the plague?" cried the Comte, with a look of horror. "Pierrotin, put me out!"

"Get on, Pierrotin," said Mistigris. "You hear that the plague was suppressed," he went on, addressing Monsieur de Sérisy. "It was the sort of plague that goes down in the course of conversation."

"The plague of which one merely says, 'Plague take it!'" cried the artist.

"Or plague take the man!" added Mistigris.

"Mistigris," said his master, "I shall put you out to walk if you get into mischief. So you have been in the East, Monsieur?" he went on, turning to Georges.

"Yes, Monsieur. First in Egypt and then in Greece where I served under Ali Pasha of Janina, with whom I had a desperate row. The climate is too much for most men, and the excitements of all kinds that are part of an Oriental life wrecked my liver."

"Oh, ho! A soldier?" said the burly farmer. "Why, how old are you?"

"I am twenty-nine," said Georges, and all his fellow travellers looked at him. "At eighteen I served as a private in the famous campaign of 1813, but I only was present at the Battle of Hanau where I won the rank of sergeant major. In France, at Montereau,* I was made sub-lieutenant, and I was decorated by . . . (no spies here?) by the Emperor."

"And you do not wear the cross of your order?" said Oscar.

"A cross given by the present set? Thank you for nothing. Besides, who that is anybody wears his decorations when travelling? Look at Monsieur," he went on, indicating the Comte de Sérisy, "I will bet you anything you please——"

"Betting anything you please is the same thing in France as not betting at all," said Mistigris's master.

"I will bet you anything you please," Georges repeated pompously, "that he is covered with stars."

"I have, in fact," said Monsieur de Sérisy, with a laugh, "the Grand Cross of the Legion of Honour, the Grand Cross of Saint Andrew of Russia, of the Eagle of Prussia, of the Order of the Annunciada of Sardinia,* and of the Golden Fleece."

"Is that all?" said Mistigris. "And it all rides in a public chaise?"

"He is going it, is the brick-red man!" said Georges in a whisper to Oscar. "What did I tell you?" he remarked aloud. "I make no secret of it, I am devoted to the Emperor!"

"I served under him," said the Comte.

"And what a man! wasn't he?" cried Georges.

"A man to whom I am under great obligations," replied the Comte, with a well-affected air of stupidity.

"For your crosses?" said Mistigris.

"And what quantities of snuff he took!" replied Monsieur de Sérisy.

"Yes, he took it loose in his waistcoat pockets."

"So I have been told," said the farmer, with a look of incredulity.

"And not only that, but he chewed and smoked," Georges went on. "I saw him smoking in the oddest way at Waterloo when Marshal Soult lifted him up bodily and flung him into his travelling carriage, just as he had seized a musket and wanted to charge the English!"

"So you were at Waterloo?" said Oscar, opening his eyes very wide.

"Yes, young man, I went through the campaign of 1815. At Mont Saint-Jean* I was made captain, and I retired on the Loire when we were disbanded. But, on my honour, I was sick of France, and I could not stay. No, I should have got myself into some scrape. So I went off with two or three others of the same sort—Selves, Besson, and some more—who are in Egypt to this day in the service of Mohammed Pasha,* and a queer fellow he is, I can tell you! He was a tobacconist at La Cavalle, and is on the high way to be a reigning prince. You have seen him in Horace Vernet's picture of the *Massacre of the Mamelukes*.* Such a handsome man! I never would abjure the faith of my fathers and adopt Islam, all the more because the ceremony involves a surgical operation for which I had no liking. Besides, no one respects a renegade. If they had offered me a hundred thousand francs a year, then, indeed—and yet—no. The Pasha made me a present of a thousand *talari*."

"How much is that?" asked Oscar, who was all ears.

"Oh, no great matter. The *talaro* is much the same as a five franc piece. And, on my honour, I did not earn enough to pay for the vices I learned in that thundering vile country—if you can call it a country. I cannot live now without smoking my narghileh twice a day, and it is very expensive——"

"And what is Egypt like?" asked Monsieur de Sérisy.

"Egypt is all sand," replied Georges, quite undaunted. "There is nothing green but the Nile valley. Draw a green strip on a sheet of yellow paper, and there you have Egypt. The Egyptians, the *fellaheen*, have, I may remark, one great advantage over us: there are no gendarmes. You may go from one end of Egypt to the other, and you will not find one."

"I suppose there are a good many Egyptians there," said Mistigris.

"Not so many as you would think," answered Georges. "There are more Abyssinians, Giaours, Vechabites,* Bedouins, and Copts. However, all these creatures are so very far from amusing that I was only too glad to embark on a Genoese polacre bound for the Ionian Islands, to take up powder and ammunition for Ali of Tebelen. As you know, the English sell powder and ammunition to all nations, to the Turks and the Greeks; they would sell them to the Devil if the Devil had money. So from Zante we were to luff up to the coast of Greece. And, I tell you, take me as you see me, the name of Georges is famous in those parts. I am the grandson of that famous Czerni-Georges who made war on the Porte;* but instead of breaking it down, he was unluckily smashed up. His son took refuge in the house of the French Consul at Smyrna, and came to Paris in 1792 where he died before I, his seventh child, was born. Our treasure was stolen from us by a friend of my grandfather's, so we were ruined. My mother lived by selling her diamonds one by one, till in 1799 she married Monsieur Yung, a contractor, and my stepfather. But my mother died; I quarrelled with my stepfather, who, between ourselves, is a rascal; he is still living, but we never meet. The wretch left us all seven to our fate without a word, nor bit nor sup. And that is how, in 1813, in sheer despair, I went off as a conscript. You cannot imagine with what joy Ali of Tebelen hailed the grandson of Czerni-Georges. Here I call myself simply Georges. The Pasha gave me a seraglio——"

"You had a seraglio?" said Oscar.

"Were you a Pasha with many tails?"* asked Mistigris.

"How is it that you don't know that there is but one Sultan who can create pashas?" said Georges, "and my friend Tebelen—for we were friends, like two Bourbons—was a rebel against the Padishah. You know—or you don't know—that the Grand Seigneur's correct title is Padishah, and not the Grand Turk or the Sultan. Do not suppose that a seraglio is any great matter. You might just as well have a flock of goats. Their women are great fools, and I like the grisettes of the *Chaumière* at Mont-Parnasse* a thousand times better."

"And they are much nearer," said the Comte de Sérisy.

"These women of the seraglio never know a word of French, and language is indispensable to an understanding. Ali gave me five lawful wives and ten slave girls. At Janina that was a mere nothing. In the East, you see, it is very bad style to have wives; you have them, but as we here have our Voltaire and our Rousseau; who ever looks into his Voltaire or his Rousseau? Nobody. And yet it is quite the right thing to be jealous. You may tie a woman up in a sack and throw her into the water on a mere suspicion by an article of their code."

"Did you throw any in?"

"I? What! A Frenchman! I was devoted to them."

Whereupon Georges twirled up his moustache and assumed a pensive air. By this time they were at Saint-Denis, and Pierrotin drew up at the door of the inn where the famous cheesecakes are sold, and where all travellers call. The Comte, really puzzled by the mixture of truth and nonsense in Georges's rhodomontade, jumped into the carriage again, looked under the cushion for the portfolio which Pierrotin had told him that this mysterious youth had bestowed there, and saw on it in gilt letters the words, "Master Crottat, Notary." The Comte at once took the liberty of opening the case, fearing, with good reason, that if he did not, farmer Léger might be possessed with similar curiosity, and taking out the deed relating to the Moulineaux farm, he folded it up, put it in the side pocket of his coat, and came back to join his fellow travellers.

"This Georges is neither more nor less than Crottat's junior clerk. I will send my regards to his master, who ought to have sent his head clerk," he said to himself.

From the respectful attention of the farmer and Oscar, Georges perceived that in them at least he had two ardent admirers. Of course, he put on lordly airs; he treated them to cheesecakes and a glass of Alicante,* and then did the same to Mistigris and his master, asking them their names on the strength of this munificence.

"Oh, Monsieur," said the elder, "I am not the proud owner of so illustrious a name as yours, and I have not come home from Asia . . ."

The Comte, who had made haste to get back to the vast inn kitchen so as to excite no suspicions, came in time to hear the end of the reply.

". . . I am simply a poor painter just returned from Rome where I went at the expense of the government after winning the Grand Prix five years ago. My name is Schinner . . ."

"Hallo, Master, may I offer you a glass of Alicante and some cheesecakes?" cried Georges to the Comte.

"Thank you, no," said the Comte. "I never come out till I have had my cup of coffee."

"And you never eat anything between meals? How Marais, Place Royale, and Île Saint-Louis!"* exclaimed Georges. "When he *shammed* us just now about his orders, I fancied him better fun than he is," he went on in a low voice to the painter, "but we will get him on to that subject again—the little tallow chandler. Come, *mon brave,*" said he to Oscar, "drink the glass that was poured out for the grocer, it will make your moustache grow."

Oscar, anxious to play the man, drank the second glass of wine, and ate three more cheesecakes.

"Very good wine it is!" said old Léger, smacking his tongue.

"And all the better," remarked Georges, "because it comes from Bercy.* I have been to Alicante, and, I tell you, this is no more like the wine of that country than my arm is like a windmill. Our manufactured wines are far better than the natural products. Come, Pierrotin, have a glass. What a pity it is that your horses cannot each drink one; we should get on faster!"

"Oh, that is unnecessary as I have a grey horse already,"* said Pierrotin.

Oscar, as he heard the vulgar pun, thought Pierrotin a marvel of wit.

"Off!" cried Pierrotin, cracking his whip as soon as the passengers had once more packed themselves into the vehicle. It was by this time eleven o'clock. The weather, which had been rather dull, now cleared; the wind swept away the clouds; the blue sky shone out here and there, and by the time Pierrotin's chaise was fairly started on the ribbon of road between Saint-Denis and Pierrefitte, the sun had finally drunk up the last filmy haze that hung like a diaphanous veil over the views from this famous suburb.

"Well, and why did you throw over your friend the Pasha?" said the farmer to Georges.

"He was a very queer customer," replied Georges, with an air of hiding many mysteries. "Only think, he put me in command of his cavalry! Very well——"

"That," thought poor Oscar, "is why he wears spurs."

"At that time, Ali of Tebelen wanted to rid himself of Chosrew Pasha, another queer fish. Chaureff you call him here, but in Turkey they call him Cosserev.* You

must have read in the papers at the time that old Ali had
beaten Chosrew, and pretty soundly too. Well, but for
me, Ali would have been done for some days sooner. I
led the right wing, and I saw Chosrew, the old sneak, just
charging the centre—oh, yes, I can tell you, as straight
and steady a move as if he had been Murat. Good! I took
my time, and I charged at full speed, cutting Chosrew's
column in two parts, for he had pushed through our
centre and had no cover. You understand—after it was
all over Ali fairly hugged me."

"Is that the custom in the East?" said the Comte de
Sérisy, with a touch of irony.

"Yes, Monsieur, as it is everywhere," answered the
painter.

"We drove Chosrew back over thirty leagues of country—like a hunt, I tell you," Georges went on. "Splendid
horsemen are the Turks. Ali gave me yataghans, guns,
and swords—'take as many as you like.' When we got
back to the capital, that incredible creature made pro-
posals to me that did not suit my views at all. He wanted
to adopt me as his favourite, his heir. But I had had
enough of the life, for, after all, Ali of Tebelen was a rebel
against the Porte, and I thought it wiser to clear out. But
I must do Monsieur de Tebelen justice, he loaded me
with presents: diamonds, ten thousand talari, a thousand pieces of gold, a fair Greek girl for a page, a little
Arnaute maid* for company, and an Arab horse. Well,
there! Ali, the Pasha of Janina, is an unappreciated man;
he lacks a historian. Nowhere but in the East do you
meet with these iron souls who, for twenty years, strain
every nerve, only to be able to take a revenge one fine
morning. In the first place, he had the grandest white
beard you ever saw, and a hard, stern face——"

"But what became of your treasure?" asked the farmer.

"Ah! There you are! Those people have no state funds
nor Bank of France, so I packed my moneybags on board
a Greek tartane, which was captured by the Capitan-

Pasha himself. Then I myself, as you see me, was within an ace of being impaled at Smyrna. Yes, on my honour, but for Monsieur de Rivière, the ambassador,* who happened to be on the spot, I should have been executed as an ally of Ali Pasha's. I saved my head, or I could not speak so plainly, but as for the ten thousand talari, the thousand pieces of gold, and the weapons, oh! that was all swallowed down by that *drunkard* the Capitan-Pasha. My position was all the more ticklish because the Capitan-Pasha was Chosrew himself. After the dressing he had had, the scamp had got this post, which is that of high admiral in France."

"But he had been in the cavalry, as I understood?" said old Léger, who had been listening attentively to this long story.

"That shows how little the East is understood in the département of Seine-et-Oise!" exclaimed Georges. "Monsieur, the Turks are like that. You are a farmer, the Padishah makes you a field marshal; if you do not fulfil your duties to his satisfaction, so much the worse for you. Off with your head! That is his way of dismissing you. A gardener is made prefect, and a prime minister is a private once more. The Ottomans know no laws of promotion or hierarchy. Chosrew, who had been a horseman, was now a sailor. The Padishah Mohammed* had instructed him to fall on Ali by sea, and he had, in fact, mastered him, but only by the help of the English, who got the best of the booty, the thieves! They laid hands on the treasure. This Chosrew, who had not forgotten the riding lesson I had given him, recognised me at once. As you may suppose, I was settled—oh! done for!—if it had not occurred to me to appeal, as a Frenchman and a troubadour, to Monsieur de Rivière. The ambassador, delighted to assert himself, demanded my release. The Turks have this great merit: they are as ready to let you go as to cut off your head; they are indifferent to everything. The French consul, a charming man and a friend of Chosrew's, got him to restore two thousand talari, and his name, I may say, is graven on my heart——"

"And his name?" asked Monsieur de Sérisy.

He could not forbear a look of surprise when Georges, in fact, mentioned the name of one of our most distinguished consuls general, who was at Smyrna at the time.

"I was present, as it fell out, at the execution of the Commandant of Smyrna, the Padishah having ordered Chosrew to put him to death—one of the most curious things I ever saw, though I have seen many. I will tell you all about it by and by at breakfast. From Smyrna I went to Spain, on hearing there was a revolution there. I went straight to Mina, who took me for an aide-de-camp, and gave me the rank of colonel. So I fought for the constitutionalists, who will surely be defeated, for we shall march into Spain one of these days."*

"And you a French officer!" said the Comte de Sérisy severely. "You are trusting very rashly to the discretion of your hearers."

"There are no spies among them," said Georges.

"And does it not occur to you, Colonel Georges," said the Comte, "that at this very time a conspiracy is being inquired into by the Chamber of Peers, which makes the government very strict in its dealings with soldiers who bear arms against France, or who aid in intrigues abroad tending to the overthrow of any legitimate sovereign?"

At this ominous remark, the painter reddened up to his ears and glanced at Mistigris, who was speechless.

"Well, and what then?" asked old Léger.

"Why, if I by chance were a magistrate, would it not be my duty to call on the gendarmes of the brigade at Pierrefitte to arrest Mina's aide-de-camp," said the Comte, "and to summons all who are in this chaise as witnesses?"

This speech silenced Georges all the more effectually because the vehicle was just passing the gendarmerie station where the white flag was, to use a classical phrase, floating on the breeze.

"You have too many orders to be guilty of such mean conduct," said Oscar.

"We will play him a trick yet," whispered Georges to Oscar.

"Colonel," said Léger, very much discomfited by the Comte's outburst and anxious to change the subject, "in the countries where you have travelled, what is the farming like? What are their crops in rotation?"

"In the first place, my good friend, you must understand that the people are too busy smoking weeds to burn them on the land . . . (the Comte could not help smiling, and his smile reassured the narrator) . . . and they have a way of cultivating the land which you will think strange. They do not cultivate it all; that is their system. The Turks and Greeks eat onions or rice; they collect opium from their poppies, which yields a large revenue, and tobacco grows almost wild—their famous Latakia. Then there are dates, bunches of sugarplums, that grow without any trouble. It is a country of endless resources and trade. Quantities of carpets are made at Smyrna, and quite cheaply."

"Ay," said the farmer, "but if the carpets are made of wool, wool comes from sheep, and to have sheep they must have fields, farms, and farming——"

"There must, no doubt, be something of the kind," replied Georges, "but rice, in the first place, grows in water, and then I have always been near the coast and have only seen the country devastated by war. Besides, I have a perfect horror of statistics."

"And the taxes?" said the farmer.

"Ah! The taxes are heavy. The people are robbed of everything, and allowed to keep the rest. The Pasha of Egypt,* struck by the merits of this system, was organising his administration on that basis when I left."

"But how?" said old Léger, who was utterly puzzled.

"How?" echoed Georges. "There are collectors who seize the crops, leaving the peasants just enough to live on. And by that system there is no trouble with papers and red tape, the plague of France. There you are!"

"But what right have they to do it?" asked the farmer.

"It is the land of despotism, that's all. Did you never hear Montesquieu's fine definition of despotism—'Like the savage, it cuts the tree down to gather the fruit.'"

"And that is what they want to bring us back to!" cried Mistigris. "But *a burnt rat dreads the mire.*"*

"And it is what we shall come to," exclaimed the Comte de Sérisy. "Those who hold land will be wise to sell it. Monsieur Schinner must have seen how such things are done in Italy."

"*Corpo di Bacco!** The Pope is not behind his times. But they are used to it there. The Italians are such good people! So long as they are allowed to do a little highway murdering of travellers, they are quite content."

"But you, too, do not wear the ribbon of the Legion of Honour that was given you in 1819," remarked the Comte. "Is the fashion universal?"

Mistigris and the false Schinner reddened up to their hair.

"Oh, with me it is different," replied Schinner. "I do not wish to be recognised. Do not betray me, Monsieur. I mean to pass for a quite unimportant painter—in fact, a mere decorator. I am going to a gentleman's house where I am anxious to excite no suspicion."

"Oh, ho!" said the Comte, "A lady! A love affair! How happy you are to be young!"

Oscar, who was bursting in his skin with envy at being nobody and having nothing to say, looked from Colonel Czerni-Georges to Schinner the great artist, wondering whether he could not make something of himself. But what could he be, a boy of nineteen, packed off to spend a fortnight or three weeks in the country with the steward of Presles? The Alicante had gone to his head, and his conceit was making the blood boil in his veins. Thus, when the sham Schinner seemed to hint at some romantic adventure of which the joys must be equal to the danger, he gazed at him with eyes flashing with rage and envy.

"Ah!" said the Comte, with a look half of envy and half of incredulity, "you must love a woman very much to make such sacrifices for her sake."

"What sacrifices?" asked Mistigris.

"Don't you know, my little friend, that a ceiling painted by so great a master is covered with gold in payment?" replied the Comte. "Why, if the Civil List* pays you thirty thousand francs for those of the two rooms in the Louvre," he went on, turning to Schinner, "you would certainly charge a humble individual, a *bourgeois*, as you call us in your studios, twenty thousand for a ceiling, while an unknown decorator would hardly get two thousand francs."

"The money loss is not the worst of it," replied Mistigris. "You must consider that it will be a masterpiece, and that he must not sign it for fear of compromising *her*."

"Ah! I would gladly restore all my orders to the sovereigns of Europe to be loved as a young man must be, to be moved to such devotion!" cried Monsieur de Sérisy.

"Ay, there you are," said Mistigris. "A man who is young is beloved of many women, and, as the saying goes, *there is safety in grumblers.*"*

"And what does Madame Schinner say to it?" asked the Comte, "for you married for love the charming Adélaïde de Rouville, the niece of old Admiral Kergarouët, who got you the work at the Louvre, I believe, through the interest of his nephew the Comte de Fontaine."

"Is a painter ever a married man when he is travelling?" asked Mistigris.

"That, then, is studio morality?" exclaimed the Comte in an idiotic way.

"Is the morality of the courts where you got your orders any better?" said Schinner, who had recovered his presence of mind, which had deserted him for a moment when he heard that the Comte was so well informed as to the commission given to the real Schinner.

"I never asked for one," replied the Comte. "I flatter myself that they were all honestly earned."

"And it becomes you *like a pig in dress boots*,"* said Mistigris.

Monsieur de Sérisy would not betray himself; he put on an air of stupid good nature as he looked out over the valley of Groslay, into which they diverged where the roads fork, taking the road to Saint-Brice, and leaving that to Chantilly on their right.

"Ay, take that!" said Oscar between his teeth.

"And is Rome as fine as it is said to be?" Georges asked of the painter.

"Rome is fine only to those who love it—you must have a passion for it to be happy there—but, as a town, I prefer Venice, though I was near being assassinated there."

"My word! But for me," said Mistigris, "your goose would have been cooked! It was that rascal Lord Byron who played you that trick. That devil of an Englishman was as mad as a hatter!"

"Hold your tongue," said Schinner. "I won't have anything known of my affair with Lord Byron."

"But you must confess," said Mistigris, "that you were very glad that I had learned to box in our French fashion?"*

Now and again Pierrotin and the Comte exchanged significant glances which would have disturbed men a little more worldly-wise than these five fellow travellers.

"Lords and pashas, and ceilings worth thirty thousand francs! Bless me!" cried the L'Isle-Adam carrier, "I have crowned heads on board today. What handsome tips I shall get!"

"To say nothing of the places being paid for," said Mistigris slily.

"It comes in the nick of time," Pierrotin went on. "For, you know, my fine new coach, Père Léger, for which I paid two thousand francs on account—well, those swindling coach builders, to whom I am to pay two thousand five hundred francs tomorrow, would not take fifteen hundred francs down and a bill for a thousand at two months. The vultures insist on it all in ready money. Fancy being as hard as that on a man who has travelled this road for eight years, the father of a family, and putting him in danger of losing everything, money and coach both, for lack of a wretched sum of a thousand francs! Gee up, Bichette. They would not dare do it to one of the big companies, I lay a wager."

"Bless me! *No thong, no crupper!*"* said the *rapin*.

"You have only eight hundred francs to seek," replied the Comte, understanding that this speech addressed to the farmer was a sort of bill drawn on himself.

"That's true," said Pierrotin. "Come up, Rougeot!"

"You must have seen some fine painted ceilings at Venice," said the Comte, speaking to Schinner.

"I was too desperately in love to pay any attention to what at the time seemed to me mere trifles," replied Schinner. "And yet I might have been cured of love affairs, for in the Venetian States themselves, in Dalmatia, I had just had a sharp lesson."

"Can you tell the tale?" asked Georges. "I know Dalmatia."

"Well, then, if you have been there you know, of course, that up in that corner of the Adriatic they are all old pirates, outlaws, and corsairs retired from business, when they have escaped hanging, all——"

"Uscoques,* in short," said Georges.

On hearing this, the right name, the Comte, whom

Napoléon had sent into the provinces of Illyria, looked sharply round, so much was he astonished.

"It was in the town where the maraschino is made," said Schinner, seeming to try to remember a name.

"Zara!"* said Georges. "Yes, I have been there; it is on the coast."

"You have hit it," said the painter. "I went there to see the country, for I have a passion for landscape. Twenty times have I made up my mind to try landscape painting, which no one understands, in my opinion, but Mistigris, who will one of these days be a Hobbema, Ruysdael, Claude Lorraine, Poussin, and all the tribe in one."

"Well," exclaimed the Comte, "if he is but one of them, he will do."

"If you interrupt so often, Monsieur," said Oscar, "we shall never know where we are."

"Besides, our friend here is not speaking to you," added Georges to the Comte.

"It is not good manners to interrupt," said Mistigris sententiously. "However, we did the same, and we should all be the losers if we didn't diversify the conversation by an exchange of reflections. All Frenchmen are equal in a public chaise, as the grandson of Czerni-Georges told us. So pray go on, delightful old man, more of your *bunkum*. It is quite the correct thing in the best society, and you know the saying, *do in Turkey as the turkeys do*."*

"I had heard wonders of Dalmatia," Schinner went on. "So off I went, leaving Mistigris at the inn at Venice."

"At the *locanda*," said Mistigris, "put in the local colour."

"Zara is, as I have been told, a vile hole——"

"Yes," said Georges, "but it is fortified."

"I should say so!" replied Schinner, "and the fortifications are an important feature in my story. At Zara there are a great many apothecaries, and I lodged with one of them. In foreign countries the principal business of every native is to let lodgings, his trade is purely accessory. In the evening, when I had changed my shirt, I went out on my balcony. Now on the opposite balcony I perceived a woman—oh!—but a woman! A Greek, that says everything, the loveliest creature in all the town. Almond eyes, eyelids that came down over them like blinds, and lashes like paintbrushes; an oval face that might have turned Raphael's brain, a complexion of exquisite hue, melting tones, a skin of velvet—hands—oh!"

"And not moulded in butter like those of David's school," said Mistigris.

"You insist on talking like a painter!" cried Georges.

"There, you see! *Drive nature out with a pitchfork and it comes back in a paintbox,*"* replied Mistigris.

"And her costume—a genuine Greek costume," Schinner went on. "As you may suppose, I was in flames. I questioned my Diafoirus,* and he informed me that my fair neighbour's name was Zéna. I changed my shirt. To marry Zéna, her husband, an old villain, had paid her parents three hundred thousand francs; the girl's beauty was so famous, and she really was the loveliest creature in all Dalmatia, Illyria, and the Adriatic. In that part of the world you buy your wife, and without having seen her——"

"I will not go there," said old Léger.

"My sleep, some nights, is illuminated by Zéna's eyes," said Schinner. "Her adoring young husband was sixty-seven. Good! But he was as jealous—not as a tiger, for they say a tiger is as jealous as a Dalmatian, and my man was worse than a Dalmatian; he was equal to three Dalmatians and a half. He was an Uscoque, a turkey cock, a high cockalorum gamecock!"

"In short, *the worthy hero of a cock-and-bull story,*"* said Mistigris.

"Good for you!" replied Georges, laughing.

"After being a corsair, and perhaps a pirate, my man thought no more of spitting a Christian than I do of spitting out of the window," Schinner went on. "A pretty lookout for me. And rich—rolling in millions, the old villain! And as ugly as a pirate may be, for some Pasha had wanted his ears, and he had dropped an eye somewhere on his travels. But my Uscoque made good use of the one he had, and you may take my word for it when I tell you he had eyes all round his head. 'Never does he let his wife out of his sight,' said my little Diafoirus. 'If she should require your services, I would take your place in disguise,' said I. 'It is a trick that is very successful in our stage plays.' It would take too long to describe the most delightful period of my life, three days, to wit, that I spent at my window ogling Zéna, and putting on a clean shirt every morning. The situation was all the more ticklish and exciting because the least gesture bore some dangerous meaning. Finally, Zéna, no doubt, came to the conclusion that in all the world none but a foreigner, a Frenchman, and an artist would be capable of making eyes at her in the midst of the perils that surrounded him, so, as she execrated her hideous pirate, she responded to my gaze with glances that were enough to lift a man into the vault of Paradise without any need of pulleys—I was screwed up higher and higher! I was tuned to the pitch of Don Quixote. At last I exclaimed, 'Well, the old wretch may kill me, but here goes!' Not a landscape did I study; I was studying my corsair's lair. At night, having put on my most highly scented clean shirt, I crossed the street and I went in——"

"Into the house?" said Oscar.

"Into the house?" said Georges.

"Into the house," repeated Schinner.

"Well! You are as bold as brass!" cried the farmer. "I wouldn't have gone, that's all I can say——"

"With all the more reason that you would have stuck in the door," replied Schinner. "Well, I went in," he continued, "and I felt two hands which took hold of mine. I said nothing, for those hands, as smooth as the skin of an onion, impressed silence on me. A whisper in my ear said in Venetian, 'He is asleep.' Then, being sure that no one would meet us, Zéna and I went out on the ramparts for an airing, but escorted, if you please, by an old duenna as ugly as sin, who stuck to us like a shadow, and I could not induce Madame la Pirate to dismiss this ridiculous attendant. Next evening we did the same; I wanted to send the old woman home; Zéna refused. As my fair one spoke Greek, and I spoke Venetian, we could come to no understanding—we parted in anger! Said I to myself, as I changed my shirt, 'Next time surely there will be no old woman, and we can make friends again, each in our mother tongue.' Well, and it was the old woman that saved me, as you shall hear. It was so fine that, to divert suspicion, I went out to look about me, after we had made it up, of course. After walking round the ramparts, I was coming quietly home with my hands in my pockets when I saw the street packed full of people. Such a crowd!—as if there was an execution. This crowd rushed at me. I was arrested, handcuffed, and led off in charge of the police. No, you cannot imagine, and I hope you may never know, what it is to be supposed to be a murderer by a frenzied mob, throwing stones at you, yelling after you from top to bottom of the high street of a country town, and pursuing you with threats of death! Every eye is a flame of fire, abuse is on every lip, these firebrands of loathing flare up above a hideous cry of 'Kill him! Down with the murderer!' a sort of bass in the background."

"So your Dalmatians yelled in French?" said the Comte. "You describe the scene as if it had happened yesterday."

Schinner was for the moment dumbfounded.

"The mob speaks the same language everywhere," said Mistigris the politician.

"Finally," Schinner went on again, "when I was in the local court of justice and in the presence of the judges of that country, I was informed that the diabolical corsair was dead, poisoned by Zéna. How I wished I could put on a clean shirt! On my soul, I knew nothing about this melodrama. It would seem that the fair Greek was wont to add a little opium—poppies are so plentiful there, as Monsieur has told you—to her pirate's grog to secure a few minutes' liberty to take a walk, and the night before the poor woman had made a mistake in the dose. It was the damned corsair's money that made the trouble for my Zéna, but she accounted for everything so simply that I was released at once on the strength of the old woman's affidavit, with an order from the mayor of the town and the Austrian Commissioner of Police to remove myself to Rome. Zéna, who allowed the heirs and the officers of the law to help themselves liberally to the Uscoque's wealth, was let off, I was told, with two years' seclusion in a convent, where she still is. I will go back and paint her portrait, for in a few years everything will be forgotten. And these are the follies of eighteen!"

"Yes, and you left me without a sou in the *locanda* at Venice," said Mistigris. "I made my way from Venice to Rome, to see if I could find you, by daubing portraits at five francs a head, and never got paid, but it was a jolly time! *Happiness*, they say, *does not dwell under gilt hoofs*."*

"You may imagine the reflections that choked me with bile in a Dalmatian prison, thrown there without a protector, having to answer to the Dalmatian Austrians, and threatened with the loss of my head for having twice taken a walk with a woman who insisted on being followed by her housekeeper. That is what I call bad luck!" cried Schinner.

"What," said Oscar guilelessly, "did that happen to you?"

"Why not to this gentleman, since it had already happened during the French occupation of Illyria to one of our most distinguished artillery officers?" said the Comte with meaning.

"And did you believe the artillery man?" asked Mistigris slily.

"And is that all?" asked Oscar.

"Well," said Mistigris, "he cannot tell you that he had his head cut off. *Those who live last live longest.*"*

"And are there any farms out there?" asked old Léger. "What do they grow there?"

"There is the maraschino crop," said Mistigris. "A plant that grows just as high as your lips and yields the liqueur of that name."

"Ah!" said Léger.

"I was only three days in the town and a fortnight in prison," replied Schinner. "I saw nothing, not even the fields where they grow the maraschino."

"They are making game of you," said Georges to the farmer, "maraschino grows in cases."

Pierrotin's chaise was now on the way down one of the steep sides of the valley of Saint-Brice, towards the inn in the middle of that large village, where he was to wait an hour to let his horses take breath, eat their oats, and get a drink. It was now about half-past one.

"Hallo! It is farmer Léger!" cried the innkeeper, as the vehicle drew up at his door. "Do you take breakfast?"

"Once every day," replied the burly customer. "We can eat a snack."

"Order breakfast for us," said Georges, carrying his cane as if he were shouldering a musket, in a cavalier style that bewitched Oscar.

Oscar felt a pang of frenzy when he saw this reckless adventurer take a fancy straw cigar case out of his side pocket, and from it a beautiful tan coloured cigar, which he smoked in the doorway while waiting for the meal.

"Do you smoke?" said Georges to Oscar.

"Sometimes," said the schoolboy, puffing out his little chest and assuming a dashing style.

Georges held out the open cigar case to Oscar and to Schinner.

"The devil!" said the great painter. "Ten sous cigars!"

"The remains of what I brought from Spain," said the adventurer. "Are you going to have breakfast?"

"No," said the artist. "They will wait for me at the château. Besides, I had some food before starting."

"And you?" said Georges to Oscar.

"I have had breakfast," said Oscar.

Station à l'auberge de Saint-Brice.

Plate V

Oscar would have given ten years of his life to have boots and trouser straps. He stood sneezing, and choking, and spitting, and sucking up the smoke with ill-disguised grimaces.

"You don't know how to smoke," said Schinner. "Look here," and Schinner, without moving a muscle, drew in the smoke of his cigar and blew it out through his nose without the slightest effort. Then again he kept the smoke in his throat, took the cigar out of his mouth, and exhaled it gracefully.

"There, young man," said the painter.

"And this, young man, is another way," said Georges, imitating Schinner, but swallowing the smoke so that none returned.

"And my parents fancy that I am educated," thought poor Oscar, trying to smoke with some grace.

But he felt so mortally sick that he allowed Mistigris to bone his cigar and to say, as he puffed at it with conspicuous satisfaction—"I suppose you have nothing catching."

But Oscar wished he were only strong enough to hit Mistigris. "Why," said he, pointing to Colonel Georges, "eight francs for Alicante and cheesecakes, forty sous in cigars, and his breakfast, which will cost——"

"Ten francs at least," said Mistigris. "But so it is, *little dishes make long bills.*"*

"Well, Père Léger, we can crack a bottle of Bordeaux apiece?" said Georges to the farmer.

"His breakfast will cost him twenty francs!" cried Oscar. "Why, that comes to more than thirty francs!"

Crushed by the sense of his inferiority, Oscar sat down on the cornerstone lost in a reverie, which hindered his observing that his trousers, hitched up as he sat, showed the line of union between an old stocking leg and a new foot to it, a masterpiece of his mother's skill.

"Our understandings are twins, if not our soles," said Mistigris, pulling one leg of his trousers a little way up to show a similar effect. *"But a baker's children are always worst bread."**

The jest made Monsieur de Sérisy smile as he stood with folded arms under the gateway behind the two lads. Heedless as they were, the solemn statesman envied them their faults; he liked their bounce, and admired the quickness of their fun.

"Well, can you get Les Moulineaux? for you went to Paris to fetch the money," said the innkeeper to old Léger, having just shown him a nag for sale in his stables. "It will be a fine joke to *screw a bit* out of the Comte de Sérisy, a Peer of France and a state minister."

The wily old courtier betrayed nothing in his face, but he looked round to watch the farmer.

"His goose is cooked!" replied Léger in a low voice.

"So much the better; I love to see your bigwigs *done*. And if you want a score or so thousand francs, I will lend you the money. But François, the driver of Touchards' six o'clock coach, told me as he went through that Monsieur Margueron is invited to dine with the Comte de Sérisy himself today at Presles."

"That is His Excellency's plan, but we have our little notions too," replied the farmer.

"Ah, but the Comte will find a place for Monsieur Margueron's son, and you have no places to give away," said the innkeeper.

"No, but if the Comte has the ministers on his side, I have King Louis XVIII on mine," said Léger in the innkeeper's ear, "and forty thousand of his effigies handed over to Master Moreau will enable me to buy Les Moulineaux for two hundred and sixty thousand francs before Monsieur de Sérisy can step in, and he will be glad enough to take it off my hands for three hundred and sixty thousand rather than have the lands valued lot by lot."

"Not a bad turn, Master," said his friend.

"How is that for a stroke of business?" said the farmer.

"And, after all, the farm lands are worth it to him," said the innkeeper.

"Les Moulineaux pays six thousand francs a year in kind, and I mean to renew the lease at seven thousand five hundred for eighteen years. So as he invests at more than two and a half percent, Monsieur le Comte won't be robbed. Not to commit Monsieur Moreau, I am to be proposed to the Comte by him as a tenant; he will seem to be taking care of his master's interests by finding him nearly three percent, for his money and a farmer who will pay regularly——"

"And what will Moreau get out of the job altogether?"

"Well, if the Comte makes him a present of ten thousand francs, he will clear fifty thousand on the transaction, but he will have earned them fairly."

"And, after all, what does the Comte care for Presles? He is so rich," said the innkeeper. "I have never set eyes on him myself."

"Nor I neither," said the farmer. "But he is coming at last to live there; he would not otherwise be laying out two hundred thousand francs on redecorating the rooms. It is as fine as the King's palace."

"Well, then," replied the other, "it is high time that Moreau should feather his nest."

"Yes, yes, for when once the master and mistress are on the spot, they will not keep their eyes in their pockets."

Though the conversation was carried on in a low tone, the Comte had kept his ears open.

"Here I have all the evidence I was going in search of," thought he, looking at the burly farmer as he went back into the kitchen. "But perhaps it is no more than a scheme as yet. Perhaps Moreau has not closed with the offer!" So averse was he to believe that the land steward was capable of mixing himself up in such a plot.

Pierrotin now came out to give his horses water. The Comte supposed that the driver would breakfast with the innkeeper and Léger, and what he had overheard made him fear the least betrayal.

"The whole posse are in league," thought he, "it serves them right to thwart their scheming. Pierrotin," said he in a low voice as he went up to the driver, "I promised you ten louis to keep my secret, but if you will take care not to let out my name (and I shall know whether you have mentioned it, or given the least due to it to any living soul, even at L'Isle-Adam) tomorrow morning, as you pass the château, I will give you the thousand francs to pay for your new coach. And for greater safety," added he, slapping Pierrotin's back, "do without your breakfast; stay outside with your horses."

Pierrotin had turned pale with joy.

"I understand, Monsieur le Comte, trust me. It is old Père Léger——"

"It concerns every living soul," replied the Comte.

"Be easy. Come, hurry up," said Pierrotin, half opening the kitchen door, "we are late already. Listen, Père Léger, there is the hill before us, you know; I am not hungry; I will go on slowly, and you will easily catch me up. A walk will do you good."

"'The man is in a devil of a hurry!" said the innkeeper. "Won't you come and join us? The Colonel is standing wine at fifty sous, and a bottle of champagne."

"No, I can't. I have a fish on board to be delivered at Stors by three o'clock for a big dinner, and such customers don't see a joke any more than the fish."

"All right," said Léger to the innkeeper, "put the horse you want me to buy in the shafts of your gig, and you can drive us on to pick up Pierrotin. Then we can breakfast in peace, and I shall see what the nag can do. Three of us can very well ride in your trap."

To the Comte's great satisfaction, Pierrotin himself brought out his horses. Schinner and Mistigris had walked forward. Pierrotin picked up the two artists halfway between Saint-Brice and Poncelles, and just as he reached the top of the hill, whence they had a view of Écouen, the belfry of Le Mesnil,* and the woods which encircle that beautiful landscape, the sound of a galloping horse drawing a gig that rattled and jingled announced the pursuit of Père Léger and Mina's Colonel, who settled themselves into the chaise again. As Pierrotin zigzagged down the hill into Moisselles, Georges, who had never ceased expatiating to old Léger on the beauty of the innkeeper's wife at Saint-Brice, exclaimed—"I say, this is not amiss by way of landscape, Great Painter?"

"It ought not to astonish you, who have seen Spain and the East."

"And I have two of the Spanish cigars left. If nobody objects, will you finish them off, Schinner? The little man had enough with a mouthful or two."

Old Léger and the Comte kept silence, which was taken for consent.

Oscar, annoyed at being spoken of as 'a little man,' retorted while the others were lighting their cigars— "Though I have not been Mina's aide-de-camp, Monsieur, and have not been in the East, I may go there yet. The career for which my parents intend me will, I hope, relieve me of the necessity of riding in a public chaise when I am as old as you are. When once I am a person of importance and get a place, I will stay in it——"

"*Et cetera punctum!*" said Mistigris, imitating the sort of hoarse crow which made Oscar's speech even more ridiculous, for the poor boy was at the age when the beard begins to grow and the voice to break. "After all," added Mistigris, "*extremes bleat.*"*

"My word!" said Schinner, "the horses can scarcely drag such a weight of dignity."

"So your parents intend to start you in a career," said Georges very seriously. "And what may it be?"

"In diplomacy," said Oscar.

Three shouts of laughter went forth like three rockets from Mistigris, Schinner, and the old farmer. Even the Comte could not help smiling. Georges kept his countenance.

"By Allah! But there is nothing to laugh at," said the Colonel. "Only, young man," he went on, addressing Oscar, "it struck me that your respectable mother is not for the moment in a social position wholly beseeming an ambassadress. She had a most venerable straw bag and a patch on her shoe."

"My mother, Monsieur!" said Oscar, fuming with indignation. "It was our housekeeper."

"'*Our*' is most aristocratic!" cried the Comte, interrupting Oscar.

"The King says *our*," replied Oscar haughtily.

A look from Georges checked a general burst of laughter; it conveyed to the painter and to Mistigris the desirability of dealing judiciously with Oscar so as to make the most of this mine of amusement.

"Monsieur is right," said the painter to the Comte, designating Oscar. "Gentlefolks talk of *our* house; only second-rate people talk of *my* house. Everybody has a mania for seeming to have what he has not. For a man loaded with decorations——"

"Then, Monsieur also is a decorator?" asked Mistigris.

"You know nothing of court language. I beg the favour of your protection, Your Excellency," added Schinner, turning to Oscar.

"I must congratulate myself," said the Comte, "on having travelled with three men who are or will be famous—a painter who is already illustrious, a future general, and a young diplomatist who will some day reunite Belgium to France."

But Oscar, having so basely denied his mother and furious at perceiving that his companions were making game of him, determined to convince their incredulity at any cost.

"All is not gold that glitters!" said he, flashing lightning from his eyes.

"You've got it wrong," cried Mistigris. "*All is not told that titters.** You will not go far in diplomacy if you do not know your proverbs better than that."

"If I do not know my proverbs, I know my way."

"It must be leading you a long way," said Georges, "for your family housekeeper gave you provisions enough for a sea voyage—biscuits, chocolate——"

"A particular roll and some chocolate, yes, Monsieur," returned Oscar. "My stomach is much too delicate to digest the *ratatouille* you get at an inn."

"*Ratatouille* is as delicate as your digestion," retorted Georges.

"*Ratatouille* is good!" said the great painter.

"The word is in use in the best circles," said Mistigris; "I use it myself at the coffeehouse of the Poule Noire."*

"Your tutor was, no doubt, some famous professor— Monsieur Andrieux of the Academy, or Monsieur Royer-Collard?"* asked Schinner.

"My tutor was the Abbé Loraux, now the Vicar of St. Sulpice,"* replied Oscar, remembering the name of the confessor of the school.

"You did very wisely to have a private tutor," said Mistigris, "*for the fountain—of learning—brought forth a mouse,** and you will do something for your abbé, of course?"

"Certainly; he will be a bishop some day."

"Through your family interest?" asked Georges quite gravely.

"We may perhaps contribute to his due promotion, for the Abbé Frayssinous* often comes to our house."

"Oh, do you know the Abbé Frayssinous?" asked the Comte.

"He is under obligations to my father," replied Oscar.

"And you are on your way to your estates no doubt?" said Georges.

"No, Monsieur, but I have no objection to saying where I am going. I am on my way to the château of Presles, the Comte de Sérisy's."

"The devil you are! To Presles?" cried Schinner, turning crimson.

"Then you know Monseigneur the Comte de Sérisy?" asked Georges.

Farmer Léger turned so as to look at Oscar with a bewildered gaze, exclaiming—"And Monsieur le Comte is at Presles?"

"So it would seem, as I am going there," replied Oscar.

"Then you have often seen the Comte?" asked Monsieur de Sérisy.

"As plainly as I see you. I am great friends with his son, who is about my age, nineteen, and we ride together almost every day."

"Kings have been known to harry beggar maids,"* said Mistigris sapiently.

A wink from Pierrotin had relieved the farmer's alarm.

"On my honour," said the Comte to Oscar, "I am delighted to find myself in the company of a young gentleman who can speak with authority of that nobleman. I am anxious to secure his favour in a somewhat important business in which his help will cost him nothing. It is a little claim against the American Government. I should be glad to learn something as to the sort of man he is."

"Oh, if you hope to succeed," replied Oscar, with an assumption of competence, "do not apply to him, but to his wife; he is madly in love with her, no one knows that better than I, and his wife cannot endure him."

"Why?" asked Georges.

"The Comte has some skin disease that makes him hideous, and Doctor Alibert* has tried in vain to cure it. Monsieur de Sérisy would give half of his immense fortune to have a chest like mine," said Oscar, opening his shirt and showing a clean pink skin like a child's.

"He lives alone, secluded in his house. You need a good introduction to see him at all. In the first place, he gets up very early in the morning and works from three till eight, after eight he follows various treatments, sulphur baths or vapour baths. They stew him in a sort of iron tank, for he is always hoping to be cured."

"If he is so intimate with the King, why is he not 'touched' by him?" asked Georges.

"Then the lady keeps her husband in hot water,"* said Mistigris.

"The Comte has promised thirty thousand francs to a famous Scotch physician who is prescribing for him now," Oscar went on.

"Then his wife can hardly be blamed for giving herself the best——" Schinner began, but he did not finish his sentence.

"To be sure," said Oscar. "The poor man is so shrivelled, so decrepit, you would think he was eighty. He is as dry as parchment, and to add to his misfortune, he feels his position——"

"And feels it hot, I should think," remarked the farmer facetiously.

"Monsieur, he worships his wife, and dares not blame her," replied Oscar. "He performs the most ridiculous scenes with her; you would die of laughing—exactly like Arnolphe in Molière's play."*

The Comte, in blank dismay, looked at Pierrotin, who seeing him apparently unmoved, concluded that Madame Clapart's son was inventing a pack of slander.

"So, Monsieur, if you wish to succeed," said Oscar to the Comte, "apply to the Marquis d'Aiglemont. If you have Madame's venerable adorer on your side, you will at one stroke secure both the lady and her husband."

"That is what we call *killing two-thirds with one bone*,"* said Mistigris.

"Dear me!" said the painter, "have you seen the Comte undressed? Are you his valet?"

"His valet!" cried Oscar.

"By the Mass! A man does not say such things about his friends in a public conveyance," added Mistigris. "*Prudence*, my young friend, *is the mother of Deafness*. I simply don't hear you."

"It is certainly a case of *tell me whom you know, and I will tell you whom you hate*," exclaimed Schinner.

"But you must learn, Great Painter," said Georges pompously, "that no man can speak ill of those he does not know. The boy has proved at any rate that he knows his Sérisy by heart. Now, if he had only talked of Madame, it might have been supposed that he was on terms——"

"Not another word about the Comtesse de Sérisy, young men!" cried the Comte. "Her brother, the Marquis de Ronquerolles, is a friend of mine, and the man who is so rash as to cast a doubt on the Comtesse's honour will answer to me for his speech."

"Monsieur is right," said the artist, "there should be no *talking rubbish* about women."

"God, Honour, and the Ladies! I saw a melodrama of that name,"* said Mistigris.

"Though I do not know Mina, I know the Keeper of the Seals,"* said the Comte, looking at Georges. "And though I do not display my orders," he added, turning to the painter, "I can hinder their being given to those who do not deserve them. In short, I know so many people that I know Monsieur Grindot, the architect of Presles. Stop, Pierrotin, I am going to get out."

Pierrotin drove on to the village of Moisselles, and there, at a little country inn, the travellers alighted. This bit of road was passed in utter silence.

"Where on earth is that little rascal going?" asked the Comte, leading Pierrotin into the inn yard.

"To stay with your steward. He is the son of a poor lady who lives in the Rue de la Cerisaie, and to whom I often carry fruit and game and poultry—a certain Madame Husson."

"Who is that gentleman?" old Léger asked Pierrotin when the Comte had turned away.

"I don't know," said Pierrotin. "He never rode with me before, but he may be the prince who owns the château of Maffliers. He has just told me where to set him down on the road; he is not going so far as L'Isle-Adam."

"Pierrotin fancies he is the owner of Maffliers," said the farmer to Georges, getting back into the chaise.

At this stage the three young fellows, looking as silly as pilferers caught in the act, did not dare meet each other's eye, and seemed lost in reflections on the upshot of their fictions.

"That is what I call *a great lie and little wool*,"* observed Mistigris.

"You see, I know the Comte," said Oscar.

"Possibly, but you will never be an ambassador," replied Georges. "If you must talk in a public carriage, learn to talk like me and tell nothing."

"*The mother of mischief is no more than a midge's sting*,"* said Mistigris conclusively.

The Comte now got into the chaise, and Pierrotin drove on; perfect silence reigned.

"Well, my good friends," said the Comte, as they reached the wood of Carreau,* "we are all as mute as if we were going to an execution."

"We must know when to *creep* silent," said Mistigris with an air.

"It is a fine day," remarked Georges.

"What place is that?" asked Oscar, pointing to the château of Franconville, which shows so finely on the slope of the great forest of Saint-Martin.*

"What!" said the Comte, "you, who have been so often to Presles, do not know Franconville when you see it?"

"Monsieur knows more of men than of houses," said Mistigris.

"An apprentice diplomat may sometimes be oblivious," exclaimed Georges.

"Remember my name!" cried Oscar in a fury, "it is Oscar Husson, and in ten years' time I shall be famous."

After this speech, pronounced with great bravado, Oscar huddled himself into his corner.

"Husson de—what?" asked Mistigris.

"A great family," replied the Comte. "The Hussons de la Cerisaie. Monsieur was born at the foot of the Imperial throne."

Oscar blushed to the roots of his hair in an agony of alarm. They were about to descend the steep hill by La Cave, at the bottom of which, in a narrow valley, on the skirt of the forest of Saint-Martin, stands the splendid château of Presles.

"Messieurs," said Monsieur de Sérisy, "I wish you well in your several careers. You, Monsieur le Colonel, make your peace with the King of France; the Czerni-Georges must be on good terms with the Bourbons. I have no forecast for you, my dear Monsieur Schinner; your fame is already made, and you have won it nobly by splendid work. But you are such a dangerous man that I, who have a wife, should not dare to offer you a commission under my roof. As to Monsieur Husson, he needs no interest; he is the master of statesmen's secrets, and can make them tremble. Monsieur Léger is going to steal a march on the Comte de Sérisy; I only hope that he may hold his own. Put me down here, Pierrotin, and you can take me up at the same spot tomorrow!" added the Comte, who got out, leaving his fellow travellers quite confounded.

"*When you take to your heels you can't take too much,*"* remarked Mistigris, seeing how nimbly the traveller vanished in a sunken path.

"Oh, he must be the Comte who has taken Franconville; he is going that way," said Père Léger.

"If ever again I should happen to *talk rubbish* in a public carriage, I will call myself out," said the false

Schinner. "It is partly your fault too, Mistigris," said he, giving his boy a rap on his cap.

"Oh, ho! I—who only followed you to Venice," replied Mistigris. "But *play a dog a bad game and slang him.*"*

"Do you know," said Georges to Oscar, "that if by any chance that was the Comte de Sérisy, I should be sorry to find myself in your skin, although it is so free from disease."

Oscar, reminded by these words of his mother's advice, turned pale, and was quite sobered.

"Here you are, Messieurs," said Pierrotin, pulling up at a handsome gate.

"What, already?" exclaimed the painter, Georges, and Oscar all in a breath.

"That's a stiff one!" cried Pierrotin. "Do you mean to say, Messieurs, that neither of you has ever been here before? There stands the château of Presles!"

"All right," said Georges, recovering himself. "I am going on to the farm of Les Moulineaux," he added, not choosing to tell his fellow travellers that he was bound for the house.

"Then you are coming with me," said Léger.

"How is that?"

"I am the farmer at Les Moulineaux. And what do you want of me, Colonel?"

"A taste of your butter," said Georges, pulling out his portfolio.

"Pierrotin, drop my things at the steward's," said Oscar; "I am going straight to the house."

And he plunged into a cross path without knowing whither it led.

"Hallo! Monsieur Ambassador," cried Pierrotin, "you are going into the forest. If you want to get to the château, go in by the side gate."

Thus compelled to go in, Oscar made his way into the spacious courtyard with a huge stone-edged flowerbed in the middle and stone posts all round with chains between. While Père Léger stood watching Oscar, Georges, thunderstruck at hearing the burly farmer describe himself as the owner of Les Moulineaux, vanished so nimbly that when the fat man looked round for his Colonel, he could not find him. At Pierrotin's request the gate was opened, and he went in with much dignity to deposit the Great Schinner's multifarious properties at the lodge. Oscar was in dismay at seeing Mistigris and the artist, the witnesses of his brag, really admitted to the château. In ten minutes Pierrotin had unloaded the chaise of the painter's paraphernalia, Oscar Husson's luggage, and the neat leather portmanteau, which he mysteriously confided to the lodge keeper. Then he turned his machine, cracking his whip energetically, and went on his way to the woods of L'Isle-Adam, his face still wearing the artful expression of a peasant summing up his profits. Nothing was wanting to his satisfaction. On the morrow he would have his thousand francs.

Oscar, with his tail between his legs, so to speak, wandered round the great court, waiting to see what would become of his travelling companions, when he presently saw Monsieur Moreau come out of the large entrance hall, known as the guardroom, on to the front steps. The land steward, who wore a long blue riding coat down to his heels, had on nankin-coloured breeches and hunting boots, and carried a crop in his hand.

"Well, my boy, so here you are? And how is the dear mother?" said he, shaking hands with Oscar. "Good morning, Messieurs; you, no doubt, are the painters promised us by Monsieur Grindot the architect?" said he to the artists.

He whistled twice, using the end of his riding whip, and the lodge keeper came forward.

"Take these gentlemen to their rooms—numbers 14 and 15; Madame Moreau will give you the keys. Light fires this evening if necessary and carry up their things. I am instructed by Monsieur le Comte to ask you to dine with me," he added, addressing the artists. "At five, as in Paris. If you are sportsmen, you can be well amused. I have permission to shoot and fish, and we have twelve thousand acres of shooting outside our own grounds."

Oscar, the painter, and Mistigris, one as much disconcerted as the other, exchanged glances. Still, Mistigris, faithful to his instincts, exclaimed—"Bah! *Never throw the candle after the shade!** On we go!"

Little Husson followed the steward, who led the way, walking quickly across the park.

"Jacques," said he to one of his sons, "go and tell your mother that young Husson has arrived, and say that I am obliged to go over to Les Moulineaux for a few minutes."

Moreau, now about fifty years of age, a dark man of medium height, had a stern expression. His bilious complexion, highly coloured nevertheless by a country life, suggested, at first sight, a character very unlike what his really was. Everything contributed to the illusion. His hair was turning grey, his blue eyes and a large aquiline nose gave him a sinister expression, all the more so because his eyes were too close together; still, his full lips, the shape of his face, and the good humour of his address, would, to a keen observer, have been indications of kindliness. His very decided manner and abrupt way of speech impressed Oscar immensely with a sense of his penetration, arising from his real affection for the boy. Brought up by his mother to look up to the steward as a great man, Oscar always felt small in Moreau's presence, and now, finding himself at Presles, he felt an oppressive uneasiness, as if he had some ill to fear from this fatherly friend who was his only protector.

"Why, my dear Oscar, you do not look glad to be here," said the steward. "But you will have plenty to amuse you; you can learn to ride, to shoot, and hunt."

"I know nothing of such things," said Oscar dully.

"But I have asked you here on purpose to teach you."

"Mama told me not to stay more than a fortnight, because Madame Moreau——"

"Oh, well, we shall see," replied Moreau, almost offended by Oscar's doubts of his conjugal influence.

Moreau's youngest son, a lad of fifteen, active and brisk, now came running up.

"Here," said his father, "take your new companion to your mother."

And the steward himself went off by the shortest path to the gamekeeper's house between the park and the wood.

The handsome lodge, given by the Comte to his land steward as a residence, had been built some years before the Revolution by the owner of the famous estate of Cassan where Bergeret, a farmer-general of enormous wealth who made himself as notorious for extravagance as Bodard, Pâris, and Bouret, had planted gardens, diverted rivers, and built hermitages, Chinese temples, and other costly magnificences.

This house, in the middle of a large garden, of which one wall divided it from the outbuildings of Presles, had formerly had its entrance on the village high street. Monsieur de Sérisy's father, when he purchased the property, had only to pull down the dividing wall and build up the front gate to make this plot and house part of the outbuildings. Then, by pulling down another wall, he added to his park all the garden land that the former owner had purchased to complete his ring fence. The lodge, built of freestone, was in the Louis XV style, with linen pattern panels under the windows, like those on the colonnades of the Place Louis XV,* in stiff, angular folds; it consisted, on the ground floor, of a fine drawing room opening into a bedroom, and of a dining room with a billiard room adjoining. These two suites, parallel to each other, were divided by a sort of anteroom or hall, and the stairs. The hall was decorated by the doors of the drawing room and dining room, both handsomely ornamental. The kitchen was under the dining room, for there was a flight of ten outside steps.

Madame Moreau had taken the first floor for her own, and had transformed what had been the best bedroom into a boudoir; this boudoir, and the drawing room below, handsomely fitted up with the best pickings of the old furniture from the château, would certainly have done no discredit to the mansion of a lady of fashion. The drawing room, hung with blue and white damask, the spoils of a state bed, and with old gilt wood furniture upholstered with the same silk, displayed ample curtains to the doors and windows. Some pictures that had formerly been panels, with flower stands, a few modern tables, and handsome lamps, besides an antique hanging chandelier of cut glass, gave the room a very dignified effect. The carpet was old Persian. The boudoir was altogether modern and fitted to Madame Moreau's taste, in imitation of a tent, with blue silk ropes on a light grey ground. There was the usual divan with pillows and cushions for the feet, and the flower stands, carefully cherished by the head gardener, were a joy to the eye with their pyramids of flowers. The dining room and billiard room were fitted with mahogany. All round the house the steward's lady had planned a flower garden, beautifully kept, and beyond it lay the park. Clumps of foreign shrubs shut out the stables, and to give admission from the road to her visitors she had opened a gate where the old entrance had been built up.

Thus, the dependent position filled by the Moreaus was cleverly glossed over, and they were the better able to figure as rich folks managing a friend's estate for their pleasure, because neither the Comte nor the Comtesse ever came to quash their pretensions, and the liberality of Monsieur de Sérisy's concessions allowed of their living in abundance, the luxury of country homes. Dairy produce, eggs, poultry, game, fruit, forage, flowers, wood, and vegetables—the steward and his wife had all of these in profusion, and bought literally nothing but butcher's meat and the wine and foreign produce necessary to their lordly extravagance. The poultry wife made the bread, and, in fact, for the last few years, Moreau had paid his butcher's bill with the pigs of the farm, keeping only as much pork as he needed. One day the Comtesse, always very generous to her former lady's maid, made Madame Moreau a present, as a souvenir perhaps, of a little travelling chaise of a past fashion which Moreau had furbished up, and in which his wife drove out behind a pair of good horses, useful at other times in the grounds. Besides this pair, the steward had his saddle horse. He ploughed part of the parkland and raised grain enough to feed the beasts and servants; he cut three hundred tons more or less of good hay, accounting for no more than one hundred, encroaching on the license vaguely granted by the Comte, and instead of using his share of the produce on the premises, he sold it. He kept his poultry farm, his pigeons, and his cows on the crops from the parkland, but then the manure from his stables was used in the Comte's garden. Each of these pilfering acts had an excuse ready. Madame Moreau's house servant was the daughter of one of the gardeners, and waited on her and cooked; she was helped in the housework by a girl who also attended to the poultry and dairy. Moreau had engaged an invalided soldier named Brochon to look after the horses and do the dirty work.

At Nerville, at Chauvry,* at Beaumont, at Maffliers, at Préroles, and at Nointel, the steward's pretty wife was everywhere received by persons who did not, or affected not to know her original position in life. And Moreau could confer obligations. He could use his master's interest in matters which are of immense importance in the depths of the country, though trivial in Paris. After securing for friends the appointments of Justice of the Peace at Beaumont and at L'Isle-Adam, he had, in the course of the same year, saved an inspector of forest-lands from dismissal, and obtained the Cross of the Legion of Honour for the quartermaster at Beaumont. So there was never a festivity among the more respectable neighbours without Monsieur and Madame Moreau being invited. The Curé and the Mayor of Presles were to be seen every evening at their house. A man can hardly help being a good fellow when he has made himself so comfortable.

A pretty and simpering woman like every grand lady's servant who, when she marries, likes to imitate her mistress, the steward's wife introduced the latest fashions, wore the most expensive shoes, and never walked out but in fine weather. Though her husband gave her no more than five hundred francs a year for dress, this in the country is a very large sum, especially when judiciously spent, and his "lady"—fair, bright, and fresh looking at the age of thirty-six, and still slight, neat, and attractive in spite of her three children—still played the girl, and gave herself the airs of a princess. If, as she drove past in her open chaise on her way to Beaumont, some stranger happened to inquire, "Who is that?" Madame Moreau was furious if a native of the place replied, "She is the steward's wife at Presles." She aimed at being taken for the mistress of the château. She amused herself with patronising the villagers as a great lady might have done. Her husband's power with the Comte, proved in so many ways, hindered the townsfolk from laughing at Madame Moreau, who was a person of importance in the eyes of the peasantry. Estelle, however (her name was Estelle) did not interfere in the management any more than a stockbroker's wife interferes in dealings on the Bourse; she even relied on her husband for the administration of the house and of their income. Quite confident in her own *powers of pleasing,* she was miles away from imagining that this delightful life, which had gone on for seventeen years, could ever be in danger; however, on hearing that the Comte had resolved on restoring the splendid château of Presles, she understood that all her enjoyments were imperilled, and she had persuaded her husband to come to terms with Léger so as to have a retreat at L'Isle-Adam. She could not have borne to find herself in an almost servile position in the presence of her former mistress, who would undoubtedly laugh at her on finding her established at the lodge in a style that aped the lady of fashion.

The origin of the deep-seated enmity between the Reyberts and the Moreaus lay in a stab inflicted on Madame Moreau by Madame de Reybert in revenge for a pinprick that the steward's wife had dared to give on the first arrival of the Reyberts, lest her supremacy should be infringed on by the lady *née* de Corroy. Madame de Reybert had mentioned, and perhaps for the first time informed the neighbourhood, of Madame Moreau's original calling. The words *lady's maid* flew from lip to lip. All those who envied the Moreaus—and they must have been many—at Beaumont, at L'Isle-Adam, at Maffliers, at Champagne, at Nerville, at Chauvry, at Baillet, and at Moisselles, made such pregnant comments that more than one spark from this conflagration fell into the Moreaus' home. For four years now, the Reyberts, excommunicated by their pretty rival, had become the object of so much hostile animadversion from her partisans that their position would have been untenable but for the thought of vengeance, which had sustained them to this day.

The Moreaus, who were very good friends with Grindot the architect, had been told by him of the arrival ere long of a painter commissioned to finish the decorative panels at the château, Schinner having executed the more important pieces. This great painter recommended the artist we have seen travelling with Mistigris to paint the borders, arabesques, and other accessory decorations. Hence, for two days past, Madame Moreau had been preparing her war paint and sitting expectant. An artist who was to board with her for some weeks was worthy of some outlay. Schinner and his wife had been quartered in the château, where, by the Comte's orders, they had been treated like Her Ladyship herself. Grindot, who boarded with the Moreaus, had treated the great artist with so much respect that neither the steward nor his wife had ventured on any familiarity. And, indeed, the richest and most noble landowners in the district had vied with each other in entertaining Schinner and his wife. So now Madame Moreau, much pleased at the prospect of turning the tables, promised herself that she would sound the trumpet before the artist who was to be her guest, and make him out a match in talent for Schinner.

Although on the two previous days she had achieved very coquettish toilettes, the steward's pretty wife had husbanded her resources too well not to have reserved the most bewitching till the Saturday, never doubting that on that day at any rate the artist would arrive to dinner. She had shod herself in bronze kid with fine thread stockings. A dress of finely striped pink and white muslin, a pink belt with a chased gold buckle, a cross and heart round her neck, and wristlets of black velvet on her bare arms (Madame de Sérisy had fine arms, and was fond of displaying them) gave Madame Moreau the style of a fashionable Parisian. She put on a very handsome Leghorn hat, graced with a bunch of moss roses made by Nattier, and under its broad shade her fair hair flowed in glossy curls. Having ordered a first-rate dinner and carefully inspected the rooms, she went out at an hour which brought her to the large flowerbed in the court of the château, like the lady of the house, just when the coach would pass. Over her head she held an elegant pink silk parasol lined with white and trimmed with fringe. On seeing Pierrotin hand over to the lodge keeper the artist's extraordinary looking luggage, and perceiving no owner, Estelle had returned home lamenting the waste of another carefully arranged dress. And, like most people who have dressed for an occasion, she felt quite incapable of any occupation but that of doing nothing in her drawing room while waiting for the passing of the Beaumont coach which should come through an hour after Pierrotin's, though it did not start from Paris till one o'clock; thus she was waiting at home while the two young artists were dressing for dinner. In fact, the young painter and Mistigris were so overcome by the description of lovely Madame Moreau given them by the gardener whom they had questioned, that it was obvious to them both that they must get themselves into their best *toggery*. So they donned their very best before presenting themselves at the steward's house, whither they were conducted by Jacques Moreau, the eldest of the children, a stalwart youth, dressed in the English fashion in a round jacket with a turned down collar, and as happy during the holidays as a fish in water, here on the estate where his mother reigned supreme.

"Mama," said he, "here are the two artists come from Monsieur Schinner."

Madame Moreau, very agreeably surprised, rose, bid her son set chairs, and displayed all her graces.

"Mama, little Husson is with father; I am to go to fetch him," whispered the boy in her ear.

"There is no hurry, you can stop and amuse him," said the mother.

The mere words *there is no hurry* showed the two artists how entirely unimportant was their travelling companion, but the tone also betrayed the indifference of a stepmother for her stepchild. In fact, Madame Moreau, who, after seventeen years of married life, could not fail to be aware of her husband's attachment to Madame

Clapart and young Husson, hated the mother and son in so overt a manner that it is easy to understand why Moreau had never till now ventured to invite Oscar to Presles.

"We are enjoined, my husband and I," said she to the two artists, "to do the honours of the château. We are fond of art, and more especially of artists," said she, with a simper, "and I beg you to consider yourselves quite at home here. In the country, you see, there is no ceremony; liberty is indispensable, otherwise life is too insipid. We have had Monsieur Schinner here already——"

Mistigris gave his companion a mischievous wink.

"You know him, of course," said Estelle, after a pause.

"Who does not know him, Madame?" replied the painter.

"He is as well known *as the parish birch*," added Mistigris.

"Monsieur Grindot mentioned your name," said Madame Moreau, "but really I——"

"Joseph Bridau, Madame," replied the artist, extremely puzzled as to what this woman could be.

Mistigris was beginning to fume inwardly at this fair lady's patronising tone; still, he waited, as Bridau did too, for some movement, some chance word to enlighten them: one of those expressions of assumed fine-ladyism which painters, those born and cruel observers of folly—the perennial food of their pencil—seize on in an instant. In the first place, Estelle's large hands and feet, those of a peasant from the district of Saint-Lô, struck them at once, and before long one or two lady's maid's phrases, modes of speech that gave the lie to the elegance of her dress, betrayed their prey into the hands of the artist and his apprentice. They exchanged a look which pledged them both to take Estelle quite seriously as a pastime during their stay.

"You are so fond of art, perhaps you cultivate it with success, Madame?" said Joseph Bridau.

"No. Though my education was not neglected, it was purely commercial. But I have such a marked and delicate feeling for art that Monsieur Schinner always begged me, when he had finished a piece, to give him my opinion."

"Just as Molière consulted Laforêt," said Mistigris.

Not knowing that Laforêt was a servant girl, Madame Moreau responded with a graceful droop, showing that in her ignorance she regarded this speech as a compliment.

"How is it that he did not propose just to knock off your head?" said Bridau. "Painters are generally on the lookout for handsome women."

"What is your meaning, pray?" said Madame Moreau, on whose face dawned the wrath of an offended queen.

"In studio slang, to knock a thing off is to sketch it," said Mistigris, in an ingratiating tone, "and all we ask is to have handsome heads to sketch. And we sometimes say in admiration that *a woman's beauty has knocked us over*."

"Ah, I did not know the origin of the phrase!" replied she, with a look of languishing sweetness at Mistigris.

"My pupil, Monsieur Léon de Lora," said Bridau, "has a great talent for likeness. He would be only too happy, fair lady, to leave you a souvenir of his skill by painting your charming face."

And Bridau signalled to Mistigris, as much as to say, "Come, drive it home, she really is not amiss!" Taking this hint, Léon de Lora moved to the sofa by Estelle's side and took her hand, which she left in his.

"Oh! if only as a surprise to *your husband*. Madame, if you could give me a few sittings in secret, I would try to excel myself. You are so lovely, so young, so charming! A man devoid of talent might become a genius with you for his model! In your eyes he would find——"

"And we would represent your sweet children in our arabesques," said Joseph, interrupting Mistigris.

"I would rather have them in my own drawing room, but that would be asking too much," said she, looking coquettishly at Bridau.

"Beauty, Madame, is a queen whom painters worship, and who has every right to command them."

"They are quite charming," thought Madame Moreau. "Do you like driving out in the evening, after dinner, in an open carriage, in the woods?"

"Oh! oh! oh! oh!" cried Mistigris in ecstatic tones at each added detail. "Why, Presles will be an earthly paradise."

"With a fair-haired Eve, a young and bewitching woman," added Bridau.

Just as Madame Moreau was preening herself and soaring into the seventh heaven, she was brought down again like a kite by a tug at the cord.

"Madame!" exclaimed the maid, bouncing in like a cannonball.

"Bless me, Rosalie, what can justify you in coming in like this without being called?"

Rosalie did not trouble her head about this apostrophe, but said in her mistress's ear—"Monsieur le Comte is here."

"Did he ask for me?" said the steward's wife.

"No, Madame—but—he wants his portmanteau and the key of his room."

"Let him have them then," said she, with a cross shrug to disguise her uneasiness.

"Mama, here is Oscar Husson!" cried her youngest son, bringing in Oscar, who, as red as a poppy, dared not come forward as he saw the two painters in different dress.

"So here you are at last, boy," said Estelle coldly. "You are going to dress, I hope?" she went on, after looking at him from head to foot with great contempt. "I suppose your mother has not brought you up to dine in company in such clothes as those."

"Oh, no," said the ruthless Mistigris, "a future diplomat must surely have *a seat—to his trousers! A coat to dine saves wine.*"*

"A future diplomat?" cried Madame Moreau.

The tears rose to poor Oscar's eyes as he looked from Joseph to Léon.

"Only a jest by the way," replied Joseph, who wished to help Oscar in his straits.

"The boy wanted to make fun as we did, and he tried to *tell tales*," said the merciless Mistigris. "And now he finds himself *the ass with a lion's grin*."

"Madame," said Rosalie, coming back to the drawing room door, "His Excellency has ordered dinner for eight persons at six o'clock; what is to be done?"

While Estelle and her maid were holding counsel, the artists and Oscar gazed at each other, their eyes big with terrible apprehensions.

"His Excellency—who?" said Joseph Bridau.

"Why, Monsieur le Comte de Sérisy," replied little Moreau.

"Was it he, by chance, in the *coucou?*" said Léon de Lora.

"Oh!" exclaimed Oscar, "the Comte de Sérisy would surely never travel but in a coach and four."

"How did he come, Madame—the Comte de Sérisy?" the painter asked of Madame Moreau when she came back very much upset.

"I have no idea," said she. "I cannot account for his coming, nor guess what he has come for. And Moreau is out!"

"His Excellency begs you will go over to the château, Monsieur Schinner," said a gardener coming to the door, "and he begs you will give him the pleasure of your company at dinner, as well as Monsieur Mistigris."

"Our goose is cooked!" said the lad with a laugh; "The man we took for a country worthy in Pierrotin's chaise was the Comte. So true is it that *what you seek you never bind*."

Oscar was almost turning to a pillar of salt, for on hearing this his throat felt as salty as the sea.

"And you! Who told him all about his wife's adorers and his skin disease?" said Mistigris to Oscar.

"What do you mean?" cried the steward's wife, looking at the two artists, who went off laughing at Oscar's face.

Oscar stood speechless, thunderstruck, hearing nothing, though Madame Moreau was questioning him and shaking him violently by one of his arms, which she had seized and clutched tightly, but she was obliged to leave him where he was without having extracted a reply, for Rosalie called her again to give out linen and silver plate, and to request her to attend in person to the numerous orders given by the Comte. The house servants, the gardeners, everybody on the place was rushing to and fro in such confusion as may be imagined. The master had in fact dropped on the household like a shell from a mortar.

From above La Cave the Comte had made his way by a path familiar to him to the gamekeeper's house, and reached it before Moreau. The gamekeeper was amazed to see his real master.

"Is Moreau here, I see his horse waiting?" asked Monsieur de Sérisy.

"No, Monseigneur, but as he is going over to Les Moulineaux before dinner, he left his horse here while he ran across to give some orders at the house."

The gamekeeper had no idea of the effect of this reply, which, under existing circumstances, was, in the eyes of a clear-sighted man, tantamount to assurance.

"If you value your place," said the Comte to the keeper, "ride as fast as you can pelt to Beaumont on this horse, and deliver to Monsieur Margueron a note I will give you."

The Comte went into the man's lodge, wrote a line, folded it in such a manner that it could not be opened without detection, and gave it to the man as soon as he was in the saddle.

"Not a word to any living soul," said he. "And you, Madame," he added to the keeper's wife, "if Moreau is surprised at not finding his horse, tell him that I took it."

And the Comte went off across the park, through the gate which was opened for him at his nod. Inured though a man may be to the turmoil of political life with its excitement and vicissitudes, the soul of a man who, at the Comte's age, is still firm enough to love, is also young enough to feel a betrayal. It was so hard to believe that Moreau was deceiving him, that at Saint-Brice Monsieur de Sérisy had supposed him to be not so much in league with Léger and the notary as, in fact, led away by them. And so, standing in the inn gateway as he heard Père Léger talking to the innkeeper, he intended to forgive his land steward after a severe reproof. And then, strange to say, the dishonesty of his trusted agent had seemed no more than an episode when Oscar had blurted out the noble infirmities of the intrepid traveller, the minister of Napoléon. Secrets so strictly kept could only have been revealed by Moreau, who had no doubt spoken contemptuously of his benefactor to Madame de Sérisy's maid, or to the erewhile Aspasia of the Directory. As he made his way down the cross road to the château, the Peer of France, the great minister, had shed bitter tears, weeping as a boy weeps. They were his last tears that he shed! Every human feeling at once was so cruelly, so mercilessly attacked, that this self-controlled man rushed on across his park like a hunted animal.

When Moreau asked for his horse, and the keeper's wife replied—"Monsieur le Comte has just taken it," he cried "Who—Monsieur le Comte?"

"Monsieur le Comte de Sérisy, the master," said she. "Perhaps he is at the château," added she, to get rid of the steward, who, quite bewildered by this occurrence, went off towards the house.

But he presently returned to question the keeper's wife, for it had struck him that there was some serious motive for his master's secret arrival and unwonted conduct. The woman, terrified at finding herself in a vice, as it were, between the Comte and the steward, had shut herself into her lodge, quite determined only to open the door to her husband. Moreau, more and more uneasy, hurried across to the gatekeeper's lodge where he was told that the Comte was dressing. Rosalie, whom he met, announced: "Seven people to dine at the Comte's table."

Moreau next went home, where he found the poultry girl in heated discussion with an odd-looking young man.

"Monsieur le Comte told us, 'Mina's aide-de-camp and a colonel,'" the girl insisted.

"I am not a colonel," replied Georges.

"Well, but is your name Georges?"

"What is the matter?" asked the steward, intervening.

"Monsieur, my name is Georges Marest; I am the son of a rich hardware dealer, wholesale, in the Rue Saint-Martin,* and I have come on business to Monsieur le Comte de Sérisy from Master Crottat, his notary—I am his second clerk."

"And I can only repeat, Monsieur, what Monseigneur said to me: 'a gentleman will come,' says he, 'a Colonel Czerni-Georges, aide-de-camp to Mina, who travelled down in Pierrotin's chaise. If he asks for me, show him into the drawing room.'"

"There is no joking with His Excellency," said the steward. "You had better go in, Monsieur. But how is it that His Excellency came down without announcing his purpose? And how does he know that you travelled by Pierrotin's chaise?"

"It is perfectly clear," said the clerk, "that the Comte is the gentleman who, but for the civility of a young man, would have had to ride on the front seat of Pierrotin's *coucou*."

"On the front seat of Pierrotin's *coucou?*" cried the steward and the farm girl.

"I am quite sure of it from what this girl tells me," said Georges Marest.

"But how——?" the steward began.

"Ah, there you are!" cried Georges. "To jest with the other travellers, I told them a heap of cock-and-bull stories about Egypt, Greece, and Spain. I had spurs on, and I gave myself out as a colonel in the cavalry—a mere joke."

"And what was the gentleman like, whom you believe to be the Comte?" asked Moreau.

"Why, he has a face the colour of brick," said Georges, "with perfectly white hair and black eyebrows."

"That is the man!"

"I am done for!" said Georges Marest.

"Why?"

"I made fun of his orders."

"Bah! He is a thoroughly good fellow; you will have amused him. Come to the château forthwith," said Moreau. "I am going up to the Comte. Where did he leave you?"

"At the top of the hill."

"I can make neither head nor tail of it!" cried Moreau.

"After all, I *poked fun* at him, but I did not insult him," said the clerk to himself.

"And what are you here for?" asked the steward.

"I have brought the deed of sale of the farmlands of Les Moulineaux, ready made out."

"*Mon Dieu!*" exclaimed Moreau.

"I don't understand!"

Moreau felt his heart beat painfully when, after knocking two raps on his master's door, he heard in reply—"Is that you, *Monsieur* Moreau?"

"Yes, Monseigneur."

"Come in."

The Comte was dressed in white trousers and thin boots, a white waistcoat, and a black coat on which glittered, on the right-hand side, the star of the Grand Cross of the Legion of Honour, and on the left, from a buttonhole, hung that of the Golden Fleece from a gold chain; the blue ribbon was conspicuous across his waistcoat. He had dressed his hair himself, and had no doubt got himself up to do the honours of Presles to Margueron, and, perhaps, to impress that worthy with the atmosphere of grandeur.

"Well, Monsieur," said the Comte, who remained sitting, but allowed Moreau to stand, "so we cannot come to terms with Margueron?"

"At the present moment he wants too much for his farm."

"But why should he not come over here to talk about it?" said the Comte in an absent-minded way.

"He is ill, Monseigneur——"

"Are you sure?"

"I went over there——"

"Monsieur," said the Comte, assuming a stern expression that was terrible, "what would you do to a man whom you had allowed to see you dress a wound you wished to keep secret, and who went off to make game of it with a street trollop?"

"I should give him a sound thrashing."

"And if, in addition to this, you discovered that he was cheating your confidence and robbing you?"

"I should try to catch him out and send him to the galleys."

"Listen, *Monsieur* Moreau. You have, I suppose, discussed my health with Madame Clapart and made fun at her house of my devotion to my wife, for little Husson was giving to the passengers in a public conveyance a vast deal of information with reference to my cures, in my presence, this very morning, and in what words! God knows! He dared to slander my wife. Again, I heard from farmer Léger's own lips, as he returned from Paris in Pierrotin's chaise, of the plan concocted by the notary of Beaumont with him, and with you, with reference to Les Moulineaux. If you have been at all to see Margueron, it was to instruct him to sham illness; he is so little ill that I expect him to dinner, and he is coming. Well, Monsieur, as to your having made a fortune of two hundred and fifty thousand francs in seventeen years—I forgive you. I understand it. If you had but asked me for what you took from me, or what others offered you, I would have given it to you; you have a family to provide for. Even with your want of delicacy you have treated me better than another might have done, that I believe—but that you, who know all that I have done for my country, for France, you who have seen me sit up a hundred nights and more to work for the Emperor, or toiling eighteen hours a day for three months on end; that you, who know my worship of Madame de Sérisy, should have gossiped about it before a boy, have betrayed my secrets to the mockery of a Madame Husson——"

"Monseigneur!"

"It is unpardonable. To damage a man's interest is nothing, but to strike at his heart! Ah! You do not know what you have done!" The Comte covered his face with his hands and was silent for a moment. "I leave you in possession of what you have," he went on, "and I will forget you. As a point of dignity, of honour, we will part without quarrelling, for, at this moment, I can remember what your father did for mine. You must come to terms—good terms—with Monsieur de Reybert, your successor. Be calm, as I am. Do not make yourself a spectacle for fools. Above all, no bluster and no haggling. Though you have forfeited my confidence, try to preserve the decorum of wealth. As to the little wretch who has half-killed me, he is not to sleep at Presles. Send him to the inn; I cannot answer for what I might do if he crossed my path."

"I do not deserve such leniency, Monseigneur," said Moreau, with tears in his eyes. "If I had been utterly dishonest I should have five hundred thousand francs, and indeed I will gladly account for every franc in detail! But permit me to assure you, Monseigneur, that when I spoke of you to Madame Clapart it was never in derision. On the contrary, it was to deplore your condition and to ask her whether she did not know of some remedy, unfamiliar to the medical profession, which the common people use. I have spoken of you in the boy's presence when he was asleep (but he heard me, it would seem!) and always in terms of the deepest affection and respect. Unfortunately, a blunder is sometimes punished as a crime. Still, while I bow to the decisions of your just anger, I would have you to know what really happened. Yes, it was heart to heart that I spoke of you to Madame Clapart. And only ask my wife; never have I mentioned these matters to her——"

"That will do," said the Comte, whose conviction was complete. "We are not children; the past is irrevocable. Go and set your affairs and mine in order. You may remain in the lodge till the month of October. Monsieur and Madame de Reybert will live in the château. Above all, try to live with them as gentlemen should—hating each other, but keeping up appearances."

The Comte and Moreau went downstairs, Moreau as white as the Comte's hair, Monsieur de Sérisy calm and dignified.

While this scene was going forward, the Beaumont coach, leaving Paris at one o'clock, had stopped at the gate of Presles to set down Master Crottat, who, in obedience to the Comte's orders, was shown into the drawing room to wait for him; there he found his clerk excessively crestfallen, in company with the two painters, all three conspicuously uncomfortable. Monsieur de Reybert, a man of fifty with a very surly expression, had brought with him old Margueron and the notary from Beaumont, who held a bundle of leases and title deeds. When this assembled party saw the Comte appear in full court costume, Georges Marest had a spasm in the stomach and Joseph Bridau felt a qualm, but Mistigris, who was himself in his Sunday clothes, and who indeed had no crime on his conscience, said loud enough to be heard—"Well, he looks much nicer now."

"You little rascal," said the Comte, drawing him towards him by one ear, "so we both deal in decorations! Do you recognise your work, my dear Schinner?" he went on, pointing to the ceiling.

"Monseigneur," said the artist, "I was so foolish as to assume so famous a name out of bravado, but today's experience makes it incumbent on me to do something good and win glory for that of Joseph Bridau."

"You took my part," said the Comte eagerly, "and I hope you will do me the pleasure of dining with me—you and our witty Mistigris."

"You do not know what you are exposing yourself to," said the audacious youngster. "*An empty stomach knows no peers.*"*

"Bridau," said the Comte, struck by a sudden reminiscence, "are you related to one of the greatest workers under the Empire, a brigadier in command who died a victim to his zeal?"

"I am his son, Monseigneur," said Joseph, bowing.

"Then you are welcome here," replied the Comte, taking the artist's hand in both his own; "I knew your father, and you may depend on me as on—an American uncle," said Monsieur de Sérisy, smiling. "But you are too young to have a pupil—to whom does Mistigris belong?"

"To my friend Schinner, who has lent him to me," replied Joseph. "Mistigris's name is Léon de Lora.

Monseigneur, if you remember my father, will you condescend to bear in mind his other son, who stands accused of conspiring against the State, and is on trial before the Court of Peers——"

"To be sure," said the Comte. "I will bear it in mind, believe me. As to Prince Czerni-Georges, Ali Pasha's ally, and Mina's aide-de-camp——" said the Comte, turning to Georges.

"He? My second clerk?" cried Crottat.

"You are under a mistake, Master Crottat," said Monsieur de Sérisy, very severely. "A clerk who hopes ever to become a notary does not leave important documents in a diligence at the mercy of his fellow travellers! A clerk who hopes to become a notary does not spend twenty francs between Paris and Moisselles! A clerk who hopes to become a notary does not expose himself to arrest as a deserter——"

"Monseigneur," said Georges Marest, "I may have amused myself by playing a practical joke on a party of travellers, but——"

"Do not interrupt His Excellency," said his master, giving him a violent nudge in the ribs.

"A notary ought to develop early the gifts of discretion, prudence, and discernment, and not mistake a Minister of State for a candlemaker."

"I accept sentence for my errors," said Georges, "but I did not leave my papers at the mercy——"

"You are at this moment committing the error of giving the lie to a Minister of State, a Peer of France, a gentleman, an old man—and a client. Look for your deed of sale."

The clerk turned over the papers in his portfolio.

"Do not make a mess of your papers," said the Comte, taking the document out of his pocket. "Here is the deed you are seeking."

Crottat turned it over three times, so much was he amazed at receiving it from the hands of his noble client.

"What, Monsieur!" he at last began, addressing Georges.

"If I had not taken it," the Comte went on, "Père Léger—who is not such a fool as you fancy him from his questions as to agriculture, since they might have taught you that a man should always be thinking of his business—Père Léger might have got hold of it and discovered my plans. You also will give me the pleasure of your company at dinner, but on condition of telling us the history of the Moslem's execution at Smyrna, and of finishing the memoirs of some client which you read, no doubt, before publication."

"*A trouncing for a bouncing!*"* said Léon de Lora, in a low voice to Joseph Bridau.

"Messieurs," said the Comte to the notary from Beaumont, to Crottat, Margueron, and Reybert, "come into the other room. We will not sit down to dinner till we have concluded our bargain, for, as my friend Mistigris says, 'we must know when to *creep* silent.'"

"Well, he is a thoroughly good fellow," said Léon de Lora to Georges Marest.

"Yes, but if he is a good fellow, my employer is not, and he will request me to play my tricks elsewhere."

"Well, you like travelling," said Bridau.

"What a dressing that boy will get from Monsieur and Madame Moreau!" cried Léon de Lora.

"The little idiot!" said Georges. "But for him the Comte would have thought it all very good fun. Well, well, it is a useful lesson, and if I am caught chattering in a coach again——"

"Oh, it is a stupid thing to do," said Joseph Bridau.

"And vulgar too," said Mistigris. "Keep your tongue to clean your teeth."

While the business of the farm was being discussed between Monsieur Margueron and the Comte de Sérisy, with the assistance of three notaries, and in the presence of Monsieur de Reybert, Moreau was slowly making his way home. He went in without looking about him, and sat down on a sofa in the drawing room, while Oscar Husson crept into a corner out of sight, so terrified was he by the steward's white face.

"Well, my dear," said Estelle, coming in, fairly tired out by all she had had to do, "what is the matter?"

"My dear, we are ruined, lost beyond redemption. I am no longer land steward of Presles! The Comte has withdrawn his confidence."

"And what has caused——?"

"Old Léger, who was in Pierrotin's chaise, let out all about the farm of Les Moulineaux, but it is not that which has cut me off forever from his favour——"

"What, then?"

"Oscar spoke ill of the Comtesse, and talked of Monseigneur's ailments——"

"Oscar?" cried Madame Moreau. "You are punished by your own act! A pretty viper you have nursed in your bosom! How often have I told you——"

"That will do," said Moreau hoarsely.

At this instant Estelle and her husband detected Oscar huddled in a corner. Moreau pounced on the luckless boy like a hawk on its prey, seized him by the collar of his olive-green coat, and dragged him into the daylight of a window.

"Speak! What did you say to Monseigneur in the coach? What devil loosened your tongue, when you always stand moonstruck if I ask you a question? What did you do it for?" said the steward with terrific violence.

Oscar, too much scared for tears, kept silence, as motionless as a statue.

"Come and ask His Excellency's pardon!" said Moreau.

"As if His Excellency cared about a vermin like him!" shrieked Estelle in a fury.

"Come—come to the château!" Moreau repeated. Oscar collapsed, a lifeless heap on the floor.

"Will you come, I say?" said Moreau, his rage increasing every moment.

"No, no—have pity!" cried Oscar, who could not face a punishment worse than death.

Moreau took the boy by the collar and dragged him like a corpse across the courtyard, which rang with the boy's cries and sobs; he hauled him up the steps and flung him howling, and as rigid as a post, into the drawing room at the feet of the Comte, who, having settled for the purchase of Les Moulineaux, was just passing into the dining room with his company.

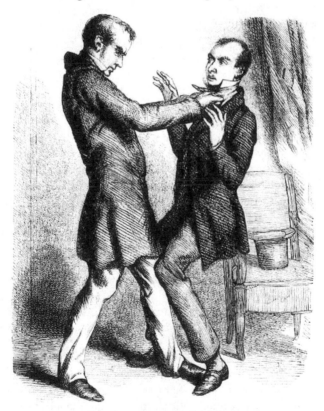

Moreau l'empoigna par le collet de sa redingote.

Plate VI

"On your knees, on your knees, wretched boy! Ask pardon of the man who has fed your mind by getting you a scholarship at college!" cried Moreau.

Oscar lay with his face on the ground, foaming with rage. Everybody was startled. Moreau, quite beside himself, was purple in the face from the rush of blood to his head.

"This boy is mere vanity," said the Comte, after waiting in vain for Oscar's apology. "Pride can humble itself, for there is dignity in some self-humiliation. I am afraid you will never make anything of this fellow."

And the minister passed on.

Moreau led Oscar away and back to his own house. While the horses were being harnessed to the travelling chaise, he wrote the following letter to Madame Clapart:

Oscar, my dear, has brought me to ruin. In the course of his journey in Pierrotin's chaise this morning he spoke of the flirtations of Madame la Comtesse to His Excellency himself, who was travelling incognito, and told the Comte his own secrets as to the skin disease brought on by long nights of hard work in his various high offices. After dismissing me from my place, the Comte desired me not to allow Oscar to sleep at Presles, but to send him home. In obedience to his orders I am having my horses put to my wife's carriage, and Brochon, my groom, will take the little wretch home. My wife and I are in a state of despair, which you may imagine, but which I cannot attempt to describe. I will go to see you in a few days, for I must make my plans. I have three children; I must think of the future, and I do not yet know what to decide on, for I am determined to show the Comte the value of seventeen years of the life of such a man as I. I have two hundred and sixty thousand francs, and I mean to acquire such a fortune as will allow me to be, some day, not much less than His Excellency's equal. At this instant I feel that I could remove mountains and conquer insurmountable difficulties. What a lever is such a humiliating scene! Whose blood can Oscar have in his veins? I cannot compliment you on your son; his behaviour is that of a buzzard. At this moment of writing he has not yet uttered a word in reply to my questions and my wife's. Is he becoming idiotic, or is he idiotic already? My dear friend, did you not give him due injunctions before he started? How much misfortune you would have spared me by coming with him, as I begged you. If you were afraid of Estelle, you could have stayed at Moisselles. However, it is all over now. Farewell till we meet, soon.

Your faithful friend and servant,
MOREAU

Demande pardon à celui qui t'a donné le pain de l'âme...

Plate VII

At eight o'clock that evening Madame Clapart had come in from a little walk with her husband, and sat knitting stockings for Oscar by the light of a single dip. Monsieur Clapart was expecting a friend named Poiret, who sometimes came in for a game of dominoes, for he never trusted himself to spend an evening in a café. In spite of temperance, enforced on him by his narrow means, Clapart could not have answered for his abstinence when in the midst of food and drink, and surrounded by other men, whose laughter might have nettled him.

"I am afraid Poiret may have been and gone," said he to his wife.

"The lodge keeper would have told us, my dear," replied his wife.

"She may have forgotten."

"Why should she forget?"

"It would not be the first time she has forgotten things that concern us; God knows, anything is good enough for people who have no servants!"

"Well, well," said the poor woman, to change the subject and escape her husband's pin stabs. "Oscar is at Presles by this time; he will be very happy in that beautiful place, that fine park——"

"Oh yes, expect great things!" retorted Clapart. "He will make hay there with a vengeance!"

"Will you never cease to be spiteful to that poor boy? What harm has he done you? *Mon Dieu!* If ever we are in easy circumstances we shall owe it to him perhaps, for he has a good heart."

"Our bones will be gelatin long before that boy succeeds in the world!" said Clapart. "And he will have altered very considerably! Why, you don't know your own boy; he is a braggart, a liar, lazy, incapable——"

"Supposing you were to go to fetch Poiret," said the hapless mother, struck to the heart by the diatribe she had brought down on her own head.

"A boy who never took a prize at school!" added Clapart.

In the eyes of the commoner sort, bringing home prizes from school is positive proof of future success in life.

"Did you ever take a prize?" retorted his wife. "Oscar got the fourth *accessit** in philosophy."

This speech reduced Clapart to silence for a moment.

"And besides," he presently went on, "Madame Moreau must love him as she loves a nail—you know where; she will try to set her husband against him. Oscar steward at Presles! Why, he must understand land surveying and agriculture——"

"He can learn."

"He? Never! I bet you that if he got a place there he would not be in it a week before he had done something clumsy and was packed off by the Comte de Sérisy——"

"*Mon Dieu!* How can you be so vicious about the future prospects of a poor boy, full of good points, as sweet as an angel, and incapable of doing an ill turn to any living soul?"

At this moment the cracking of a postboy's whip and the clatter of a chaise at top speed, with the hoofs of horses pulled up sharply at the outer gate, had roused the whole street. Clapart, hearing every window flung open, went out on the landing.

"Oscar, sent back by post!" cried he in a tone in which his satisfaction gave way to genuine alarm.

"Oh! *Mon Dieu*, what can have happened?" said the poor mother, trembling as a leaf is shaken by an autumn wind.

Brochon came upstairs, followed by Oscar and Poiret.

"*Mon Dieu!* What has happened?" repeated she, appealing to the groom.

"I don't know, but Monsieur Moreau is no longer steward of Presles; they say it is your son's doing, and

Monseigneur has ordered him home again. However, here is a letter from poor Monsieur Moreau, who is so altered, Madame, it is dreadful to see."

"Clapart, a glass of wine for the postboy and one for Monsieur," said his wife, who dropped into an armchair and read the terrible letter. "Oscar," she went on, dragging herself to her bed, "you want to kill your mother! After all I said to you this morning——"

But Madame Clapart did not finish her sentence; she fainted with misery.

Oscar remained standing, speechless. Madame Clapart, as she recovered her senses, heard her husband saying to the boy as he shook him by the arm—"Will you speak?"

"Go to bed at once, Monsieur," said she to her son. "And leave him in peace, Monsieur Clapart; do not drive him out of his wits, for he is dreadfully altered!"

Oscar did not hear his mother's remark; he had made for bed the instant he was told.

Those who have any recollection of their own boyhood will not be surprised to hear that, after a day so full of events and agitations, Oscar slept the sleep of the just in spite of the enormity of his sins. Nay, next day he did not find the whole face of nature so much changed as he expected, and was astonished to find that he was hungry, after regarding himself the day before as unworthy to live. He had suffered only in mind, and at that age mental impressions succeed each other so rapidly that each wipes out the last, however deep it may have seemed. Hence corporal punishment, though philanthropists have made a strong stand against it of late years, is in some cases necessary for children; also, it is perfectly natural, for Nature herself has no other means but the infliction of pain to produce a lasting impression of her lessons. If to give weight to the shame, unhappily too transient, which had overwhelmed Oscar, the steward had given him a sound thrashing, the lesson might have been effectual. The discernment needed for the proper infliction of such corrections is the chief argument against their use, for Nature never makes a mistake, while the teacher must often blunder.

Madame Clapart took care to send her husband out next morning to have her son to herself. She was in a pitiable condition. Her eyes red with weeping, her face worn by a sleepless night, her voice broken; everything in her seemed to sue for mercy by the signs of such grief as she could not have endured a second time. When Oscar entered the room, she beckoned to him to sit down by her, and in a mild but feeling voice reminded him of all the kindness done them by the steward of Presles. She explained to Oscar that for the last six years especially she had lived on Moreau's ingenious charity. Monsieur Clapart's appointment, which they owed, no less than Oscar's scholarship, to the Comte de Sérisy, he would some day cease to hold. Clapart could not claim a pension, not having served long enough either in the Treasury or the city to ask for one. And when Monsieur Clapart should be shelved, what was to become of them?

"I," she said, "by becoming a sick nurse or taking a place as housekeeper in some gentleman's house, could make my living and keep Monsieur Clapart, but what would become of you? You have no fortune, and you must work for your living. There are but four openings for lads like you: trade, the civil service, the liberal professions, and military service. A young man who has no capital must contribute faithful service and brains, but great discretion is needed in business, and your behaviour yesterday makes your success very doubtful. For an official career you have to begin, for years perhaps, as a supernumerary, and need interest to back you, and you have alienated the only protector we ever had—a man high in power. And besides, even if you were blest with the exceptional gifts which enable a young man to rise rapidly, either in business or in an official position, where are we to find the money for food and clothing while you are learning your work?"

And here his mother, like all women, went off into wordy lamentations. What could she do now that she was deprived of the gifts of produce which Moreau was able to send her while managing Presles? Oscar had overthrown his best friend. Next to trade and office work, of which her son need not even think, came the legal profession as a notary, a pleader, an attorney, or an usher. But then he must study law for three years at least and pay heavy fees for his admission, his examinations, his theses and diploma; the number of competitors was so great that superior talent was indispensable, and how was he to live? That was the constantly recurring question.

"Oscar," she said in conclusion, "all my pride, all my life were centred in you. I could bear to look forward to an old age of poverty, for I kept my eyes on you; I saw you entering on a prosperous career and succeeding in it. That hope has given me courage to endure the privations I have gone through during the last six years to keep you at school, for it has cost seven or eight hundred francs a year besides the half-scholarship. Now that my hopes are crushed, I dread to think of your future fate. I must not spend a sou of Monsieur Clapart's salary on my own son. What do you propose to do? You are not a good enough mathematician to pass into a specialist college, and, besides, where could I find the three thousand francs a year for your training? This is life, my dear child! Well, you are eighteen, and a strong lad—enlist as a soldier; it is the only way you can make a living."

Oscar as yet knew nothing of life. Like all boys who have been brought up in ignorance of the poverty at home, he had no idea of the need to work for his living; the word Commerce conveyed no idea to his mind and the word Administration did not mean much, for he knew nothing of the work. He listened with a look of submission, which he tried to make penitential, but his mother's remonstrances were lost in the air. However, at the idea of being a soldier, and on seeing the tears in his mother's eyes, the boy too was ready to weep. As soon as Madame Clapart saw the drops on her boy's cheeks, she was quite disarmed, and, like all mothers in a similar position, she fell back on the generalities which wind up this sort of attack, in which they suffer all their own sorrows and their children's at the same time.

"Come, Oscar, *promise me* to be more cautious for the future, not to blurt out whatever comes uppermost, to moderate your absurd conceit——" and so on.

Oscar was ready to promise all his mother asked, and pressing him gently to her heart, Madame Clapart ended by embracing him to comfort him for the scolding he had had.

"Now," said she, "you will listen to your mother and follow her advice, for a mother can give her son none but good advice. We will go and see your Uncle Cardot. He is our last hope. Cardot owed a great deal to your father, who, by allowing him to marry his sister with what was then an immense marriage portion, enabled him to make a large fortune in silk. I fancy he would place you with Monsieur Camusot, his son-in-law and successor in the Rue des Bourdonnais.* Still, your Uncle Cardot has four children of his own. He made over his shop, the Cocon d'Or,* to his eldest daughter, Madame Camusot. Though Camusot has millions, there are the four children by two wives, and he hardly knows of our existence. Marianne, his second girl, married Monsieur Protez, of Protez & Chiffreville. He paid four hundred thousand francs to put his eldest son in business as a notary, and he has just invested for his second son Joseph as a partner in the business of Matifat, drug importers. Thus your Uncle Cardot may very well not choose to be troubled about you, whom he sees but four times a year. He has never been to call on me here, but he could come to see me when I was in Madame Mère's household, to be allowed to supply silks to their Imperial Highnesses, and the Emperor, and the grandees at court. And now the Camusots are Ultras!* Camusot's eldest son, by his first wife, married the daughter of a gentleman-usher to the King! Well, when the world stoops it grows hunchbacked. And, after all, it is a good business; the Cocon d'Or has the custom of the court under the Bourbons as it had under the Emperor. Tomorrow we will go to see your Uncle Cardot, and I hope you will contrive to behave, for, as I tell you, in him is our last hope."

Monsieur Jean Jérôme Séverin Cardot had lost his second wife six years since—Mademoiselle Husson, on whom, in the days of his glory, the contractor had bestowed a marriage portion of a hundred thousand francs in hard cash. Cardot, the head clerk of the Cocon d'Or, one of the old established Paris houses, had bought the business in 1793 when its owners were ruined by the maximum,* and Mademoiselle Husson's money to back him had enabled him to make an almost colossal fortune in ten years. To provide handsomely for his children, he had very ingeniously invested three hundred thousand francs in annuities for himself and his wife, which brought him in thirty thousand francs a year. The rest of his capital he divided into three portions of four hundred thousand francs for his younger children, and the shop was taken as representing that sum by Camusot when he married the eldest girl. Thus the old fellow, now nearly seventy, could dispose of his thirty thousand francs a year without damaging his children's interests; they were all well married, and no avaricious hopes could interfere with their filial affection. Uncle Cardot lived at Belleville in one of the first houses just above La Courtille. He rented a first floor, whence there was a fine view over the Seine valley, an apartment for which he paid a thousand francs a year, facing south, with the exclusive enjoyment of a large garden; thus he never troubled himself about the three or four other families inhabiting the spacious country house. Secure, by a long lease, of ending his days there, he lived rather shabbily, waited on by his old cook and by a maid who had been attached to his late wife, both of whom looked forward to an annuity of some six hundred francs at his death, and consequently did not rob him. These two women took incredible care of their master, and with all the more devotion since no one could be less fractious or fidgety than he. The rooms, furnished by the late Madame Cardot, had remained unaltered for six years, and the old man was quite content; he did not spend a thousand crowns a year there, for he dined out in Paris five days a week, and came home at midnight in a private fly that he took at the Barrière de la Courtille.* They had hardly anything to do beyond providing him with breakfast. The old man breakfasted at eleven o'clock, then he dressed and scented himself and went to Paris. A man usually gives notice when he means to dine out; Monsieur Cardot gave notice when he was to dine at home.

This little old gentleman—plump, rosy, square, and hearty—was always as neat as a pin, as the saying goes, that is to say, always in black silk stockings, corded silk knee breeches, a white marcella waistcoat, dazzlingly white linen, and a dark blue coat; he wore violet silk gloves, gold buckles to his shoes and breeches, a touch of powder on his hair, and a small queue tied with black ribbon. His face was noticeable for the thick, bushy eyebrows beneath which sparkled his grey eyes, and a large squarely-cut nose that made him look like some venerable prebendary. This countenance did not belie the man.

Old Cardot was, in fact, one of the race of frisky *Gérontes** who are disappearing day by day, and who played the part of Turcaret in all the romances and comedies of the eighteenth century. Uncle Cardot would speak to a woman as *belle dame!*—he would take home any woman in a coach who had no other protector—he was "theirs to command," to use his own expression, with a chivalrous flourish. His calm face and snowy hair were the adjuncts of an old age wholly devoted to pleasure. Among men he boldly professed Epicureanism, and allowed himself rather a broad style of jokes. He had made no objection when his son-in-law Camusot attached himself to Coralie, the fascinating actress, for he was, in secret, the Mæcenas of Mademoiselle Florentine, *première danseuse* at the Gaîté theatre.* Still, nothing appeared on the surface, or in his evident conduct, to tell tales of these opinions and this mode of life. Uncle Cardot, grave and polite, was supposed to be almost cold, such a display did he make of the proprieties, but a pious woman would have called him a hypocrite. This worthy gentleman particularly detested the priesthood; he was one of the large body of silly people who subscribe to the *Constitutionnel*, and was much exercised about the refusal of rights of burial.* He adored Voltaire, though his preference as a matter of taste was for Piron, Verdé, and Collé.* Of course he admired Béranger, of whom he spoke ingeniously as the *high priest of the religion of Lisette*.* His daughters, Madame Camusot and Madame Protez, and his two sons would indeed have been knocked flat, to use a vulgar phrase, if anyone had told them what their father meant by singing "*La Mère Godichon.*"* The shrewd old man had never told his children of his annuity, and they, seeing him live so poorly, all believed that he had stripped himself of his fortune for them, and overwhelmed him with care and affection. And he would sometimes say to his sons, "Do not lose your money, for I have none to leave you." Camusot, who was a man after his own heart, and whom he liked well enough to allow him to join his little parties, was the only one who knew of his annuity of thirty thousand francs. Camusot highly applauded the old fellow's philosophy, thinking that after providing so liberally for his children and doing his duty so thoroughly, he had a right to end his days jovially. "You see, my dear fellow," the old master of the Cocon d'Or would say to his son-in-law, "I might have married again, no doubt, and a young wife would have had children. Oh, yes, I should have had children, I was at an age when men always have children. Well, Florentine does not cost me so much as a wife, she never bores me, she will not plague me with children, and will not make a hole in your fortune."

And Camusot discovered in old Cardot an admirable feeling for the family, regarding him as a perfect father-in-law. "He succeeds," he would say, "in reconciling the interests of his children with the pleasures it is natural to indulge in in old age after having gone through all the anxieties of business."

Neither the Cardots, nor the Camusots, nor the Protez suspected what the existence was of their old aunt Madame Clapart. Their communications had always been restricted to sending formal letters on the occasions of a death or a marriage and visiting cards on New Year's Day. Madame Clapart was too proud to sacrifice her feelings for anything but her Oscar's interests, and acted under the influence of her regard for Moreau, the only person who had remained faithful to her in misfortune. She had never wearied old Cardot by her presence or her importunities, but she had clung to him as to a hope. She called on him once a quarter and talked to him of Oscar Husson, the nephew of the late respected Madame Cardot, taking the lad to see Uncle Cardot three times a year during the holidays. On each occasion the old man took Oscar to dine at the Cadran-bleu,* and to the Gâité in the evening, taking him home afterwards to the Rue de la Cerisaie. On one occasion, after giving him a new suit of clothes, he had made him a present of the silver mug and spoon and fork required as part of every schoolboy's equipment. Oscar's mother had tried to convince the old man that Oscar was very fond of him, and she was always talking of the silver mug and spoon and the beautiful suit, of which nothing now survived but the waistcoat. But these little insinuating attentions did Oscar more harm than good with so cunning an old fox as Uncle Cardot. Old Cardot had not been devoted to his late lamented, a bony red-haired woman; also he knew the circumstances of the deceased Husson's marriage to Oscar's mother, and without looking down on her in any way, he knew that Oscar had been born after his father's death, so his poor nephew seemed an absolute alien to the Cardot family. Unable to foresee disaster, Oscar's mother had not made up for this lack of natural ties between the boy and his uncle, and had not succeeded in implanting in the old merchant any liking for her boy in his earliest youth. Like all women who are absorbed in the one idea of motherhood, Madame Clapart could not put herself in Uncle Cardot's place; she thought he ought to be deeply interested in such a charming boy whose name, too, was that of the late Madame Cardot.

"Monsieur, here is the mother of your nephew Oscar," said the maid to Monsieur Cardot, who was airing himself in the garden before breakfast, after being shaved and having his head dressed by the barber.

"Good morning, *belle dame*," said the old silk merchant, bowing to Madame Clapart while he wrapped his white quilted dressing gown across him. "Ah, ha! Your youngster is growing apace," he added, pulling Oscar by the ear.

"He has finished his schooling, and he was very sorry that his dear uncle was not present at the distribution of prizes at the Collège Henri IV, for he was named. The name of Husson—of which, let us hope, he may prove worthy—was honourably mentioned."

"The deuce it was!" said the little man, stopping short. He was walking with Madame Clapart and Oscar on a terrace where there were orange trees, myrtles, and pomegranate shrubs. "And what did he get?"

"The fourth *accessit* in philosophy," said the mother triumphantly.

"Oh, ho! He has some way to go yet to make up for lost time," cried Uncle Cardot. "To end with an *accessit* is not the treasure of Peru. You will breakfast with me?" said he.

"We are at your commands," replied Madame Clapart. "Oh, my dear Monsieur Cardot, what a comfort it is to a father and mother when their children make a good start in life. From that point of view, as indeed from every other," she put in, correcting herself, "you are one of the happiest fathers I know. In the hands of your admirable son-in-law and your amiable daughter, the Cocon d'Or is still the best shop of the kind in Paris. Your eldest son has been for years as a notary at the head of the best known business in Paris, and he married a rich woman. Your youngest is a partner in a first-rate druggist's business. And you have the sweetest grandchildren! You are the head of four flourishing families. Oscar, leave us; go and walk round the garden, and do not touch the flowers."

"Why, he is eighteen!" exclaimed Uncle Cardot, smiling at this injunction, "as though Oscar was a child!"

"Alas! Indeed he is, my dear Monsieur Cardot, and after bringing him up to that age neither crooked nor bandy, sound in mind and body, after sacrificing everything to give him an education, it would be hard indeed not to see him start in the way to fortune."

"Well, Monsieur Moreau, who got you his half-scholarship at the Collège Henri IV, will start him on the right road," said Uncle Cardot, hiding his hypocrisy under an affectation of bluntness.

"Monsieur Moreau may die," said she. "Besides, he has quarrelled beyond remedy with Monsieur le Comte de Sérisy, his patron."

"The deuce he has! Listen, Madame, I see what you are coming to———"

"No, Monsieur," said Oscar's mother, cutting the old man short, while he, out of respect for a *belle dame*, controlled the impulse of annoyance at being interrupted. "Alas! You can know nothing of the anguish of a mother who for seven years has been obliged to take six hundred francs a year out of her husband's salary of eighteen hundred. Yes, Monsieur, that is our whole income. So what can I do for my Oscar? Monsieur Clapart so intensely hates the poor boy that I really cannot keep him at home. What can a poor woman do under such circumstances but come to consult the only relative her boy has under heaven?"

"You did quite right," replied Monsieur Cardot, "you never said anything of all this before———"

"Indeed, Monsieur," replied Madame Clapart with pride, "you are the last person to whom I would confess the depth of my poverty. It is all my own fault; I married a man whose incapacity is beyond belief. Oh! I am a most miserable woman."

"Listen, Madame," said the little old man gravely, "do not cry. I cannot tell you how much it pains me to see a *belle dame* in tears. After all, your boy's name is Husson, and if the dear departed were alive, she would do something for the sake of her father's and brother's name———"

"She truly loved her brother!" cried Oscar's mother.

"But all my fortune is divided among my children, who have nothing further to expect from me," the old man went on. "I divided the two million francs I had among them; I wished to see them happy in my lifetime. I kept nothing for myself but an annuity, and at my time of life a man clings to his habits. Do you know what you must do with this youngster?" said he, calling back Oscar and taking him by the arm. "Put him to study law, I will pay for his matriculation and preliminary fees.

Place him with an attorney; let him learn all the tricks of the trade; if he does well, and gets on and likes the work, and if I am still alive, each of my children will, when the time comes, lend him a quarter of the sum necessary to purchase a connection; I will stand surety for him. From now till then you have only to feed and clothe him; he will know some hard times no doubt, but he will learn what life is. Why, why! I set out from Lyons with two double louis given me by my grandmother; I came to Paris on foot—and here I am! Short commons are good for the health. Young man, with discretion, honesty, and hard work success is certain. It is a great pleasure to make your own fortune, and when a man has kept his teeth he eats what he likes in his old age, singing "*La Mère Godichon*" every now and then, as I do. Mark my words: honesty, hard work, and discretion."

"You hear, Oscar," said his mother. "Your uncle has put in four words the sum total of all my teaching, and you ought to stamp the last on your mind in letters of fire."

"Oh, it is there!" replied Oscar.

"Well, then, thank your uncle; do you not understand that he is providing for you in the future? You may be an attorney in Paris."

"He does not appreciate the splendour of his destiny," said the old man, seeing Oscar's bewildered face. "He has but just left school. Listen to me: I am not given to wasting words," his uncle went on. "Remember that at your age honesty is only secured by resisting temptations, and in a great city like Paris you meet them at every turn. Live in a garret under your mother's roof; go straight to your lecture and from that to your office; work away morning, noon, and night, and study at home; be a second clerk by the time you are twenty-two and a head clerk at twenty-four. Get learning and you are a made man. And then if you should not like that line of work, you might go into my son's office as a notary and succeed him. So work, patience, honesty, and discretion—these are your watchwords."

"And God grant you may live another thirty years to see your fifth child realise all our expectations!" cried Madame Clapart, taking the old man's hand and pressing it with a dignity worthy of her young days.

"Come, breakfast," said the kind old man, leading Oscar in by the ear.

During the meal Uncle Cardot watched his nephew on the sly, and soon discovered that he knew nothing of life.

"Send him to see me now and then," said he, as he took leave of her, with a nod to indicate Oscar. "I will lick him into shape."

This visit soothed the poor woman's worst grief, for she had not looked for such a happy result. For a fortnight she took Oscar out walking, watched over him almost tyrannically, and thus time went on till the end of October. One morning Oscar saw the terrible steward walk in to find the wretched party in the Rue de la Cerisaie breakfasting off a salad of herring and lettuce, with a cup of milk to wash it down.

"We have settled in Paris, but we do not live as we did at Presles," said Moreau, who intended thus to make Madame Clapart aware of the change in their circumstances brought about by Oscar's misdemeanour. "But I shall not often be in town. I have gone into partnership with old Léger and old Margueron of Beaumont. We are land agents, and we began by buying the estate of Persan. I am the head of the firm, which has got together a million francs, for I have borrowed on my property. When I find an opening, Père Léger and I go into the matter, and my partners each take a quarter and I half of the profits, for I have all the trouble; I shall always be on the road. My wife lives in Paris very quietly, in the Faubourg du Roule.* When we have fairly started in business, and shall only be risking the interest on our money, if we are satisfied with Oscar, we may perhaps give him work."

"Well, after all, my friend, my unlucky boy's blunder will no doubt turn out to be the cause of your making a fine fortune, for you really were wasting your talents and energy at Presles."

Madame Clapart then told the story of her visit to Uncle Cardot, to show Moreau that she and her son might be no further expense to them.

"The old man is quite right," said the ex-steward. "Oscar must be kept to his work with a hand of iron, and he will no doubt make a notary or an attorney. But he must not wander from the line traced out for him. Ah! I know the man you want. The custom of an estate agent is valuable. I have been told of an attorney who has bought a practice without any connection. He is a young man, but as stiff as an iron bar—a tremendous worker, a perfect horse for energy and go; his name is Desroches. I will offer him all our business on condition of his taking Oscar in hand. I will offer him a premium of nine hundred francs, of which I will pay three hundred; thus your son will cost you only six hundred, and I will recommend him strongly to his master. If the boy is ever to become a man, it will be under that iron rule, for he will come out a notary, a pleader, or an attorney."

"Come, Oscar, thank Monsieur Moreau for his kindness; you stand there like a mummy. It is not every youth who blunders that is lucky enough to find friends to take an interest in him after being injured by him——"

"The best way to make matters up with me," said Moreau, taking Oscar's hand, "is to work steadily and behave well."

Ten days after this Oscar was introduced by Monsieur Moreau to Master Desroches, attorney, lately established in the Rue de Béthisy,* in spacious rooms at the end of a narrow court, at a relatively low rent. Desroches, a young man of twenty-six, the son of poor parents, austerely brought up by an excessively severe father, had himself known what it was to be in Oscar's position; he therefore took an interest in him, but only in the way of which he was himself capable, with all the hardness of his character. The manner of this tall, lean young lawyer with a dull complexion and his hair cut short all over his head—sharp in his speech, keen-eyed, and gloomy though hasty—terrified poor Oscar.

"We work day and night here," said the lawyer from the depths of his chair, and from behind a long table on which papers were piled in alps. "Monsieur Moreau, we will not kill him, but he will have to go our pace. Monsieur Godeschal!" he called out.

Although it was Sunday, the head clerk appeared with a pen in his hand.

"Monsieur Godeschal, this is the articled pupil of whom I spoke, and in whom Monsieur Moreau takes the greatest interest; he will dine with us, and sleep in the little attic next to your room. You must allow him exactly time enough to get to the law schools and back, so that he has not five minutes to lose; see that he learns the Code* and does well at lecture; that is to say, give him law books to read up when he has done his school work. In short, he is to be under your immediate direction, and I will keep an eye on him. We want to turn him out what you are yourself—a capital head clerk by the time he is ready to be sworn in as an attorney. Go with Godeschal, my little friend; he will show you your room, and you can move into it. You see Godeschal?" Desroches went on, addressing Moreau. "He is a youngster without a sou like myself; he is Mariette's brother, and she is saving for him so that he may buy a connection ten years hence. All my clerks are youngsters who have nothing to depend on but their ten fingers to make their fortune. And my five clerks and I work like any dozen of other men. In ten years I shall have the finest practice in Paris. We take a passionate interest here in our business and our clients, and that is beginning to be known. I got Godeschal from my greater brother in the law, Derville; with him he was second clerk, and only for a fortnight, but we had made friends in that huge office. I give Godeschal a thousand francs a year with board and lodging. The fellow is worth it to me; he is indefatigable! I like that boy! He managed to live on six hundred francs a year as I did when I was a clerk. What I absolutely insist on is stainless honesty, and the man who can practise it in poverty *is* a man. The slightest failing on that score, and a clerk of mine goes!"

"Come, the boy is in a good school," said Moreau.

For two whole years Oscar lived in the Rue de Béthisy in a den of the law, for if ever this old-fashioned term could be applied to a lawyer's office, it was to this of Desroches. Under this minute and strict supervision, he was kept so rigidly to hours and to work, that his life in the heart of Paris was like that of a monk.

At five in the morning, in all weathers, Godeschal woke. He went down to the office with Oscar to save a fire, and they always found the "chief" up and at work. Oscar did the errands and prepared his schoolwork—studies on an enormous scale. Godeschal, and often the chief himself, showed their pupil what authors to compare and the difficulties to be met. Oscar never was allowed to pass from one chapter of the Code to the next till he had thoroughly mastered it and had satisfied both Desroches and Godeschal, who put him through preliminary examinations far longer and harder than those of the law schools. On his return from the schools, where he did not spend much time, he resumed his seat in the office and worked again; sometimes he went into the courts, and he was at the bidding of the merciless Godeschal till dinnertime. Dinner, which he shared with his masters, consisted of a large dish of meat, a dish of vegetables, and a salad; for dessert there was a bit of Gruyère cheese. After dinner, Godeschal and Oscar went back to the office and worked there till the evening. Once a month Oscar went to breakfast with his Uncle Cardot, and spent Sundays with his mother. From time to time, Moreau, when he came to the office on business, would take Oscar to dine at the Palais-Royal and treat him to a play. Oscar had been so thoroughly snubbed by Godeschal and Desroches on the subject of his craving after fashion that he had ceased to think about dress.

"A good clerk," said Godeschal, "should have two black coats (one old and one new), black trousers, black stockings and shoes. Boots cost too much. You may have boots when you are an attorney. A clerk ought not to spent more than seven hundred francs in all. He should wear good, strong shirts of stout linen. Oh, when you start from zero to make a fortune, you must know how to limit yourself to what is strictly needful. Look at Monsieur Desroches! He did as we are doing, and you see he has succeeded."

Godeschal practised what he preached. Professing the strictest principles of honour, reticence, and honesty, he acted on them without any display as simply as he walked and breathed. It was the natural working of his soul, as walking and breathing are the working of certain organs. Eighteen months after Oscar's arrival, the second clerk had made, for the second time, a small mistake in the accounts of his little cashbox. Godeschal addressed him in the presence of all the clerks—"My dear Gaudet, leave on your own account; let no one say that the chief turned you out. You are either inaccurate or careless, and neither of those faults is of any use here. The chief shall not know, and that is the best I can do for an old fellow clerk."

Thus, at the age of twenty, Oscar was third clerk in Master Desroches's office. Though he earned no salary yet, he was fed and lodged, for he did the work of a second clerk. Desroches employed two managing clerks, and the second clerk was overdone with work. By the time he had got through his second year at the schools, Oscar, who knew more than many a man who has taken out his license, did the work of the courts very intelligently, and occasionally pleaded in chambers. In fact, Desroches and Godeschal were satisfied. Still, though he had become almost sensible, he betrayed a love of pleasure and a desire to shine, which were only subdued by the stern discipline and incessant toil of the life he led. The estate agent, satisfied with the boy's progress, then relaxed his strictness, and when, in the month of July 1825, Oscar passed his final examination, Moreau gave him enough money to buy some good clothes. Madame Clapart, very happy and proud of her son, prepared a magnificent outfit for the qualified attorney, the second clerk, as he was soon to be. In poor families a gift always takes the form of something useful. When the courts reopened in the month of November, Oscar took the second clerk's room and his place with a salary of eight hundred francs, board and lodging. And Uncle Cardot, who came privately to make inquiries about his nephew of Desroches, promised Madame Clapart that he would put Oscar in a position to buy a connection if he went on as he had begun.

In spite of such seeming wisdom, Oscar Husson was torn by many yearnings in the bottom of his soul. Sometimes he felt as if he must fly from a life so entirely opposed to his taste and character; a galley slave, he thought, was happier than he. Galled by his iron collar, he was sometimes tempted to run away when he compared himself with some well-dressed youth he met in the street. Now and then an impulse of folly with regard to women would surge up in him, and his resignation was only a part of his disgust of life. Kept steady by Godeschal's example, he was dragged rather than led by his will to follow so thorny a path. Godeschal, who watched Oscar, made it his rule not to put his ward in the way of temptation. The boy had usually no money, or so little that he could not run into excesses. During the last year the worthy Godeschal had five or six times taken Oscar out for some lark, paying the cost, for he perceived that the cord round this tethered kid's neck must be loosened, and these excesses, as the austere head clerk termed them, helped Oscar to endure life. He found little to amuse him at his uncle's house, and still less at his mother's, for she lived even more frugally than Desroches. Moreau could not, like Godeschal, make himself familiar with Oscar, and it is probable that this true protector made Godeschal his deputy in initiating the poor boy into the many mysteries of life. Oscar, thus learning discretion, could at last appreciate the enormity of the blunder he had committed during his ill-starred journey in the *coucou*; still, as the greater part of his fancies were so far suppressed, the follies of youth might yet lead him astray. However, as by degrees he acquired knowledge of the world and its ways, his reason developed, and so long as Godeschal did not lose sight of him, Moreau hoped to train Madame Clapart's son to a good end.

"How is he going on?" the estate agent asked on his return from a journey which had kept him away from Paris for some months.

"Still much too vain," replied Godeschal. "You give him good clothes and fine linen, he wears shirt frills like a stockbroker, and my gentleman goes to walk in the Tuileries on Sundays in search of adventures. What can I say? He is young. He teases me to introduce him to my sister, in whose house he would meet a famous crew: actresses, dancers, dandies, men who are eating themselves out of house and home. He is not cut out for an attorney, I fear. Still, he does not speak badly; he might become a pleader. He could argue a case from a well-prepared brief."

In November 1825, when Oscar Husson was made second clerk and was preparing his thesis for taking out his license, a new fourth clerk came to Desroches's office to fill up the gap made by Oscar's promotion.

This fourth clerk, whose name was Frédéric Marest, was intended for the higher walks of the law, and was now ending his third year at the schools. From information received by the inquiring minds of the office, he was a handsome fellow of twenty-three who had inherited about twelve thousand francs a year at the death of a bachelor uncle, and the son of a Madame Marest, the widow of a rich timber merchant. The future judge, filled with the laudable desire to know his business in its minutest details, placed himself under Desroches, intending to study procedure, so as to be fit to take the place of a managing clerk in two years' time. His purpose was to go through his first stages as a pleader in Paris so as to be fully prepared for an appointment, which, as a young man of wealth, he would certainly get. To see himself a public prosecutor, at the age of thirty, was the height of his ambition. Though Frédéric was the first cousin of Georges Marest, the practical joker of the journey to Presles, young Husson knew him only by the name of Georges; the name of Frédéric Marest had no associations for him.

"Messieurs," said Godeschal at breakfast, addressing all his underlings, "I have to announce the advent of a new student in law, and as he is very rich, we shall, I hope, make him pay his footing handsomely."

"Bring out the book," cried Oscar to the youngest clerk, "and let us be serious, pray."

The boy clambered like a squirrel along the pigeon-holes to reach a volume lying on the top shelf, so as to collect all the dust.

"It is finely coloured!" said the lad, holding it up.

We must now explain the perennial pleasantry which at that time gave rise to the existence of such a book in almost every lawyer's office. An old saying of the eight-eenth century—*clerks only breakfast, farmers generally dine, and lords sup*—is still true, as regards the faculty of law, of every man who has spent two or three years studying procedure under an attorney, or the technicalities of a notary's business under some master of that branch. In the life of a lawyer's clerk, work is so unremitting that pleasure is enjoyed all the more keenly for its rarity, and a practical joke especially is relished with rapture. This, indeed, is what explains up to a certain point Georges Marest's behaviour in Pierrotin's chaise. The gloomiest of law clerks is always a prey to the craving for farcical buffoonery. The instinct with which a practical joke or an occasion for fooling is jumped at and utilised among law clerks is marvellous to behold, and is found in no other class but among artists. The studio and the law-yer's office are, in this respect, better than the stage. Desroches, having started in an office without a con-nection, had, as it were, founded a new dynasty. This "Restoration" had interrupted the traditions of the office with regard to the footing of a newcomer. Desroches, indeed, settling in quarters where stamped paper had never yet been seen, had put in new tables and clean new file boxes of white millboard edged with blue. His staff consisted of clerks who had come from other of-fices with no connection between them, thrown together by surprise, as it were. But Godeschal, who had learned his fence under Derville, was not the man to allow the precious tradition of the bienvenue to be lost. The bi-envenue is the breakfast which every new pupil must give to the "old boys" of the office to which he is arti-cled. Now, just at the time when Oscar joined the office, in the first six months of Desroches's career, one win-ter afternoon when work was got through earlier than usual and the clerks were warming themselves before going home, Godeschal hit upon the notion of concoct-ing a sham register of the *fasti* and High Festivals of the

Minions of the Law, a relic of great antiquity saved from the storms of the Revolution and handed down from the office of the great Bordin, Attorney to the Châtelet* and the immediate predecessor of Sauvagnest, the attorney from whom Desroches had taken the office. The first thing was to find in some stationer's old stock a ledger with paper bearing an eighteenth century watermark, and properly bound in parchment, in which to enter the decrees of the Grand Council. Having discovered such a volume, it was tossed in the dust, in the ash pan, in the fireplace, in the kitchen; it was even left in what the clerks called the consulting room, and it had acquired a tint of mildew that would have enchanted a bookworm along with its cracks of primeval antiquity and corners so worn that the mice might have nibbled them off. The edges were rubbed with infinite skill. The book being thus perfected, here are a few passages which will explain to the dullest the uses to which Desroches's clerks devoted it, the first sixty pages being filled with sham reports of cases.

In the name of the Father and of the Son and of the Holy Ghost. So be it. Whereas, on this day the Festival of our Lady Saint Geneviève, patron saint of this good city of Paris, under whose protection the scribes and scriveners of this office have dwelt since the year of our Lord 1525, we, the undersigned clerks and scriveners of this office of Master Jérôme-Sebastien Bordin, successor here to the deceased Guerbet, who in his lifetime served as attorney to the Châtelet, have recognised the need for us to replace the register and archives of installations of clerks in this glorious office, being ourselves distinguished members of the Faculty of the Law, which former register is now filled with the roll and record of our well-beloved predecessors, and we have besought the Keeper of the Palace Archives to bestow it with those of other offices, and we have all attended High Mass in the parish church of Saint-Séverin* to solemnise the opening of this our new register.

In token whereof, we here sign and affix our names.

> MALIN, Head Clerk
> GREVIN, Second Clerk
> ATHANASE FERET, Clerk
> JACQUES HUET, Clerk
> REGNALD DE SAINT-JEAN-D'ANGELY, Clerk
> BEDEAU, Office Boy and Gutter Jumper
> In the year of our Lord 1787

Having attended Mass, we went in a body to La Courtille, and had a great breakfast, which lasted until seven in the morning.

This was a miracle of caligraphy. An expert could have sworn that the writing dated from the eighteenth century. Twenty-seven reports of "welcome" breakfasts then followed, the last dating from the fatal year 1792.* After a gap of fourteen years, the register reopened in 1806 with the appointment of Bordin to be attorney to the lower Court of the Seine. And this was the record of the reconstitution of the Kingdom of Basoche:*

God in His clemency has granted that in the midst of the storms which have devastated France, now a great Empire, the precious archives of the most illustrious office of Master Bordin should be preserved. And we, the undersigned clerks of the most honourable and most worshipful Master Bordin, do not hesitate to ascribe this their marvellous escape, when so many other title deeds, charters, and letters patent have vanished, to the protection of Saint Geneviève, the patron saint of this office, as likewise to the reverence paid by the last of the attorneys of the old block to all ancient use and custom. And whereas we know not what share to ascribe to the Lady Saint Geneviève and what to Master Bordin in the working of this miracle, we have resolved to go to the Church of Saint Etienne-du-Mont,* there to attend a mass to be said at the altar of that saintly shepherdess who sendeth us so many lambs to fleece, and to invite our chief and master to breakfast, in the hope that he may bear the charges thereof. And to this we set our hand.

> OIGNARD, Head Clerk
> POIDEVIN, Second Clerk
> PROUST, Clerk
> BRIGNOLET, Clerk
> DERVILLE, Clerk
> AUGUSTEN CORET, Office Boy
> At the office, this 10th day of November 1806

At three o'clock of the afternoon of the next day, the undersigned, being the clerks of this office, record their gratitude to their very worshipful chief, who hath feasted them at Rolland's, a restaurant in the Rue du Hasard,* on good wines of three districts, Bordeaux, Champagne, and Burgundy, and on meats of good savour, from four o'clock of the afternoon until half-past seven, with coffee, liqueurs, and ices galore. Yet hath the presence of the worshipful master hindered us from the singing of laudes in clerkly modes,* nor hath any clerk overstepped the limits of pleasing levity, inasmuch as our worthy, worshipful, and generous master had promised to take us his clerks to see Talma in Britannicus at the Théâtre Français.* Long may he flourish! May Heaven shed blessings on our worshipful master! May he get a good price for this his glorious office! May rich clients come to his heart's desire! May his bills of costs be paid in gold on the nail! May all our future masters be like him! May he be ever beloved of his clerks, even when he is no more!

Next came thirty-three reports in due form of the receptions of clerks who had joined the office, distinguished by various handwritings in different shades of ink, distinct phraseology, and different signatures, and containing such laudatory accounts of the good cheer and wines as seemed to prove that the reports were drawn up on the spot and *inter pocula.**

Finally, in the month of June 1822, at the time when Desroches himself had taken the oaths, there was this page of businesslike prose:

I, the undersigned François Claude Marie Godeschal, being called by Master Desroches to fulfil the difficult duties of head clerk in an office where there are as yet no clients, having heard from Master Derville, whose chambers I have quitted, of the existence of certain famous archives of Basochian banquets and festivals famous in the courts, I besought our worshipful master to require them of his predecessor, for it was important to recover that document which bore the date 1786, and was the sequel to the archives, deposited with those of the courts of law, of which the existence was certified by Messieurs Terrasse and Duclos, keepers of the said archives, going back to the year 1525, and giving historical details of the highest value as to the manners and cookery of the law clerks in those days.

This having been granted, the office was put in possession as at this time of these evidences of the worship constantly paid by our predecessors to the *Dive Bouteille** and to good cheer.

Whereupon, for the edification of those that come after us, and to continue the sequence of time and cup, I have invited Messieurs Doublet, second clerk; Vassal, third clerk; Hérisson and Grandemain, assistant clerks; Dumets, office boy, to breakfast on Sunday next at the Cheval Rouge on the Quai Saint-Bernard,* where we will celebrate the recovery of this volume containing the charter of our guzzlings.

On this day, Sunday, June 27th, one dozen bottles of various wines were drunk and found excellent. Noteworthy, likewise, were two melons, pies *au jus romanum* a fillet of beef, and a toast *Agaricibus*.* Mademoiselle Mariette, the illustrious sister of the head clerk, and leading lady at the Royal Academy of Music and Dancing, having given to the clerks of this office stalls for that evening's performance, she is hereby to be remembered for her act of generosity. And it is furthermore resolved that the said clerks shall proceed in a body to return thanks to that noble damsel, and to assure her that on the occasion of her first lawsuit, if the Devil involves her in one, she shall pay no more than the bare costs; to which all set their hand.

Godeschal was proclaimed the pride of his profession and the best of good fellows. May the man who treats others so handsomely soon be treating for a business of his own!

The document was spattered with wine spots and with blots and flourishes like fireworks. To give a complete idea of the stamp of truth impressed on this great work, it will suffice to extract the report of the reception supposed to have been provided by Oscar:

Today, Monday, the 25th day of November 1822, after a meeting held yesterday in the Rue de la Cerisaie, hard by the Arsenal, at the house of Madame Clapart, the mother of the new pupil, by name Oscar Husson, we, the undersigned, declare that the breakfast far surpassed our expectations. It included radishes (red and black), gherkins, anchovies, butter, and olives as introductory *hors-d'œuvres*; of a noble rice broth that bore witness to a mother's care, inasmuch as we recognised in it a delicious flavour of fowl, and by the courtesy of the founder of the feast we were, in fact, informed that the trimmings of a handsome cold dish prepared by Madame Clapart had been judiciously added to the stock concocted at home with such care as is known only in private kitchens.

Item, the aforementioned cold fowl, surrounded by a sea of jelly, the work of the aforenamed mother.

Item, an ox tongue, *aux tomates*, on which we proved ourselves by no means au-tomata.

Item, a stew of pigeons of such flavour as led us to believe that angels had watched over the pot.

Item, a dish of macaroni flanked by cups of chocolate custard.

Item, dessert, consisting of eleven dishes, among which, in spite of the intoxication resulting from sixteen bottles of excellent wine, we discerned the flavour of an exquisitely and superlatively delicious preserve of peaches.

The wines of Roussillon and of the Côte du Rhône quite outdid those of Champagne and Burgundy. A bottle of maraschino, and one of Kirsch, finally, and in spite of delicious coffee, brought us to such a pitch of œnological rapture, that one of us—namely, Master Hérisson—found himself in the Bois de Boulogne when he believed he was still on the Boulevard du Temple,* and that Jacquinaut, the gutter jumper, aged fourteen, spoke to citizens' wives of fifty-seven, taking them for women of the street; to which all set their hand.

Now, in the statutes of our Order there is a law strictly observed, which is, that those who aspire to the benefits and honours of the profession of the law shall restrict the magnificence of their "welcome" to the due proportion with their fortune, inasmuch as it is a matter of public notoriety that no man with a private income serves Themis,* and that all clerks are kept short of cash by their fond parents; wherefore, it is with great admiration that we here record the munificence of Madame Clapart, widow after her first marriage of Monsieur Husson, the new licentiate's father, and declare that it was worthy of the cheers we gave her at dessert; to which all set their hand.

This rigmarole had already taken in three newcomers, and three real breakfasts were duly recorded in this imposing volume.

On the day when a neophyte first made his appearance in the office, the boy always laid the archives on the desk in front of his seat, and the clerks chuckled as they watched the face of the new student while he read these grotesque passages. Each in turn, *inter pocula*, had been initiated into the secret of this practical joke, and the revelation, as may be supposed, filled them with the hope of mystifying other clerks in the future.

So, now, my readers can imagine the countenances of the four clerks and the boy when Oscar, now in his turn the practical joker, uttered the words, "Bring out the book."

Ten minutes later, a handsome young man came in, well grown and pleasant looking, asked for Monsieur Desroches, and gave his name at once to Godeschal.

"I am Frédéric Marest," said he, "and have come to fill the place of third clerk here."

"Monsieur Husson," said Godeschal, "show the gentleman his seat, and induct him into our ways of work."

Next morning the new clerk found the book lying on his writing pad, but after reading the first pages he only laughed, gave no invitation, and put the book aside on his desk.

"Messieurs," said he, as he was leaving at five o'clock, "I have a cousin who is managing clerk to Master Léopold Hannequin, the notary, and I will consult him as to what I should do to pay my footing."

"This looks badly," cried Godeschal. "Our future magistrate is no novice!"

"Oh! We will lead him a life!" said Oscar.

Next afternoon, at about two o'clock, Oscar saw a visitor come in, and recognised in Hannequin's head clerk Georges Marest.

"Why, here is Ali Pasha's friend!" said he, in an airy tone.

"What? You here, Monsieur Ambassador?" retorted Georges, remembering Oscar.

"Oh, ho! Then you are old acquaintances?" said Godeschal to Georges.

"I believe you! We played the fool in company," said Georges, "above two years ago. Yes, I left Crottat to go to Hannequin in consequence of that very affair."

"What affair?" asked Godeschal.

"Oh, a mere nothing," replied Georges, with a wink at Oscar. "We tried to make game of a Peer of France, and it was he who made us look foolish. And now, I hear you want to draw my cousin."

"We do not draw anything," said Oscar with dignity. "Here is our charter."

And he held out the famous volume at a page where sentence of excommunication was recorded against a refractory student who had been fairly driven out of the office for stinginess in 1788.

"Still, I seem to smell game," said Georges, "for here is the trail," and he pointed to the farcical archives. "However, my cousin and I can afford it, and we will give you a feast such as you never had, and which will stimulate your imagination when recording it here. Tomorrow, Sunday, at the Rocher de Cancale,* two o'clock. And I will take you afterwards to spend the evening with Madame la Marquise de las Florentinas y Cabirolos, where we will gamble, and you will meet the elite of fashion. And so, gentlemen of the lower court," he went on, with the arrogance of a notary, "let us have your best behaviour, and carry your wine like gentlemen of the Regency."

"*Hurrah!*" cried the clerks like one man. "*Bravo! Very well! Vivat!* Long live the Marests!"

"*Pontins!*"* added the boy.

"What is up?" asked Desroches, coming out of his private room. "Ah! You are here, Georges," said he to the visitor. "I know you, you are leading my clerks into mischief." And he went back into his own room, calling Oscar. "Here," said he, opening his cashbox, "are five hundred francs; go to the Palais and get the judgment in the case of Vandenesse v. Vandenesse out of the copying clerk's office; it must be sent in this evening if possible. I promised Simon a refresher of twenty francs; wait for the copy if it is not ready, and do not let yourself be put off. Derville is quite capable of putting a drag on our wheels if it will serve his client. Comte Félix de Vandenesse is more influential than his brother the ambassador, our client. So keep your eyes open, and if the least difficulty arises, come to me at once."

Oscar set out, determined to distinguish himself in this little skirmish, the first job that had come to him since his promotion.

When Georges and Oscar were both gone, Godeschal tried to pump the new clerk as to what jest might lie, as he felt sure, under the name of the Marquise de las Florentinas y Cabirolos, but Frédéric carried on his cousin's joke with the coolness and gravity of a judge, and by his replies and his manner contrived to convey to all the clerks that the Marquise de las Florentinas was the widow of a Spanish grandee, whom his cousin was courting. Born in Mexico, and the daughter of a Creole, this wealthy young widow was remarkable for the free-and-easy demeanour characteristic of the women of the Tropics.

"'She likes to laugh, she likes to drink, she likes to sing as we do,'"* said he, quoting a famous song by Béranger. "And Georges," he went on, "is very rich; he inherited a fortune from his father, who was a widower, and who left him eighteen thousand francs a year, which, with twelve thousand left to each of us by an uncle, make an income of thirty thousand francs. And he hopes to be Marquis de las Florentinas, for the young widow bears her title in her own right and can confer it on her husband."

Though the clerks remained very doubtful as to the Marquise, the prospect of a breakfast at the Rocher de Cancale, and of a fashionable soirée, filled them with joy. They *reserved their opinion* as to the Spanish lady, to judge her *without appeal* after having seen her.

The Marquise de las Florentinas was, in fact, neither more nor less than Mademoiselle Agathe-Florentine Cabirolle, leading dancer at the Gaîté Théâtre, at whose house Uncle Cardot sang *"La Mère Godichon."* Within a year of the very reparable loss of the late Madame Cardot, the fortunate merchant met Florentine one evening coming out of Coulon's dancing school.* Dazzled by the beauty of this flower of the ballet—Florentine was then but thirteen—the retired shopkeeper followed her to the Rue Pastourelle, where he had the satisfaction of learning that the future divinity of the dance owed her existence to a humble doorkeeper. The mother and daughter, transplanted within a fortnight to the Rue de Crussol,* there found themselves in modest but easy circumstances. So it was to this "Patron of the Arts," to use a time-honoured phrase, that the stage was indebted for the budding artist.

The generous Mæcenas almost turned their simple brains by giving them mahogany furniture, curtains, carpets, and a well-fitted kitchen; he enabled them to keep a servant, and allowed them two hundred and fifty francs a month. Old Cardot, with his *ailes de pigeon*,* to them seemed an angel, and was treated as a benefactor should be. This was *the golden age* of the old man's passion.

For three years the singer of "*La Mère Godichon*" was so judicious as to keep Mademoiselle Cabirolle and her mother in this unpretentious house, close to the theatre; then, for love of the Terpsichorean art, he placed his protégée under Vestris. And, in 1820, he was pleased to see Florentine dance her first steps in the ballet of a spectacular melodrama called *Les Ruines de Babylone*.* Florentine was now sixteen. Soon after this first appearance, Uncle Cardot had already become *an old miser* in the young lady's estimation; however, as he had tact enough to understand that a dancer at the Gaîté Théâtre must keep up a position, he raised her monthly allowance to five hundred francs a month—if he was no longer an angel, he was at least *a friend for life*, a second father. This was *the age of silver*.

Between 1820 and 1823, Florentine went through the experience which must come to every ballet dancer of nineteen or twenty. Her friends were the famous opera singers Mariette and Tullia; Florine and poor Coralie, so early snatched from Art, Love, and Camusot. And as little Uncle Cardot himself was now five years older, he had drifted into the indulgence of that half-fatherly affection which old men feel for the young talents they have trained, and whose successes are theirs. Besides, how and where should a man of sixty-eight have formed such another attachment as this with Florentine, who knew his ways, and at whose house he could sing "*La Mère Godichon*" with his friends? So the little man found himself under a half-matrimonial yoke of irresistible weight. This was *the age of brass*.

In the course of the five years of the ages of gold and of silver, Cardot had saved ninety thousand francs. The old man had had much experience; he foresaw that by the time he was seventy Florentine would be of age; she would probably come out on the opera stage, and, of course, expect the luxury and splendour of a leading lady. Only a few days before the evening now to be described, Cardot had spent forty-five thousand francs in establishing his Florentine in a suitable style, and had taken for her the apartment where the now dead Coralie had been the joy of Camusot. In Paris, apartments and houses, like streets, have a destiny. Enriched with a magnificent set of silverware, the leading lady of the Gaîté gave handsome dinners, spent three hundred francs a month on dress, never went out but in a private fly, and kept a maid, a cook, and a page. What she aimed at indeed was a command to dance at the opera. The Cocon d'Or laid its handsomest products at the feet of its former master to please Mademoiselle Cabirolle, known as Florentine, just as, three years since, it had gratified every wish of Coralie's, but still without the knowledge of Uncle Cardot's daughter, for the father and his son-in-law had always agreed that decorum must be respected at home. Madame Camusot knew nothing of her husband's extravagance or her father's habits. Now, after being the master for seven years, Cardot felt himself in tow of a pilot whose power of caprice was unlimited. But the unhappy old fellow was in love! Florentine alone must close his eyes, and he meant to leave her a hundred thousand francs. *The age of iron* had begun!

Georges Marest, handsome, young, and rich, with thirty thousand francs a year, was paying court to Florentine. All dancers affect the pretension of loving their protectors as much as they love them, and want to have a young man who will escort them out walking and arrange wild parties for them in the country. And, however disinterested, the affections of a leading lady are always a luxury, costing *the happy object* of her choice some little trifle. Dinners at the best restaurants, boxes at the play, carriages for driving in the environs of Paris, and choice wines lavishly consumed—for ballet dancers live now like the athletes of antiquity. Georges, in short, amused himself as young men do who suddenly find themselves independent of paternal discipline, and his uncle's death, almost doubling his income, enlarged his ideas. So long as he had but the eighteen thousand francs a year left him by his parents he intended to be a notary, but, as his cousin remarked to Desroches's clerks, a man would be senseless to start in a profession with as much money as others have when they give it up. So the retiring law clerk was celebrating his first day of freedom by this breakfast, which was also to pay his cousin's footing. Frédéric, more prudent than Georges, persisted in his legal career. As a fine young fellow like Georges might very well marry a rich creole, and the Marquis de las Florentinas y Cabirolos might very well in the decline of life—as Frédéric hinted to his new companions—have preferred to marry for beauty rather than for noble birth, the clerks of Desroches's office—all belonging to impecunious families, and having no acquaintance with the fashionable world—got themselves up in their Sunday clothes, all impatient to see the Mexican Marquesa de las Florentinas y Cabirolos.

"What good luck," said Oscar to Godeschal as he dressed in the morning, "that I should have just ordered a new coat, waistcoat, and trousers, and a pair of boots, and that my precious mother should have given me a new outfit on my promotion to be second clerk. I have six fine shirts with frills out of the dozen she gave me. We will make a good show? Oh! If only one of us could carry off the Marquise from that Georges Marest!"

"A pretty thing for a clerk in Master Desroches's office!" cried Godeschal. "Will you never be cured of your vanity—brat!"

"Oh, Monsieur," said Madame Clapart, who had just come in to bring her son some ties, and heard the managing clerk's remarks, "would to God that Oscar would follow your good advice! It is what I am always saying to him, 'Imitate Monsieur Godeschal, take his advice,' is what I say."

"He is getting on, Madame," said Godeschal, "but he must not often be so clumsy as he was yesterday, or he will lose his place in the master's good graces. Master Desroches cannot stand a man who is beaten. He sent your son on his first errand yesterday to fetch away the copy of the judgment delivered in a will case in which two brothers, men of high rank, are fighting against each other, and Oscar allowed himself to be circumvented. The master was furious. It was all I could do to set things straight by going at six this morning to find the copying clerk, and I made him promise to let me have the judgment in black and white by seven tomorrow morning."

"Oh, Godeschal," cried Oscar, going up to his superior and grasping his hand, "you are a true friend!"

"Yes, Monsieur," said Madame Clapart, "it is a happy thing for a mother to feel that her son has such a friend as you, and you may believe that my gratitude will end only with my life. Oscar, beware of this Georges Marest; he has already been the cause of your first misfortune in life."

"How was that?" asked Godeschal.

The too-confiding mother briefly told the head clerk the story of poor Oscar's adventure in Pierrotin's chaise.

"I am certain," added Godeschal, "that this *joker* of ours will play some trick on us this evening. I shall not go to the Marquise de las Florentinas. My sister needs my help in drawing up a fresh engagement, so I shall leave you at dessert. But be on your guard, Oscar. Perhaps they will make you gamble, and Desroches's office must not make a poor mouth. Here, you can stake for us both; here are a hundred francs," said the kind fellow, giving the money to Oscar, whose purse had been drained by the tailor and bootmaker. "Be careful; do not dream of playing beyond the hundred francs; do not let play or wine go to your head. By the Mass! Even a second clerk has a position to respect; he must not play on promissory paper, nor overstep a due limit in anything. When a man is second clerk he must remember that he will presently be an attorney. So not to drink, not to play high, and to be moderate in all things must be your rule of conduct. Above all, be in by midnight, for you must be at the courts by seven to fetch away the copy of that judgment. There is no law against some fun, but business holds the first place."

"Do you hear, Oscar?" said Madame Clapart. "And see how indulgent Monsieur Godeschal is, and how he combines the enjoyments of youth with the demands of duty."

Madame Clapart, seeing the tailor and bootmaker waiting for Oscar, remained behind a moment with Godeschal to return the hundred francs he had just lent the boy.

"A mother's blessing be on you, Monsieur, and on all you do," said she.

The mother had the supreme delight of seeing her boy well dressed; she had bought him a gold watch, purchased out of her savings, as a reward for his good conduct.

"You are on the list for the conscription next week," said she, "and as it was necessary to be prepared in case your number should be drawn, I went to see your Uncle Cardot; he is delighted at your being so high up at the age of twenty, and at your success in the examinations at the law schools, so he has promised to find the money for a substitute. Do you not yourself feel some satisfaction in finding good conduct so well rewarded? If you still have to put up with some privations, think of the joy of being able to purchase a connection in only five years! And remember too, dear boy, how happy you make your mother."

Oscar's face, thinned down a little by hard study, had developed into a countenance to which habits of business had given a look of gravity. He had done growing and had a beard; in short, from a boy he had become a man. His mother could not but admire him, and she kissed him fondly, saying—"Yes, enjoy yourself, but remember Monsieur Godeschal's advice. By the way, I was forgetting: here is a present from our friend Moreau—a pocketbook."

"The very thing I want, for the chief gave me five hundred francs to pay for that confounded judgment in Vandenesse, and I did not want to leave them in my room."

"Are you carrying the money about with you?" said his mother in alarm. "Supposing you were to lose such a sum of money! Would you not do better to leave it with Monsieur Godeschal?"

"Godeschal!" cried Oscar, thinking his mother's idea admirable.

But Godeschal, like all clerks on Sunday, had his day to himself from ten o'clock and was already gone.

When his mother had left, Oscar went out to lounge on the boulevards till it was time for the breakfast. How could he keep himself from walking about in those resplendent clothes, which he wore with such pride and satisfaction? What young person who had begun life in circumstances as narrow as his would not understand? A neat double-breasted blue cashmere waistcoat, black kerseymere trousers made with pleats, a well-fitting black coat, and a cane with a silver-gilt knob, bought out of his little savings, were the occasion of very natural pleasure to the poor boy, who remembered the clothes he had worn on the occasion of that journey to Presles, and the effect produced on his mind by Georges. Oscar looked forward to a day of perfect bliss; he was to see the world of fashion for the first time that evening! And it must be admitted that to a lawyer's clerk starved of pleasure, who had for long been craving for a debauch, the sudden play of the senses was enough to obliterate the wise counsels of Godeschal and his mother. To the shame of the young be it said, good advice and warnings are never to seek. Apart from the morning's lecture, Oscar felt an instinctive dislike of Georges; he was humiliated in the presence of a man who had witnessed the scene in the drawing room at Presles when Moreau had dragged him to the Comte's feet.

The Moral Order has its laws, and we are always punished if we ignore them. One, especially, the very beasts obey invariably and without delay. It is that which bids us fly from anyone who has once injured us, voluntarily or involuntarily, intentionally or no. The being who has brought woe or discomfort on us is always odious. Whatever his rank, however near be the ties of affection, we must part. He is the emissary of our evil genius. Though Christian theory is opposed to such conduct, obedience to this inexorable law is essentially social and preservative. James II's daughter, who sat on her father's throne, must have inflicted more than one wound on him before her usurpation.* Judas must certainly have given Jesus some mortal thrust or ever he betrayed Him. There is within us a second sight, a mind's eye, which foresees disasters, and the repugnance we feel to the fateful being is the consequence of this prophetic sense. Though religion may command us to resist it, distrust remains and its voice should be listened to. Could Oscar, at the age of twenty, be so prudent?

Alas! When, at two o'clock, Oscar went into the room of the Rocher de Cancale where he found three guests besides his fellow clerks—to wit, an old dragoon captain named Giroudeau; Finot, a journalist who might enable Florentine to get an engagement at the opera;

and du Bruel, an author and friend of Tullia's, one of Mariette's rivals at the opera—the junior felt his hostility melt away under the first hand shaking, the first flow of talk among young men, as they sat at a table handsomely laid for twelve. And indeed Georges was charming to Oscar.

"You are," said he, "following a diplomatic career, but in private concerns, for what is the difference between an ambassador and an attorney? Merely that which divides a nation from an individual. Ambassadors are the attorneys of a people. If I can ever be of any use to you, depend on me."

"My word! I may tell you now," said Oscar, "you were the cause of a terrible catastrophe for me."

"Bah!" said Georges, after listening to the history of the lad's tribulations. "It was Monsieur de Sérisy who behaved badly. His wife? I would not have her as a gift. And although the Comte is Minister of State and Peer of France, I would not be in his red skin! He is a small-minded man, and I can afford to despise him now."

Oscar listened with pleasure to Georges's ironies on the Comte de Sérisy, for they seemed to diminish the gravity of his own fault, and he threw himself into the young man's spirit as he predicted that overthrow of the nobility of which the bourgeoisie then had visions, to be realised in 1830.* They sat down at half-past three; dessert was not on the table before eight. Each course of dishes lasted two hours. None but law clerks can eat so steadily! Digestions of eighteen and twenty are inexplicable to the medical faculty. The wine was worthy of Borrel, who had at that time succeeded the illustrious Balaine,* the creator of the very best restaurant in Paris—and that is to say in the world—for refined and perfect cookery.

A full report of this Belshazzar's feast was drawn up at dessert, beginning with *Inter pocula aurea restauranti, qui vulgo dicitur Rupes Cancali,** and from this introduction the rapturous record may be imagined which was added to the Golden Book of the High Festivals of the Law.

Godeschal disappeared after signing his name, leaving the eleven feasters, prompted by the old Captain of the Imperial Dragoons, to devote themselves to the wine, the liqueurs, and the toasts, over a dessert of pyramids of sweets and fruits like the pyramids of Thebes. By half-past ten the "boy" of the office was in a state which necessitated his removal; Georges packed him into a cab, gave the driver his mother's address, and paid his fare. Then the ten remaining guests, as drunk as Pitt and Dundas,* talked of going on foot by the boulevards, the night being very fine, as far as the residence of the Marquise, where, at a little before midnight, they would find a brilliant company. The whole party longed to fill their lungs with fresh air, but excepting Georges, Giroudeau, Finot, and du Bruel, all accustomed to Parisian orgies, no one could walk. So Georges sent for three open carriages from a job master's stables, and took the whole party for an airing on the outer boulevards for an hour, from Montmartre to the Barrière du Trône, and back by Bercy, the quays, and the boulevards to the Rue de Vendôme.*

The clerks were still floating in the paradise of fancy to which intoxication transports young people, when their Amphitryon led them into Florentine's rooms. Here sat a dazzling assembly of the queens of the stage, who, at a hint, no doubt, from Frédéric, amused themselves by aping the manners of fine ladies. Ices were handed round, the chandeliers blazed with wax lights. Tullia's footman, with those of Madame du Val-Noble and Florine, all in gaudy livery, carried round sweetmeats on silver trays. The hangings, choice products of the looms of Lyons looped with gold cord, dazzled the eye. The flowers on the carpet suggested a garden bed. Costly toys and curiosities glittered on all sides. At first, and in the obfuscated state to which Georges had brought them, the clerks, and Oscar in particular, believed in the genuineness of the Marquesa de las Florentinas y Cabirolos. On four tables set out for play, gold pieces lay in glittering heaps. In the drawing room the women were playing at vingt-et-un; Nathan, the famous author, holding the deal. Thus, after being carried tipsy and half-asleep along the dimly-lighted boulevards, the clerks woke to find themselves in Armida's Palace.* Oscar, on being introduced by Georges to the sham Marquise, stood dumbfounded, not recognising the ballet dancer from the Gaîté in an elegant dress cut aristocratically low at the neck and richly trimmed with lace—a woman looking like a vignette in a keepsake, who received them with an air and manners that had no parallel in the experience or the imagination of a youth so strictly bred as he had been. After he had admired all the splendor of the rooms, the beautiful women who displayed themselves and who had vied with each other in dress for this occasion—the inauguration of all this magnificence—Florentine took Oscar by the hand and led him to the table where vingt-et-un was going on.

"Come, let me introduce you to the lovely Marquise d'Anglade, one of my friends——"

And she took the hapless Oscar up to pretty Fanny Beaupré, who, for the last two years, had filled poor Coralie's place in Camusot's affections. The young actress had just achieved a reputation in the part of a marquise in a melodrama at the Porte-Saint-Martin called *La Famille d'Anglade,** one of the successes of the day.

"Here, my dear," said Florentine, "allow me to introduce to you a charming youth who can be your partner in the game."

"Oh! That will be very nice!" replied the actress with a fascinating smile, as she looked Oscar down from head to foot. "I am losing. We will go shares if you like."

"I am at your orders, Madame la Marquise," said Oscar, taking a seat by her side.

"You shall stake," said she, "and I will play. You will bring me luck! There, that is my last hundred francs——"

And the sham Marquise took out a purse heavily adorned with diamonds and produced five gold pieces. Oscar brought out his hundred francs in five franc pieces, already shamefaced at mingling the ignoble silver cartwheels with the gold coin. In ten rounds the actress had lost the two hundred francs.

"Come, this is stupid!" she exclaimed. "I will take the deal. We will still be partners?" she asked of Oscar.

Fanny Beaupré rose, and the lad, who, like her, was now the centre of attention to the whole table, dared not withdraw, saying that the devil alone was lodged in his purse. He was speechless, his tongue felt heavy and stuck to his palate.

"Lend me five hundred francs," said the actress to the dancer.

Florentine brought her five hundred francs which she borrowed from Georges, who had just won at écarté eight times running.

"Nathan has won twelve hundred francs," said the actress to the clerk. "The dealer always wins; do not let us be made fools of," she whispered in his ear.

Every man of feeling, imagination, or spirit will understand that poor Oscar could not help opening his pocketbook and taking out the five hundred franc note. He looked at Nathan, the famous writer, who in partnership with Florine staked high against the dealer.

"Now then, boy, sweep it in!" cried Fanny Beaupré, signing to Oscar to take up two hundred francs that Florine and Nathan had lost.

The actress did not spare the losers her banter and jests. She enlivened the game by remarks of a character which Oscar thought strange, but delight stifled these reflections, for the two first deals brought in winnings of two thousand francs. Oscar longed to be suddenly taken ill and to fly, leaving his partner to her fate, but

honour forbade it. Three more deals had carried away
the profits. Oscar felt the cold sweat down his spine; he
was quite sobered now. The two last rounds absorbed
a thousand francs staked by the partners; Oscar felt
thirsty and drank three glasses of iced punch. The actress led him into an adjoining room, talking nonsense
to divert him, but the sense of his error so completely
overwhelmed Oscar, to whom Desroches's face appeared like a vision in a dream, that he sank on to a
splendid ottoman in a dark corner and hid his face in his
handkerchief. He was fairly crying. Florentine detected
him in this attitude, too sincere not to strike an actress;
she hurried up to Oscar, pulled away the handkerchief,
and seeing his tears led him into a boudoir.

"What is the matter, *mon petit?*" said she.

To this voice, these words, this tone, Oscar, recognising
the motherliness of a courtesan's kindness, replied—
"I have lost five hundred francs that my master gave
me to pay tomorrow morning for a judgment; there is
nothing for it but to throw myself into the river; I am
disgraced."

"How can you be so silly?" cried Florentine. "Stay
where you are; I will bring you a thousand francs. Try
to recover it all, but only risk five hundred francs so as
to keep your chief's money. Georges plays a first-rate
game at écarté; bet on him."

Oscar, in his dreadful position, accepted the offer of
the mistress of the house.

"Ah!" thought he, "none but a marquise would be capable of such an action. Beautiful, noble, and immensely
rich! Georges is a lucky dog!"

He received a thousand francs in gold from the hands
of Florentine, and went to bet on the man who had
played him this trick. The punters were pleased at the
arrival of a new man, for they all, with the instinct of
gamblers, went over to the side of Giroudeau, the old
Imperial officer.

"Messieurs," said Georges, "you will be punished for your defection, for I am in luck. Come, Oscar; we will do for them."

But Georges and his backer lost five games running. Having thrown away his thousand francs, Oscar, carried away by the gambling fever, insisted on holding the cards. As a result of the luck that often favours a beginner, he won, but Georges puzzled him with advice; he told him how to discard, and frequently snatched his hand from him, so that the conflict of two wills, two minds, spoiled the run of luck. In short, by three in the morning, after many turns of fortune and unhoped-for recoveries, still drinking punch, Oscar found himself possessed of no more than a hundred francs. He rose from the table, his brain heavy and dizzy, walked a few steps, and dropped on to a sofa in the boudoir, his eyes sealed in leaden slumbers.

"Mariette," said Fanny Beaupré to Godeschal's sister, who had come in at about two in the morning, "will you dine here tomorrow? My Camusot will be here and Père Cardot; we will make them mad."

"How?" cried Florentine. "My old man has not sent me word."

"He will be here this morning to tell you that he proposes to sing '*La Mère Godichon*,'" replied Fanny Beaupré. "He must give a housewarming too, poor man."

"The devil take him and his orgies!" exclaimed Florentine. "He and his son-in-law are worse than magistrates or managers. After all, Mariette, you dine well here," she went on. "Cardot orders everything from Chevet.* Bring your Duc de Maufrigneuse; we will have fun and make them dance."

Oscar, who caught the names of Cardot and Camusot, made an effort to rouse himself, but he could only mutter a word or two which were not heard, and fell back on the silk cushion.

"You are provided, I see," said Fanny Beaupré to Florentine, with a laugh.

"Ah! Poor boy, he is drunk with punch and despair. He has lost some money his master had intrusted to him for some office business. He was going to kill himself, so I lent him a thousand francs, of which those robbers Finot and Giroudeau have fleeced him. Poor innocent!"

Oh! le pauvre garçon, il est ivre de punch et de désespoir.

Plate VIII

"But we must wake him," said Mariette. "My brother will stand no nonsense, nor his master either."

"Well, wake him if you can and get him away," said Florentine, going back into the drawing room to take leave of those who were not gone.

The party then took to dancing—character dances, as they were called, and at daybreak Florentine went to bed very tired, having forgotten Oscar, whom nobody, in fact, remembered, and who was still sleeping soundly.

At about eleven o'clock, a terrible sound awoke the lad, who, recognising his Uncle Cardot's voice and thinking that he might get out of the scrape by pretending still to be asleep, hid his face in the handsome yellow velvet cushions in which he had passed the night.

"Really, my little Florentine," the old man was saying, "it is neither good nor nice of you. You were dancing last night in the *Ruines*, and then spent the night in an orgy. Why, it is simply destruction to your freshness, not to say that it is really ungrateful of you to inaugurate this splendid apartment without me, with strangers, without my knowing it—who knows what may have happened!"

"You old monster!" cried Florentine. "Have you not a key to come in whenever you like? We danced till half-past five, and you are so cruel as to wake me at eleven."

"Half-past eleven, Titine," said the old man humbly. "I got up early to order a dinner from Chevet worthy of an archbishop. How they have spoilt the carpets! What sort of people have you been receiving here?"

"You ought to make no complaints, for Fanny Beaupré told me that you and Camusot were coming, so I have asked the others to meet you—Tullia, du Bruel, Mariette, the Duc de Maufrigneuse, Florine, and Nathan. And you will have the five loveliest women who ever stood behind the footlights, and we will dance you a *pas de Zephire*."

"It is killing work to lead such a life!" cried old Cardot. "What a heap of broken glasses, what destruction! The anteroom is a scene of horror!"

At this moment the amiable old man stood speechless and fascinated, like a bird under the gaze of a reptile. He caught sight of the outline of a young figure clothed in black cloth.

"Ah! Mademoiselle Cabirolle!" said he at last.

"Well, what now?" said she.

The girl's eyes followed the direction of Père Cardot's gaze, and when she saw the youth still there, she burst into a fit of crazy laughter which not only struck the old man dumb, but compelled Oscar to look round. Florentine pulled him up by the arm, and half choked with laughing as she saw the hangdog look of the uncle and nephew.

"You here, my nephew?"

"Ah! He is your nephew?" cried Florentine, laughing more than ever. "You never mentioned this nephew of yours. Then Mariette did not take you home?" said she to Oscar, who sat petrified. "What is to become of the poor boy?"

"Whatever he pleases!" replied old Cardot drily, and turning to the door to go away.

"One minute, Papa Cardot; you will have to help your nephew out of the mess he has got into by my fault, for he has gambled away his master's money, five hundred francs, besides a thousand francs of mine which I lent him to get it back again."

"Wretched boy, have you lost fifteen hundred francs at play—at your age?"

"Oh! Uncle, Uncle!" cried the unhappy Oscar, cast by these words into the depths of horror at his position. He fell on his knees at his uncle's feet with clasped hands. "It is twelve o'clock; I am lost, disgraced. Monsieur Desroches will show no mercy—there was an important business, a matter on which he prides himself—I was to have gone this morning to fetch away the copy of the judgment in Vandenesse v. Vandenesse! What has happened? What will become of me? Save me for my father's sake—for my aunt's. Come with me to Master Desroches and explain; find some excuse——"

The words came out in gasps between sobs and tears that might have softened the Sphinx in the desert of Luxor.

"You old skinflint!" cried the dancer in tears, "can you leave your own nephew to disgrace, the son of the man to whom you owe your fortune, since he is Oscar Husson? Save him, I say, or Titine refuses to own you as her milord!"

"But why is he here?" asked the old man.

"What! So as to forget the hour when he should have gone the errand he speaks of? Don't you see, he got drunk and dropped there, dead tired and sleepy? Georges and his cousin Frédéric treated Desroches's clerks yesterday at the Rocher de Cancale."

Cardot looked at her, still doubtful.

"Come, now, you old baboon, if it were anything more should I not have hidden him more effectually?" cried she.

"Here, then, take the five hundred francs, you scamp!" said Cardot to his nephew. "That is all you will ever have of me. Go and make matters up with your master if you can. I will repay the thousand francs Mademoiselle lent you, but never let me hear your name again."

Oscar fled, not wishing to hear more, but when he was in the street he did not know where to go.

The chance which ruins men and the chance that serves them seemed to be playing against each other on equal terms for Oscar that dreadful morning, but he was destined to fail with a master who, when he made up his mind, never changed it. Mariette, on returning home, horrified at what might befall her brother's charge, had written a message to Godeschal that told her brother of Oscar's drunken bout and the misfortunes that had befallen him, and enclosed a five-hundred franc note. The good woman, ere she went to sleep, instructed her maid to take this letter to Desroches's chambers before seven. Godeschal, on his part, waking at six, found no Oscar. He at once guessed what had happened. He took five hundred francs out of his savings and hurried off to the copying clerk to fetch the judgment, so as to lay it before Desroches for signature in his office at eight. Desroches, who always rose at four, came to his room at seven o'clock. Mariette's maid, not finding her mistress's brother in his attic, went down to the office and was there met by Desroches, to whom she very naturally gave the note.

"Is it a matter of business?" asked the lawyer. "I am Master Desroches."

"You can see, Monsieur," said the woman.

Desroches opened the letter and read it. On finding the five-hundred franc note he went back into his own room, furious with his second clerk. Then at half-past seven he heard Godeschal dictating a report on the judgment to another clerk, and a few minutes later Godeschal came into the room in triumph.

"Was it Oscar Husson who went to Simon this morning?" asked Desroches.

"Yes, Monsieur," replied Godeschal.

"Who gave him the money?" said the lawyer.

"You," said Godeschal, "on Saturday."

"It rains five-hundred franc notes, it would seem!" cried Desroches. "Look here, Godeschal, you are a good fellow, but that little wretch Husson does not deserve your generosity. I hate a fool, but yet more I hate people who will go wrong in spite of the care of those who are kind to them." He gave Godeschal Mariette's note and the five-hundred francs she had sent. "Forgive me for opening it, but the maid said it was a matter of business. You must get rid of Oscar."

"What trouble I have had with that poor little ne'er-do-well!" said Godeschal. "That scoundrel Georges Marest is his evil genius; he must avoid him like the plague, for I do not know what might happen if they met a third time."

"How is that?" asked Desroches.

Godeschal sketched the story of the practical joking on the journey to Presles.

"To be sure," said the lawyer. "I remember Joseph Bridau told me something about that at the time. It was to that meeting that we owed the Comte de Sérisy's interest in Bridau's brother."

At this moment Moreau came in, for this suit over the Vandenesse property was an important affair to him. The Marquis wanted to sell the Vandenesse estate in lots, and his brother opposed such a proceeding. Thus the land agent was the recipient of the justifiable complaints and sinister prophecies fulminated by Desroches against his second clerk, and the unhappy boy's most friendly protector was forced to the conclusion that Oscar's vanity was incorrigible.

"Make a pleader of him," said Desroches; "he only has to pass his final; in that branch of the law his faults may prove to be useful qualities, for conceit spurs the tongue of half of our advocates."

As it happened, Clapart was at this time out of health and nursed by his wife: a painful and thankless task. The man worried the poor soul, who had hitherto never known how odious the nagging and spiteful taunts can be in which a half-imbecile creature gives vent to his irritation when poverty drives him into a sort of cunning rage. Delighted to have a sharp dagger that he could drive home to her motherly heart, he had suspected the fears for the future which were suggested to the hapless woman by Oscar's conduct and faults. In fact, when a mother has received such a blow as she had felt from the adventure at Presles she lives in perpetual alarms, and by the way in which Madame Clapart praised Oscar whenever he achieved a success, Clapart understood all her secret fears and would stir them up on the slightest pretext.

"Well, well, Oscar is getting on better than I expected of him; I always said his journey to Presles was only a blunder due to inexperience. Where is the young man who never made a mistake? Poor boy, he is heroic in his endurance of the privations he would never have known if his father had lived. God grant he may control his passions!" and so on.

So, while so many disasters were crowding on each other in the Rue de Vendôme and the Rue de Béthisy, Clapart, sitting by the fire wrapped in a shabby dressing gown, was watching his wife busily cooking over the bedroom fire some broth, Clapart's herb tea, and her own breakfast.

"*Mon Dieu*, I wish I knew how things fell out yesterday. Oscar was to breakfast at the Rocher de Cancale and spend the evening with some marquise——"

"Oh! Don't be in a hurry; sooner or later *murder will out*," retorted her husband. "Do you believe in the Marquise? Go on; a boy who has his five senses and a love of extravagance—as Oscar has, after all—can find marquises in Spain costing their weight in gold! He will come home some day loaded with debt——"

"You do nothing but drive me to despair!" exclaimed Madame Clapart. "You complained that my son ate up all your salary, and he never cost you a sou. For two years you have not had a fault to find with Oscar, and now he is second clerk, his uncle and Monsieur Moreau provide him with everything, and he has eight hundred francs a year of his own earning. If we have bread in our old age, we shall owe it to that dear boy. You really are too unjust."

"You consider my foresight an injustice?" said the sick man sourly.

There came at this moment a sharp ring at the bell. Madame Clapart ran to open the door, and then remained in the outer room, talking to Moreau, who had come himself to soften the blow that the news of Oscar's levity must be to his poor mother.

"What! He lost his master's money?" cried Madame Clapart in tears.

"Aha! What did I tell you?" said Clapart, who appeared like a spectre in the doorway of the drawing room, to which he had shuffled across under the prompting of curiosity.

"But what is to be done with him?" said his wife, whose distress left her insensible to this stab.

"Well, if he bore my name," said Moreau, "I should calmly allow him to be drawn for the conscription, and if he should be called to serve, I would not pay for a substitute. This is the second time that sheer vanity has brought him into mischief. Well, vanity may lead him to some brilliant action which will win him promotion as a soldier. Six years' service will at any rate add a little weight to his featherbrain, and as he has only his final examination to pass, he will not do so badly if he finds himself a pleader at twenty-six, if he chooses to go to the bar after paying the blood tax, as they say. This time, at any rate, he will have had his punishment, he will gain experience and acquire habits of subordination. He will have served his apprenticeship to life before serving it in the law courts."

"If that is the sentence you would pronounce on a son," said Madame Clapart, "I see that a father's heart is very unlike a mother's. My poor Oscar—a soldier?"

"Would you rather see him jump headfirst into the Seine after doing something to disgrace himself? He can never now be an attorney; do you think he is fitted yet to be an advocate? While waiting till he reaches years of discretion, what will he become? A thorough scamp; military discipline will at any rate preserve him from that."

"Could he not go into another office? His Uncle Cardot would certainly pay for a substitute—and Oscar will dedicate his thesis to him——"

The clatter of a cab, in which was piled all Oscar's personal property, announced the wretched lad's return, and in a few minutes he made his appearance.

"So here you are, Monsieur *Joli-Cœur!*"* cried Clapart.

Oscar kissed his mother and held out a hand to Monsieur Moreau that he refused to shake; Oscar responded to this show of contempt with a reproachful look that revealed a certain boldness as yet unseen in him.

"Listen, Monsieur Clapart," said the boy, so suddenly grown to be a man, "you worry my poor mother beyond endurance, and you have a right to do so—she is, unfortunately for her, your wife. But it is different with me. In a few months I shall be of age, and you have no power over me even while I am a minor. I have never asked you for anything. Thanks to this gentleman, I have never cost you one sou, and I owe you no sort of gratitude, so have the goodness to leave me in peace."

Clapart, startled by this apostrophe, went back to his armchair by the fire. The reasoning of the lawyer's clerk and the suppressed fury of a young man of twenty, who had just had a sharp lecture from his friend Godeschal, had reduced the sick man's imbecility to silence, once and for all.

"An error into which you would have been led quite as easily as I, at my age," said Oscar to Moreau, "made me commit a fault which Desroches thinks serious, but which is really trivial enough; I am far more vexed with myself for having taken Florentine, of the Gaîté theatre, for a marquise, and actresses for women of rank, than for having lost fifteen hundred francs at a little orgy where everybody, even Godeschal, was as drunk as a lord. This time, at any rate, I have hurt no one but myself. I am thoroughly cured. If you will help me, Monsieur Moreau, I swear to you that in the course of the six years during which I must remain a clerk before I can practise——"

"Stop a bit!" said Moreau. "I have three children; I can make no promises."

"Well, well," said Madame Clapart, with a reproachful look at Moreau, "your Uncle Cardot——"

"No more Uncle Cardot for me," replied Oscar, and he related the adventure of the Rue de Vendôme.

Madame Clapart, feeling her knees give way under the weight of her body, dropped on one of the dining room chairs as if a thunderbolt had fallen.

"Every possible misfortune at once!" said she, and fainted away.

Moreau lifted the poor woman in his arms and carried her to her bed. Oscar stood motionless and speechless.

"There is nothing for you but to serve as a soldier," said the estate agent, coming back again. "That idiot Clapart will not last three months longer, it seems to me; your mother will not have a sou in the world; ought I not rather to keep for her the little money I can spare? This was what I could not say to you in her presence. As a soldier, you will earn your bread, and you may meditate on what life is to the penniless."

"I might draw a lucky number," said Oscar.

"And if you do? Your mother has been a very good mother to you. She gave you an education, she started you in a good way; you have lost it; what could you do now? Without money a man is helpless, as you now know, and you are not the man to begin all over again by pulling off your coat and putting on a workman's or artisan's blouse. And then your mother worships you. Do you want to kill her? For she would die of seeing you fallen so low."

Oscar sat down, and could no longer control his tears, which flowed freely. He understood now a form of appeal which had been perfectly incomprehensible at the time of his first error.

"People without money have to be perfect!" said Moreau to himself, not appreciating how deeply true this cruel verdict was.

"My fate will soon be decided," said Oscar; "the numbers are drawn the day after tomorrow. Between this and then I will come to some decision."

Moreau, deeply grieved in spite of his austerity, left the family in the Rue de la Cerisaie to their despair. Three days after, Oscar drew number 27. To help the poor lad, the ex-steward of Presles found courage enough to go to the Comte de Sérisy and beg his interest to get Oscar into the cavalry. As it happened, the Comte's son, having come out well at his last examination on leaving the École Polytechnique,* had been passed by favour, with the rank of sub-lieutenant, into the cavalry regiment commanded by the Duc de Manfrigneuse. And so, in the midst of his fall, Oscar had the small piece of luck of being enlisted in this fine regiment at the Comte de Sérisy's recommendation, with the promise of promotion to be quartermaster in a year's time. Thus chance placed the lawyer's clerk under the command of Monsieur de Sérisy's son.

After some days of pining, Madame Clapart, who was deeply stricken by all these misfortunes, gave herself up to the remorse which is apt to come over mothers whose conduct has not been blameless, and who, as they grow old, are led to repent. She thought of herself as one accursed. She ascribed the miseries of her second marriage and all her son's ill-fortune to the vengeance of God, who was punishing her in expiation of the sins and pleasures of her youth. This idea soon became a conviction. The poor soul went to confession, for the first time in forty years, to the Vicar of the Church of Saint-Paul,* the Abbé Gaudron, who plunged her into the practices of religion. But a spirit so crushed and so loving as Madame Clapart's could not fail to become simply pious. The Aspasia of the Directory yearned to atone for her sins that she might bring the blessing of God down on the head of her beloved Oscar, and before long she had given herself up to the most earnest practices of devotion and works of piety. She believed that she had earned the favour of Heaven when she had succeeded in saving Monsieur Clapart, who, thanks to her care, lived to torment her, but she persisted in seeing in the tyranny of this half-witted old man the trials inflicted by Him who loves while He chastens us. Oscar's conduct meanwhile was so satisfactory that in 1830 he was first quartermaster of the company under the Vicomte de Sérisy, equivalent in rank to a sub-lieutenant of the line, as the Duc de Maufrigneuse's regiment was attached to the Royal Guard. Oscar Husson was now twenty-five. As the regiments of guards were always quartered in Paris, or within thirty leagues of the capital, he could see his mother from time to time and confide his sorrows to her, for he was clear-sighted enough to perceive that he could never rise to be an officer. At that time cavalry officers were almost always chosen from among the younger sons of the nobility, and men without the distinguishing *de* got on but slowly. Oscar's whole ambition was to get out of the guards and enter some cavalry regiment of the line as a sub-lieutenant, and in the month of February 1830 Madame Clapart, through the interest of the Abbé Gaudron, now at the head of his parish, gained the favour of the Dauphiness,* which secured Oscar's promotion.

Although the ambitious young soldier professed ardent devotion to the Bourbons, he was at heart a liberal. In the struggle of 1830, he took the side of the people. This defection, which was important due to the point where it took place, drew public attention to Oscar Husson. In the moment of triumph, in the month of August, Oscar, promoted to be lieutenant, received the Cross of the Legion of Honour, and succeeded in obtaining the post of aide-de-camp to Lafayette, who made him captain in 1832. When this devotee to "the best of all Republics"* was deprived of his command of the National Guard, Oscar Husson, whose devotion to the new royal family was almost fanaticism, was sent as major with a regiment to Africa on the occasion of the first expedition undertaken by the Prince. The Vicomte de Sérisy was now lieutenant colonel of that regiment. At the fight at the Macta,* where the Arabs remained masters of the field, Monsieur de Sérisy was left wounded under his dead horse. Oscar addressed his company:

"It is riding to our death," said he, "but we cannot desert our Colonel." He was the first to charge the enemy, and his men, quite electrified, followed. The Arabs, in the shock of surprise at this furious and unexpected attack, allowed Oscar to pick up his Colonel, whom he took on his horse and rode off at a pelting gallop, though in this act, carried out in the midst of furious fighting, he had two cuts from a yataghan on the left arm. Oscar's valiant conduct was rewarded by the Cross of an Officer of the Legion of Honour and promotion to the rank of lieutenant colonel. He nursed the Vicomte de Sérisy with devoted affection; the Comtesse de Sérisy joined her son and carried him to Toulon, where, as all the world knows, he died of his wounds. Madame de Sérisy did not part her son from the man who, after rescuing him from the Arabs, had cared for him with such unfailing devotion. Oscar himself was so severely wounded that the surgeons called in by the Comtesse to attend her son pronounced amputation necessary. The Comte forgave Oscar his follies on the occasion of the journey to Presles, and even regarded himself as the young man's debtor when he had buried his only surviving son in the chapel of the Château de Sérisy.

A long time after the battle of the Macta, an old lady dressed in black, leaning on the arm of a man of thirty-four, at once recognisable as a retired officer by the loss of one arm and the rosette of the Legion of Honour at his buttonhole, was to be seen at eight o'clock one morning,

Oscar était si grièvement blessé que l'amputation du bras
gauche fut jugée nécessaire.....

UN DÉBUT DANS LA VIE.

Plate IX

waiting under the gateway of the Lion-d'Argent, Rue du Faubourg Saint-Denis, till the diligence should be ready to start. Pierrotin, the manager of the coach services of the valley of the Oise, passing by Saint-Leu-Taverny and L'Isle-Adam, as far as Beaumont, would hardly have recognised in this bronzed officer that little Oscar Husson whom he had once driven to Presles. Madame Clapart, a widow at last, was quite as unrecognisable as her son. Clapart, one of the victims of Fieschi's machine,* had done his wife a better turn by the manner of his death than he had ever done her in his life.

Of course, Clapart, the idler, the lounger, had taken up a place on *his* boulevard to see *his* legion reviewed. Thus the poor devotee had found her name down for a pension of fifteen hundred francs a year by the decree which indemnified the victims of this infernal machine.

The vehicle, to which four dappled grey horses were now being harnessed—steeds worthy of the *Messageries royales*—was in four divisions: the coupé, the *intérieur*, the *rotonde* behind, and the *imperiale* at top. It was identically the same as the diligences called *gondoles* which, in our day, still maintain a rivalry on the Versailles road with two lines of railway. Strong and light, well painted and clean, lined with good blue cloth, furnished with blinds of arabesque design and red morocco cushions, the *Hirondelle de l'Oise** could carry nineteen travellers. Pierrotin, though he was by this time fifty-six, was little changed. He still wore a blouse over his black coat and still smoked his short pipe, as he watched two porters in stable livery piling numerous packages on the roof of his coach.

"Have you taken seats?" he asked of Madame Clapart and Oscar, looking at them as if he were searching his memory for some association of ideas.

"Yes, two inside places, name of Belle-Jambe, my servant," said Oscar. "He was to take them when he left the house last evening."

"Oh, then Monsieur is the new collector at Beaumont," said Pierrotin. "You are going down to take the place of Monsieur Margueron's nephew?"

"Yes," replied Oscar, pressing his mother's arm as a hint to her to say nothing.

For now he in his turn wished to remain unknown for a time.

At this instant Oscar was startled by recognising Georges's voice calling from the street—"Have you a seat left, Pierrotin?"

"It strikes me that you might say Monsieur Pierrotin without breaking your jaw," said the coach owner angrily.

But for the tone of his voice Oscar could never have recognised the practical joker who had twice brought him such ill luck. Georges, almost bald, had but three or four locks of hair left above his ears, and carefully combed up to disguise his bald crown as far as possible. A development of fat in the wrong place, a bulbous stomach, had spoiled the elegant figure of the once handsome young man. Almost vulgar in shape and mien, Georges showed the traces of disaster in love, and of a life of constant debauchery, in a spotty red complexion, and thickened, vinous features. His eyes had lost the sparkle and eagerness of youth, which can only be preserved by decorous and studious habits. Georges, dressed with evident indifference to his appearance, wore a pair of trousers with straps, but which were rather shabby, and of a style that demanded patent leather boots; the boots he wore, thick and badly polished, were at least three-quarters of a year old, which is in Paris as much as three years anywhere else. A shabby waistcoat, a tie elaborately knotted though it was but an old bandanna, betrayed the covert penury to which a decayed dandy may be reduced. To crown all, at this early hour of the day Georges wore a dress coat instead of a morning coat, the symptom of positive poverty. This coat, which must have danced at many a ball, had fallen, like its owner, from the opulence it once represented, to the duties of daily scrub. The seams of the black cloth showed white ridges, the collar was greasy, and wear had pinked out the cuffs into a dog's tooth edge. Still, Georges was bold enough to invite attention by wearing lemon-coloured gloves—rather dirty, to be sure, and on one finger the outline of a large ring was visible in black. Round his tie, of which the ends were slipped through a pretentious gold ring, twined a brown silk chain in imitation of hair, ending no doubt in a watch. His hat, though stuck on with an air, showed more evidently than all these other symptoms the poverty of a man who never has sixteen francs to spend at the hatter's when he lives from hand to mouth. Florentine's ci-devant lover flourished a cane with a chased handle, silver-gilt, but horribly dented. His blue trousers, tartan waistcoat, sky-blue tie, and red-striped cotton shirt bore witness, in spite of so much squalor, to such a passion for *show* that the contrast was not merely laughable, but a lesson.

"And this is Georges?" said Oscar to himself. "A man I left in possession of thirty thousand francs a year!"

"Has Monsieur *de* Pierrotin still a vacant seat in his coupé?" asked Georges ironically.

"No, my coupé is taken by a Peer of France, Monsieur Moreau's son-in-law, Monsieur le Baron de Canalis, with his wife and his mother-in-law. I have only a seat in the body of the coach."

"The deuce! It would seem that under every form of government Peers of France travel in Pierrotin's conveyances! I will take the seat in the *intérieur*," said Georges, with a reminiscence of the journey with Monsieur de Sérisy.

He turned to stare at Oscar and the widow, but recognised neither mother nor son. Oscar was deeply tanned by the African sun; he had a very thick moustache and whiskers; his hollow cheeks and marked features were in harmony with his military deportment. The officer's rosette, the loss of an arm, the plain dark dress, would all have been enough to mislead Georges's memory, if indeed he remembered his former victim. As to Madame Clapart, whom he had scarcely seen on the former occasion, ten years spent in pious exercises of the severest kind had absolutely transformed her. No one could have imagined that this sort of Grey Sister* hid one of the Aspasias of 1797.

A huge old man, plainly but very comfortably dressed, in whom Oscar recognised old Léger, came up slowly and heavily; he nodded familiarly to Pierrotin, who seemed to regard him with the respect due in all countries to millionaires.

"Heh! Why, it is Père Léger! More ponderous than ever!" cried Georges.

"Whom have I the honour of addressing?" asked the farmer very drily.

"What! Don't you remember Colonel Georges, Ali Pasha's friend? We travelled this road together, once upon a time, with the Comte de Sérisy, who preserved his incognito."

One of the commonest follies of persons who have come down in the world is insisting on recognising people, and on being recognised.

"You are very much changed," said the old land agent, now worth two million francs.

"Everything changes," said Georges. "Look at the Lion-d'Argent and at Pierrotin's coach, and see if they are the same as they were fourteen years since."

"Pierrotin is now owner of all the coaches that serve the Oise valley, and has very good vehicles," said Monsieur Léger. "He is a citizen now of Beaumont, and keeps an inn there where his coaches put up; he has a wife and daughter who know their business——"

An old man of about seventy came out of the inn and

joined the group of travellers who were waiting to be told to get in.

"Come along, Papa Reybert!" said Léger. "We have no one to wait for now but your great man."

"Here he is," said the land steward of Presles, turning to Joseph Bridau.

Neither Oscar nor Georges would have recognised the famous painter, for his face was the strangely worn countenance now so well known, and his manner was marked by the confidence born of success. His black overcoat displayed the ribbon of the Legion of Honour. His dress, which was careful in all points, showed that he was on his way to some country fête.

At this moment a clerk with a paper in his hand bustled out of an office constructed at one end of the old kitchen of the Lion-d'Argent, and stood in front of the still unoccupied coupé.

"Monsieur and Madame de Canalis, three places!" he called out; then, coming to the *intérieur*, he said, "Monsieur Belle-Jambe, two places; Monsieur Reybert, three; Monsieur—your name?" added he to Georges.

"Georges Marest," muttered the fallen hero.

The clerk then went to the *rotonde*, round which stood a little crowd of nurses, country folks, and small shop-keepers taking leave of each other. After packing the six travellers, the clerk called the names of four youths who clambered up on to the seat on the *imperiale* and then said, "Right behind!" as the signal for starting. Pierrotin took his place by the driver, a young man in a blouse, who in his turn said, "Get up," to his horses.

The coach, set in motion by four horses purchased at Roye, was pulled up the hill of the Faubourg Saint-Denis at a gentle trot, but having once gained the level above Saint-Laurent,* it spun along like a mail coach as far as Saint-Denis for forty minutes. They did not stop at the inn famous for cheesecakes, but turned off to the left of Saint-Denis, down the valley of Montmorency.

It was here, as they turned, that Georges broke the silence which had been kept so far by the travellers who were studying each other.

"We keep rather better time than we did fifteen years ago," said he, taking out a silver watch. "Heh! Père Léger?"

"People are so condescending as to address me as Monsieur Léger," retorted the millionaire.

"Why, this is our *blusterer* of my first journey to Presles," exclaimed Joseph Bridau. "Well, and have you been fighting new campaigns in Asia, Africa, and America?" asked the great painter.

"*Sacrebleu!* I helped in the Revolution of July, and that was enough, for it ruined me."

"Oho! You helped in the Revolution of July, did you?" said Bridau. "I am not surprised, for I never could believe what I was told, that it made itself."

"How strangely meetings come about," said Monsieur Léger, turning to Reybert. "Here, Papa Reybert, you see the notary's clerk to whom you owe indirectly your place as steward of the estates of Sérisy."

"But we miss Mistigris, now so famous as Léon de Lora," said Joseph Bridau, "and the little fellow who was such a fool as to tell the Comte all about his skin complaints—which he has cured at last—and his wife, from whom he has parted to die in peace."

"Monsieur le Comte is missing too," said Reybert.

"Oh!" said Bridau sadly, "I am afraid that the last expedition he will ever make will be to L'Isle-Adam, to be present at my wedding."

"He still drives out in the park, now and then," remarked old Reybert.

"Does his wife come often to see him?" asked Léger.

"Once a month," replied Reybert. "She still prefers Paris; she arranged the marriage of her favourite niece, Mademoiselle du Rouvre, to a very rich young Pole, Count Laginski, in September last——"

"And who will inherit Monsieur de Sérisy's property?" asked Madame Clapart.

"His wife, she will bury him," replied Georges. "The Comtesse is still handsome for a woman of fifty-four, still very elegant, and at a distance quite illusory——"

"Elusive, you mean? She will always elude you," Léger put in, wishing, perhaps, to turn the tables on the man who had mystified him.

"I respect her," said Georges in reply. "But, by the way, what became of that steward who was so abruptly dismissed in those days?"

"Moreau?" said Léger. "He is deputy now for Seine-et-Oise."

"Oh, the famous *centrier** Moreau of L'Oise?" said Georges.

"Yes," replied Léger. "*Monsieur* Moreau of L'Oise. He helped rather more than you in the Revolution of July, and he has lately bought the splendid estate of Pointel, between Presles and Beaumont."

"What, close to the place he managed, and so near his old master! That is in very bad taste," cried Georges.

"Do not talk so loud," said Monsieur de Reybert, "for Madame Moreau and her daughter, the Baronne de Canalis, and her son-in-law, the old minister, are in the coupé."

"What fortune did he give her that the great orator would marry his daughter?"

"Well, somewhere about two millions," said Léger.

"He had a pretty taste in millions," said Georges, smiling, and in an undertone, "He began feathering his nest at Presles——"

"Say no more about Monsieur Moreau," exclaimed Oscar. "It seems to me that you might have learned to hold your tongue in a public conveyance!"

Joseph Bridau looked for a few seconds at the one-armed officer, and then said—"Monsieur is not an ambassador, but his rosette shows that he has risen in the world, and nobly too, for my brother and General Giroudeau have often mentioned you in their despatches——"

"Oscar Husson!" exclaimed Georges. "On my honour, but for your voice, I should never have recognised you."

"Ah! Is this the gentleman who so bravely carried off the Vicomte Jules de Sérisy from the Arabs?" asked Reybert, "and to whom Monsieur le Comte has given the collectorship at Beaumont pending his appointment to Pontoise?"

"Yes, Monsieur," said Oscar.

"Well, then," said the painter, "I hope, Monsieur, that you will do me the pleasure of being present at my marriage, at L'Isle-Adam."

"Whom are you marrying?" asked Oscar.

"Mademoiselle Léger, Monsieur de Reybert's granddaughter. Monsieur le Comte de Sérisy was good enough to arrange the matter for me. I owe him much as an artist, and he was anxious to establish my fortune before his death—I had scarcely thought of it——"

"Then Père Léger married?" said Georges.

"My daughter," said Monsieur de Reybert, "and without any money."

"And he has children?"

"One daughter. Quite enough for a widower who had no other children," said Père Léger. "And, like my partner Moreau, I shall have a famous man for my son-in-law."

"So you still live at L'Isle-Adam?" said Georges to Monsieur Léger, almost respectfully.

"Yes, I purchased Cassan."

"Well, I am happy in having chosen this particular day for *doing* the Oise valley," said Georges, "for you may do me a service, Messieurs."

"In what way?" asked Léger.

"Well, thus," said Georges. "I am employed by the Society of *L'Espérance*,* which has just been incorporated, and its bylaws approved by letters patent from the King. This institution is, in ten years, to give marriage portions to girls and annuities to old people; it will pay for the education of children; in short, it takes care of everybody——"

"So I should think!" said old Léger, laughing. "In short, you are an insurance agent."

"No, Monsieur, I am inspector general, instructed to establish agencies and correspondents with the company throughout France; I am acting only till the agents are appointed, for it is a delicate and difficult matter to find honest men——"

"But how did you lose your thirty thousand francs a year?" asked Oscar.

"As you lost your arm!" the ex-notary's clerk replied sharply to the ex-attorney's clerk.

"Then you invested your fortune in some brilliant deed?" said Oscar, with somewhat bitter irony.

"*Parbleu!* My investments are a sore subject. I have more deeds than enough."

They had reached Saint-Leu-Taverny where the travellers got out while they changed horses. Oscar admired the briskness with which Pierrotin unbuckled the straps of the swing bar while his driver took out the leaders.

"Poor Pierrotin!" thought he. "Like me, he has not risen much in life. Georges has sunk into poverty. All the others, by speculation and skill, have made fortunes. Do we breakfast here, Pierrotin?" he asked, clapping the man on the shoulder.

"I am not the driver," said Pierrotin.

"What are you, then?" asked Colonel Husson.

"I am the owner," replied Pierrotin.

"Well, well, do not quarrel with an old friend," said Oscar, pointing to his mother, but still with a patronising air; "do you not remember Madame Clapart?"

It was the more graceful of Oscar to name his mother to Pierrotin, because at this moment Madame Moreau de l'Oise had got out of the coupé and looked scornfully at Oscar and his mother as she heard the name.

"On my honour, Madame, I should never have known you, nor you either, Monsieur. You *get it hot* in Africa, it would seem?"

The disdainful pity Oscar had felt for Pierrotin was the last blunder into which vanity betrayed the hero of this scene, and for that he was punished, though not too severely. Here is how.

Two months after he had settled at Beaumont-sur-Oise, Oscar paid his court to Mademoiselle Georgette Pierrotin, whose fortune amounted to a hundred and fifty thousand francs, and by the end of the winter of 1838 he married the daughter of the owner of the Oise valley coach service.

The results of the journey to Presles had given Oscar discretion, the evening at Florentine's had disciplined his honesty, the hardships of a military life had taught him the value of social distinctions and submission to fate. He was prudent, capable, and consequently happy. The Comte de Sérisy, before his death, obtained for Oscar the place of revenue collector at Pontoise. The influence of Monsieur Moreau de l'Oise, of the Comtesse de Sérisy, and of Monsieur le Baron de Canalis, who, sooner or later, will again have a seat in the ministry, will secure Monsieur Husson's promotion to the post of receiver general, and the Camusots now recognise him as a relation.

Oscar is a commonplace man: gentle, unpretentious, and modest—faithful, like the government he serves, to the happy medium in all things. He invites neither envy nor scorn. In short, he is the modern French citizen.

Paris, February 1842

Oscar Husson.

Plate X

The following personages appear or are mentioned
in other volumes of *The Human Comedy*.

Beaupré, Fanny

II: *Modest Mignon*
XIV: *The Muse of the Department*
XIX: *The Splendours and Miseries of Courtesans*

Bridau, Joseph

I: *Letters of Two Brides*
II: *The Purse, Modeste Mignon*
XIII: *The Rabouilleuse*
IX: *Another Study of Woman*
XVI: *Lost Illusions*
XX: *Pierre Grassou*
XXI: *Cousin Bette*
XXVIII: *The Deputy for Arcis*

Bruel, Jean François du

IV: *A Daughter of Eve*
XIII: *The Rabouilleuse*
XVI: *Lost Illusions*
XXIII: *A Prince of Bohemia*
XXIV: *The Bureaucrats*
XXV: *The Petits Bourgeois*

Cabirolle, Madame

XIII: *The Rabouilleuse*

Cabirolle, Agathe-Florentine

XIII: *The Rabouilleuse*
XVI: *Lost Illusions*

Albert Savarus
May 1842

*To Madame Émile de Girardin**

Amédée de Souhs.

Plate XI

One of the few drawing rooms where, under the Restoration,* the Archbishop of Besançon was sometimes to be seen, was that of the Baronne de Watteville, to whom he was particularly attached on account of her religious sentiments. A word as to this lady, perhaps the most significant female figure in Besançon.

Monsieur de Watteville, a descendant of the famous Watteville, the most successful and illustrious of murderers and renegades—his extraordinary adventures are too much a part of history to be related here—this nineteenth century Monsieur de Watteville was as gentle and peaceable as his ancestor of the *Grand Siècle** had been passionate and turbulent. After living in the Comté* like a wood louse in the crack of a wainscot, he had married the heiress of the celebrated house of Rupt. Mademoiselle de Rupt brought twenty thousand francs a year in the funds to add to the ten thousand francs a year in real estate of the Baron de Watteville. The Swiss gentleman's coat of arms (the Wattevilles are Swiss) was then borne as an escutcheon of pretence* on the old shield of the Rupts. The marriage, arranged in 1802, was solemnised in 1815 after the second Restoration. Within three years of the birth of a daughter all Madame de Watteville's grandparents were dead, and their estates wound up. Monsieur de Watteville's house was then sold, and they settled in the Rue de la Préfecture in the fine old mansion of the Rupts, with an immense garden stretching to the Rue du Perron. Madame de Watteville, devout as a girl, became even more so after her marriage. She is one of the queens of the saintly brotherhood which gives the upper circles of Besançon a solemn air and prudish manners in harmony with the character of the town.*

Monsieur le Baron de Watteville, a dry, lean man devoid of intelligence, looked worn out without anyone knowing whereby, for he enjoyed the profoundest ignorance, but as his wife was a red-haired woman, and of a stern nature that became proverbial (we still say "as sharp as Madame de Watteville"), some wits of the legal profession declared that he had been worn against that rock—*Rupt* is obviously derived from *rupes*.* Scientific students of social phenomena will not fail to have observed that Rosalie was the only offspring of the union between the Wattevilles and the Rupts.

Monsieur de Watteville spent his existence in a handsome workshop with a lathe; he was a turner! As subsidiary to this pursuit, he took up a fancy for making collections. Philosophical doctors, devoted to the study of madness, regard this tendency towards collecting as a first degree of mental aberration when it is set on small things. The Baron de Watteville treasured shells and geological fragments of the neighbourhood of Besançon. Some contradictory folk, especially women, would say of Monsieur de Watteville, "He has a noble soul! He perceived from the first days of his married life that he would never be his wife's master, so he threw himself into a mechanical occupation and good living."

The house of the Rupts was not devoid of a certain magnificence worthy of Louis XIV, and bore traces of the nobility of the two families who had mingled in 1815. The chandeliers of glass cut in the shape of leaves, the brocades, the damask, the carpets, the gilt furniture, were all in harmony with the old liveries and the old servants. Though served in blackened family plate, round a looking glass tray furnished with Dresden china, the food was exquisite. The wines selected by

Monsieur de Watteville, who, to occupy his time and vary his employments, was his own butler, enjoyed a sort of fame throughout the département. Madame de Watteville's fortune was a fine one; while her husband's, which consisted only of the estate of Rouxey, worth about ten thousand francs a year, was not increased by inheritance. It is needless to add that in consequence of Madame de Watteville's close intimacy with the Archbishop, the three or four clever or remarkable abbés of the diocese who were not averse to good feeding were very much at home at her house.

At a ceremonial dinner given in honour of I know not whose wedding, at the beginning of September 1834, when the women were standing in a circle round the drawing room fire, and the men in groups by the windows, everyone exclaimed with pleasure at the entrance of Monsieur l'Abbé de Grancey, who was announced.

"Well, and the lawsuit?" they all cried.

"Won!" replied the Vicar-General. "The verdict of the court, from which we had no hope, you know why——"

This was an allusion to the composition of the Royal Court since 1830; virtually every one of the legitimists had resigned.*

"The verdict is in our favour on every point, and reverses the decision of the lower court."

"Everybody thought you were done for."

"And we should have been, but for me. I told our advocate to be off to Paris, and at the crucial moment I was able to secure a new pleader, to whom we owe our victory, a wonderful man——"

"At Besançon?" said Monsieur de Watteville, guilelessly.

"At Besançon," replied the Abbé de Grancey.

"Oh yes, Savaron," said a handsome young man sitting near the Baronne, and named de Soulas.

"He spent five or six nights over it; he devoured documents and briefs; he had seven or eight interviews of several hours with me," continued Monsieur de Grancey, who had just reappeared at the Hôtel de Rupt for the first time in three weeks. "In short, Monsieur Savaron has just completely beaten the celebrated lawyer whom our adversaries had sent for from Paris. This young man is wonderful, the bigwigs say. Thus the chapter is twice victorious; it has triumphed in law and also in politics, since it has vanquished liberalism in the person of the defender of our municipality. 'Our adversaries,' so our advocate said, 'must not expect to find readiness on all sides to ruin the archbishoprics . . .' The President was obliged to enforce silence. All the townsfolk of Besançon applauded. Thus the possession of the buildings of the old convent remains with the Chapter of the Cathedral of Besançon. Monsieur Savaron, however, invited his Parisian opponent to dine with him as they came out of court. He accepted, saying, 'Honour to every conqueror,' and complimented him on his success without bitterness."

"And where did you unearth this lawyer?" said Madame de Watteville. "I never heard his name before."

"Why, you can see his windows from hence," replied the Vicar-General. "Monsieur Savaron lives in the Rue du Perron; the garden of his house joins on to yours."

"But he is not a native of the Comté," said Monsieur de Watteville.

"So little is he a native of any place, that no one knows where he comes from," said Madame de Chavoncourt.

"But who is he?" asked Madame de Watteville, taking the Abbé's arm to go into the dining room. "If he is a stranger, by what chance has he settled at Besançon? It is a strange fancy for a lawyer."

"Very strange!" echoed Amédée de Soulas, whose biography is here necessary to the understanding of this tale.

In all ages France and England have carried on an exchange of trifles, which is all the more constant because it evades the tyranny of the custom house. The fashion that is called English in Paris is called French in London, and this is reciprocal. The hostility of the two nations is suspended on two points—the uses of words and the fashion of dress. *God save the King*, the national air of England, is a tune written by Lulli for the chorus of *Esther* or of *Athalie*.* Hoops, introduced at Paris by an Englishwoman, were invented in London, it is known why, by a Frenchwoman, the notorious Duchess of Portsmouth.* They were at first so jeered at that the first Englishwoman who appeared in them at the Tuileries narrowly escaped being crushed by the crowd, but they were adopted. This fashion tyrannised over the ladies of Europe for half a century. At the peace of 1815, for a year, the long waists of the English were a standing jest; all Paris went to see Pothier and Brunet in *Les Anglaises pour rire*,* but in 1816 and 1817 the belt of the Frenchwoman, which in 1814 cut her across the bosom, gradually descended till it reached the hips. Within ten years England has made two little gifts to our language. The *incroyable*, the *merveilleux*, the *élégant*, the three successors of the *petits-maîtres* of discreditable etymology,* have made way for the *dandy* and the *lion*. The *lion* is not the parent of the *lionne*. The *lionne* is due to the famous song by Alfred de Musset: *Avez-vous vu dans Barcelone . . . C'est ma maîtresse et ma lionne*.* There has been a fusion—or, if you prefer it, a confusion—of the two words and the leading ideas. When an absurdity can amuse Paris, which devours as many masterpieces as absurdities, the provinces can hardly be deprived of them. So, as soon as the *lion* paraded Paris with his mane, his beard and moustaches, his waistcoats and his eyeglass, maintained in its place, without the help of his hands, by the contraction of his cheek and eye socket, the chief towns of some départements had their sub-lions, who protested by the smartness of their trousers straps against the untidiness of their fellow townsmen. Thus, in 1834, Besançon could boast of a *lion*, in the person of Monsieur Amédée-Sylvain de Soulas, spelt Souleyas at the time of the Spanish occupation. Amédée de Soulas is perhaps the only man in Besançon descended from a Spanish family. Spain sent men to manage her business in the Comté, but very few Spaniards settled there. The Soulas remained in consequence of their connection with Cardinal Granvelle.* Young Monsieur de Soulas was always talking of leaving Besançon, a dull town, churchgoing, and not literary, a military centre and garrison town, of which the manners and customs and physiognomy are worth describing. This opinion allowed of his lodging, like a man uncertain of the future, in three very scantily furnished rooms at the end of the Rue Neuve,* just where it opens into the Rue de la Préfecture.

Young Monsieur de Soulas could not possibly live without a tiger. This tiger was the son of one of his farmers, a small servant aged fourteen, thickset, and named Babylas. The *lion* dressed his tiger very smartly—a short tunic coat of iron-grey cloth, belted with patent leather, bright blue plush breeches, a red waistcoat, polished leather top boots, a shiny hat with black lacing, and brass buttons with the arms of Soulas. Amédée gave this boy white cotton gloves and his washing, and thirty-six francs a month to keep himself—a sum that seemed enormous to the grisettes of Besançon: four hundred and twenty francs a year to a child of fifteen, without counting extras! The extras consisted in the price for which he could sell his turned clothes, a present when Soulas exchanged one of his horses, and the perquisite of the manure. The two horses, treated with sordid economy, cost, one with another, eight hundred francs a year. His bills for articles received from Paris, such as perfumery, cravats, jewellery, patent blacking, and clothes, ran to another twelve hundred francs. Add to this the groom, or tiger, the horses, a very superior style of dress, and six hundred francs a year for rent, and you will see a grand total of three thousand francs. Now, Monsieur de Soulas's father had left him only four thousand francs a year, the income from some cottage farms in rather bad repair, which required keeping up, a charge which lent painful uncertainty to the rents. The *lion* had hardly three francs a day left for food, amusements, and gambling. He very often dined out, and breakfasted with remarkable frugality. When he was positively obliged to dine at his own cost, he sent his tiger to fetch a couple of dishes from a cookshop, never spending more than twenty-five sous.

Young Monsieur de Soulas was supposed to be a spendthrift, recklessly extravagant, whereas the poor man made the two ends meet in the year with a keenness and skill which would have done honour to a thrifty housewife. At Besançon in those days no one knew how great a tax on a man's capital were six francs spent in polish to spread on his boots or shoes, yellow gloves at fifty sous a pair, cleaned in the deepest secrecy to make them three times renewed, cravats costing ten francs, and lasting three months, four waistcoats at twenty-five francs, and trousers fitting close to the boots. How could he do otherwise, since we see women in Paris bestowing their special attention on simpletons who visit them, and cut out the most remarkable men by means of these frivolous advantages, which a man can buy for fifteen louis, and get his hair curled and a fine linen shirt into the bargain?

If this unhappy youth should seem to you to have become a *lion* on very cheap terms, you must know that Amédée de Soulas had been three times to Switzerland, by coach and in short stages, twice to Paris, and once from Paris to England. He passed as a well-informed traveller, and could say, "In England, where I went . . ." The dowagers of the town would say to him, "You, who have been in England . . ." He had been as far as Lombardy, and seen the shores of the Italian lakes.

He read new books. Finally, when he was cleaning his gloves, the tiger Babylas replied to callers, "Monsieur is very busy." An attempt had been made to withdraw Monsieur Amédée de Soulas from circulation by pronouncing him *a man of advanced ideas*. Amédée had the gift of uttering with the gravity of a native the commonplaces that were in fashion, which gave him the credit of being one of the most enlightened of the nobility. His person was garnished with fashionable trinkets, and his head furnished with ideas hallmarked by the press.

In 1834 Amédée was a young man of twenty-five, of medium height, dark, with a very prominent thorax, well-made shoulders, rather plump legs, feet already fat, white dimpled hands, a beard under his chin, moustaches worthy of the garrison, a good-natured, fat, rubicund face, a flat nose, and brown expressionless eyes; nothing Spanish about him. He was progressing rapidly in the direction of obesity, which would be fatal to his pretensions. His nails were well kept, his beard trimmed, the smallest details of his dress attended to with English precision. Hence Amédée de Soulas was looked upon as the finest man in Besançon. A hairdresser who waited upon him at a fixed hour (another luxury, costing sixty francs a year!) held him up as the sovereign authority in matters of fashion and elegance. Amédée slept late, dressed, and then around noon would ride out to one of his farms and practise pistol shooting. He attached as much importance to this exercise as Lord Byron did in his later days. Then, at three o'clock he came home, admired on horseback by the grisettes and the ladies who happened to be at their windows. After an affectation of study or business, which seemed to engage him till four, he dressed to dine out, spent the evening in the drawing rooms of the aristocracy of Besançon playing whist, and went home to bed at eleven. No life could be more above board, more prudent, or more irreproachable, for he punctually attended the services at church on Sundays and holy days.

To enable you to understand how exceptional is such a life, it is necessary to devote a few words to an account of Besançon. No town ever offered more deaf and dumb resistance to progress. At Besançon the officials, the employees, the military, in short, everyone engaged in governing it, sent thither from Paris to fill a post of any kind, are all spoken of by the expressive general name of *the Colony*. The Colony is neutral ground, the only ground where, as in church, the upper rank and the townsfolk of the place can meet. Here, fired by a word, a look, or gesture, are started those feuds between house and house, between a woman of rank and a citizen's wife, which endure till death, and widen the impassable gulf which parts the two classes of society. With the exception of the Clermont-Mont-Saint-Jean, the Beauffremont, the de Scey, and the Gramont families,* with a few others who come only to stay on their estates in the Comté, the aristocracy of Besançon dates no further back than a couple of centuries, the time of the conquest by Louis XIV. This little world is essentially of the parlement, and arrogant, stiff, solemn, uncompromising, haughty beyond all comparison, even with the Court of Vienna, for in this the nobility of Besançon would put the Viennese drawing rooms to shame. As to Victor Hugo, Nodier,* Fourier, the glories of the town, they are never mentioned, no one thinks about them. The marriages in these families are arranged in the cradle, so rigidly are the greatest things settled as well as the smallest. No stranger, no intruder, ever finds his way into one of these houses, and to obtain an introduction for the colonels or officers of title belonging to the first families in France when quartered there, requires efforts of diplomacy which Prince Talleyrand* would gladly have mastered to use at a congress. In 1834 Amédée was the only man in Besançon who wore trouser straps; this will account for the young man's being regarded as a *lion*. And a little anecdote will enable you to understand the city of Besançon.

Some time before the opening of this story, the need arose at the prefecture for bringing an editor from Paris for the official newspaper, to enable it to hold its own against the little *Gazette*, dropped at Besançon by the great *Gazette*, and the *Patriot*, which frisked in the hands of the Republicans.* Paris sent them a young man, knowing nothing about La Franche-Comté, who began by writing them a leading article of the school of the *Charivari*.* The chief of the moderate party, a member of the Hôtel-de-Ville, sent for the journalist and said to him, "You must understand, Monsieur, that we are serious, more than serious—tiresome; we resent being amused, and are furious at having been made to laugh. Be as hard of digestion as the toughest disquisitions in the *Revue des Deux Mondes*,* and you will hardly reach the level of Besançon." The editor took the hint, and thenceforth spoke the most incomprehensible philosophical lingo. His success was complete.

If young Monsieur de Soulas did not fall in the esteem of Besançon society, it was out of pure vanity on its part; the aristocracy were happy to affect a modern air, and to be able to show any Parisians of rank who visited the Comté a young man who bore some likeness to them. All this hidden labour, all this dust thrown in people's eyes, this display of folly and latent prudence, had an object, or the *lion* of Besançon would have been no son of the soil. Amédée wanted to achieve a good marriage by proving some day that his farms were not mortgaged, and that he had some savings. He wanted to be the talk of the town, to be the finest and best-dressed man there, in order to win first the attention, and then the hand, of Mademoiselle Rosalie de Watteville.

In 1830, at the time when young Monsieur de Soulas was setting up in business as a dandy, Rosalie was but fourteen. Hence, in 1834, Mademoiselle de Watteville had reached the age when young persons are easily struck by the peculiarities which attracted the attention

of the town to Amédée. There are many *lions* who become *lions* out of self-interest and speculation. The
Wattevilles, who for twelve years had been drawing an
income of fifty thousand francs, did not spend more than
twenty-four thousand francs a year, while receiving all
the upper circle of Besançon every Monday and Friday.
On Mondays they gave a dinner, on Fridays an evening
party. Thus, in twelve years, what a sum must have
accumulated from twenty-six thousand francs a year,
saved and invested with the judgment that distinguishes
those old families! It was very generally supposed that
Madame de Watteville, thinking she had land enough,
had placed her savings in the three percents, in 1830.
Rosalie's dowry would therefore, as the best informed
opined, amount to about twenty thousand francs a year.
So for the last five years Amédée had worked like a mole
to get into the highest favour of the severe Baronne,
while laying himself out to flatter Mademoiselle de
Watteville's conceit. Madame de Watteville was in the
secret of the devices by which Amédée succeeded in
keeping up his rank in Besançon, and esteemed him
highly for it. Soulas had placed himself under her wing
when she was thirty, and at that time had dared to admire her and make her his idol; he had got so far as to
be allowed—he alone in the world—to pour out to her
all the unseemly gossip which almost all very precise
women love to hear, being authorised by their superior
virtue to look into the gulf without falling, and into the
devil's snares without being caught. Do you understand
why the *lion* did not allow himself the very smallest intrigue? He lived a public life, in the street so to speak,
on purpose to play the part of a lover sacrificed to duty
by the Baronne, and to feast her mind with the sins she
had forbidden to her senses. A man who is so privileged as to be allowed to pour light stories into the ear
of a pious woman is in her eyes a charming man. If this
exemplary youth had better known the human heart,

he might without risk have allowed himself some flirtations among the grisettes of Besançon who looked up to him as a king; his affairs might perhaps have been all the more hopeful with the strict and prudish Baronne. To Rosalie our Cato affected prodigality; he professed a life of elegance, showing her in perspective the splendid part played by a woman of fashion in Paris, whither he meant to go as deputy. All these manoeuvres were crowned with complete success. In 1834 the mothers of the forty noble families composing the high society of Besançon quoted Monsieur Amédée de Soulas as the most charming young man in the town; no one would have dared to dispute his place as cock of the walk at the Hôtel de Rupt, and all Besançon regarded him as Rosalie de Watteville's future husband. There had even been some exchange of ideas on the subject between the Baronne and Amédée, to which the Baron's apparent nonentity gave some certainty.

Mademoiselle de Watteville, to whom her enormous prospective fortune at that time lent considerable importance, had been brought up exclusively within the precincts of the Hôtel de Rupt—which her mother rarely quitted, so devoted was she to her dear Archbishop—and severely repressed by an exclusively religious education, and by her mother's despotism, which held her rigidly to principles. Rosalie knew absolutely nothing. Is it knowledge to have learned geography from Guthrie, sacred history, ancient history, the history of France, and the four rules,* all passed through the sieve of an old Jesuit? Dancing and music were forbidden, as being more likely to corrupt life than to grace it. The Baronne taught her daughter every conceivable stitch in tapestry and women's work—plain sewing, embroidery, netting. At seventeen Rosalie had never read anything but the *Lettres édifiantes,** and some works on heraldry. No newspaper had ever defiled her sight. She attended Mass at the cathedral every morning, taken there by her mother, came back to breakfast, did needlework after a little walk in the garden, and received visitors, sitting with the Baronne until dinnertime. Then, after dinner, excepting on Mondays and Fridays, she accompanied Madame de Watteville to other houses to spend the evening, without being allowed to talk more than the maternal rule permitted.

At eighteen Mademoiselle de Watteville was a slight, thin girl with a flat figure, fair, colourless, and insignificant to the last degree. Her eyes, of a very light blue, borrowed beauty from their lashes, which, when downcast, threw a shadow on her cheeks. A few freckles marred the whiteness of her forehead, which was shapely enough. Her face was exactly like those of Albrecht Dürer's saints, or those of the painters before Perugino; the same plump, though slender modelling, the same delicacy saddened by ecstasy, the same severe guilelessness. Everything about her, even to her attitude, was suggestive of those virgins, whose beauty is only revealed in its mystical radiance to the eyes of the studious connoisseur. She had fine hands, though red, and a pretty foot, the foot of an aristocrat. She habitually wore simple checked cotton dresses, but on Sundays and in the evening her mother allowed her silk. The cut of her frocks, made at Besançon, almost made her ugly, while her mother tried to borrow grace, beauty, and elegance from Paris fashions, for through Monsieur de Soulas she procured the smallest trifles of her dress from thence. Rosalie had never worn a pair of silk stockings or thin boots, but always cotton stockings and leather shoes. On high days she was dressed in a muslin frock, her hair plainly dressed, and had bronze kid shoes.

This education, and her own modest demeanour, hid in Rosalie a spirit of iron. Physiologists and profound observers will tell you, perhaps to your great astonishment, that tempers, characteristics, wit, or genius reappear in families at long intervals, precisely like what

209

are known as hereditary diseases. Thus talent, like gout, sometimes skips over two generations. We have an illustrious example of this phenomenon in George Sand, in whom are resuscitated the force, the power, and the imaginative faculty of the Marshal de Saxe, whose natural granddaughter she is. The decisive character and romantic daring of the famous Watteville had reappeared in the soul of his grandniece, reinforced by the tenacity and pride of blood of the Rupts. But these qualities—or faults, if you will have it so—were as deeply buried in this young girlish soul, apparently so weak and yielding, as the seething lavas within a hill before it becomes a volcano. Madame de Watteville alone, perhaps, suspected this inheritance from two strains. She was so severe to her Rosalie, that she replied one day to the Archbishop, who blamed her for being too hard on the child, "Leave me to manage her, Monseigneur. I know her! She has more than one Beelzebub in her skin!"

The Baronne kept all the keener watch over her daughter, because she considered her honour as a mother to be at stake. After all, she had nothing else to do. Clotilde de Rupt, at this time thirty-five and as good as widowed, with a husband who turned eggcups in every variety of wood and who set his mind on making wheels with six spokes out of ironwood and manufactured snuff boxes for every one of his acquaintances, flirted in strict propriety with Amédée de Soulas. When this young man was in the house, she alternately dismissed and recalled her daughter, and tried to detect symptoms of jealousy in that youthful soul, so as to have occasion to repress them. She imitated the police in its dealings with the Republicans, but she laboured in vain. Rosalie showed no symptoms of rebellion. The cold woman of piety then accused her daughter of perfect insensibility. Rosalie knew her mother well enough to be sure that if she had thought young Monsieur de Soulas *nice,* she would have drawn down on herself a smart reproof. Thus, to all her mother's incitement she replied merely by such phrases as are wrongly called Jesuitical—wrongly, because the Jesuits were strong, and such reservations are the *chevaux-de-frise* behind which weakness takes refuge. Then the mother regarded the girl as a dissembler. If by mischance a spark of the true nature of the Wattevilles and the Rupts blazed out, the mother armed herself with the respect due from children to their parents to reduce Rosalie to passive obedience. This covert battle was carried on in the most secret seclusion of domestic life, with closed doors. The Vicar-General, the dear Abbé de Grancey, the friend of the late Archbishop, clever as he was in his capacity as the chief Father Confessor of the diocese, could not discover whether the struggle had stirred up some hatred between the mother and daughter, whether the mother were jealous in anticipation, or whether the court Amédée was paying to the girl through her mother had not overstepped its due limits. Being a friend of the family, neither mother nor daughter confessed to him.

Rosalie, a little too much harried, morally, about young de Soulas, could not abide him, to use a homely phrase, and when he spoke to her, trying to take her heart by surprise, she received him but coldly. This aversion, discerned only by her mother's eye, was a constant subject of admonition.

"Rosalie, I cannot imagine why you affect such coldness towards Amédée. Is it because he is a friend of the family, and because we like him—your father and I?"

"Well, Mama," replied the poor child one day, "if I made him welcome, should I not be still more in the wrong?"

"What do you mean by that?" cried Madame de Watteville. "What is the meaning of such words? Your mother is unjust, no doubt, and, according to you, would be so in any case! Never let such an answer pass your lips again to your mother——" and so forth.

This quarrel lasted three hours and three-quarters. Rosalie noted the time. Her mother, pale with fury, sent her to her room, where Rosalie pondered on the meaning of this scene without discovering it, so guileless was she. Thus young Monsieur de Soulas, who was supposed by everyone to be very near the end he was aiming at, all neckcloths set, and by dint of pots of patent blacking—an end which required so much waxing of his moustaches, so many smart waistcoats, wore out so many horseshoes and stays—for he wore a leather vest, the stays of the *lion*—Amédée, I say, was further away than any chance comer, although he had on his side the worthy and noble Abbé de Grancey.

"Madame," said Monsieur de Soulas, addressing the Baronne, while waiting till his soup was cool enough to swallow and affecting to give a romantic turn to his narrative, "one fine morning the mail coach dropped at the Hôtel National a gentleman from Paris, who, after seeking apartments, made up his mind in favour of the first floor in Mademoiselle Galard's house, Rue du Perron. Then the *stranger* went straight to the town hall, and had himself registered as a resident with all political qualifications. Finally, he had his name entered on the list of advocates to the court, showing his title in due form, and he left his card with all his new colleagues, the ministerial officials, the court counselors, and the members of the bench, with the name: ALBERT SAVARON."

"The name of Savaron is famous," said Mademoiselle de Watteville, who was strong in heraldic information. "The Savarons of Savarus are one of the oldest, noblest, and richest families in Belgium."

"He is a Frenchman, and no man's son," replied Amédée de Soulas. "If he wishes to bear the arms of the Savarons of Savarus, he must add a bar sinister. There is no one left of the Brabant family but a Mademoiselle de Savarus, a rich heiress, and unmarried."

"The bar sinister is, of course, the badge of a bastard,

but the bastard of a Comte de Savarus is noble," answered Rosalie.

"Enough, that will do, Rosalie!" said the Baronne.

"You insisted on her learning heraldry," said Monsieur de Watteville, "and she knows it very well."

"Go on, I beg, Monsieur de Soulas."

"You may suppose that in a town where everything is classified, known, pigeonholed, ticketed, and numbered, as in Besançon, Albert Savaron was received without hesitation by the lawyers of the town. They were satisfied to say, 'Here is a man who does not know his Besançon. Who the devil can have sent him here? What can he hope to do? Sending his card to the judges instead of calling in person! What a blunder!' And so, three days after, Savaron had ceased to exist. He took as his servant old Monsieur Galard's man—Galard being dead—Jérôme, who can cook a little. Albert Savaron was all the more completely forgotten, because no one had seen him or met him anywhere."

"Then, does he not go to Mass?" asked Madame de Chavoncourt.

"He goes on Sundays to Saint-Pierre,* but to the early service at eight in the morning. He rises every night between one and two in the morning, works till eight, has his breakfast, and then goes on working. He walks in his garden, going round fifty, or perhaps sixty times; then he goes in, dines, and goes to bed between six and seven."

"How did you learn all that?" Madame de Chavoncourt asked Monsieur de Soulas.

"In the first place, Madame, I live in the Rue Neuve, at the corner of the Rue du Perron; I look out on the house where this mysterious personage lodges; then, of course, there are communications between my tiger and Jérôme."

"And you gossip with Babylas?"

"What would you have me do out riding?"

"Well—and how was it that you engaged a stranger for your defence?" asked the Baronne, thus placing the conversation in the hands of the Vicar-General.

"The Premier President of the Court played this pleader a trick by appointing him to defend at the assizes a half-witted peasant accused of forgery. But Monsieur Savaron procured the poor man's acquittal by proving his innocence and showing that he had been a tool in the hands of the real culprits. Not only did his line of defence succeed, but it led to the arrest of two of the witnesses, who were proved guilty and condemned. His speech struck the court and the jury. One of these, a merchant, placed a difficult case next day in the hands of Monsieur Savaron, and he won it. In the position in which we found ourselves, Monsieur Berryer* finding it impossible to come to Besançon, Monsieur de Garcenault advised him to employ this Monsieur Albert Savaron, foretelling our success. As soon as I saw him and heard him, I felt faith in him, and I was not wrong."

"Is he then so extraordinary?" asked Madame de Chavoncourt.

"Certainly, Madame," replied the Vicar-General.

"Well, tell us about it," said Madame de Watteville.

"The first time I saw him," said the Abbé de Grancey, "he received me in his outer room next to the ante-room—old Galard's drawing room—which he has had painted like old oak, and which I found to be entirely lined with law books, arranged on shelves also painted as old oak. The painting and the books are the sole decoration of the room, for the furniture consists of an old writing table of carved wood, six old armchairs covered with tapestry, window curtains of grey stuff bordered with green, and a green carpet over the floor. The ante-room stove heats this library as well. As I waited there I did not picture my advocate as a young man. But this singular setting is in perfect harmony with his person, for Monsieur Savaron came out in a black merino dressing gown tied with a red cord, red slippers, a red flannel waistcoat, and a red smoking cap."

"The devil's colours!" exclaimed Madame de Watteville.

"Yes," said the Abbé, "but a magnificent head. Black hair already streaked with a little grey, hair like that of Saint Peter and Saint Paul in pictures, with thick shining curls, hair as stiff as horsehair; a round white throat like a woman's; a splendid forehead, furrowed by the strong median line which great schemes, great thoughts, deep meditations stamp on a great man's brow; an olive complexion marbled with red, a square nose, eyes of flame,

Albert Savarus.

Plate XII

215

hollow cheeks, with two long lines betraying much suffering, a mouth with a sardonic smile, and a small chin, narrow, and too short; crows' feet on his temples; deep-set eyes, moving in their sockets like burning balls; but, in spite of all these indications of a violently passionate nature, his manner was calm, deeply resigned, and his voice of penetrating sweetness, which surprised me in court by its easy flow; a true orator's voice, now clear and appealing, sometimes insinuating, but a voice of thunder when needful, and lending itself to sarcasm to become incisive. Monsieur Albert Savaron is of middle height, neither stout nor thin. And his hands are those of a prelate. The second time I called on him he received me in his bedroom, adjoining the library, and smiled at my astonishment when I saw there a wretched chest of drawers, a shabby carpet, a camp bed, and cotton window curtains. He came out of his private room, to which no one is admitted, as Jérôme informed me; the man did not go in, but merely knocked at the door. The third time he was breakfasting in his library on the most frugal fare, but on this occasion, as he had spent the night studying our documents, as I had my attorney with me, and as that worthy Monsieur Girardet is long-winded, I had leisure to study the stranger. He certainly is no ordinary man. There is more than one secret behind that face, at once so terrible and so gentle, patient and yet impatient, broad and yet hollow. I saw, too, that he stooped a little, like all men who have some heavy burden to bear."

"Why did so eloquent a man leave Paris? For what purpose did he come to Besançon?" asked pretty Madame de Chavoncourt. "Could no one tell him how little chance a stranger has of succeeding here? The good folks of Besançon will make use of him, but they will not allow him to make use of them. Why, having come, did he make so little effort that it needed a freak of the presidents to bring him forward?"

"After carefully studying that fine head," said the Abbé, looking keenly at the lady who had interrupted him, in such a way as to suggest that there was something he would not tell, "and especially after hearing him this morning reply to one of the bigwigs of the Paris bar, I believe that this man, who may be thirty-five, will by and by make a great sensation."

"Why should we discuss him? You have gained your action, and paid him," said Madame de Watteville, watching her daughter, who, all the time the Vicar-General had been speaking, seemed to hang on his lips.

The conversation changed, and no more was heard of Albert Savaron.

The portrait sketched by the cleverest of the vicars-general of the diocese had all the greater charm for Rosalie because there was a romance behind it. For the first time in her life she had come across the marvellous, the exceptional, which smiles on every youthful imagination, and which curiosity, so eager at Rosalie's age, goes forth to meet halfway. What an ideal being was this Albert—gloomy, unhappy, eloquent, laborious, as compared by Mademoiselle de Watteville to that chubby fat Comte, bursting with health, paying compliments, and talking of the fashions in the very face of the splendour of the old Comtes of Rupt. Amédée had cost her many quarrels and scoldings, and, indeed, she knew him only too well; while this Albert Savaron offered many enigmas to be solved.

"Albert Savaron de Savarus," she repeated to herself.

Now, to see him, to catch sight of him! This was the desire of the girl to whom desire was hitherto unknown. She pondered in her heart, in her fancy, in her brain, the least phrases used by the Abbé de Grancey, for all his words had told.

"A fine forehead!" she said to herself, looking at the head of every man seated at the table; "I do not see a single fine one here . . . Monsieur de Soulas's is too prominent, Monsieur de Grancey's is fine, but he is seventy and has no hair—it is impossible to see where his forehead ends."

"What is the matter, Rosalie? You are eating nothing."

"I am not hungry, Mama," said she. "A prelate's hands——" she went on to herself. "I cannot remember our handsome Archbishop's hands, though he confirmed me."

Finally, in the midst of her coming and going in the labyrinth of her meditations, she remembered a lighted window she had seen from her bed, gleaming through the trees of the two adjoining gardens, when she had happened to wake in the night . . . "Then that was his light!" thought she. "I might see him! I will see him."

"Monsieur de Grancey, is the chapter's lawsuit quite settled?" said Rosalie point-blank to the Vicar-General, during a moment of silence.

Madame de Watteville exchanged rapid glances with the Vicar-General.

"What can that matter to you, my dear child?" she said to Rosalie, with an affected sweetness which made her daughter cautious for the rest of her days.

"It might be appealed, but our adversaries will think twice about that," replied the Abbé.

"I never could have believed that Rosalie would think about a lawsuit all through a dinner," remarked Madame de Watteville.

"Nor I either," said Rosalie, in a dreamy way that made everyone laugh. "But Monsieur de Grancey spoke so well that I became interested."

The company rose from table and returned to the drawing room. All through the evening Rosalie listened in case Albert Savaron should be mentioned again, but beyond the congratulations offered by each newcomer to the Abbé on having gained his suit, to which no one added any praise of the advocate, no more was said about it. Mademoiselle de Watteville impatiently looked forward to bedtime. She had promised herself to wake at between two and three in the morning, and to look at Albert's dressing room windows. When the hour came, she felt almost pleasure in gazing at the glimmer from the lawyer's candles that shone through the trees, now almost bare of their leaves. By the help of the strong sight of a young girl, which curiosity seems to make longer, she saw Albert writing, and fancied she could distinguish the colour of the furniture, which she thought was red. From the chimney above the roof rose a thick column of smoke.

"While all the world is sleeping, he is awake—like God!" thought she.

The education of girls brings with it such serious problems—for the future of a nation is in the mother—that the University of France long since set itself the task of having nothing to do with it. Here is one of these problems.

Ought girls to be informed on all points? Ought their minds to be under restraint? It need not be said that the religious system is one of restraint. If you enlighten them, you make them demons before their time; if you keep them from thinking, you end in the sudden explosion so well shown by Molière in the character of Agnès,* and you leave this suppressed mind, so fresh and clear-seeing, as swift and as logical as that of a savage, at the mercy of an accident. This inevitable crisis was brought on in Mademoiselle de Watteville by the portrait which one of the most prudent abbots of the Chapter of Besançon imprudently allowed himself to sketch at a dinner party.

Next morning, Mademoiselle de Watteville, while dressing, necessarily looked out at Albert Savaron walking in the garden adjoining that of the Hôtel de Rupt.

"What would have become of me," thought she, "if he had lived anywhere else? Here I can, at any rate, see him. What is he thinking about?"

Having seen this extraordinary man, though at a distance, the only man whose countenance stood forth in contrast with crowds of Besançon faces she had hitherto met with, Rosalie at once jumped at the idea of getting into his home, of ascertaining the reasons of so much mystery, of hearing that eloquent voice, of winning a glance from those fine eyes. All this she set her heart on, but how could she achieve it?

All that day she drew her needle through her embroidery with the obtuse concentration of a girl who, like Agnès, seems to be thinking of nothing, but who is reflecting on things in general so deeply, that her artifice is unfailing. As a result of this profound meditation, Rosalie thought she would go to confession. Next morning, after Mass, she had a brief interview with the Abbé Giroud at Saint-Pierre, and managed so ingeniously that the hour for her confession was fixed for Sunday morning at half-past seven, before the eight o'clock Mass. She committed herself to a dozen fibs in order to find herself, just for once, in the church at the hour when the lawyer came to Mass. Then she was seized with an impulse of extreme affection for her father; she went to see him in his workroom, and asked him for all sorts of information on the art of turning, ending by advising him to turn larger pieces, columns. After persuading her father to set to work on some twisted pillars, one of the difficulties of the turner's art, she suggested that he should make use of a large heap of stones that lay in the middle of the garden to construct a sort of grotto on which he might erect a little temple or belvedere in which his twisted pillars could be used and shown off to all the world.

At the climax of the pleasure the poor unoccupied man derived from this scheme, Rosalie said, as she kissed him, "Above all, do not tell Mama who gave you the notion; she would scold me."

"Do not be afraid!" replied Monsieur de Watteville,

who groaned as bitterly as his daughter under the tyranny of the terrible descendant of the Rupts.

So Rosalie had a certain prospect of seeing ere long a charming observatory built, whence her eye would command the lawyer's private room. And there are men for whose sake young girls can carry out such masterstrokes of diplomacy, while, for the most part, like Albert Savaron, they know it not.

The Sunday so impatiently looked for arrived, and Rosalie dressed with such carefulness as made Mariette, the lady's maid, smile.

"It is the first time I ever knew Mademoiselle to be so fidgety," said Mariette.

"It strikes me," said Rosalie, with a glance at Mariette, which brought poppies to her cheeks, "that you too are more particular on some days than on others."

As she went down the steps, across the courtyard, and through the gates, Rosalie's heart beat, as everybody's does in anticipation of a great event. Hitherto, she had never known what it was to walk in the streets; for a moment she had felt as though her mother must read her schemes on her brow and forbid her going to confession, and she now felt new blood in her feet; she lifted them as though she trod on fire. She had, of course, arranged to be with her confessor at a quarter-past eight, telling her mother eight, so as to have about a quarter of an hour near Albert. She got to church before Mass, and after a short prayer, went to see if the Abbé Giroud were in his confessional, simply to pass the time, and she thus placed herself in such a way as to see Albert as he came into church. The man must have been atrociously ugly who did not seem handsome to Mademoiselle de Watteville in the frame of mind produced by her curiosity. And Albert Savaron, who was really very striking, made all the more impression on Rosalie because his mien, his walk, his carriage, everything down to his clothing, had the indescribable stamp which can only be expressed by the word *mystery*. He came in. The church, till now gloomy, seemed to Rosalie to be illuminated. The girl was fascinated by his slow and solemn demeanour, as of a man who bears a world on his shoulders, and whose deep gaze, whose very gestures, combine to express a devastating or absorbing thought. Rosalie now understood the Vicar-General's words in their fullest extent. Yes, those eyes of tawny brown, shot with golden lights, covered an ardour which revealed itself in sudden flashes. Rosalie, with a recklessness which Mariette noted, stood in the lawyer's way, so as to exchange glances with him, and this glance turned her blood, for it seethed and boiled as though its warmth were doubled. As soon as Albert had taken a seat, Mademoiselle de Watteville quickly found a place whence she could see him perfectly during all the time the Abbé might leave her. When Mariette said, "Here is Monsieur Giroud," it seemed to Rosalie that the interval had lasted no more than a few minutes. By the time she came out from the confessional, Mass was over. Albert had left the church.

"The Vicar-General was right," thought she. "*He* is unhappy. Why should this eagle—for he has the eyes of an eagle—swoop down on Besançon? Oh, I must know everything! But how?"

Under the smart of this new desire, Rosalie set the stitches of her worsted work with exquisite precision, and hid her meditations under a little innocent air, which shammed simplicity to deceive Madame de Watteville. From that Sunday, when Mademoiselle de Watteville had met that look, or, if you please, received this baptism of fire—a fine expression of Napoléon's which may be well applied to love—she eagerly promoted the plan for the belvedere.

"Mama," said she one day when two columns were turned, "my father has taken a singular idea into his head; he is turning columns for a belvedere he intends to erect on the heap of stones in the middle of the garden. Do you approve of it? It seems to me——"

"I approve of everything your father does," said Madame de Watteville drily, "and it is a wife's duty to submit to her husband even if she does not approve of his ideas. Why should I object to a thing which is of no importance in itself, if only it amuses Monsieur de Watteville?"

"Well, because from thence we shall see into Monsieur de Soulas's rooms, and Monsieur de Soulas will see us when we are there. Perhaps remarks may be made——"

"Do you presume, Rosalie, to guide your parents, and think you know more than they do of life and the proprieties?"

"I say no more, Mama. Besides, my father said that there would be a room in the grotto where it would be cool, and where we can take coffee."

"Your father has had an excellent idea," said Madame de Watteville, who forthwith went to look at the columns.

She gave her entire approbation to the Baron de Watteville's design, while choosing for the erection of this monument a spot at the bottom of the garden, which could not be seen from Monsieur de Soulas's windows, but whence they could perfectly see into Albert Savaron's rooms. A builder was sent for, who undertook to construct a grotto, of which the top should be reached by a path three feet wide through the rock work, where periwinkles would grow along with iris, clematis, ivy, honeysuckle, and Virginia creeper. The Baronne desired that the inside should be lined with rustic woodwork, such as was then the fashion for flower stands, with a looking glass against the wall, an ottoman forming a box, and a table of inlaid bark. Monsieur de Soulas proposed that the floor should be of asphalt. Rosalie suggested a hanging chandelier of rustic wood.

"The Wattevilles are having something charming done in their garden," was rumoured in Besançon.

"They are rich, and can afford a thousand écus for a whim——"

"A thousand écus!" exclaimed Madame de Chavoncourt.

"Yes, a thousand écus," cried young Monsieur de Soulas. "A man has been sent for from Paris to rusticate the interior, but it will be very pretty. Monsieur de Watteville himself is making the chandelier, and has begun to carve the wood."

"Berquet is to make a cellar under it," said an abbot.

"No," replied young Monsieur de Soulas, "he is raising the kiosk on a concrete foundation, that it may not be damp."

"You know the very least things that are done in that house," said Madame de Chavoncourt sourly, as she looked at one of her eldest girls waiting to be married for a year past.

Mademoiselle de Watteville, with a little flush of pride in thinking of the success of her belvedere, discerned in herself a vast superiority over everyone about her. No one guessed that a little girl, supposed to be a witless goose, had simply made up her mind to get a closer view of the lawyer Savaron's private study.

Albert Savaron's brilliant defence of the Cathedral Chapter was all the sooner forgotten because the envy of the other lawyers was aroused. Also, Savaron, faithful to his seclusion, went nowhere. Having no friends to praise him, and seeing no one, he increased the chances of being forgotten which are common to strangers in such a town as Besançon. Nevertheless, he pleaded three times at the commercial court in three knotty cases which had to be carried to the superior court. He thus gained as clients four of the chief merchants of the place, who discerned in him so much good sense and sound legal purview that they placed their claims in his hands. On the day when the Watteville family

inaugurated the belvedere, Savaron also was founding a monument. Thanks to the connections he had
obscurely formed among the upper class of merchants
in Besançon, he was starting a fortnightly paper called
the *Revue de l'Est** with the help of forty shares of five
hundred francs each, taken up by his first ten clients, on
whom he had impressed the necessity for promoting the
interests of Besançon, the town where the traffic should
meet between Mulhouse and Lyons, and the chief centre between Mulhouse and the Rhone.

To compete with Strasbourg, was it not needful that
Besançon should become a focus of enlightenment as
well as of trade? The leading questions relating to the
interests of eastern France could only be dealt with in
a revue. What a glorious task to rob Strasbourg and
Dijon of their literary importance, to bring light to the
East of France, and compete with the centralising influence of Paris! These reflections, put forward by Albert,
were repeated by the ten merchants who believed them
to be their own.

Monsieur Savaron did not commit the blunder of
putting his name in front; he left the finances of the concern to his chief client, Monsieur Boucher, connected by
marriage with one of the great publishers of important
ecclesiastical works, but he kept the editorship with a
share of the profits as founder. The commercial interest
appealed to Dôle, to Dijon, to Salins, to Neufchâtel, to
the Jura, Bourg, Nantua,* Lous-le-Saulnier. The concur-
rence was invited of the learning and energy of every
scientific student in the districts of Le Bugey, La Bresse,*
and Franche-Comté. By the influence of commercial interests and common feeling, five hundred subscribers
were booked in consideration of the low price: the *Revue*
cost eight francs a quarter. To avoid hurting the conceit
of the provincials by refusing their articles, the lawyer
hit on the good idea of suggesting a desire for the literary management of this *Revue* to Monsieur Boucher's

eldest son, a young man of twenty-two, very eager for fame, to whom the snares and woes of literary responsibilities were utterly unknown. Albert quietly kept the upper hand, and made Alfred Boucher his devoted adherent. Alfred was the only man in Besançon with whom the King of the Bar was on familiar terms. Alfred came in the morning to discuss the articles for the next number with Albert in the garden. It is needless to say that the trial number contained a *Meditation* by Alfred, which Savaron approved. In his conversations with Alfred, Albert would let drop some great ideas, subjects for articles of which Alfred availed himself. And thus the merchant's son fancied he was making capital out of the great man. To Alfred, Albert was a man of genius, of profound politics. The commercial world, enchanted at the success of the *Revue*, had to pay up only three-tenths of their shares. Two hundred more subscribers, and the periodical would pay a dividend to the shareholders of five percent, the editor remaining unpaid. This editing, indeed, was beyond price.

After the third number, the *Revue* was recognised for exchange by all the papers published in France, which Albert henceforth read at home. This third number included a tale signed "A.S.," and was attributed to the famous lawyer. In spite of the small attention paid by the higher circles of Besançon to the *Revue*, which was accused of liberalism, this, the first novel produced in the Comté, came under discussion that midwinter at Madame de Chavoncourt's.

"Papa," said Rosalie, "a review is published in Besançon; you ought to take it in and keep it in your room, for Mama would not let me read it, but you will lend it to me."

Monsieur de Watteville, eager to obey his dear Rosalie, who for the last five months had given him so many proofs of filial affection—Monsieur de Watteville went in person to subscribe for a year to the *Revue de l'Est*, and lent the four numbers already out to his daughter. In the course of the night Rosalie devoured the tale—the first she had ever read in her life—but she had only known life for two months past. Hence the effect produced on her by this work must not be judged by ordinary rules. Without prejudice of any kind as to the greater or less merit of this composition from the pen of a Parisian who had thus imported into the province the manner, the brilliancy, if you will, of the new literary school, it could not fail to be a masterpiece to a young girl abandoning all her intelligence and her innocent heart to her first reading of this kind. Also, from what she had heard said, Rosalie had by intuition conceived a notion of it which strangely enhanced the interest of this novel. She hoped to find in it the sentiments, and perhaps something of the life of Albert. From the first pages this opinion took so strong a hold on her, that after reading the fragment to the end she was certain that it was no mistake. Here, then, is this confession, in which, according to the critics of Madame de Chavoncourt's drawing room, Albert had imitated some modern writers who, for lack of inventiveness, relate their private joys, their private griefs, or the mysterious events of their own life.

AMBITION FOR LOVE'S SAKE

In 1823 two young men, having agreed as a plan for a holiday to make a tour through Switzerland, set out from Lucerne one fine morning in the month of July in a boat pulled by three oarsmen. They started for Fluelen, intending to stop at every notable spot on the Lake of the Four Cantons.* The views which shut in the waters on the way from Lucerne to Fluelen offer every combination that the most exacting fancy can demand of mountains and rivers, lakes and rocks, brooks and pastures, trees and torrents. Here are austere solitudes and charming headlands, smiling and trimly kept meadows, forests crowning perpendicular granite cliffs like plumes, deserted but verdant reaches opening out, and valleys whose beauty seems the lovelier in the dreamy distance.

As they passed the pretty hamlet of Gersau,* one of the friends looked for a long time at a wooden house which seemed to have been recently built, enclosed by a paling and standing on a promontory, almost bathed by the waters. As the boat rowed past, a woman's head was raised against the background of the room on the upper story of this house to admire the effect of the boat on the lake. One of the young men met the glance thus indifferently given by the unknown lady.

"Let us stop here," said he to his friend. "We meant to make Lucerne our headquarters for seeing Switzerland; you will not take it amiss, Léopold, if I change my mind and stay here to take charge of our possessions. Then you can go where you please; my journey is ended. Pull to land, men, and put us out at this village; we will breakfast here. I will go back to Lucerne to fetch all our luggage, and before you leave you will know in which house I take a lodging, where you will find me on your return."

"Here or at Lucerne," replied Léopold, "the difference is not so great that I need hinder you from following your whim."

These two youths were friends in the truest sense of the word. They were of the same age; they had learned at the same school, and after studying the law they were spending their holiday in a classical tour of Switzerland. Léopold, by his father's determination, was already pledged to a place in a notary's office in Paris. His spirit of rectitude, his gentleness, and the coolness of his senses and his brain guaranteed him to be a docile pupil. Léopold could see himself a notary in Paris: his life lay before him like one of the high roads that cross the plains of France, and he looked along its whole length with philosophical resignation.

The character of his companion, whom we will call Rodolphe, presented a strong contrast with Léopold's, and their antagonism had no doubt had the result of tightening the bond that united them. Rodolphe was the natural son of a man of rank, who was carried off by a premature death before he could make any arrangements for securing the means of existence to a woman he fondly loved and to Rodolphe. Thus cheated by a stroke of fate, Rodolphe's mother had recourse to a heroic measure. She sold everything she owed to the munificence of her child's father for a sum of more than a hundred thousand francs, bought with it a life annuity for herself at a high rate, and thus acquired an income of about fifteen thousand francs, resolving to devote the whole of it to the education of her son, so as to give him all the personal advantages that might help to make his fortune, while saving, by strict economy, a small capital to be his when he came of age. It was bold; it was counting on her own life; but without this boldness the good mother would certainly have found it impossible to live and to bring her child up suitably, and he was her only hope, her future, the spring of all her joys. Rodolphe, the son of a most charming Parisian woman and a man of mark, a nobleman of Brabant, was cursed with extreme sensitiveness. From his infancy he had in everything shown a most ardent nature. In him mere Desire became a guiding force and the motive power of his whole being, the stimulus to his imagination, the reason of his actions. Notwithstanding the pains taken by a clever mother, who was alarmed when she detected this predisposition, Rodolphe wished for things as a poet imagines, as a mathematician calculates, as a painter sketches, as a musician creates melodies. Tender-hearted, like his mother, he dashed with inconceivable violence and impetus of thought after the object of his desires; he annihilated time. While dreaming of the fulfilment of his schemes, he always overlooked the means of attainment.

"When my son has children," said his mother, "he will want them born grown up."

This fine ardour, carefully directed, enabled Rodolphe to achieve his studies with brilliant results, and to become what the English call an accomplished gentleman. His mother was then proud of him, though still fearing a catastrophe if ever a passion should possess a heart at once so tender and so susceptible, so vehement and so kind. Therefore, the judicious mother had encouraged the friendship which bound Léopold to Rodolphe and Rodolphe to Léopold, since she saw in the cold and faithful young notary a guardian, a comrade, who might to a certain extent take her place if by some misfortune she should be lost to her son. Rodolphe's mother, still handsome at forty-three, had inspired Léopold with an ardent passion. This circumstance made the two young men even more intimate.

So Léopold, knowing Rodolphe well, was not surprised to find him stopping at a village and giving up the projected journey to Saint-Gothard on the strength of a single glance at the upper window of a house. While breakfast was prepared for them at the Auberge du Cygne, the friends walked round the hamlet and came to the neighbourhood of the pretty new house; here, while gazing about him and talking to the inhabitants, Rodolphe discovered the residence of some decent folk who were willing to take him as a boarder, a very frequent custom in Switzerland. They offered him a bedroom looking over the lake and the mountains, and from whence he had a view of one of those immense sweeping reaches which, in this lake, are the admiration of every traveller. This house was divided by a roadway and a little creek from the new house where Rodolphe had caught sight of the unknown fair one's face.

For a hundred francs a month Rodolphe was relieved of all thought for the necessaries of life. But, in consideration of the outlay the Stopfer couple expected to make, they bargained for three months' residence and a month's payment in advance. Rub a Swiss never so little, and you find the usurer. After breakfast, Rodolphe at once made himself at home by depositing in his room such property as he had brought with him for the journey to the Saint-Gothard, and he watched Léopold as he set out, moved by the spirit of routine, to carry out the excursion for himself and his friend. When Rodolphe, sitting on a fallen rock on the shore, could no longer see Léopold's boat, he turned to examine the new house with stolen glances, hoping to see the fair unknown. Alas! He went in without its having given a sign of life. During dinner, in the company of Monsieur and Madame Stopfer, retired coopers from Neufchâtel, he questioned them as to the neighbourhood, and ended by learning all he wanted to know about the lady, thanks to his hosts' loquacity, for they were ready to pour out their budget of gossip without any pressing.

The fair stranger's name was Fanny Lovelace. This name (pronounced *Loveless*) is that of an old English family, but Richardson has given it to a creation whose fame eclipses all others!* Miss Lovelace had come to settle by the lake for her father's health, the physicians having recommended him the air of Lucerne. These two English people had arrived with no other servant than a little girl of fourteen, a dumb child, much attached to Miss Fanny, on whom she waited very intelligently, and had settled, two winters since, with Monsieur and Madame Bergmann, the retired head gardeners of His Excellency Count Borromeo of Isola Bella and Isola Madre in the Lago Maggiore.* These Swiss, who were possessed of an income of about a thousand écus a year, had let the top story of their house to the Lovelaces for three years at a rent of two hundred francs a year. Old Lovelace, a man of ninety, and much broken, was too poor to allow himself any gratifications, and very rarely went out; his daughter worked to maintain him, translating English books, and writing some herself, it was said. The Lovelaces could not afford to hire boats to row on the lake, or horses and guides to explore the neighbourhood. Poverty demanding such privation as this excites all the greater compassion among the Swiss, because it deprives them of a chance of profit. The cook of the establishment fed the three English boarders for a hundred francs a month inclusive. In Gersau it was generally believed, however, that the gardener and his wife, in spite of their pretensions, used the cook's name as a screen to net the little profits of this bargain. The Bergmanns had made beautiful gardens round their house, and had built a hothouse. The flowers, the fruit, and the botanical rarities of this spot were what had induced the young lady to settle on it as she passed through Gersau. Miss Fanny was said to be nineteen years old; she was the old man's youngest child, and the object of his adulation. About two months ago she had hired a piano from Lucerne, for she seemed to be simply mad about music.

"She loves flowers and music, and she is unmarried!" thought Rodolphe; "what good luck!"

The next day Rodolphe went to ask leave to visit the hothouses and gardens, which were beginning to be somewhat famous. The permission was not immediately granted. The retired gardeners asked, strangely enough, to see Rodolphe's passport; it was sent to them at once. The paper was not returned to him till next morning, by the hands of the cook, who expressed her master's pleasure in showing him their place. Rodolphe went to the Bergmanns, not without a certain trepidation, known only to persons of strong feelings, who go through as much passion in a moment as some men experience in a whole lifetime.. After dressing himself carefully to gratify the old gardeners of the Borromean Islands, whom he regarded as the warders of his treasure, he went all over the grounds, looking at the house now and again, but with much caution; the old couple treated him with evident distrust. But his attention was soon attracted by the little English deaf-mute, in whom his discernment, though young as yet, enabled him to recognise a girl of African, or at least of Sicilian, origin. The child had the golden-brown colour of a Havannah cigar, eyes of fire, Armenian eyelids with lashes of very un-British length, hair blacker than black, and under this almost olive skin, sinews of extraordinary strength and feverish alertness. She looked at Rodolphe with amazing curiosity and effrontery, watching his every movement.

"To whom does that little Moresco belong?" he asked the worthy Madame Bergmann.

"To the English," Monsieur Bergmann replied.

"But she never was born in England!"

"They may have brought her from the Indies," said Madame Bergmann.

"I have been told that Miss Lovelace is fond of music. I should be delighted if, during the residence by the lake to which I am condemned by my doctor's orders, she would allow me to join her."

"They receive no one, and will not see anybody," said the old gardener.

Rodolphe bit his lip and went away, without having been invited into the house, or taken into the part of the garden that lay between the front of the house and the shore of the little promontory. On that side, the house had a balcony above the first floor made of wood and covered by the roof, which projected deeply like the roof of a chalet on all four sides of the building, in the Swiss fashion. Rodolphe had loudly praised the elegance of this arrangement, and talked of the view from that balcony, but all in vain. When he had taken leave of the Bergmanns it struck him that he was a simpleton, like any man of spirit and imagination disappointed of the results of a plan which he had believed would succeed.

In the evening he, of course, went out in a boat on the lake, round and about the spit of land, to Brunnen and to Schwytz,* and came in at nightfall. From afar he saw the window open and brightly lighted; he heard the sound of a piano and the tones of an exquisite voice. He made the boatmen stop, and gave himself up to the pleasure of listening to an Italian air delightfully sung. When the singing ceased, Rodolphe landed and sent away the boat and rowers. At the cost of wetting his feet, he went to sit down under the water-worn granite shelf crowned by a thick hedge of thorny acacia, by the side of which ran a long lime avenue in the Bergmanns' garden. By the end of an hour he heard steps and voices just above him, but the words that reached his ears were all Italian, and spoken by two women. He took advantage of the moment when the two speakers were at one end of the walk to slip noiselessly to the other. After half an hour of struggling, he got to the end of the avenue and there took up a position whence, without being seen or heard, he could watch the two women without being observed by them as they came towards him. What was Rodolphe's amazement on recognising the deafmute as one of them; she was talking to Miss Lovelace in Italian. It was now eleven o'clock at night. The stillness was so perfect on the lake and around the dwelling, that the two women must have thought themselves safe; in all Gersau there could be no eyes open but theirs. Rodolphe supposed that the girl's dumbness must be a necessary deception. From the way in which they both spoke Italian, Rodolphe suspected that it was the mother tongue of both girls, and concluded that the English name also hid some disguise.

"They are Italian refugees," said he to himself, "outlaws in fear of the Austrian or Sardinian police.* The young lady waits till it is dark to walk and talk in security."

He lay down by the side of the hedge, and crawled like a snake to find a way between two acacia shrubs. At the risk of leaving his coat behind him, or tearing deep scratches in his back, he got through the hedge when the so-called Miss Fanny and her pretended deaf-and-dumb maid were at the other end of the path; then, when they had come within twenty yards of him without seeing him, for he was in the shadow of the hedge, and the moon was shining brightly, he suddenly rose.

"Fear nothing," said he in French to the Italian girl, "I am not a spy. You are refugees, I have guessed that. I am a Frenchman whom one look from you has fixed at Gersau."

Rodolphe, startled by the acute pain caused by some steel instrument piercing his side, fell like a log.

"*Nel lago con pietra!*"* said the terrible dumb girl.

"Oh, Gina!" exclaimed the Italian.

"She has missed me," said Rodolphe, pulling from the wound a stiletto, which had been turned by one of the false ribs. "But a little higher up it would have been deep in my heart. I was wrong, Francesca," he went on, remembering the name he had heard little Gina repeat several times; "I owe her no grudge, do not scold her. The happiness of speaking to you is well worth the prick of a stiletto. Only show me the way out; I must get back to the Stopfers' house. Be easy; I shall tell nothing."

Francesca, recovering from her astonishment, helped Rodolphe to rise, and said a few words to Gina, whose eyes filled with tears. The two girls made him sit down on a bench and take off his coat, his waistcoat, and his cravat. Then Gina opened his shirt and sucked the wound strongly. Francesca, who had left them, returned with a large piece of sticking plaster, which she applied to the wound.

"You can walk now as far as your house," she said.

Each took an arm, and Rodolphe was conducted to a side gate, of which the key was in Francesca's apron pocket.

"Does Gina speak French?" said Rodolphe to Francesca.

"No. But do not excite yourself," replied Francesca with some impatience.

"Let me look at you," said Rodolphe pathetically, "for it may be long before I am able to come again——"

He leaned against one of the gateposts contemplating the beautiful Italian, who allowed him to gaze at her for a moment under the sweetest silence and the sweetest night which ever, perhaps, shone on this lake, the king of Swiss lakes. Francesca was quite of the classic Italian type, and such as imagination supposes or pictures, or, if you will, dreams, that Italian women are. What first struck Rodolphe was the grace and elegance of a figure evidently powerful, though so slender as to appear fragile. An amber paleness overspread her face, betraying sudden interest, but it did not dim the voluptuous glance of her liquid eyes of velvety blackness. A pair of hands as beautiful as ever a Greek sculptor added to the polished arms of a statue grasped Rodolphe's arm, and their whiteness gleamed against his black coat. The rash Frenchman could but just discern the long, oval shape of her face, and a melancholy mouth showing brilliant teeth between the parted lips—full, fresh, and brightly red. The exquisite lines of this face guaranteed to Francesca permanent beauty; but what most struck Rodolphe was the adorable freedom, the Italian frankness of this woman, wholly absorbed as she was in her pity for him.

La petite muette

Plate XIII

Francesca said a word to Gina, who gave Rodolphe her arm as far as the Stopfers' door, and fled like a swallow as soon as she had rung.

"These patriots do not play at killing!" said Rodolphe to himself as he felt his sufferings when he found himself in his bed. "'*Nel lago!*' Gina would have pitched me into the lake with a stone tied to my neck."

Next day he sent to Lucerne for the best surgeon there, and when he came, enjoined on him absolute secrecy, giving him to understand that his honour depended on it. Léopold returned from his excursion on the day when his friend first got out of bed. Rodolphe made up a story, and begged him to go to Lucerne to fetch their luggage and letters. Léopold brought back the most fatal, the most dreadful news: Rodolphe's mother was dead. While the two friends were on their way from Basel to Lucerne, the fatal letter, written by Léopold's father, had reached Lucerne the day they left for Fluelen. In spite of Léopold's utmost precautions, Rodolphe fell ill of a nervous fever. As soon as Léopold saw his friend out of danger, he set out for France with a power of attorney, and Rodolphe could thus remain at Gersau, the only place in the world where his grief could grow calmer. The young Frenchman's 1position—his despair, the circumstances which made such a loss worse for him than for any other man—became known, and secured him the pity and interest of everyone at Gersau. Every morning the pretended dumb girl came to see him and bring news of her mistress.

As soon as Rodolphe could go out, he went to the Bergmanns' house to thank Miss Fanny Lovelace and her father for the interest they had taken in his sorrow and his illness. For the first time since he had lodged with the Bergmanns, the old Italian admitted a stranger to his room, where Rodolphe was received with the cordiality due to his misfortunes and to his being a Frenchman, which excluded all distrust of him. Francesca looked so lovely by candlelight that first evening that she shed a ray of brightness on his grieving heart. Her smiles flung the roses of hope on his woe. She sang, not indeed gay songs, but grave and solemn melodies suited to the state of Rodolphe's heart, and he observed this touching care. At about eight o'clock, the old man left the young people without any sign of uneasiness, and went to his room. When Francesca was tired of singing, she led Rodolphe on to the balcony whence they perceived the sublime scenery of the lake, and signed to him to be seated by her on a rustic wooden bench.

"Am I very indiscreet in asking how old you are, *cara* Francesca?" said Rodolphe.

"Nineteen," said she, "well past."

"If anything in the world could soothe my sorrow," he went on, "it would be the hope of winning you from your father, whatever your fortune may be. So beautiful as you are, you seem to me richer than a prince's daughter. And I tremble as I confess to you the feelings with which you have inspired me; they are deep—they are eternal."

"*Zitto!*"* said Francesca, laying a finger of her right hand on her lips. "Say no more: I am not free. I have been married these three years."

For a few minutes utter silence reigned. When the Italian girl, alarmed at Rodolphe's stillness, went close to him, she found that he had fainted.

"*Povero!*" she said to herself. "And I thought him cold."

She fetched some salts, and revived Rodolphe by making him smell at them.

"Married!" said Rodolphe, looking at Francesca. And then his tears flowed freely.

"Child!" said she. "But there still is hope. My husband is——"

"Eighty?" Rodolphe put in.

"No," said she with a smile, "but sixty-five. He has disguised himself as much older to mislead the police."

"Dearest," said Rodolphe, "a few more shocks of this kind and I shall die. Only when you have known me twenty years will you understand the strength and power of my heart and the nature of its aspirations for happiness. This plant," he went on, pointing to the yellow jasmine which covered the balustrade, "does not climb more eagerly to spread itself in the sunbeams than I have clung to you for this month past. I love you with unique passion. That love will be the secret fount of my life—I may possibly die of it."

"Oh! Frenchman, Frenchman!" said she, emphasising her exclamation with a little incredulous grimace.

"Shall I not be forced to wait, to accept you at the hands of Time?" said he gravely. "But know this: if you are in earnest in what you have allowed to escape you, I will wait for you faithfully without suffering any other attachment to grow up in my heart."

She looked at him doubtfully.

"None," said he, "not even a passing fancy. I have my fortune to make; you must have a splendid one, nature created you a princess——"

At this word Francesca could not repress a faint smile, which gave her face the most bewitching expression, something subtle, like what the great Leonardo has so well depicted in the *Gioconda*. This smile made Rodolphe pause.

"Ah yes!" he went on, "you must suffer much from the destitution to which exile has brought you. Oh, if you would make me happy above all men, and consecrate my love, you would treat me as a friend. Ought I not to be your friend? My poor mother has left sixty thousand francs of savings; take half."

Francesca looked steadily at him. This piercing gaze went to the bottom of Rodolphe's soul.

"We want nothing; my work amply supplies our luxuries," she replied in a grave voice.

"And can I endure that a Francesca should work?" cried he. "One day you will return to your country and find all you left there." Again the Italian girl looked at Rodolphe. "And you will then repay me what you may have condescended to borrow," he added, with an expression full of delicate feeling.

"Let us drop this subject," said she, with incomparable dignity of gesture, expression, and attitude. "Make a splendid fortune, be one of the remarkable men of your country; that is my desire. Fame is a drawbridge which may serve to cross a deep gulf. Be ambitious if you must. I believe you have great and powerful talents, but use them rather for the happiness of mankind than to deserve me; you will be all the greater in my eyes."

In the course of this conversation, which lasted two hours, Rodolphe discovered that Francesca was an enthusiast for liberal ideas, and for that worship of liberty which had led to the three revolutions in Naples, Piedmont, and Spain.*

On leaving, he was shown to the door by Gina, the so-called mute. At eleven o'clock no one was astir in the village, there was no fear of listeners; Rodolphe took Gina into a corner and asked her in a low voice and in bad Italian, "Who are your master and mistress, child? Tell me, I will give you this fine new gold piece."

"Monsieur," said the girl, taking the coin, "my master is the famous bookseller Lamporani of Milan, one of the leaders of the revolution and the conspirator of all others, whom Austria would most like to have in the Spielberg."*

"A bookseller's wife! Ah, so much the better," thought he; "we are on an equal footing. And what is her family?" he added, "for she looks like a queen."

"All Italian women do," replied Gina proudly. "Her father's name is Colonna."

Emboldened by Francesca's modest rank, Rodolphe had an awning fitted to his boat and cushions placed in the stern. When this was done, the lover came to propose to Francesca to come out on the lake. The Italian accepted, no doubt to carry out her part of a young English miss in the eyes of the villagers, but she brought Gina with her. Francesca Colonna's lightest actions betrayed a superior education and the highest social rank. By the way in which she took her place at the end of the boat, Rodolphe felt himself in some sort cut off from her, and, in the face of a look of pride worthy of an aristocrat, the familiarity he had intended fell dead. By a glance Francesca made herself a princess, with all the prerogatives she might have enjoyed in the Middle Ages. She seemed to have read the thoughts of this vassal who was so audacious as to constitute himself her protector. Already, in the furniture of the room where Francesca had received him, in her dress, and in the various trifles she made use of, Rodolphe had detected indications of a superior character and a fine fortune. All these observations now returned to his mind; he became thoughtful after having been trampled on, as it were, by Francesca's dignity. Gina, her half-grown-up confidante, also seemed to have a mocking expression as she gave a covert or side glance at Rodolphe. This obvious disagreement between the Italian lady's rank and her manners was a fresh puzzle to Rodolphe, who suspected some further trick like Gina's assumed dumbness.

"Where would you go, *Signora Lamporani?*" he asked.

"Towards Lucerne," replied Francesca in French.

"Good!" said Rodolphe to himself, "she is not startled by hearing me speak her name; she had, no doubt, foreseen that I should ask Gina—she is so cunning. What is your quarrel with me?" he went on, going at last to sit down by her side and asking her by a gesture to give him her hand, which she withdrew. "You are cold and ceremonious; what, in colloquial language, we should call *short*."

"It is true," she replied with a smile. "I am wrong. It is not good manners; it is vulgar. In French you would call it inartistic. It is better to be frank than to harbor cold or hostile feelings towards a friend, and you have already proved yourself my friend. Perhaps I have gone too far with you. You must take me to be a very ordinary woman"—Rodolphe made many signs of denial—"yes," said the bookseller's wife, going on without acknowledging this pantomime, which, however, she plainly saw. "I have detected that, and naturally I have reconsidered my conduct. Well! I will put an end to everything by a few words of deep truth. Understand this, Rodolphe: I feel in myself the strength to stifle a feeling if it were not in harmony with my ideas or anticipation of what true love is. I could love—as we can love in Italy, but I know my duty. No intoxication can make me forget it. Married without my consent to that poor old man, I might take advantage of the liberty he so generously gives me; but three years of married life imply acceptance of its laws. Hence the most vehement passion would never make me utter, even involuntarily, a wish to find myself free. Émilio knows my character. He knows that without my heart, which is my own, and which I might give away, I should never allow anyone to take my hand. That is why I have just refused it to you. I desire to be loved and waited for with fidelity, nobleness, and ardour, while all I can give is infinite tenderness of which the expression may not overstep the boundary of the heart, the permitted neutral ground. All this being thoroughly understood—Oh!" she went on with a girlish gesture, "I will be as coquettish, as gay, as glad, as a child who knows nothing of the dangers of familiarity."

This plain and frank declaration was made in a tone, an

accent, and supported by a look which gave it the deepest stamp of truth.

"A Princess Colonna could not have spoken better," said Rodolphe, smiling.

"Is that," she answered with some haughtiness, "a reflection on the humbleness of my birth? Must your love flaunt a coat of arms? At Milan the noblest names are written over shop doors: Sforza, Canova, Visconti, Trivulzio, Ursini; there are Archintos apothecaries, but, believe me, though I keep a shop, I have the feelings of a duchess."

"A reflection? Nay, Madame, I meant it for praise."

"By a comparison?" she said archly.

"Ah, once and for all," said he, "do not torture me if my words should ill express my feelings, understand that my love is perfect; it carries with it absolute obedience and respect."

She bowed as a woman satisfied, and said, "Then Monsieur accepts the treaty?"

"Yes," said he. "I can understand that in a rich and powerful feminine nature the faculty of loving ought not to be wasted, and that you, out of delicacy, wished to restrain it. Ah! Francesca, at my age tenderness requited, and by so sublime, so royally beautiful a creature as you are—why, it is the fulfilment of all my wishes. To love you as you desire to be loved—is not that enough to make a young man guard himself against every evil folly? Is it not to concentrate all his powers in a noble passion, of which in the future he may be proud, and which can leave none but lovely memories? If you could but know with what hues you have clothed the chain of Pilatus, the Rigi, and this superb lake——"

"I want to know," said she, with the Italian artlessness which has always a touch of artfulness.

"Well, this hour will shine on all my life like a diamond on a queen's brow."

Francesca's only reply was to lay her hand on Rodolphe's.

"Oh dearest! Forever dearest! Tell me, have you never loved?"

"Never."

"And you allow me to love you nobly, looking to heaven for the utmost fulfilment?" he asked.

She gently bent her head. Two large tears rolled down Rodolphe's cheeks.

"Why! what is the matter?" she cried, abandoning her imperial manner.

"I have now no mother whom I can tell of my happiness; she left this earth without seeing what would have mitigated her agony——"

"What?" said she.

"Her tenderness replaced by an equal tenderness——"

"*Povero mio!*"* exclaimed the Italian, much touched. "Believe me," she went on after a pause, "it is a very sweet thing, and to a woman, a strong element of fidelity to know that she is everything in the world to the man she loves; to find him lonely, with no family, with nothing in his heart but his love—in short, to have him wholly to herself."

When two lovers thus understand each other, the heart feels delicious peace, supreme tranquillity. Certainty is the basis for which human feelings crave, for it is never lacking to religious sentiment; man is always certain of being fully repaid by God. Love never believes itself secure but by this resemblance to divine love. And the raptures of that moment must have been fully felt to be understood; it is unique in life; it cannot return any more than can the emotions of youth. To believe in a woman, to make her your human religion, the fount of life, the secret luminary of all your least thoughts! Is this not a second birth? And a young man mingles with this love a little of the feeling he had for his mother. Rodolphe and Francesca for some time remained in perfect silence, answering each other by sympathetic glances full of thoughts. They understood each other in the midst of one of the most beautiful scenes of nature, whose glories, interpreted by the glory in their hearts, helped to stamp on their minds the most fugitive details of that unique hour. There had not been the slightest shade of frivolity in Francesca's conduct. It was noble, large, and without any second thought. This magnanimity struck Rodolphe greatly, for in it he recognized the difference between the Italian and the Frenchwoman. The waters, the land, the sky, the woman, all were grandiose and full of wonder; even their love in the midst of this picture, so vast in its expanse, so rich in detail, where the sternness of the snowy peaks and their hard folds stood out clearly against the blue sky, reminded Rodolphe of the circumstances which limited his happiness: a lovely country encircled by snow.

This delightful intoxication of soul was destined to be disturbed. A boat was approaching from Lucerne; Gina, who had been watching it attentively, gave a joyful start, though faithful to her part as a mute. The bark came nearer; when at length Francesca could distinguish the faces on board, she exclaimed, "Tito!" as she perceived a young man. She stood up, and remained standing at the risk of being drowned. "Tito! Tito!" cried she, waving her handkerchief. Tito desired the boatmen to slacken, and the two boats pulled side by side. Francesca and Tito spoke with such extreme rapidity, and in a dialect unfamiliar to a man who hardly knew even the Italian of books, that Rodolphe could neither hear nor guess the drift of this conversation. But Tito's handsome face, Francesca's familiarity, and Gina's expression of delight, all aggrieved him. And indeed no lover can help being ill pleased at finding himself neglected for another, whoever he may be. Tito tossed a little leather bag to Gina, full of gold no doubt, and a packet of letters to Francesca, who began to read them with a farewell wave of the hand to Tito.

"Get quickly back to Gersau," she said to the boatmen, "I will not let my poor Émilio pine ten minutes longer than need be."

"What has happened?" asked Rodolphe, as he saw Francesca finish reading the last letter.

"*La libertà!*" she exclaimed, with an artist's enthusiasm.

"*E denaro!*"* added Gina, like an echo, for she had found her tongue.

"Yes," said Francesca, "no more poverty! For more than eleven months have I been working, and I was beginning to be tired of it. I am certainly not a literary woman."

"Who is this Tito?" asked Rodolphe.

"The Secretary of State to the financial department of the humble shop of the Colonnas—in other words, the son of our *ragionato*. Poor boy! He could not come by the Saint-Gothard, nor by the Mont-Cenis, nor by the Simplon; he came by sea, by Marseilles, and had to cross France. Well, in three weeks we shall be at Geneva, and living at our ease.

Come, Rodolphe," she added, seeing sadness overspread the Parisian's face, "is not the Lake of Geneva quite as good as the Lake of Lucerne?"

"But allow me to bestow a regret on the Bergmanns' delightful house," said Rodolphe, pointing to the little promontory.

"Come and dine with us to add to your associations, *povero mio*," said she. "This is a great day; we are out of danger. My mother writes that within a year there will be an amnesty. Oh! *La cara patria!*"*

These three words made Gina weep. "Another winter here," said she, "and I should have been dead!"

"My poor little Sicilian lamb!" said Francesca, stroking Gina's head with an expression and an affection which made Rodolphe long to be so caressed, even if it were without love. The boat grounded; Rodolphe sprang on to the sand, offered his hand to the Italian lady, escorted her to the door of the Bergmanns' house, and went to dress and return as soon as possible.

When he joined the bookseller and his wife, who were sitting on the balcony, Rodolphe could scarcely repress an exclamation of surprise at seeing the prodigious change which the good news had produced in the old man. He now saw a man of about sixty, extremely well preserved, lean and as straight as an I, with hair still black, though thin and showing a white skull, bright-eyed, a full set of white teeth, a face like Caesar, and on his diplomatic lips a sardonic smile, the almost false smile under which a man of good breeding hides his real feelings.

"Here is my husband under his natural form," said Francesca gravely.

"He is quite a new acquaintance," replied Rodolphe, bewildered.

"Quite," said the bookseller; "I have played many a part, and know well how to make up. Ah! I played one in Paris under the Empire with Bourrienne, Madame Murat, Madame d'Abrantès,* *è tutti quanti*. Everything we take the trouble to learn in our youth, even the most futile, is of use. If my wife had not received a man's education—an unheard-of thing in Italy—I should have been obliged to chop wood to make my living here. *Povera* Francesca! Who would have told me that she would some day maintain me!"

As he listened to this worthy bookseller—so easy, so affable, so hale—Rodolphe scented some mystification, and preserved the watchful silence of a man who has been duped.

"*Che avete, signor?*"* Francesca asked with simplicity. "Does our happiness sadden you?"

"Your husband is a young man," he whispered in her ear.

She broke into such a frank, infectious laugh that Rodolphe was still more puzzled.

"He is but sixty-five, at your service," said she; "but I can assure you that even that is something—to be thankful for!"

"I do not like to hear you jest about an affection so sacred as this, of which you yourself prescribed the conditions."

"*Zitto!*" said she, stamping her foot, and looking whether her husband were listening. "Never disturb the peace of mind of that dear man, as simple as a child, and with whom I can do what I please. He is under my protection," she added. "If you could know with what generosity he risked his life and fortune because I was a liberal! For he does not share my political opinions. Is not that love, Monsieur Frenchman? But they are like that in his family. Émilio's younger brother was deserted for a handsome youth by the woman he loved. He thrust his sword through his own heart ten minutes after he had said to his servant, 'I could of course kill my rival, but that would grieve the *Diva* too deeply.'"

This mixture of dignity and banter, of haughtiness and playfulness, made Francesca at this moment the most fascinating creature in the world. The dinner and the evening were full of cheerfulness, justified, indeed, by the relief of the two refugees, but depressing to Rodolphe.

"Can she be fickle?" he asked himself as he returned to the Stopfers' house. "She sympathized in my sorrow, and I cannot take part in her joy!"

He blamed himself, justifying this girl-wife.

"She has no taint of hypocrisy and is carried away by impulse," thought he, "and I want her to be like a Parisian woman."

The next day and the following days, in fact, for twenty days after, Rodolphe spent all his time at the Bergmanns' watching Francesca without having determined to watch her. In some souls admiration is not independent of a certain penetration. The young Frenchman discerned in Francesca the imprudence of girlhood, the true nature of a woman as yet unbroken, sometimes struggling against her love, and at other moments yielding and carried away by it. The old man certainly behaved to her as a father to his daughter, and Francesca treated him with a deeply felt gratitude which roused her instinctive nobleness. The situation and the woman were to Rodolphe an impenetrable enigma, of which the solution attracted him more and more.

These last days were full of secret joys, alternating with melancholy moods, with tiffs and quarrels even more delightful than the hours when Rodolphe and Francesca were of one mind. And he was more and more fascinated by this tenderness apart from wit, always and in all things the same, an affection that was jealous of mere nothings—already!

"You care very much for luxury?" said he one evening to Francesca, who was expressing her wish to get away from Gersau, where she missed many things.

"I!" cried she. "I love luxury as I love the arts, as I love a picture by Raphael, a fine horse, a beautiful day, or the Bay of Naples. Émilio," she went on, "have I ever complained here during our days of privation?"

"You would not have been yourself if you had," replied the old man gravely.

"After all, is it not in the nature of plain folks to aspire to grandeur?" she asked, with a mischievous glance at Rodolphe and at her husband. "Were my feet made for fatigue?" she added, putting out two pretty little feet. "My hands"—and she held one out to Rodolphe—"were those hands made to work? Leave us," she said to her husband; "I want to speak to him."

The old man went into the drawing room with sublime good faith; he was sure of his wife.

"I will not have you come with us to Geneva," she said to Rodolphe. "It is a gossiping town. Though I am far above the nonsense the world talks, I do not choose to be calumniated, not for my own sake, but for *his*. I make it my pride to be the glory of that old man, who is, after all, my only protector. We are leaving; stay here a few days. When you come to Geneva, call first on my husband and let him introduce you to me. Let us hide our great and unchangeable affection from the eyes of the world. I love you; you know it, but this is how I will prove it to you—you shall never discern in my conduct anything whatever that may arouse your jealousy."

She drew him into a corner of the balcony, kissed him on the forehead, and fled, leaving him in amazement.

The next day Rodolphe heard that the lodgers at the Bergmanns' had left at daybreak. It then seemed to him intolerable to remain at Gersau, and he set out for Vevay* by the longest route, starting sooner than was necessary. Attracted to the waters of the lake where the beautiful Italian awaited him, he reached Geneva by the end of October. To avoid the discomforts of the town he took rooms in a house at Eaux-Vives,* outside the walls. As soon as he was settled, his first care was to ask his landlord, a retired jeweller, whether some Italian refugees from Milan had not lately come to reside at Geneva. "Not so far as I know," replied the man. "Prince and Princess Colonna of Rome have taken Monsieur Jeanrenaud's place for three years; it is one of the finest on the lake. It is situated between the Villa Diodati* and that of Monsieur Lafin-de-Dieu, let to the Vicomtesse de Beauséant. Prince Colonna has come to see his daughter and his son-in-law Prince Gandolphini, a Neopolitan, or if you like, a Sicilian, an old adherent of King Murat's, and a victim of the last revolution. These are the last arrivals at Geneva, and they are not Milanese. Serious steps had to be taken, and the Pope's interest in the Colonna family was invoked, to obtain permission from the foreign powers and the King of Naples for the Prince and Princess Gandolphini to live here. Geneva is anxious to do nothing to displease the Holy Alliance to which it owes its independence.* *Our* part is not to ruffle foreign courts: there are many foreigners here, Russians and English."

"Even some Genevese."

"Yes, Monsieur, our lake is so fine! Lord Byron lived here about seven years at the Villa Diodati, which everyone goes to see now, like Coppet and Ferney."*

"You cannot tell me whether within a week or so a bookseller from Milan has come with his wife—named Lamporani, one of the leaders of the last revolution?"

"I could easily find out by going to the Cercle des Étrangers,"* said the jeweller.

Rodolphe's first walk was very naturally to the Villa Diodati, the residence of Lord Byron, whose recent death added to its attractiveness: for is not death the consecration of genius? The road to Eaux-Vives follows the shore of the lake, and, like all the roads in Switzerland, is very narrow; in some spots, in consequence of the configuration of the hilly ground, there is scarcely space for two carriages to pass each other. At a few yards from the Jeanrenauds' house, which he was approaching without knowing it, Rodolphe heard the sound of a carriage behind him, and, finding himself in a sunk road, he climbed to the top of a rock to leave the road free. Of course he looked at the approaching carriage—an elegant English phaeton, with a splendid pair of English horses. He felt quite dizzy as he beheld in this carriage Francesca, beautifully dressed, by the side of an old lady as hard as a cameo. A servant blazing with gold lace stood behind. Francesca recognised Rodolphe, and smiled at seeing him like a statue on a pedestal. The carriage, which the lover followed with his eyes as he climbed the hill, turned in at the gate of a country house, towards which he ran.

"Who lives here?" he asked of the gardener.

"Prince and Princess Colonna, and Prince and Princess Gandolphini."

"Have they not just driven in?"

"Yes, Monsieur."

In that instant a veil fell from Rodolphe's eyes; he saw clearly the meaning of the past.

"If only this is her last piece of trickery!" thought the thunderstruck lover to himself.

He trembled lest he should have been the plaything of a whim, for he had heard what a *capriccio* might mean in an Italian. But what a crime had he committed in the eyes of a woman—in accepting a born princess as a citizen's wife!—in believing that a daughter of one of the most illustrious houses of the Middle Ages was the wife of a bookseller! The consciousness of his blunders increased Rodolphe's desire to know whether he would be ignored and repelled. He asked for Prince Gandolphini, sending in his card, and was immediately received by the false Lamporani, who came forward to meet him, welcomed him with the best possible grace, and took him to walk on a terrace whence there was a view of Geneva, the Jura, the hills covered with villas, and below them a wide expanse of the lake.

"My wife is faithful to the lakes, you see," he remarked, after pointing out the details to his visitor. "We have a sort of concert this evening," he added, as they returned to the splendid Villa Jeanrenaud. "I hope you will do me and the Princess the pleasure of seeing you. Two months of poverty endured in intimacy are equal to years of friendship."

Though he was consumed by curiosity, Rodolphe dared not ask to see the Princess; he slowly made his way back to Eaux-Vives, looking forward to the evening. In a few hours his passion, great as it had already been, was augmented by his anxiety and by suspense as to future events. He now understood the necessity for making himself famous, that he might some day find himself, socially speaking, on a level with his idol. In his eyes Francesca was made really great by the simplicity and ease of her conduct at Gersau. Princess Colonna's haughtiness, so evidently natural to her, alarmed Rodolphe, who would find enemies in Francesca's father and mother—at least so he might expect, and the secrecy which Princess Gandolphini had so strictly enjoined on him now struck him as a wonderful proof of affection. By not choosing to compromise the future, had she not confessed that she loved him?

At last nine o'clock struck; Rodolphe could get into a carriage and say with an emotion that is very intelligible, "To the Villa Jeanrenaud—to Prince Gandolphini's."

At last he saw Francesca, but without being seen by her. The Princess was standing quite near the piano. Her beautiful hair, so thick and long, was bound with a golden fillet. Her face, in the light of wax candles, had the brilliant pallor peculiar to Italians, and which looks its best only by artificial light. She was in full evening dress, showing her fascinating shoulders, the figure of a girl, and the arms of an antique statue. Her sublime beauty was beyond all possible rivalry, though there were some charming English and Russian ladies present, the prettiest women of Geneva, and other Italians, among them the dazzling and illustrious Princess Varèse, and the famous singer Tinti, who was at that moment singing. Rodolphe, leaning against the doorpost, looked at the Princess, turning on her the fixed, tenacious, attracting gaze, charged with the full, insistent will which is concentrated in the feeling called *desire*, and thus assumes the nature of a vehement command. Did the flame of that gaze reach Francesca? Was Francesca expecting each instant to see Rodolphe? In a few minutes she stole a glance at the door as though magnetised by this current of love, and her eyes, without reserve, looked deep into Rodolphe's. A slight thrill quivered through that superb face and beautiful body; the shock to her spirit reacted: Francesca blushed! Rodolphe felt a whole life in this exchange of looks, so swift that it can only be compared to a lightning flash. But to what could his happiness compare? He was loved. The lofty Princess, in the midst of her world, in this handsome villa, kept the pledge given by the disguised exile, the capricious beauty of Bergmanns' lodgings. The intoxication of such a moment enslaves a man for life! A faint smile, refined and subtle, candid and triumphant, curled Princess Gandolphini's lips, and at a moment when she did not feel herself observed she looked at Rodolphe with an expression which seemed to ask his pardon for having deceived him as to her rank. When the song was ended, Rodolphe could make his way to the Prince, who graciously led him to his wife. Rodolphe went through the ceremony of a formal introduction to Princess and Prince Colonna, and to Francesca. When this was over, the Princess had to take part in the famous quartet, *Mi manca la voce*,* which was sung by her with Tinti, with the famous tenor Génovèse, and with a well-known Italian prince then in exile, whose voice, if he had not been a prince, would have made him one of the Princes of Art.

"Take that seat," said Francesca to Rodolphe, pointing to her own chair. "*Oimè!*" I think there is some mistake in my name; I have for the last minute been Princess Rodolphini."

It was said with an artless grace which revived, in this avowal hidden beneath a jest, the happy days at Gersau. Rodolphe revelled in the exquisite sensation of listening to the voice of the woman he adored, while sitting so close to her that one cheek was almost touched by the stuff of her dress and the gauze of her scarf. But when, at such a moment, *Mi manca la voce* is being sung, and by the finest voices in Italy, it is easy to understand what it was that brought the tears to Rodolphe's eyes.

In love, as perhaps in everything else, there are certain trivial circumstances, the outcome of a thousand little previous incidents, the importance of which is immense, because they epitomize the past and link themselves to the future. A hundred times already we have felt the preciousness of the one we love, but a trifle—the perfect touch of two souls united during a walk perhaps by a single word, by some unlooked-for *proof* of affection, will carry the feeling to its supremest pitch. In short, to express this truth by an image which has been preeminently successful from the earliest ages of the world, there are in a long chain points of attachment needed where the cohesion is stronger than in the intermediate loops of rings. This recognition between Rodolphe and Francesca, at this party, in the face of the world, was one of those intense moments which join the future to the past, and rivet a real attachment more deeply in the heart. It was perhaps of these incidental rivets that Bossuet spoke when he compared them to the rarity of happy moments in our lives—he who had such a living and secret experience of love!

Next to the pleasure of admiring the woman we love comes that of seeing her admired by everyone else. Rodolphe was enjoying both at once. Love is a treasury of memories, and though Rodolphe's was already full, he added to it pearls of great price; smiles shed aside for him alone, stolen glances, tones in her singing which Francesca addressed to him alone, but which made Tinti pale with jealousy, they were so much applauded. All his strength of desire, the special expression of his soul, was thrown over the beautiful Roman, who became unchangeably the beginning and the end of all his thoughts and actions. Rodolphe loved as every woman may dream of being loved, with a force, a constancy, a tenacity, which made Francesca the very substance of his heart; he felt her mingling with his blood as purer blood, with his soul as a more perfect soul; she would henceforth underlie the least efforts of his life as the golden sand of the Mediterranean lies beneath the waves. In short, Rodolphe's lightest aspiration was now a living hope.

At the end of a few days, Francesca understood this boundless love, but it was so natural, and so perfectly shared by her, that it did not surprise her. She was worthy of it.

"What is there that is strange?" said she to Rodolphe, as they walked on the garden terrace, when he had been betrayed into one of those outbursts of conceit which come so naturally to Frenchmen in the expression of their feelings, "what is extraordinary in the fact of your loving a young and beautiful woman, artist enough to be able to earn her living like Tinti, and of giving you some of the pleasures of vanity? What lout but would then become an Amadis? This is not in question between you and me. What is needed is that we both love faithfully, persistently—at a distance from each other for years, with no satisfaction but that of knowing that we are loved."

"Alas!" said Rodolphe, "will you not consider my fidelity as devoid of all merit when you see me absorbed in the efforts of devouring ambition? Do you imagine that I can wish to see you one day exchange the fine name of Gandolphini for that of a man who is a nobody? I want to become one of the most remarkable men of my country, to be rich, great—that you may be as proud of my name as of your own name of Colonna."

"I should be grieved to see you without such sentiments in your heart," she replied, with a bewitching smile. "But do not wear yourself out too soon in your ambitious labours. Remain young. They say that politics soon makes a man old."

One of the rarest gifts in women is a certain gaiety which does not detract from tenderness. This combination of deep feeling with the lightness of youth added an enchanting grace at this moment to Francesca's charms. This is the key to her character: she laughs and she is touched; she becomes enthusiastic and returns to arch raillery with a readiness, a facility, which make her the charming and exquisite creature she is, and for which her reputation is known outside Italy. Under the graces of a woman she conceals vast learning, thanks to the excessively monotonous, and almost monastic life she led in the castle of the old Colonnas. This rich heiress was at first intended for the cloister, being the fourth child of Prince and Princess Colonna, but the death of her two brothers and of her elder sister suddenly brought her out of her retirement and made her one of the most brilliant matches in the Papal States. Her elder sister had been betrothed to Prince Gandolphini, one of the richest landowners in Sicily, and Francesca was married to him instead, so that nothing might be changed in the position of the family. The Colonnas and Gandolphinis had always intermarried. From the age of nine till she was sixteen, Francesca, under the direction of a cardinal of the family, had read all through the library of the Colonnas, to make weight against her ardent imagination by studying science, art, and letters. But in these studies she acquired the taste for independence and liberal ideas which threw her, with her husband, into the ranks of the revolution. Rodolphe had not yet learned that, besides five living languages, Francesca knew Greek, Latin, and Hebrew. The charming creature perfectly understood that, for a woman, the first condition of being learned is to keep it deeply hidden.

Rodolphe spent the whole winter at Geneva. This winter passed like a day. When spring returned, notwithstanding the infinite delights of the society of a clever woman, wonderfully well informed, young and lovely, the lover went through cruel sufferings, endured indeed with courage, but which were sometimes legible in his countenance, and betrayed themselves in his manners or speech, perhaps because he believed that Francesca shared them. Now and again it annoyed him to admire her calmness. Like an Englishwoman, she seemed to pride herself on expressing nothing in her face; its serenity defied love; he longed to see her agitated; he accused her of having no feeling, for he believed in the tradition which ascribes to Italian women a feverish excitability.

"I am a Roman!" Francesca gravely replied one day when she took quite seriously some banter on this subject from Rodolphe.

There was a depth of tone in her reply which gave it the appearance of scathing irony, and which set Rodolphe's pulses throbbing. The month of May spread before them the treasures of her fresh verdure; the sun was sometimes as powerful as at midsummer. The two lovers happened to be at a part of the terrace where the rock rises abruptly from the lake, and were leaning over the stone parapet that crowns the wall above a flight of steps leading down to a landing stage. From the neighbouring villa, where there is a similar stairway, a boat presently shot out like a swan, its flag flaming, its crimson awning spread over a lovely woman comfortably reclining on red cushions, her hair wreathed with real flowers; the boatman was a young man dressed like a sailor, and rowing with all the more grace because he was under the lady's eye.

"They are happy!" exclaimed Rodolphe, with bitter emphasis. "Claire de Bourgogne, the last survivor of the only house which could ever vie with the royal family of France——"

"Oh! of a bastard branch, and that a female line."

"At any rate, she is Vicomtesse de Beauséant, and she did not——"

"Did not hesitate, you would say, to bury herself here with Monsieur Gaston de Nueil, you would say," replied the daughter of the Colonnas. "She is only a Frenchwoman; I am an Italian, Monsieur!"

Francesca turned away from the parapet, leaving Rodolphe, and went to the further end of the terrace, whence there is a wide prospect of the lake. Watching her as she slowly walked away, Rodolphe suspected that he had wounded her soul, at once so simple and so wise, so proud and so humble. It turned him cold; he followed Francesca, who signed to him to leave her to herself. But he did not heed the warning, and detected her wiping away her tears. Tears in so strong a nature! "Francesca," said he, taking her hand, "is there a single regret in your heart?"

She was silent, disengaged her hand which held her embroidered handkerchief, and again dried her eyes.

"Forgive me!" he said. And with a rush, he kissed her eyes to wipe away the tears.

Francesca did not seem aware of his passionate impulse, she was so violently agitated. Rodolphe, thinking she consented, grew bolder; he put his arm round her, clasped her to his heart, and snatched a kiss. But she freed herself by a dignified movement of offended modesty, and, standing a yard off, she looked at him without anger, but with firm determination. "Go this evening," she said. "We meet no more till we meet at Naples."

The order was stern, but it was obeyed, for it was Francesca's will.

On his return to Paris, Rodolphe found in his rooms a portrait of Princess Gandolphini painted by Schinner, as Schinner can paint. The artist had passed through Geneva on his way to Italy. As he had positively refused to paint the portraits of several women, Rodolphe did not believe that the Prince, anxious as he was for a portrait of his wife, would be able to conquer the great painter's objections, but Francesca, no doubt, had bewitched him and obtained from him—which was almost a miracle—an original portrait for Rodolphe, and a duplicate for Émilio. She told him this in a charming and delightful letter, in which the mind indemnified itself for the reserve required by the worship of the proprieties. The lover replied. Thus began, never to cease, a regular correspondence between Rodolphe and Francesca, the only indulgence they allowed themselves.

Partez ce soir, dit-elle.

Plate XIV

Rodolphe, possessed by an ambition sanctified by his love, set to work. First he longed to make his fortune, and risked his all in an undertaking to which he devoted all his faculties as well as his capital; but he, an inexperienced youth, had to contend against duplicity, which won the day. Thus three years were lost in a vast enterprise, three years of struggling and courage.

The Villèle ministry* fell just when Rodolphe was ruined. The valiant lover thought he would seek in Politics what commercial Industry had refused him, but before braving the storms of this career, he went, all wounded and sick at heart, to have his bruises healed and his courage revived at Naples, where the Prince and Princess had been reinstated in their place and rights on the King's accession.* This, in the midst of his warfare, was a respite full of delights; he spent three months at the Villa Gandolphini, rocked in hope.

Rodolphe then began again to construct his fortune. His talents were already known; he was about to attain the desires of his ambition; a high position was promised him as the reward of his zeal, his devotion, and his past services, when the storm of July 1830* broke, and again his bark was swamped.

She and God! These are the only witnesses of the brave efforts, the daring attempts of a young man gifted with fine qualities, but to whom, so far, the protection of luck—the god of fools—has been denied. And this indefatigable wrestler, upheld by love, comes back to fresh struggles, lighted on his way by an always friendly eye, an ever faithful heart. Lovers! pray for him!

As she finished the tale, Mademoiselle de Watteville's cheeks were on fire; there was a fever in her blood. She was crying—but with rage. This little novel, inspired by the literary style then in fashion, was the first reading of the kind that Rosalie had ever had the chance of devouring. Love was depicted in it, if not by a master hand, at any rate by a man who seemed to give his own impressions, and truth, even if unskilled, could not fail to touch a virgin soul. Here lay the secret of Rosalie's terrible agitation, of her fever and her tears; she was jealous of Francesca Colonna. She never for an instant doubted the sincerity of this poetical flight; Albert had taken pleasure in telling the story of his passion, while changing the names of persons and perhaps of places. Rosalie was possessed by infernal curiosity. What woman but would, like her, have wanted to know her rival's name—for she too loved! As she read these pages, to her really contagious, she had said solemnly to herself, "I love him!" She loved Albert, and felt in her heart a gnawing desire to fight for him, to snatch him from this unknown rival. She reflected that she knew nothing of music, and that she was not beautiful.

"He will never love me!" thought she.

This conclusion aggravated her anxiety to know whether she might not be mistaken, whether Albert really loved an Italian princess, and was loved by her. In the course of this fateful night, the power of swift decision, which had characterised the famous Watteville, was fully developed in his descendant. She devised those whimsical schemes, round which hovers the imagination of most young girls when, in the solitude to which some injudicious mothers confine them, they are aroused by some tremendous event which the system of repression to which they are subjected could neither foresee nor prevent. She dreamed of descending by a ladder from the kiosk into the garden of the house occupied by Albert, of taking advantage of the lawyer's being asleep to look through the window into his private room. She thought of writing to him, or of bursting the fetters of Besançon society by introducing Albert to the drawing room of the Hôtel de Rupt. This enterprise, which to the Abbé de Grancey even would have seemed the climax of the impossible, was a mere passing thought.

"Ah!" said she to herself, "my father has a dispute pending as to his land at Les Rouxey. I will go there! If there is no lawsuit, I will manage to make one, and *he* shall come into our drawing room!" she cried, as she sprang out of bed and to the window to look at the fascinating gleam which shone through Albert's nights. The clock struck one; he was still asleep.

"I shall see him when he gets up; perhaps he will come to his window!"

At this instant Mademoiselle de Watteville was witness to an incident which promised to place in her power the means of knowing Albert's secrets. By the light of the moon she saw a pair of arms stretched out from the kiosk to help Jérôme, Albert's servant, to get across the coping of the wall and step into the little building. In Jérôme's accomplice Rosalie at once recognised Mariette, the lady's maid.

"Mariette and Jérôme!" said she to herself. "Mariette, such an ugly girl! Certainly they must be ashamed of themselves."

Though Mariette was horribly ugly and thirty-six, she had inherited several plots of land. She had been seventeen years with Madame de Watteville, who valued her highly for her devotion, her honesty, and long service, and she had no doubt saved money and invested her wages and perquisites. Hence, earning about ten louis a year, she probably had by this time, including compound interest and her little inheritance, not less than ten thousand francs. In Jérôme's eyes ten thousand francs could alter the laws of optics; he saw in Mariette a neat figure; he did not perceive the pits and seams which virulent smallpox had left on her flat, parched face; to him the crooked mouth was straight, and ever since Savaron, by taking him into his service, had brought him so near to the Wattevilles' house, he had laid siege systematically to the maid, who was as prim and sanctimonious as her mistress, and who, like every ugly old maid, was far more exacting than the handsomest. If the night scene in the kiosk is thus fully accounted for to all perspicacious readers, it was not so

to Rosalie, though she derived from it the most dangerous lesson that can be given, that of a bad example. A
mother brings her daughter up strictly, keeps her under
her wing for seventeen years, and then, in one hour, a
servant girl destroys the long and painful work, sometimes by a word, often indeed by a gesture! Rosalie got
into bed again, not without considering how she might
take advantage of her discovery. Next morning, as she
went to Mass accompanied by Mariette (her mother was
not well), Rosalie took the maid's arm, which surprised
the country wench not a little.

"Mariette," said she, "does Jérôme have his master's
trust?"

"I do not know, Mademoiselle."

"Do not play the innocent with me," said Mademoiselle
de Watteville drily. "You let him kiss you last night under the kiosk; I no longer wonder that you so warmly
approved of my mother's ideas for the improvements
she planned."

Rosalie could feel how Mariette was trembling by the
shaking of her arm.

"I wish you no ill," Rosalie went on. "Be quite easy;
I shall not say a word to my mother, and you can meet
Jérôme as often as you please."

"But, Mademoiselle," replied Mariette, "it is perfectly
respectable; Jérôme honestly means to marry me——"

"But then," said Rosalie, "why meet at night?"

Mariette was dumbfounded, and could make no reply.

"Listen, Mariette; I am in love too! In secret and without any return. I am, after all, my father's and mother's
only child. You have more to hope for from me than
from anyone else in the world——"

"Certainly, Mademoiselle, and you may count on us
for life or death," exclaimed Mariette, rejoiced at the
unexpected turn of affairs.

"In the first place, silence for silence," said Rosalie. "I
will not marry Monsieur de Soulas, but one thing I will

have, and must have: my help and favour are yours on one condition only."

"What is that?"

"I must see the letters which Monsieur Savaron sends to the post by Jérôme."

"But what for?" said Mariette in alarm.

"Oh! merely to read them, and you yourself shall post them afterwards. It will cause a little delay, that is all."

At this moment they went into church, and each of them, instead of reading the order of Mass, fell into her own train of thought.

"*Mon Dieu!* How many sins are there in all that?" thought Mariette.

Rosalie, whose soul, brain, and heart were completely upset by reading the story, by this time regarded it as history, written for her rival. By dint of thinking of nothing else, like a child, she ended by believing that the *Revue de l'Est* was no doubt forwarded to Albert's lady love.

"Oh!" said she to herself, her head buried in her hands in the attitude of a person lost in prayer; "Oh! how can I get my father to look through the list of people to whom the *Revue* is sent?"

After breakfast she took a turn in the garden with her father, coaxing and cajoling him, and brought him to the kiosk.

"Do you suppose, my dear little Papa, that our *Revue* is ever read abroad?"

"It is but just started——"

"Well, I will wager that it is."

"It is hardly possible."

"Just go and find out, and note the names of any subscribers out of France."

Two hours later Monsieur de Watteville said to his daughter—"I was right; there is not one foreign subscriber as yet. They hope to get some at Neufchâtel, at

Berne, and at Geneva. One copy is, in fact, sent to Italy, but it is not paid for—to a Milanese lady at her country house at Belgirate,* on Lago Maggiore."

"What is her name?"

"The Duchesse d'Argaiolo."

"Do you know her, Papa?"

"I have heard about her. She was by birth a Princess Soderini, a Florentine, a very great lady, and quite as rich as her husband, who has one of the largest fortunes in Lombardy. Their villa on the Lago Maggiore is one of the sights of Italy."

La connaiss/-vous u on piie?

Plate XV

Two days after, Mariette placed the following letter in Mademoiselle de Watteville's hands:—

ALBERT SAVARON TO LÉOPOLD HANNEQUIN

Yes, 'tis so, my dear friend; I am at Besançon, while you thought I was travelling. I would not tell you anything till success should begin, and now it is dawning. Yes, my dear Léopold, after so many abortive undertakings, over which I have shed the best of my blood, have wasted so many efforts, spent so much courage, I have made up my mind to do as you have done—to start on a beaten path, on the high road, as the longest but the safest. I can see you jump with surprise in your lawyer's chair! But do not suppose that anything is changed in my personal life, of which you alone in the world know the secret, and that under the reservations *she* insists on. I did not tell you, my friend, but I was horribly weary of Paris. The outcome of the first enterprise, on which I had founded all my hopes, and which came to a bad end in consequence of the utter rascality of my two partners, who combined to cheat and fleece me—me, though everything was done by my energy—made me give up the pursuit of a fortune after the loss of three years of my life. One of these years was spent in the law courts, and perhaps I should have come worse out of the scrape if I had not been made to study law when I was twenty. I made up my mind to go into politics solely, to the end that I may some day find my name in a list for promotion to the Senate under the title of Comte Albert Savaron de Savarus, and so revive in France a good name now extinct in Belgium—though indeed I am neither legitimate nor legitimised!

"Ah! I knew it! He is of noble birth!" exclaimed Rosalie, dropping the letter.

You know how conscientiously I studied, how faithful and useful I was as an obscure journalist, and how excellent a secretary to the statesman who, on his part, was true to me in 1829. Flung to the depths once more by the Revolution of July just when my name was becoming known, at the very moment when, as Master of Requests, I was about to find my place as a necessary wheel in the political machine, I committed the blunder of remaining faithful to the fallen and fighting for them, without them. Oh! Why was I but thirty-three, and why did I not apply to you to make me eligible? I concealed from you all my devotedness and my dangers. What would you have? I was full of faith. We should not have agreed. Ten months ago, when you saw me so gay and contented writing my political articles, I was in despair: I foresaw my fate at the age of thirty-seven, with two thousand francs for my whole fortune, without the smallest fame, just having failed in a noble undertaking, the founding, namely, of a daily paper, answering only to a need of the future instead of appealing to the passions of the moment. I did not know which way to turn, and I felt my own value! I wandered about, gloomy and hurt, through the lonely places of Paris—Paris which had slipped through my fingers—thinking of my crushed ambitions, but never giving them up. Oh, what frantic letters I wrote at that time to *her*, my second conscience, my other self! Sometimes I would say to myself, 'Why did I sketch so vast a program of life? Why demand everything? Why not wait for happiness while devoting myself to some mechanical employment?'

I then looked about me for some modest appointment by which I might live. I was about to get the editorship of a paper under a manager who did not know much about it, a man of wealth and ambition, when I took fright.

'Would *she* ever accept as her husband a man who had stooped so low?' I wondered.

This reflection made me twenty-two again. But, oh, my dear Léopold, how the soul is worn by these perplexities! What must not caged eagles suffer, and imprisoned lions! They suffer what Napoléon suffered, not at Saint Helena, but on the Quay of the Tuileries on the 10th of August when he saw Louis XVI defending himself so badly while he could have quelled the insurrection, as he actually did, on the same spot, a little later, in Vendémiaire.* Well, my life has been a torment of that kind, extending over four years. How many a speech to the chamber have I not delivered in the deserted alleys of the Bois de Boulogne!* These wasted harangues have at any rate sharpened my tongue and accustomed my mind to formulate its ideas in words. And while I was undergoing this secret torture, you were getting married, you had paid for your business, you were made law clerk to the mayor of your arrondissement, after gaining the cross for a wound at Saint-Merri.*

Now, listen. When I was a small boy and tortured cock-chafers, the poor insects had one form of struggle which used almost to put me in a fever. It was when I saw them making repeated efforts to fly but without getting away, though they could spread their wings. We used to say: *they are marking time!* Now, was this sympathy? Was it a vision of my own future? Oh! to spread my wings and yet be unable to fly! That has been my predicament since that fine undertaking by which I was disgusted, but which has now made four families rich.

At last, seven months ago, I determined to make myself a name at the Paris bar, seeing how many vacancies had been left by the promotion of several lawyers to eminent positions. But when I remembered the rivalry I had seen among men of the press, and how difficult it is to achieve anything of any kind in Paris, the arena where so many champions meet, I came to a determination painful to myself, but certain in its results, and perhaps quicker than any other. In the course of our conversations you had given me a picture of the society of Besançon, of the impossibility for a stranger to get on there, to produce the smallest effect, to get into society, or to succeed in any way whatever. It was there that I determined to set up my flag, thinking, and rightly, that I should meet with no opposition, but find myself alone to canvass for the election. The people of the Comté will not meet the outsider? The outsider will not meet them! They refuse to admit him to their drawing rooms, he will never go there! He never shows himself anywhere, not even in the streets! But there is one class that elects the deputies—the commercial class. I am going especially to study commercial questions, with which I am already familiar; I will gain their lawsuits, I will effect compromises, I will be the greatest pleader in Besançon. By and by I will start a review in which I will defend the interests of the country, will create them, or preserve them, or resuscitate them. When

I shall have won a sufficient number of votes, my name will come out of the urn. For a long time the unknown advocate will be treated with contempt, but some circumstance will arise to bring him to the front—some unpaid defence, or a case which no other pleader will undertake. Well, my dear Léopold, I packed up my books in eleven cases, I bought such law books as might prove useful, and I sent everything off, furniture and all, by carrier to Besançon. I collected my diplomas, and I went to bid you good-bye. The mail coach dropped me at Besançon, where, in three days' time, I chose a little set of rooms looking out over some gardens. I sumptuously arranged the mysterious private room where I spend my nights and days, and where the portrait of my divinity reigns—of her to whom my life is dedicate, who fills it wholly, who is the mainspring of my efforts, the secret of my courage, the cause of my talents. Then, as soon as the furniture and books had come, I engaged an intelligent manservant, and there I sat for five months like a hibernating marmot. My name had, however, been entered on the list of lawyers in the town. At last I was called one day to defend an unhappy wretch at the assizes, no doubt in order to hear me speak for once! One of the most influential merchants of Besançon was on the jury; he had a difficult task to fulfil; I did my utmost for the man, and my success was absolute and complete. My client was innocent; I very dramatically secured the arrest of the real criminals, who had come forward as witnesses. In short, the court and the public were united in their admiration. I managed to save the examining magistrate's pride by pointing out the impossibility of detecting a plot so skillfully planned. Then I had to fight a case for my merchant, and won his suit. The Cathedral Chapter next chose me to defend a tremendous action against the town which had been going on for four years; I won that. Thus, after three trials, I had become the most famous advocate of Franche-Comté. But I bury my life in the deepest mystery, and so hide my aims. I have adopted habits which prevent my accepting any invitations. I am only to be consulted between six and eight in the morning; I go to bed after my dinner and work at night. The Vicar-General, a man of parts, and very influential, who placed the chapter's case in my hands after they had lost it in the lower court, of course professed their gratitude. 'Monsieur,' said I, 'I will win your suit, but I want no fee; I want more' (start of alarm on the Abbé's part). 'You must know that I am a great loser by putting myself forward in antagonism to the town. I came here only to leave the place as deputy. I mean to engage only in commercial cases, because commercial men return the members; they will distrust me if I defend *the priests*—for to them you are simply *the priests*. If I undertake your defence, it is because I was, in 1828, private secretary to such a minister' (again a start of surprise on the part of my Abbé), 'and Master of Appeals, under the name of Albert de Savarus' (another start). 'I have remained faithful to monarchical opinions, but, as you have not the majority of votes in Besançon, I must gain votes among the citizens. So the fee I ask of you is the votes you may be able secretly to secure for me at the opportune moment. Let us each keep our own counsel, and I will defend, for nothing, every case to which a priest of this diocese may be a party. Not a word about my previous life, and we will be true to each other.' When he came to thank me afterwards, he gave me a note for five hundred francs, and said in my ear, 'The votes are a bargain all the same.' I have in the course of five interviews made a friend, I think, of this Vicar-General. Now I am overwhelmed with business, and I undertake no cases but those brought me by merchants, saying that commercial questions are my specialty. This line of conduct attaches business men to me, and allows me to make friends with influential persons. So all goes well. Within a few months I shall have found a house to purchase in Besançon, so as to secure a qualification. I count on your lending me the necessary capital for this investment. If I should die, if I should fail, the loss would be too small to be any consideration between you and me. You will get the interest out of the rental, and I shall take good care to look out for something cheap so that you may lose nothing by this mortgage, which is indispensable.

Oh! my dear Léopold, no gambler with the last remains of his fortune in his pocket, bent on staking it at the Cercle des Étrangers for the last time one night, when he must come away rich or ruined, ever felt such a perpetual ringing in his ears, such a nervous moisture on his palms, such a fevered tumult in his brain, such inward qualms in his body as I go through every day now that I am playing my last card in the game ambition. Alas! My dear and only friend, for near ten years now have I been struggling. This battle with men and things, in which I have unceasingly poured out my strength and energy, and so constantly worn the springs of desire, has, so to speak, undermined my vitality. With all the appearance of a strong man of good health I feel myself a wreck. Every day carries with it a shred of my inmost life. At every fresh effort I feel that I should never be able to begin again. I have no power, no vigour left but for happiness, and if it should never come to crown my head with roses, the *me* that is really me would cease to exist, I should be a ruined thing. I should wish for nothing more in the world. I should want to cease from living. You know that power and fame, the vast moral empire that I crave, is but secondary; it is to me only a means to happiness, the pedestal for my idol.

To reach the goal and die, like the runner of antiquity! To see fortune and death stand on the threshold hand in hand! To win the beloved woman just when love is extinct! To lose the faculty of enjoyment after earning the right to be happy! Of how many men has this been the fate!

But there surely is a moment when Tantalus rebels, crosses his arms, and defies hell, throwing up his part of the eternal dupe. That is what I shall come to if anything should thwart my plan; if, after stooping to the dust of provincial life, prowling like a starving tiger round these tradesmen, these electors, to secure their votes; if, after wrangling in these squalid cases, and giving them my time—the time I might have spent on Lago Maggiore, seeing the waters she sees, basking in her gaze, hearing her voice—if, after all, I failed to scale the tribune and conquer the glory that should surround the name that is to succeed to that of Argaiolo! Nay, more than this, Léopold; there are days when I feel a heady languor; deep disgust surges up from the depths of my soul, especially when, abandoned to long daydreams, I have lost myself in anticipation of the joys of blissful love! May it not be that our desire has only a certain modicum of power, and that it perishes, perhaps, of a too lavish effusion of its essence? For, after all, at this present, my life is fair, illuminated by faith, work, and love. Farewell, my friend; I send love to your children, and beg you to remember me to your excellent wife.

Yours, ALBERT

Rosalie read this letter twice through, and its general purport was stamped on her heart. She suddenly saw the whole of Albert's previous existence, for her quick intelligence threw light on all the details, and enabled her to take it all in. By adding this information to the little novel published in the *Revue*, she now fully understood Albert. Of course, she exaggerated the greatness, remarkable as it was, of this lofty soul and potent will, and her love for Albert thenceforth became a passion, its violence enhanced by all the strength of her youth, the weariness of her solitude, and the unspent energy of her character. Love in a young girl is the effect of a natural law, but when her craving for affection is centred in an exceptional man, it is mingled with the enthusiasm which overflows in a youthful heart. Thus Mademoiselle de Watteville had in a few days reached a morbid and very dangerous stage of enamoured infatuation.

The Baronne was much pleased with her daughter, who, being under the spell of her absorbing thoughts, never resisted her will, seemed to be devoted to feminine occupations, and realised her mother's ideal of a docile daughter.

The lawyer was now engaged in court two or three times a week. Though he was overwhelmed with business, he found time to attend the trials, call on the litigious merchants, and conduct the *Revue*, all the while keeping up his personal mystery, from the conviction that the more covert and hidden was his influence, the more real it would be. But he neglected no means of success, reading up the list of the electors of Besançon and finding out their interests, their characters, their various friendships and antipathies. Did ever a cardinal hoping to be made Pope give himself more trouble?

One evening Mariette, on coming to dress Rosalie for an evening party, handed to her, not without many groans over this treachery, a letter of which the address made Mademoiselle de Watteville shiver and redden and turn pale again as she read the address:—

TO MADAME LA DUCHESSE D'ARGAIOLO
(*née Princess Soderini*),
At Belgirate,
Lago Maggiore, Italy

In her eyes this direction blazed as the words *Mene, Tekel, Upharsin*, did in the eyes of Belshazzar.* After concealing the letter, Rosalie went downstairs to accompany her mother to Madame de Chavoncourt's, and as long as the endless evening lasted, she was tormented by remorse and scruples. She had already felt shame at having violated the secrecy of Albert's letter to Léopold; she had several times asked herself whether, if he knew of her crime, infamous inasmuch as it necessarily goes unpunished, the high-minded Albert could esteem her. Her conscience answered an uncompromising "No!" She had expiated her sin by self-imposed penances; she fasted, she mortified herself by remaining on her knees, her arms outstretched for hours, and repeating prayers all the time. She had compelled Mariette to similar acts of repentance; her passion was mingled with genuine asceticism, and was all the more dangerous.

"Shall I read that letter, shall I not?" she asked herself, while listening to the Chavoncourt girls. One was sixteen, the other seventeen and a half. Rosalie looked upon her two friends as mere children because they were not secretly in love.

"If I read it," she finally decided, after hesitating for an hour between yes and no, "it shall, at any rate, be the last. Since I have gone so far as to see what he wrote to his friend, why should I not know what he says to *her?* If it is a horrible crime, is it not a proof of love? Oh, Albert! am I not your wife?"

When Rosalie was in bed she opened the letter, dated from day to day, so as to give the Duchesse a faithful picture of Albert's life and feelings.

25th

My dear soul, all is well. To my other conquests I have just added an invaluable one: I have done a service to one of the most influential men who work the elections. Like the critics, who make other men's reputations but can never make their own, he makes deputies though he never can become one. The worthy man wanted to show his gratitude without loosening his purse strings by saying to me, 'Would you care to sit in the chamber? I can get you returned as deputy.' 'If I ever made up my mind to enter on a political career,' replied I hypocritically, 'it would be to devote myself to the Comté, which I love, and where I am appreciated.' 'Well,' he said, 'we will persuade you, and through you we shall have weight in the chamber, for you will distinguish yourself there.'

And so, my beloved angel, say what you will, my perseverance will be rewarded. Ere long I shall, from the high place of the French Tribune, come before my country, before Europe. My name will be flung to you by the hundred voices of the French press!

Yes, as you tell me, I was old when I came to Besançon, and Besançon has aged me more; but, like Sixtus V, I shall be young again the day after my election. I shall enter on my true life, my own sphere. Shall we not then stand in the same line? Comte Savaron de Savarus, an ambassador to I know not where, may surely marry a Princess Soderini, the widow of the Duc d'Argaiolo! Triumph restores the youth of men who have been preserved by incessant struggles. Oh, my life! With what gladness did I fly from my library to my private room, to tell your portrait of this progress before writing to you! Yes, the votes I can command, those of the Vicar-General, of the persons I can oblige, and of this client, make my election already sure.

26th

We have entered on the twelfth year since that blest evening when, by a look, the beautiful Duchesse sealed the promises made by the exile Francesca. You, dear, are thirty-two, I am thirty-five; the dear Duc is seventy-seven—that is to say, ten years more than yours and mine put together, and he still keeps well! My patience is almost as great as my love, and indeed I need a few years yet to rise to the level of your name. As you see, I am in good spirits today, I can laugh; that is the effect of hope. Sadness or gladness, it all comes to me through you. The hope of success always carries me back to the day following that on which I saw you for the first time, when my life became one with yours as the earth turns to the light. *Qual pianto** are these eleven years, for this is the 26th of December, the anniversary of my arrival at your villa on the Lake of Geneva. For eleven years have I been crying to you, while you shine like a star set too high for man to reach it!

27th

No, dearest, do not go to Milan; stay at Belgirate. Milan terrifies me. I do not like that odious Milanese fashion of chatting at the Scala* every evening with a dozen persons, among whom it is hard if no one says something sweet. To me solitude is like the lump of amber in whose heart an insect lives forever in unchanging beauty. Thus the heart and soul of a woman remain pure and unaltered in the form of their first youth. Is it the *Tedeschi* that you regret?*

28th

Is your statue never to be finished? I should wish to have you in marble, in painting, in miniature, in every possible form, to beguile my impatience. I still am waiting for the view of Belgirate from the south, and that of the balcony; these are all that I now lack. I am so extremely busy that today I can only write you nothing—but that nothing is everything. Was it not of nothing that God made the world? That nothing is a word, God's word: *I love you!*

30th

Ah! I have received your journal. Thank you for your punctuality! So you found great pleasure in seeing all the details of our first acquaintance thus set down? Alas! Even while disguising them I was sorely afraid of offending you. We had no stories, and a review without stories is a beauty without hair. Not being *inventive* by nature, and in sheer despair, I took the only poetry in my soul, the only adventure in my memory, and pitched it in the key in which it would bear telling, nor did I ever cease to think of you while writing the only literary production that will ever come from my heart, I cannot say from my pen. Did not the transformation of your fierce Sormano into Gina make you laugh?

You ask after my health. Well, it is better than in Paris. Though I work enormously, the peacefulness of the surroundings has its effect on the mind. What really tries and ages me, dear angel, is the anguish of mortified vanity, the perpetual friction of Paris life, the struggle of rival ambitions. This peace is a balm. If you could imagine the pleasure your letter gives me!—the long, kind letter in which you tell me the most trivial incidents of your life. No! You women can never know to what a degree a true lover is interested in these trifles. It was an immense pleasure to see the pattern of your new dress. Can it be a matter of indifference to me to know what you wear? If your lofty brow is knit? If our writers amuse you? If Canalis's songs delight you? I read the books you read. Even to your boating on the lake every incident touched me. Your letter is as lovely, as sweet as your soul! Oh! flower of heaven, perpetually adored, could I have lived without those dear letters, which for eleven years have upheld me in my difficult path like a light, like a perfume, like a steady chant, like some divine nourishment, like everything which can soothe and comfort life? Do not fail me! If you knew what anxiety I suffer the day before they are due, or the pain a day's delay can give me! Is she ill? Is *he?* I am midway between hell and paradise. *O mia cara diva,** keep up your music, exercise your voice, practise. I am enchanted with the coincidence of employments and hours by which, though separated by the Alps, we live by precisely the same rule. The thought charms me and gives me courage. The first time I undertook to plead here—I forgot to tell you this—I fancied that you were listening to me, and I suddenly felt the flash of inspiration which lifts the poet above mankind. If I am returned to the chamber—oh! You must come to Paris to be present at my first appearance there!

30th, evening

Good heavens, how I love you! Alas! I have intrusted too much to my love and my hopes. An accident which should sink that overloaded bark would end my life! For three years now I have not seen you, and at the thought of going to Belgirate my heart beats so wildly that I am forced to stop. To see you, to hear that girlish caressing voice! To embrace in my gaze that ivory skin, glistening under the candlelight, and through which I can read your noble mind! To admire your fingers playing on the keys, to drink in your whole soul in a look, in the tone of an *Oimè* or an *Alberto!* To walk by the blossoming orange trees, to live a few months in the bosom of that glorious scenery! That is life. What folly it is to run after power, a name, fortune! But at Belgirate there is everything; there is poetry, there is glory! I ought to have made myself your steward, or, as that dear tyrant whom we cannot hate proposed to me, live there as *cavaliere servente,*[*] only our passion was too fierce to allow of it. Farewell, my angel, forgive me my next fit of sadness in consideration of this cheerful mood; it has come as a beam of light from the torch of Hope, which has hitherto seemed to me a will-o'-the-wisp.

"How he loves her!" cried Rosalie, dropping the letter, which seemed heavy in her hand. "After eleven years, to write like this!"

"Mariette," said Mademoiselle de Watteville to her maid next morning, "go and post this letter. Tell Jérôme that I know all I wished to know, and that he is to serve Monsieur Albert faithfully. We will confess our sins, you and I, without saying to whom the letters belonged, nor to whom they were going. I was in the wrong; I alone am guilty."

"Mademoiselle has been crying?" said Mariette.

"Yes, but I do not want that my mother should perceive it; give me some very cold water."

In the midst of the storms of her passion Rosalie often listened to the voice of conscience. Touched by the beautiful fidelity of these two hearts, she had just said her prayers, telling herself that there was nothing left to her but to be resigned, and to respect the happiness of two beings worthy of each other, submissive to fate, looking to God for everything, without allowing themselves any criminal acts or wishes. She felt a better woman, and had a certain sense of satisfaction after coming to this resolution, inspired by the natural rectitude of youth. And she was confirmed in it by a girl's idea: she was sacrificing herself for *him!*

"She does not know how to love," thought she. "Ah! If it were I—I would give up everything to a man who loved me so. To be loved! When, by whom shall I be loved? That little Monsieur de Soulas only loves my money; if I were poor, he would not even look at me."

"Rosalie, my child, what are you thinking about? You are working beyond the outline," said the Baronne to her daughter, who was making worsted work slippers for the Baron.

Rosalie spent the winter of 1834-35 torn by secret tumults, but in the spring, in the month of April, when she reached the age of nineteen, she sometimes thought that it would be a fine thing to triumph over a Duchesse d'Argaiolo. In silence and solitude the prospect of this struggle had fanned her passion and her evil thoughts. She encouraged her romantic daring by making plan after plan. Although such characters are an exception, there are, unfortunately, too many Rosalies in the world, and this story contains a moral which ought to serve them as a warning. In the course of this winter, Albert de Savarus had quietly made considerable progress in Besançon. Confident of success, he now impatiently awaited the dissolution of the chamber. Among the men of the moderate party he had won the suffrages of one of the makers of Besançon, a rich contractor, who had very wide influence.

Wherever they settled, the Romans took immense pains and spent enormous sums to have an unlimited supply of good water in every town of their empire. At Besançon they drank the water from Arcier, a hill at some considerable distance from Besançon. The town stands in a horseshoe circumscribed by the river Doubs. Thus, to restore an aqueduct in order to drink the same water that the Romans drank, in a town watered by the Doubs, is one of those absurdities which only succeed in a country place where the most exemplary gravity prevails. If this whim could be brought home to the hearts of the citizens, it would lead to considerable outlay, and this expenditure would benefit the influential contractor. Albert Savaron de Savarus opined that the water of the river was good for nothing but to flow under a suspension bridge, and that the only drinkable water was that from Arcier. Articles were printed in the *Revue* which merely expressed the views of the commercial interest of Besançon. The nobility and the citizens, the moderates and the legitimists, the government party and the opposition, everybody, in short, was agreed that they must drink the same water as the Romans, and boast of a suspension bridge. The question of the Arcier water was the order of the day at Besançon. At Besançon—as in the matter of the two railways to Versailles*—as for every standing abuse—there were private interests unconfessed which gave vital force to this idea. The reasonable folk in opposition to this scheme, who were indeed but few, were regarded as *fools*. No one talked of anything but of Savaron's two projects. And thus, after eighteen months of underground labour, the ambitious lawyer had succeeded in stirring to its depths the most stagnant town in France, the most unyielding to foreign influence, in finding the length of its foot, to use a vulgar phrase, and exerting a preponderant influence without stirring from his own room. He had solved the singular problem of how to be powerful without being popular. In the course of this winter he won seven lawsuits for various priests of Besançon. At moments he could breathe freely at the thought of his coming triumph. This intense desire, which made him work so many interests and devise so many springs, absorbed the last strength of his terribly overstrung soul. His disinterestedness was lauded, and he took his clients' fees without comment. But this disinterestedness was, in truth, moral usury; he counted on a reward far greater to him than all the gold in the world. In the month of October 1834 he had bought, ostensibly to serve a merchant who was in difficulties, with money lent him by Léopold Hannequin, a house which gave him a qualification for election. He had not seemed to seek or desire this advantageous bargain.

"You are really a remarkable man," said the Abbé de Grancey, who, of course, had watched and understood the lawyer. The Vicar-General had come to introduce to him a canon who needed his professional advice. "You are a priest who has taken the wrong turning." This observation struck Savarus.

Rosalie, on her part, had made up her mind, in her strong girl's head, to get Monsieur de Savarus into the drawing room and acquainted with the society of the Hôtel de Rupt. So far she had limited her desires to seeing and hearing Albert. She had compounded, so to speak, and a composition is often no more than a truce.

Les Rouxey, the inherited estate of the Wattevilles, was worth just ten thousand francs a year, but in other hands it would have yielded a great deal more. The Baron in his indifference—for his wife was to have, and in fact had, forty thousand francs a year—left the management of Les Rouxey to a sort of factotum, an old servant of the

Wattevilles named Modinier. Nevertheless, whenever the Baron and his wife wished to go out of the town, they went to Les Rouxey, which is very picturesquely situated. The château and the park were, in fact, created by the famous Watteville, who in his active old age was passionately attached to this magnificent spot.

Between two precipitous hills—little peaks with bare summits known as the great and the little Rouxey—in the heart of a ravine where the torrents from the heights, with the Dent de Vilard* at their head, come tumbling to join the lovely upper waters of the Doubs, Watteville had a huge dam constructed, leaving two cuttings for the overflow. Above this dam he made a beautiful lake, and below it two cascades, and these, uniting a few yards below the falls, formed a lovely little river to irrigate the barren, uncultivated valley, hitherto devastated by the torrent. This lake, this valley, and these two hills he enclosed in a ring fence, and built himself a retreat on the dam, which he widened to two acres by accumulating above it all the soil which had to be removed to make a channel for the river and the irrigation canals. When the Baron de Watteville thus obtained the lake above his dam he was owner of the two hills, but not of the upper valley thus flooded, through which there had been at all times a right of way to where it ends in a horseshoe under the Dent de Vilard. But this ferocious old man was so widely dreaded, that so long as he lived no claim was urged by the inhabitants of Riceys, the little village on the further side of the Dent de Vilard. When the Baron died, he left the slopes of the two Rouxey hills joined by a strong wall, to protect from inundation the two lateral valleys opening into the valley of Rouxey, to the right and left at the foot of the Dent de Vilard. Thus he died the master of the Dent de Vilard. His heirs asserted their protectorate of the village of Riceys, and so maintained the usurpation. The old assassin, the old renegade, the old Abbé Watteville, ended his career by planting trees and making a fine road over the shoulder of one of the Rouxey hills to join the highroad. The estate belonging to this park and house was extensive, but badly cultivated; there were chalets on both hills and neglected forests of timber. It was all wild and deserted, left to the care of nature, abandoned to chance growths, but full of sublime and unexpected beauty. You may now imagine Les Rouxey.

It is unnecessary to complicate this story by relating all the prodigious trouble and the inventiveness stamped with genius, by which Rosalie achieved her end without allowing it to be suspected. It is enough to say that it was in obedience to her mother that she left Besançon in the month of May 1835, in an antique travelling carriage drawn by a pair of sturdy hired horses, and accompanied her father to Les Rouxey.

To a young girl love lurks in everything. When she rose, the morning after her arrival, Mademoiselle de Watteville saw from her bedroom window the fine expanse of water, from which the light mists rose like smoke, and were caught in the firs and larches, rolling up and along the hills till they reached the heights, and she gave a cry of admiration.

"*They* loved by the lakes! *She* lives by a lake! A lake is certainly full of love!" she thought.

A lake fed by snows has opalescent colours and a translucency that make it one huge diamond, but when it is shut in like that of Les Rouxey, between two granite masses covered with pines, when silence broods over it like that of the savannas or the steppes, then everyone must exclaim as Rosalie did.

"We owe that," said her father, "to the notorious Watteville."

"On my word," said the girl, "he did his best to earn forgiveness. Let us go in a boat to the further end; it will give us an appetite for breakfast."

The Baron called two gardener lads who knew how

to row, and took with him his prime minister Modinier. The lake was about six acres in breadth, in some places ten or twelve, and four hundred in length. Rosalie soon found herself at the upper end shut in by the Dent de Vilard, the Jungfrau of that little Switzerland.

"Here we are, Monsieur le Baron," said Modinier, signing to the gardeners to tie up the boat; "will you come and look?"

Les deux jardiniers.

Plate XVI

"Look at what?" asked Rosalie.

"Oh, nothing!" exclaimed the Baron. "But you are a sensible girl; we have some little secrets between us, and I may tell you what ruffles my mind. Some difficulties have arisen since 1830 between the commune of Riceys and me, on account of this very Dent de Vilard, and I want to settle the matter without your mother's knowing anything about it, for she is stubborn; she is capable of flinging fire and flames, particularly if she should hear that the Mayor of Riceys, a Republican, got up this action as a sop to his people."

Rosalie had presence of mind enough to disguise her delight, so as to work more effectually on her father.

"What action?" said she.

"Mademoiselle, the people of Riceys," said Modinier, "have long enjoyed the right of grazing and cutting fodder on their side of the Dent de Vilard. Now Monsieur Chantonnit, the mayor since 1830, declares that the whole Dent belongs to his commune, and maintains that a hundred years ago, or more, there was a way through our grounds. You understand that in that case we should no longer have them to ourselves. Then this barbarian would end by saying, what the old men in the village say, that the ground occupied by the lake was appropriated by the Abbé de Watteville. That would be the end of Les Rouxey—what next?"

"Indeed, my child, between ourselves, it is the truth," said Monsieur de Watteville simply. "The land is an usurpation, with no title deed but lapse of time. And, therefore, to avoid all worry, I should wish to come to a friendly understanding as to my border line on this side of the Dent de Vilard, and I will then raise a wall."

"If you give way to the municipality, it will swallow you up. You ought to have threatened Riceys."

"That is just what I told the master last evening," said Modinier. "But in confirmation of that view I proposed that he should come to see whether, on this side of the

Dent or on the other, there may not be, high or low, some traces of an enclosure."

For a century the Dent de Vilard had been used by both parties without coming to extremities; it stood as a sort of party wall between the communes of Riceys and Les Rouxey, yielding little profit. Indeed, the object in dispute, being covered with snow for six months in the year, was of a nature to cool their ardour. Thus it required all the hot blast by which the revolution of 1830 inflamed the advocates of the people to stir up this matter, by which Monsieur Chantonnit, the Mayor of Riceys, hoped to give a dramatic turn to his career on the peaceful frontier of Switzerland, and to immortalise his term of office. Chantonnit, as his name shows, was a native of Neufchâtel.

"My dear Father," said Rosalie, as they got into the boat again, "I agree with Modinier. If you wish to secure the joint possession of the Dent de Vilard, you must act with decision, and get a legal opinion which will protect you against this enterprising Chantonnit. Why should you be afraid? Get the famous lawyer Savaron—engage him at once, lest Chantonnit should place the interests of the commune in his hands. The man who won the case for the chapter against the town can certainly win that of Watteville versus Riceys! Besides," she added, "Les Rouxey will some day be mine (not for a long time yet, I trust). Well, then, do not leave me with a lawsuit on my hands. I like this place; I shall often live here, and add to it as much as possible. On those banks," and she pointed to the feet of the two hills, "I shall cut flowerbeds and make the loveliest English gardens. Let us go to Besançon and bring back with us the Abbé de Grancey, Monsieur Savaron, and my mother, if she cares to come. You can then make up your mind; but in your place I should have done so already. Your name is Watteville, and you are afraid of a fight! If you should lose your case—well, I will never reproach you by a word!"

"Oh, if that is the way you take it," said the Baron, "I am quite ready; I will see the lawyer."

"Besides, a lawsuit is really great fun. It brings some interest into life, with coming and going and raging over it. You will have a great deal to do before you can get hold of the judges. We did not see the Abbé de Grancey for three weeks, he was so busy!"

"But the very existence of the chapter was involved," said Monsieur de Watteville; "and then the Archbishop's pride, his conscience, everything that makes up the life of the priesthood, was at stake. That Savaron does not know what he did for the chapter! He saved it!"

"Listen to me," said his daughter in his ear, "if you secure Monsieur de Savaron, you will gain your suit, won't you? Well, then, let me advise you. You cannot get at Monsieur Savaron excepting through Monsieur de Grancey. Take my word for it, and let us together talk to the dear Abbé without my mother's presence at the interview, for I know a way of persuading him to bring the lawyer to us."

"It will be very difficult to avoid mentioning it to your mother!"

"The Abbé de Grancey will settle that afterwards. But just make up your mind to promise your vote to Monsieur Savaron at the next election, and you will see!"

"Go to the election! Take the oath?" cried the Baron de Watteville.

"What then!" said she.

"And what will your mother say?"

"She may even desire you to do it," replied Rosalie, knowing as she did from Albert's letter to Léopold how deeply the Vicar-General had pledged himself.

Four days after, the Abbé de Grancey called very early one morning on Albert de Savarus, having announced his visit the day before. The old priest had come to win over the great lawyer to the house of the Wattevilles, a proceeding which shows how much tact and subtlety Rosalie must have employed in an underhand way.

"What can I do for you, Monsieur le Vicar-General?" asked Savarus.

The Abbé, who told his story with admirable frankness, was coldly heard by Albert.

"Monsieur l'Abbé," said he, "it is out of the question that I should defend the interests of the Wattevilles, and you shall understand why. My part in this town is to remain perfectly neutral. I will display no colours; I must remain a mystery till the eve of my election. Now, to plead for the Wattevilles would mean nothing in Paris, but here! Here, where everything is discussed, I should be supposed by everyone to be an ally of your Faubourg Saint-Germain."*

"What! Do you suppose that you can remain unknown on the day of the election, when the candidates must oppose each other? It must then become known that your name is Savaron de Savarus, that you have held the appointment of Master of Appeals, that you are a man of the Restoration!"

"On the day of the election," said Savarus, "I will be all I am expected to be, and I intend to speak at the preliminary meetings."

"If you have the support of Monsieur de Watteville and his party, you will get a hundred votes in a mass, and far more to be trusted than those on which you rely. It is always possible to produce division of interests; convictions are inseparable."

"The deuce is in it!" said Savarus. "I am attached to you, and I could do a great deal for you, Father! perhaps we may compound with the Devil. Whatever Monsieur de Watteville's business may be, by engaging Girardet, and prompting him, it will be possible to drag the proceedings out till the elections are over. I will not undertake to plead till the day after I am returned."

"Do this one thing," said the Abbé. "Come to the Hôtel de Rupt—there is a young person of nineteen there who, one of these days, will have a hundred thousand francs a year, and you can seem to be paying your court to her——"

"Ah! The young lady I sometimes see in the kiosk?"

"Yes, Mademoiselle Rosalie," replied the Abbé de Grancey. "You are ambitious. If she takes a fancy to you, you may be everything an ambitious man can wish— who knows? A minister perhaps. A man can always be a minister who adds a hundred thousand francs a year to your amazing talents."

"Monsieur l'Abbé, if Mademoiselle de Watteville had three times her fortune, and adored me into the bargain, it would be impossible that I should marry her——"

"You are married?" exclaimed the Abbé.

"Not in church nor before the mayor, but morally speaking," said Savarus.

"That is even worse when a man cares about it as you seem to care," replied the Abbé. "Everything that is not done, can be undone. Do not stake your fortune and your prospects on a woman's liking, any more than a wise man counts on a dead man's shoes before starting on his way."

"Let us say no more about Mademoiselle de Watteville," said Albert gravely, "and agree as to the facts. At your desire—for I have a regard and respect for you—I will appear for Monsieur de Watteville, but after the elections. Until then Girardet must conduct the case under my instructions. That is the utmost I can do."

"But there are questions involved which can only be settled after inspection of the localities," said the Vicar-General.

"Girardet can go," said Savarus. "I cannot allow myself, in the face of a town I know so well, to take any step which might compromise the supreme interests that lie beyond my election."

The Abbé left Savarus after giving him a keen look, in which he seemed to be laughing at the young athlete's uncompromising politics, while admiring his firmness.

"Ah! I would have dragged my father into a lawsuit—I would have done anything to get him here!" cried Rosalie to herself, standing in the kiosk and looking at the lawyer in his room, the day after Albert's interview with the Abbé, who had reported the result to her father. "I would have committed any mortal sin, and you will not enter the Wattevilles' drawing room; I may not hear your fine voice! You make conditions when your help is required by the Wattevilles and the Rupts! Well, God knows, I meant to be content with these small joys; with seeing you, hearing you speak, going with you to Les Rouxey, that your presence might to me make the place sacred. That was all I asked. But now—now I mean to be your wife. Yes, yes; look at *her* portrait, at *her* drawing room, *her* bedroom, at the four sides of *her* villa, the points of view from *her* gardens. You expect *her* statue? I will make *her* marble herself towards you! After all, the woman does not love. Art, science, books, singing, music, have absorbed half her senses and her intelligence. She is old, too; she is past thirty; my Albert will not be happy!"

"What is the matter that you stay here, Rosalie?" asked her mother, interrupting her reflections. "Monsieur de Soulas is in the drawing room, and he observed your attitude, which certainly betrays more thoughtfulness than is due at your age."

"Then, is Monsieur de Soulas a foe to thought?" asked Rosalie.

"Then you were thinking?" said Madame de Watteville.

"Why, yes, Mama."

"Why, no! You were not thinking. You were staring at that lawyer's window with an attention that is neither becoming nor decent, and which Monsieur de Soulas, of all men, ought never to have observed."

"Why?" said Rosalie.

"It is time," said the Baronne, "that you should know what our intentions are. Amédée likes you, and you will not be unhappy as Comtesse de Soulas."

Rosalie, as white as a lily, made no reply, so completely was she stupefied by contending feelings. And yet, in the presence of the man she had this instant begun to hate vehemently, she forced the kind of smile which a ballet dancer puts on for the public. Nay, she could even laugh; she had the strength to conceal her rage, which presently subsided, for she was determined to make use of this fat simpleton to further her designs.

"Monsieur Amédée," said she, at a moment when her mother was walking ahead of them in the garden, affecting to leave the young people together, "were you not aware that Monsieur Albert Savaron de Savarus is a legitimist?"

"A legitimist?"

"Until 1830 he was Master of Appeals to the Council of State, attached to the presidency of the Council of Ministers, and in favour with the Dauphin and Dauphine.* It would be very good of you to say nothing against him, but it would be better still if you would attend the election this year, carry the day, and hinder that poor Monsieur de Chavoncourt from representing the town of Besançon."

"What sudden interest have you in this Savaron?"

"Monsieur Albert Savaron de Savarus, the natural son of the Comte de Savarus (pray keep the secret of my indiscretion), if he is returned deputy, will be our advocate in the suit about Les Rouxey. Les Rouxey, my father tells me, will be my property; I intend to live there, it is a lovely place! I should be brokenhearted at seeing that fine piece of the great de Watteville's work destroyed."

"The devil!" thought Amédée, as he left the house. "The heiress is not such a fool as her mother thinks her."

Monsieur de Chavoncourt is a Royalist, of the famous 221.* Hence, from the day after the Revolution of July, he always preached the salutary doctrine of taking the oaths and resisting the present order of things, after the pattern of the Tories against the Whigs in England. This doctrine was not acceptable to the legitimists, who, in their defeat, had the wit to divide in their opinions, and to trust to the force of inertia and to Providence. Monsieur de Chavoncourt was not wholly trusted by his own party, but seemed to the Moderates the best man to choose; they preferred the triumph of his half-hearted opinions to the acclamation of a Republican who should combine the votes of the enthusiasts and the patriots. Monsieur de Chavoncourt, highly respected in Besançon, was the representative of an old parliamentary family; his fortune, of about fifteen thousand francs a year, was not an offence to anybody, especially as he had a son and three daughters. With such a family, fifteen thousand francs a year are a mere nothing. Now when, under these circumstances, the father of the family is above bribery, it would be hard if the electors did not esteem him. Electors wax enthusiastic over a *beau ideal* of parliamentary virtue, just as the audience in the pit do at the representation of the generous sentiments they so little practise. Madame de Chavoncourt, at this time a woman of forty, was one of the beauties of Besançon. While the chamber was sitting, she lived meagrely in one of their country places to recoup herself by economy for Monsieur de Chavoncourt's expenses in Paris. In the winter she received very creditably once a week, on Tuesdays, understanding her business as mistress of the house. Young Chavoncourt, a youth of twenty-two, and another young gentleman, named Monsieur de Vauchelles, no richer than Amédée and his school friend, were his intimate allies. They made excursions together to Granvelle,* and sometimes went out shooting; they were so well known to be inseparable that they were invited to the country together. Rosalie, who was intimate with the Chavoncourt girls, knew that the three young men had no secrets from each other. She reflected that if Monsieur de Soulas should repeat her words, it would be to his two companions. Now, Monsieur de Vauchelles had his matrimonial plans, as Amédée had his; he wished to marry Victoire, the eldest of the Chavoncourts, on whom an old aunt was to settle an estate worth seven thousand francs a year, and a hundred thousand francs in hard cash, when the contract should be signed. Victoire was this aunt's goddaughter and favourite niece. Consequently, young Chavoncourt and his friend Vauchelles would be sure to warn Monsieur de Chavoncourt of the danger he was in from Albert's candidature. But this did not satisfy Rosalie. She sent the prefect of the département a letter written with her left hand, signed *"A friend to Louis-Philippe,"* in which she informed him of the secret intentions of Monsieur Albert de Savarus, pointing out the serious support a Royalist orator might give to Berryer, and revealing to him the deeply artful course pursued by the lawyer during his two years' residence at Besançon. The prefect was a capable man, a personal enemy of the Royalist party, devoted by conviction to the Government of July—in short, one of those men of whom, in the Rue de Grenelle,* the Minister of the Interior could say, "We have a capital prefect at Besançon." The prefect read the letter, and, in obedience to its instructions, he burnt it.

Rosalie aimed at preventing Albert's election, so as to keep him five years longer at Besançon.

At that time an election was a fight between parties, and in order to win, the ministry chose its ground by choosing the moment when it would give battle. The elections were therefore not to take place for three months yet. When a man's whole life depends on an election, the period that elapses between the issuing of the writs for convening the electoral bodies and the day fixed for their meetings is an interval during which ordinary vitality is suspended. Rosalie fully understood how much latitude Albert's absorbed state would leave her during these three months. By promising Mariette—as she afterwards confessed—to take both her and Jérôme into her service, she induced the maid to bring her all the letters Albert might send to Italy, and those addressed to him from that country. And all the time she was pondering these machinations, the extraordinary girl was working slippers for her father with the most innocent air in the world. She even made a greater display than ever of candour and simplicity, quite understanding how valuable that candour and innocence would be to her ends.

"My daughter grows quite charming!" said Madame de Watteville. Two months before the election a meeting was held at the house of Monsieur Boucher senior, composed of the contractor who expected to get the work for the aqueduct for the Arcier waters; of Monsieur Boucher's father-in-law; of Monsieur Granet, the influential man to whom Savarus had done a service, and who was to nominate him as a candidate; of Girardet the lawyer; of the printer of the *Revue de l'Est*; and of the President of the Tribunal of Commerce. In fact, the assembly consisted of twenty-seven persons in all, men who in the provinces are regarded as *bigwigs*. Each man represented on an average six votes, but in estimating their value they said ten, for men always begin by exaggerating their own influence. Among these twenty-seven was one who was wholly devoted to the prefect, one false brother who secretly looked for some favour from the minister, either for himself or for someone belonging to him. At this preliminary meeting, it was agreed that Savaron the lawyer should be named as candidate, a motion received with such enthusiasm as no one looked for from Besançon. Albert, waiting at home for Alfred Boucher to fetch him, was chatting with the Abbé de Grancey, who was interested in this absorbing ambition. Albert had appreciated the priest's vast political capacities, and the priest, touched by the young man's entreaties, had been willing to become his guide and adviser in this culminating struggle. The chapter did not love Monsieur de Chavoncourt, for it was his wife's brother-in-law, as President of the Tribunal, who had lost the famous suit for them in the lower court.

"You are betrayed, my dear fellow," said the shrewd and worthy Abbé, in that gentle, calm voice which old priests acquire.

"Betrayed!" cried the lover, struck to the heart.

"By whom I know not at all," the priest replied. "But at the prefecture your plans are known, and your hand read like a book. At this moment I have no advice to give you. Such affairs need consideration. As for this evening, take the bull by the horns, anticipate the blow. Tell them all your previous life, and thus you will mitigate the effect of the discovery on the good folks of Besançon."

"Oh, I was prepared for it," said Albert in a broken voice.

"You would not benefit by my advice; you had the opportunity of making an impression at the Hôtel de Rupt; you do not know the advantage you would have gained——"

"What?"

"The unanimous support of the Royalists, an immediate readiness to go to the election—in short, above a hundred votes. Adding to these what, among ourselves, we call the *ecclesiastical vote*, though you were not yet nominated, you were master of the votes by ballot. Under such circumstances, a man may temporise, may make his way——"

Alfred Boucher when he came in, full of enthusiasm, to announce the decision of the preliminary meeting, found the Vicar-General and the lawyer cold, calm, and grave.

"Adieu, Monsieur l'Abbé," said Albert. "We will talk of your business at greater length when the elections are over."

And he took Alfred's arm, after pressing Monsieur de Grancey's hand with meaning. The priest looked at the ambitious man, whose face at that moment wore the lofty expression which a general may have when he hears the first gun fired for a battle. He raised his eyes to heaven, and left the room, saying to himself, "What a priest he would make!"

Eloquence is not at the bar. The pleader rarely puts forth the real powers of his soul; if he did, he would die of it in a few years. Eloquence is, nowadays, rarely in the pulpit, but it is found on certain occasions in the Chamber of Deputies, when an ambitious man stakes all to win all, or, stung by myriad darts, at a given moment bursts into speech. But it is still more certainly found in some privileged beings, at the inevitable hour when their claims must either triumph or be wrecked, and when they are forced to speak. Thus at this meeting, Albert Savarus, feeling the necessity of winning himself some supporters, displayed all the faculties of his soul and the resources of his intellect. He entered the room well, without awkwardness or arrogance, without weakness, without cowardice, quite gravely, and was not dismayed at finding himself among twenty or thirty men. The news of the meeting and of its determination had already brought a few docile sheep to follow the bell. Before listening to Monsieur Boucher, who was about to deluge him with a speech announcing the decision of the Boucher Committee, Albert begged for silence, and, as he shook hands with Monsieur Boucher, tried to warn him, by a sign, of an unexpected danger.

"My young friend, Alfred Boucher, has just announced to me the honour you have done me. But before that decision is irrevocable," said the lawyer, "I think that I ought to explain to you who and what your candidate is, so as to leave you free to take back your word if my declarations should disturb your conscience!" This exordium was followed by profound silence. Some of the men thought it showed a noble impulse.

Albert gave a sketch of his previous career, telling them his real name, his action under the Restoration, and revealing himself as a new man since his arrival at Besançon, while pledging himself for the future. This address held his hearers breathless, it was said. These men, all with different interests, were spellbound by the brilliant eloquence boiling out of the heart and soul of this ambitious spirit. Admiration silenced reflection. Only one thing was clear—the thing which Albert wished to get into their heads.

Was it not far better for the town to have one of those men who are born to govern society at large than a mere voting machine? A statesman carries power with him. A commonplace deputy, however incorruptible, is but a conscience. What a glory for Provence to have found a Mirabeau, to return the only statesman since 1830 that the Revolution of July had produced!*

Under the pressure of this eloquence, all the audience believed it great enough to become a splendid political instrument in the hands of their representative. They all saw Savarus the minister in Albert Savaron. And, reading the secret calculations of his constituents, the clever candidate gave them to understand that they would be the first to enjoy the right of profiting by his influence.

This confession of faith, this ambitious program, this retrospect of his life and character was, according to the only man present who was capable of judging Savarus (he has since become one of the leading men of Besançon), a masterpiece of skill and of feeling, of fervour, interest, and fascination. This whirlwind carried away the electors. Never had any man had such a triumph. But, unfortunately, speech, a weapon only for close warfare, has only an immediate effect. Reflection kills the Word when the word ceases to overpower Reflection. If the votes had then been taken, Albert's name would undoubtedly have come out of the ballot box. At the moment, he was conqueror. But he must conquer every day for two months. Albert went home quivering. The townsfolk had applauded him, and he had achieved the great point of silencing beforehand the malignant talk to which his early career might give rise. The commercial interest of Besançon had nominated the lawyer, Albert Savaron de Savarus, as its candidate. Alfred Boucher's enthusiasm, at first infectious, presently became blundering.

The prefect, alarmed by this success, set to work to count the ministerial votes, and contrived to have a secret interview with Monsieur de Chavoncourt, so as to effect a coalition in their common interests. Every day, without Albert's being able to discover how, the voters in the Boucher Committee diminished in number. Nothing could resist the slow grinding of the prefecture. Three or four clever men would say to Albert's clients, "Will the deputy defend you and win your lawsuits? Will he give you advice, draw up your contracts, arrange your compromises? He will be your slave for five years longer, if, instead of returning him to the chamber, you only hold out the hope of his going there five years hence." This calculation did Savarus all the more mischief, because the wives of some of the merchants had already made it. The parties interested in the matter of the bridge and that of the water from Arcier could not hold out against a talking-to from a clever ministerialist, who proved to them that their safety lay at the prefecture, and not in the hands of an ambitious man. Each day was a check for Savarus, though each day the battle was led by him and fought by his lieutenants—a battle of words, speeches, and proceedings. He dared not go to the Vicar-General, and the Vicar-General never showed himself. Albert rose and went to bed in a fever, his brain on fire.

At last the day dawned of the first struggle, practically the show of hands; the votes are counted, the candidates estimate their chances, and clever men can prophesy their failure or success. It is a decent hustings, without the mob, but formidable; agitation, though it is not allowed any physical display, as it is in England, is not the less profound. The English fight these battles with their fists, the French with hard words. Our neighbours have a scrimmage, the French try their fate by cold combinations calmly worked out. This particular political business is carried out in opposition to the character of the two nations. The radical party named their candidate; Monsieur de Chavoncourt came forward; then Albert appeared, and was accused by the Chavoncourt Committee and the radicals of being an uncompromising man of the Right, a second Berryer. The ministry had their candidate, a stalking-horse, useful only to receive the purely ministerial votes. The votes, thus divided, gave no result. The Republican candidate had twenty, the ministry got fifty, Albert had seventy, Monsieur de Chavoncourt obtained sixty-seven. But the prefecture's party had perfidiously made thirty of its most devoted adherents vote for Albert, so as to deceive the enemy. The votes for Monsieur de Chavoncourt, added to the eighty votes—the real number—at the disposal of the prefecture would carry the election, if only the prefect could succeed in gaining over a few of the radicals. A hundred and sixty votes were not recorded: those of Monsieur de Grancey's following and the legitimists. The show of hands at an election, like a dress rehearsal at a theatre, is the most deceptive thing in the world. Albert Savarus came home, putting a brave face on the matter, but half dead. He had had the wit, the genius, or the good luck to gain, within the last fortnight, two staunch supporters—Girardet's father-in-law and a very shrewd old merchant to whom Monsieur de Grancey had sent him. These two worthy men, his self-appointed spies, affected to be Albert's most ardent opponents in the hostile camp. Towards the end of the show of hands they informed Savarus, through the medium of

Monsieur Boucher, that thirty voters, unknown, were working against him in his party, playing the same trick that they were playing for his benefit on the other side. A criminal marching to execution could not suffer as Albert suffered as he went home from the hall where his fate was at stake. The despairing lover could endure no companionship. He walked through the streets alone, between eleven o'clock and midnight.

At one in the morning, Albert, to whom sleep had been unknown for the past three days, was sitting in his library in a deep armchair, his face as pale as if he were dying, his hands hanging limp in a forlorn attitude worthy of the Magdalene. Tears hung on his long lashes, tears that dim the eyes but do not fall; fierce thought drinks them up, the fire of the soul consumes them. Alone, he might weep. And then, under the kiosk, he saw a white figure, which reminded him of Francesca.

"And for three months I have had no letter from *her*! What has become of her? I have not written for two months, but I warned her. Is she ill? Oh my love! My life! Will you ever know what I have gone through? What a wretched constitution is mine! Have I an aneurism?" he asked himself, feeling his heart beat so violently that its pulses seemed audible in the silence like little grains of sand dropping on a big drum.

At this moment three distinct taps sounded on his door; Albert hastened to open it, and almost fainted with joy at seeing the Vicar-General's cheerful and triumphant mien. Without a word, he threw his arms round the Abbé de Grancey, held him fast, and clasped him closely, letting his head fall on the old man's shoulder. He was a child again; he cried as he had cried on hearing that Francesca Soderini was a married woman. He betrayed his weakness to no one but to this priest, on whose face shone the light of hope. The priest had been sublime, and as shrewd as he was sublime.

"Forgive me, dear Abbé, but you come at one of those moments when the man vanishes, for you are not to think me vulgarly ambitious."

"Oh! I know," replied the Abbé. "You wrote AMBITION FOR LOVE'S SAKE! Ah! my son, it was love in despair that made me a priest in 1786, at the age of twenty-two. In 1788 I was in charge of a parish. I know life. I have refused three bishoprics already; I mean to die at Besançon."

"Come and see *her!*" cried Savarus, seizing a candle, and leading the Abbé into the handsome room where hung the portrait of the Duchesse d'Argaiolo, which he lighted up.

"She is one of those women who are born to reign!" said the Vicar-General, understanding how great an affection Albert showed him by this mark of confidence. "But there is pride on that brow; it is implacable; she would never forgive an insult! It is the Archangel Michael, the angel of execution, the inexorable angel— 'All or nothing' is the motto of this type of angel. There is something divinely pitiless in that head."

"You have guessed well," cried Savarus. "But, my dear Abbé, for more than twelve years now she has reigned over my life, and I have not a thought for which to blame myself——"

"Ah! If you could only say the same of God!" said the priest with simplicity. "Now, to talk of your affairs. For ten days I have been at work for you. If you are a real politician, this time you will follow my advice. You would not be where you are now if you would have gone to the Wattevilles when I first told you. But you must go there tomorrow; I will take you in the evening. The Rouxey estates are in danger; the case must be defended within three days. The election will not be over in three days. They will take good care not to appoint examiners the first day. There will be several voting days, and you will be elected by ballot——"

"How can that be?" asked Savarus.

"By winning the Rouxey lawsuit you will gain eighty legitimist votes; add them to the thirty I can command, and you have a hundred and ten. Then, as twenty remain to you of the Boucher Committee, you will have a hundred and thirty in all."

"Well," said Albert, "we must get seventy-five more."

"Yes," said the priest, "since all the rest are ministerial. But, my son, you have two hundred votes, and the prefecture no more than a hundred and eighty."

"I have two hundred votes?" said Albert, standing stupid with amazement, after starting to his feet as if shot up by a spring.

"You have those of Monsieur de Chavoncourt," said the Abbé.

"How?" said Albert.

"You will marry Mademoiselle Sidonie de Chavoncourt."

"Never!"

"You will marry Mademoiselle Sidonie de Chavoncourt," the priest repeated coldly.

"But you see—she is inexorable," said Albert, pointing to Francesca.

"You will marry Mademoiselle Sidonie de Chavoncourt," said the Abbé calmly for the third time.

This time Albert understood. The Vicar-General would not be implicated in the scheme which at last smiled on the despairing politician. A word more would have compromised the priest's dignity and honour.

"Tomorrow evening at the Hôtel de Rupt you will meet Madame de Chavoncourt and her second daughter. You can thank her beforehand for what she is going to do for you, and tell her that your gratitude is unbounded, that you are hers body and soul, that henceforth your future is that of her family. You are quite disinterested, for you have so much confidence in yourself that you regard the nomination as deputy as a sufficient fortune. You will have a struggle with Madame de

Chavoncourt; she will want you to pledge your word. All your future life, my son, lies in that evening. But, understand clearly, I have nothing to do with it. I am answerable only for the legitimist voters; I have secured Madame de Watteville, and that means all the aristocracy of Besançon. Amédée de Soulas and Vauchelles, who will both vote for you, have won over the young men; Madame de Watteville will get the old ones. As to my electors, they are infallible."

"And who on earth has gained over Madame de Chavoncourt?" asked Savarus.

"Ask me no questions," replied the Abbé. "Monsieur de Chavoncourt, who has three daughters to marry, is not capable of increasing his wealth. Though Vauchelles marries the eldest without anything from her father, because her old aunt is to settle something on her, what is to become of the two others? Sidonie is sixteen, and your ambition is as good as a gold mine. Someone has told Madame de Chavoncourt that she will do better by getting her daughter married than by sending her husband to waste his money in Paris. That someone manages Madame de Chavoncourt, and Madame de Chavoncourt manages her husband."

"That is enough, my dear Abbé. I understand. When once I am returned as deputy, I have somebody's fortune to make, and by making it large enough I shall be released from my promise. In me you have a son, a man who will owe his happiness to you. *Mon Dieu!* What have I done to deserve so true a friend?"

"You won a triumph for the chapter," said the Vicar-General, smiling. "Now, as to all this, be as secret as the tomb. We are nothing, we have done nothing. If we were known to have meddled in election matters, we should be eaten up alive by the Puritans of the Left—who do worse—and blamed by some of our own party, who want everything. Madame de Chavoncourt has no suspicion of my share in all this. I have confided in no one but Madame de Watteville, whom we may trust as we trust ourselves."

"I will bring the Duchesse to you to be blessed!" cried Savarus.

After seeing out the old priest, Albert went to bed in the swaddling clothes of power.

Next evening, as may well be supposed, by nine o'clock Madame la Baronne de Watteville's rooms were crowded by the aristocracy of Besançon in an extraordinary convocation. They were discussing the *exceptional* step of going to the poll, to oblige the daughter of the de Rupts. It was known that the former Master of Appeals, the secretary of one of the most faithful ministers under the elder branch,* was to be presented that evening. Madame de Chavoncourt was there with her second daughter Sidonie, exquisitely dressed, while her elder sister, secure of her lover, had not indulged in any of the arts of the toilette. In country towns these little things are remarked. The Abbé de Grancey's fine and clever head was to be seen moving from group to group, listening to everything, seeming to be apart from it all, but uttering those incisive phrases which sum up a question and direct the issue.

"If the elder branch were to return," said he to an old statesman of seventy, "what politicians would they find?"—"Berryer, alone on his bench, does not know which way to turn; if he had sixty votes, he would often scotch the wheels of the government and upset ministries!"—"The Duc de Fitz-James is to be nominated at Toulouse."*—"You will enable Monsieur de Watteville to win his lawsuit."—"If you vote for Monsieur Savarus, the Republicans will vote with you rather than with the Moderates!" Etc., etc.

At nine o'clock Albert had not arrived. Madame de Watteville was disposed to regard such delay as an impertinence.

"My dear Baronne," said Madame de Chavoncourt, "do not let such serious issues turn on such a trifle. The varnish on his boots is not dry—or a consultation, perhaps, detains Monsieur de Savarus."

Rosalie shot a side glance at Madame de Chavoncourt.

"She is very lenient to Monsieur de Savarus," she whispered to her mother.

"You see," said the Baronne with a smile, "there is a question of a marriage between Sidonie and Monsieur de Savarus." Mademoiselle de Watteville hastily went to a window looking out over the garden. At ten o'clock Albert de Savarus had not yet appeared. The storm that threatened now burst. Some of the gentlemen sat down to cards, finding the thing intolerable. The Abbé de Grancey, who did not know what to think, went to the window where Rosalie was hidden, and exclaimed aloud in his amazement, "He must be dead!" The Vicar-General stepped out into the garden, followed by Monsieur de Watteville and his daughter, and they all three went up to the kiosk. In Albert's rooms all was dark; not a light was to be seen.

"Jérôme!" cried Rosalie, seeing the servant in the yard below. The Abbé looked at her with astonishment. "Where in the world is your master?" she asked the man, who came to the foot of the wall.

"Gone! in a post chaise, Mademoiselle."

"He is ruined!" exclaimed the Abbé de Grancey, "or he is happy!"

The joy of triumph was not so effectually concealed on Rosalie's face that the Vicar-General could not detect it. He affected to see nothing.

"What can this girl have had to do with this business?" he asked himself.

They all three returned to the drawing room, where Monsieur de Watteville announced the strange, the extraordinary, the prodigious news of the lawyer's departure, without any reason assigned for his evasion. By half-past eleven only fifteen persons remained, among them Madame de Chavoncourt and the Abbé de Godenars, another vicar-general, a man of about forty, who hoped for a bishopric, the two Chavoncourt girls, and Monsieur de Vauchelles, the Abbé de Grancey, Rosalie, Amédée de Soulas, and a retired magistrate, one of the most influential members of the upper circle of Besançon, who had been very eager for Albert's election. The Abbé de Grancey sat down by the Baronne in such a position as to watch Rosalie, whose face, usually pale, wore a feverish flush.

"What can have happened to Monsieur de Savarus?" said Madame de Chavoncourt.

At this moment a servant in livery brought in a letter for the Abbé de Grancey on a silver tray.

"Pray read it," said the Baronne.

The Vicar-General read the letter; he saw Rosalie suddenly turn as white as her kerchief.

"She recognises the writing," said he to himself, after glancing at the girl over his spectacles. He folded up the letter, and calmly put it in his pocket without a word. In three minutes he had met three looks from Rosalie which were enough to make him guess everything. "She is in love with Albert Savarus!" thought the Vicar-General. He rose and took leave. He was going towards the door when, in the next room, he was overtaken by Rosalie, who said—

"Monsieur de Grancey, it was from *Albert!*"

"How do you know that it was his writing, to recognise it from so far?"

The girl's reply, caught as she was in the toils of her impatience and rage, seemed to the Abbé sublime.

"Because I love him! What is the matter?" she said after a pause.

"He gives up the election."

Rosalie put her finger to her lip.

"I ask you to be as secret as if it were a confession," said she before returning to the drawing room. "If there is an end of the election, there is an end of the marriage with Sidonie."

In the morning, on her way to Mass, Mademoiselle de Watteville heard from Mariette some of the circumstances which had prompted Albert's disappearance at the most critical moment of his life.

"Mademoiselle, an old gentleman from Paris arrived yesterday morning at the Hôtel National; he came in his own carriage with four horses, and a courier in front, and a servant. Indeed, Jérôme, who saw the carriage returning, declares he could only be a prince or a *milord*."

"Was there a coronet on the carriage?" asked Rosalie.

"I do not know," said Mariette. "Just as two was striking he came to call on Monsieur Savarus and sent in his card, and when he saw it, Jérôme says Monsieur turned as pale as a sheet, and said he was to be shown in. As he himself locked the door, it is impossible to tell what the old gentleman and the lawyer said to each other, but they were together above an hour, and then the old gentleman, with the lawyer, called up his servant. Jérôme saw the servant go out again with an immense package, four feet long, which looked like a great painting on canvas. The old gentleman had in his hand a large parcel of papers. Monsieur Savaron was paler than death, and he, so proud, so dignified, was in a state to be pitied. But he treated the old gentleman so respectfully that he could not have been politer to the King himself. Jérôme and Monsieur Albert Savaron escorted the gentleman to his carriage, which was standing with the horses. The courier started on the stroke of three. Monsieur Savaron went straight to the prefecture, and from that to Monsieur Gentillet, who sold him the old travelling carriage that used to belong to Madame de Saint-Vier before she died, then he ordered post horses for six o'clock. He went home to pack; no doubt he wrote a lot of letters; finally, he settled everything with Monsieur Girardet, who went to him and stayed till seven. Jérôme carried a note to Monsieur Boucher, with whom his master was to have dined, and then, at half-past seven, the lawyer set out, leaving Jérôme with three months' wages, and telling him to find another place. He left his keys with Monsieur Girardet, whom he took home, and at his house, Jérôme says, he took a plate of soup, for at half-past seven Monsieur Girardet had not yet dined. When Monsieur Savaron got into the carriage again he looked like death. Jérôme, who, of course, saw his master off, heard him tell the postillion 'The Geneva Road!'"

"Did Jérôme ask the name of the stranger at the Hôtel National?"

"As the old gentleman did not mean to stay, he was not asked for it. The servant, by his orders no doubt, pretended not to speak French."

"And the letter which came so late to the Abbé de Grancey?" said Rosalie.

"It was Monsieur Girardet, no doubt, who ought to have delivered it, but Jérôme says that poor Monsieur Girardet, who was much attached to lawyer Savaron, was as much upset as he was. So he who came so mysteriously, as Mademoiselle Galard says, is gone away just as mysteriously."

After hearing this narrative, Mademoiselle de Watteville fell into a brooding and absent mood, which everybody could see. It is useless to say anything of the commotion that arose in Besançon on the disappearance of Monsieur Savaron. It was understood that the prefect had obliged him with the greatest readiness by giving him at once a passport across the frontier, for he was thus quit of his only opponent. Next day Monsieur de Chavoncourt was carried to the top by a majority of a hundred and forty votes.

"Jack is gone by the way he came," said an elector on hearing of Albert Savaron's flight.

This event lent weight to the prevailing prejudice at Besançon against strangers; indeed, two years previously they had received confirmation from the affair of the Republican newspaper. Ten days later Albert de Savarus was never spoken of again. Only three persons—Girardet the attorney, the Vicar-General, and Rosalie—were seriously affected by his disappearance. Girardet knew that the white-haired stranger was Prince Soderini, for he had seen his card, and he told the Vicar-General; but Rosalie, better informed than either of them, had known for three months past that the Duc d'Argaiolo was dead.

In the month of April 1836, no one had had any news from or of Albert de Savarus. Jérôme and Mariette were to be married, but the Baronne confidentially desired her maid to wait till her daughter was married, saying that the two weddings might take place at the same time.

"It is time that Rosalie should be married," said the Baronne one day to Monsieur de Watteville. "She is nineteen, and she is fearfully altered in these last months."

"I do not know what ails her," said the Baron.

"When fathers do not know what ails their daughters, mothers can guess," said the Baronne; "we must get her married."

"I am quite willing," said the Baron. "I shall give her Les Rouxey now that the court has settled our quarrel with the authorities of Riceys by fixing the boundary line at three hundred feet up the side of the Dent de Vilard. I am having a trench made to collect all the water and carry it into the lake. The commune did not appeal, so the decision is final."

"It has never yet occurred to you," said Madame de Watteville, "that this decision cost me thirty thousand francs handed over to Chantonnit. That peasant would take nothing else; he sold us peace. If you give away Les Rouxey, you will have nothing left," said the Baronne.

"I do not need much," said the Baron; "I am breaking up."

"You eat like an ogre!"

"Just so. But however much I may eat, I feel my legs get weaker and weaker——"

"It is from working the lathe," said his wife.

"I do not know," said he.

"We will marry Rosalie to Monsieur de Soulas; if you give her Les Rouxey, keep the life interest. I will give them fifteen thousand francs a year in the funds. Our children can live here; I do not see that they are much to be pitied."

"No. I shall give them Les Rouxey out and out. Rosalie is fond of Les Rouxey."

"You are a queer man with your daughter! It does not occur to you to ask me if I am fond of Les Rouxey?"

Rosalie, at once sent for, was informed that she was to marry Monsieur de Soulas one day early in the month of May.

"I am very much obliged to you, Mother, and to you too, Father, for having thought of settling me, but I do not mean to marry; I am very happy with you."

"Mere speeches!" said the Baronne. "You are not in love with Monsieur de Soulas, that is all."

"If you insist on the plain truth, I will never marry Monsieur de Soulas——"

"Oh! The *never* of a girl of nineteen!" retorted her mother, with a bitter smile.

"The *never* of Mademoiselle de Watteville," said Rosalie with firm decision. "My father, I imagine, has no intention of making me marry against my wishes?"

"No, indeed no!" said the poor Baron, looking affectionately at his daughter.

"Very well!" said the Baronne, sternly controlling the rage of a sanctimonious woman startled at finding herself unexpectedly defied, "you yourself, Monsieur de Watteville, may take the responsibility of settling your daughter. Consider well, Mademoiselle, for if you do not marry to my mind you will get nothing out of me!"

The quarrel thus begun between Madame de Watteville and her husband, who took his daughter's part, went so far that Rosalie and her father were obliged to spend the summer at Les Rouxey; life at the Hôtel de Rupt was unendurable. It thus became known in Besançon that Mademoiselle de Watteville had positively refused the Comte de Soulas. After their marriage Mariette and Jérôme came to Les Rouxey to succeed to Modinier in due time. The Baron restored and repaired the house to suit his daughter's taste. When she heard that these improvements had cost about sixty thousand francs, and that Rosalie and her father were building a conservatory, the Baronne understood that there was a leaven of spite in her daughter. The Baron purchased various outlying plots, and a little estate worth thirty thousand francs. Madame de Watteville was told that, away from her, Rosalie showed masterly qualities, that she was taking steps to improve the value of Les Rouxey, that she had treated herself to a riding habit and rode about; her father, whom she made very happy, who no longer complained of his health, and who was growing fat, accompanied her in her expeditions. As the Baronne's name day drew near—her name was Louise—the Vicar-General came one day to Les Rouxey, deputed, no doubt, by Madame de Watteville and Monsieur de Soulas, to negotiate a peace between the mother and daughter.

"That little Rosalie has a head on her shoulders," said the folk of Besançon.

After handsomely paying up the ninety thousand francs spent on Les Rouxey, the Baronne allowed her husband a thousand francs a month to live on; she would not put herself in the wrong. The father and daughter were perfectly willing to return to Besançon for the 15th of August, and to remain there till the end of the month. When, after dinner, the Vicar-General took Mademoiselle de Watteville apart, to open the question of the marriage, by explaining to her that it was vain to think any more of Albert, of whom they had had no news for a year past, he was stopped at once by a sign from Rosalie. The strange girl took Monsieur de Grancey by the arm, and led him to a seat under a clump of rhododendrons, whence there was a view of the lake.

"Listen, dear Abbé," said she. "To you whom I love as much as my father, for you had an affection for my Albert, I must at last confess that I committed crimes to become his wife, and he must be my husband. Here, read this."

She held out to him a number of the Gazette which she had in her apron pocket, pointing out the following paragraph under the date of Florence, May 25th:—

The wedding of Monsieur le Duc de Rhétoré, eldest son of the Duc de Chaulieu, the former ambassador, to Madame la Duchesse d'Argaiolo, née Princess Soderini, was solemnised with great splendour. Numerous entertainments given in honour of the marriage are making Florence gay. The Duchesse's fortune is one of the finest in Italy, for the late Duc left her everything.

"The woman he loved is married," said she. "I divided them."

"You? How?" asked the Abbé.

Rosalie was about to reply, when she was interrupted by a loud cry from two of the gardeners, following on the sound of a body falling into the water; she started, and ran off screaming, "Oh! Father!" The Baron had disappeared.

In trying to reach a piece of granite on which he fancied he saw the impression of a shell, a circumstance which would have contradicted some system of geology, Monsieur de Watteville had gone down the slope, lost his balance, and slipped into the lake, which, of course, was deepest close under the roadway. The men

had the greatest difficulty in enabling the Baron to catch
hold of a pole pushed down at the place where the water
was bubbling, but at last they pulled him out, covered
with mud, in which he had sunk; he was getting deeper and deeper in, by dint of struggling. Monsieur de
Watteville had dined heavily, digestion was in progress,
and was thus checked. When he had been undressed,
washed, and put to bed, he was in such evident danger that two servants at once set out on horseback: one
to ride to Besançon, and the other to fetch the nearest
doctor and surgeon.

When Madame de Watteville arrived, eight hours later, with the first medical aid from Besançon, they found
Monsieur de Watteville past all hope, in spite of the intelligent treatment of the Rouxey doctor. The fright had
produced serious effusion on the brain, and the shock to
the digestion was helping to kill the poor man.

This death, which would never have happened, said
Madame de Watteville, if her husband had stayed at
Besançon, was ascribed by her to her daughter's ob-
stinacy. She took an aversion for Rosalie, abandoning
herself to grief and regrets that were evidently exaggerated. She spoke of the Baron as *her dear lamb!* The last of
the Wattevilles was buried on an island in the lake at Les
Rouxey, where the Baronne had a little Gothic monument erected of white marble, like that called the tomb
of Héloïse at Père-Lachaise.*

A month after this catastrophe the mother and daughter had settled in the Hôtel de Rupt, where they lived in
savage silence. Rosalie was suffering from real sorrow,
which had no visible outlet; she accused herself of her
father's death, and she feared another disaster, much
greater in her eyes, and very certainly her own work;
neither Girardet the attorney nor the Abbé de Grancey
could obtain any information concerning Albert. This
silence was appalling. In a paroxysm of repentance
she felt that she must confess to the Vicar-General the

horrible machinations by which she had separated Francesca and Albert. They had been simple, but formidable. Mademoiselle de Watteville had intercepted Albert's letters to the Duchesse as well as those in which Francesca announced her husband's illness, warning her lover that she could write to him no more during the time while she was devoted, as was her duty, to the care of the dying man. Thus, while Albert was wholly occupied with election matters, the Duchesse had written him only two letters; one in which she told him that the Duc d'Argaiolo was in danger, and one announcing her widowhood—two noble and beautiful letters, which Rosalie kept back. After several nights' labour she succeeded in imitating Albert's writing very perfectly. She had substituted three letters of her own writing for three of Albert's, and the rough copies which she showed to the old priest made him shudder—the genius of evil was revealed in them to such perfection. Rosalie, writing in Albert's name, had prepared the Duchesse for a change in the Frenchman's feelings, falsely representing him as faithless, and she had answered the news of the Duc d'Argaiolo's death by announcing the marriage ere long of Albert and Mademoiselle de Watteville. The two letters, intended to cross on the road, had, in fact, done so. The infernal cleverness with which the letters were written so much astonished the Vicar-General that he read them a second time. Francesca, stabbed to the heart by a girl who wanted to kill love in her rival, had answered the last in these four words: "*You are free. Farewell.*"

"Purely moral crimes, which give no hold to human justice, are the most atrocious and detestable," said the Abbé severely. "God often punishes them on earth; herein lies the reason of the terrible catastrophes which to us seem inexplicable. Of all secret crimes buried in the mystery of private life, the most disgraceful is that of breaking the seal of a letter, or of reading it surreptitiously. Everyone, whoever it may be, and urged by whatever reason, who is guilty of such an act has stained his honour beyond retrieving. Do you not feel all that is touching, that is heavenly in the story of the youthful page, falsely accused, and carrying the letter containing the order for his execution, who sets out without a thought of ill, and whom Providence protects and saves—miraculously, we say! But do you know wherein the miracle lies? Virtue has a glory as potent as that of innocent childhood. I say these things not meaning to admonish you," said the old priest, with deep grief. "I, alas! am not your spiritual director; you are not kneeling at the feet of God; I am your friend, appalled by dread of what your punishment may be. What has become of that unhappy Albert? Has he, perhaps, killed himself? There was tremendous passion under his assumption of calm. I understand now that old Prince Soderini, the father of the Duchesse d'Argaiolo, came here to take back his daughter's letters and portraits. This was the thunderbolt that fell on Albert's head, and he went off, no doubt, to try to justify himself. But how is it that in fourteen months he has given us no news of himself?"

"Oh! If I marry him, he will be so happy!"

"Happy? He does not love you. Besides, you have no great fortune to give him. Your mother detests you; you made her a fierce reply which rankles, and which will be your ruin. When she told you yesterday that obedience was the only way to repair your errors, and reminded you of the need for marrying, mentioning Amédée—'If you are so fond of him, marry him yourself, Mother!'—Did you, or did you not, fling these words in her teeth?"

"Yes," said Rosalie.

"Well, I know her," Monsieur de Grancey went on. "In a few months she will be Comtesse de Soulas! She will be sure to have children; she will give Monsieur de Soulas forty thousand francs a year; she will benefit him in other ways, and reduce your share of her fortune as much as possible. You will be poor as long as she lives, and she is but thirty-eight! Your whole estate will be the land of Les Rouxey, and the small share left to you after your father's legal debts are settled, if, indeed, your mother should consent to forgo her claims on Les Rouxey. From the point of view of material advantages, you have done badly for yourself; from the point of view of feeling, I imagine you have wrecked your life. Instead of going to your mother——"

Rosalie shook her head fiercely.

"To your mother," the priest went on, "and to religion, where you would, at the first impulse of your heart, have found enlightenment, counsel, and guidance, you chose to act in your own way, knowing nothing of life, and listening only to passion!"

These words of wisdom terrified Mademoiselle de Watteville.

"And what ought I to do now?" she asked after a pause.

"To repair your wrongdoing, you must ascertain its extent," said the Abbé.

"Well, I will write to the only man who can know anything of Albert's fate, Monsieur Léopold Hannequin, a notary in Paris, his friend from childhood."

"Write no more, unless to do honour to truth," said the Vicar-General. "Place the real and the false letters in my hands, confess everything in detail as though I were the keeper of your conscience, asking me how you may expiate your sins, and doing as I bid you. I shall see—for, above all things, restore this unfortunate man to his innocence in the eyes of the woman he had made his divinity on earth. Though he has lost his happiness, Albert must still hope for justification."

Rosalie promised to obey the Abbé, hoping that the steps he might take would perhaps end in bringing Albert back to her.

Not long after Mademoiselle de Watteville's confession a clerk came to Besançon from Monsieur Léopold Hannequin, armed with a power of attorney from Albert; he called first on Monsieur Girardet, begging his assistance in selling the house belonging to Monsieur Savaron. The attorney undertook to do this out of friendship for Albert. The clerk from Paris sold the furniture, and with the proceeds could repay some money owed by Savaron to Girardet, who on the occasion of his inexplicable departure had lent him five thousand francs while undertaking to collect his assets. When Girardet asked what had become of the handsome and noble pleader, to whom he had been much attached, the clerk replied that no one knew but his master, and that the notary had seemed greatly distressed by the contents of the last letter he had received from Monsieur Albert de Savarus.

On hearing this, the Vicar-General wrote to Léopold. This was the worthy notary's reply:—

TO MONSIEUR L'ABBÉ DE GRANCEY, VICAR-GENERAL OF THE DIOCESE OF BESANÇON

Paris

Alas, Monsieur, it is in nobody's power to restore Albert to the life of the world; he has renounced it. He is a novice in the monastery of the Grande Chartreuse near Grenoble. You know, better than I who have but just learned it, that on the threshold of that cloister everything dies. Albert, foreseeing that I should go to him, placed the General of Chartreux between my utmost efforts and himself. I know his noble soul well enough to be sure that he is the victim of some odious plot unknown to us, but everything is at an end. The Duchesse d'Argaiolo, now Duchesse de Rhétoré, seems to me to have carried severity to an extreme. At Belgirate, which she had left when Albert flew thither, she had left instructions leading him to believe that she was living in London. From London Albert went in search of her to Naples, and from Naples to Rome, where she was now engaged to the Duc de Rhétoré. When Albert succeeded in seeing Madame d'Argaiolo, at Florence, it was at the ceremony of her marriage. Our poor friend swooned in church, and even when he was in danger of death he could never obtain any explanation from this woman, who must have had I know not what in her heart. For seven months Albert had travelled in pursuit of a cruel creature who thought it sport to escape him; he knew not where or how to catch her. I saw him on his way through Paris, and if you had seen him, as I did, you would have felt that not a word might be spoken about the Duchesse, at the risk of bringing on an attack which might have wrecked his reason. If he had known what his crime was, he might have found means to justify himself, but being falsely accused of being married! What could he do? Albert is dead, quite dead to the world. He longed for rest; let us hope that the deep silence and prayer into which he has thrown himself may give him happiness in another guise. You, Monsieur, who have known him, must greatly pity him and pity his friends also.

Yours, etc.

As soon as he received this letter, the good Vicar-General wrote to the General of Chartreux, and this was the letter he received from Albert Savarus:

FRÈRE ALBERT TO MONSIEUR L'ABBÉ DE GRANCEY, VICAR-GENERAL OF THE DIOCESE OF BESANÇON

La Grande Chartreuse

I recognised your tender soul, dear and well-beloved Vicar-General, and your still youthful heart, in all that the Reverend Père General of our Order has just told me. You have understood the only wish that lurks in the depths of my heart so far as the things of the world are concerned—to get justice done to my feelings by her who has treated me so badly! But before leaving me at liberty to avail myself of your offer, the General wanted to know that my vocation was sincere; he was so kind as to tell me his idea, on finding that I was determined to preserve absolute silence on this point. If I had yielded to the temptation to rehabilitate the man of the world, the friar would have been rejected by this monastery. Grace has certainly done her work, but, though short, the struggle was not the less keen or the less painful. Is not this enough to show you that I could never return to the world? Hence my forgiveness, which you ask for the author of so much woe, is entire and without a thought of vindictiveness. I will pray to God to forgive that young lady as I forgive her, and as I shall beseech him to give Madame de Rhétoré a life of happiness. Ah! Whether it be Death, or the obstinate hand of a young girl madly bent on being loved, or one of the blows ascribed to chance, must we not all obey God? Sorrow in some souls makes a vast void through which the Divine Voice rings. I learned too late the bearings of this life on that which awaits us; all in me is worn out; I could not serve in the ranks of the Church Militant, and I lay the remains of an almost extinct life at the foot of the altar. This is the last time I shall ever write. You alone, who loved me, and whom I loved so well, could make me break the law of oblivion I imposed on myself when I entered these headquarters of Saint-Bruno, but you are always especially named in the prayers of

FRÈRE ALBERT
November 1836

"Everything is for the best perhaps," thought the Abbé de Grancey.

When he showed this letter to Rosalie, who, with a pious impulse, kissed the lines which contained her forgiveness, he said to her—"Well, now that he is lost to you, will you not be reconciled to your mother and marry the Comte de Soulas?"

"Only if Albert should order it," said she.

"But you see it is impossible to consult him. The General of the Order would not allow it."

"If I were to go to see him?"

"No Carthusian sees any visitor. Besides, no woman but the Queen of France may enter a Carthusian monastery," said the Abbé. "So you have no longer any excuse for not marrying young Monsieur de Soulas."

"I do not wish to destroy my mother's happiness," retorted Rosalie.

"Satan!" exclaimed the Vicar-General.

Towards the end of that winter the worthy Abbé de Grancey died. This good friend no longer stood between Madame de Watteville and her daughter, to soften the impact of those two iron wills. The event he had foretold took place. In the month of August 1837 Madame

Il n'est au pouvoir de personne de rendre Albert à la vie du monde.

Plate XVII

de Watteville was married to Monsieur de Soulas in Paris, whither she went by Rosalie's advice, the girl making a show of kindness and sweetness to her mother. Madame de Watteville believed in this affection on the part of her daughter, who simply desired to go to Paris to give herself the luxury of a bitter revenge; she thought of nothing but avenging Savarus by torturing her rival.

Mademoiselle de Watteville had been declared legally of age; she was, in fact, not far from twenty-one. Her mother, to settle with her finally, had resigned her claims on Les Rouxey, and the daughter had signed a release for all the inheritance of the Baron de Watteville. Rosalie encouraged her mother to marry the Comte de Soulas and settle all her own fortune on him.

"Let us each be perfectly free," she said.

Madame de Soulas, who had been uneasy as to her daughter's intentions, was touched by this liberality, and made her a present of six thousand francs a year in the funds as conscience money. As the Comtesse de Soulas had an income of forty-eight thousand francs from her own lands, and was quite incapable of alienating them in order to diminish Rosalie's share, Mademoiselle de Watteville was still a fortune to marry, of eighteen hundred thousand francs; Les Rouxey, with the Baron's additions, and certain improvements, might yield twenty thousand francs a year, besides the value of the house, rents, and preserves. So Rosalie and her mother, who soon adopted the Paris style and fashions, easily obtained introductions to the best society. The golden key, the words: "eighteen hundred thousand francs!" embroidered on Mademoiselle de Watteville's bodice, did more for the Comtesse de Soulas than her pretensions *à la* de Rupt, her inappropriate pride, or even her rather distant great connections.

In the month of February 1838, Rosalie, who was eagerly courted by many young men, achieved the purpose which had brought her to Paris. This was to meet the Duchesse de Rhétoré, to see this wonderful woman, and to overwhelm her with perennial remorse. Rosalie gave herself up to the most bewildering elegance and vanities in order to face the Duchesse on an equal footing. They first met at a ball given annually after 1830 for the benefit of the pensioners on the old Civil List.*

A young man, prompted by Rosalie, pointed her out to the Duchesse, saying—"There is a very remarkable young person, a strong-minded young lady too! She drove a clever man into a monastery—the Grande Chartreuse—a man of immense capabilities, Albert de Savarus, whose career she wrecked. She is Mademoiselle de Watteville, the famous Besançon heiress——"

The Duchesse turned pale. Rosalie's eyes met hers with one of those flashes which, between woman and woman, are more fatal than the pistol shots of a duel. Francesca Soderini, who had suspected that Albert might be innocent, hastily quitted the ballroom, leaving the speaker at his wit's end to guess what terrible blow he had inflicted on the beautiful Duchesse de Rhétoré.

If you want to hear more about Albert, come to the opera ball on Tuesday with a marigold in your hand.

This anonymous note, sent by Rosalie to the Duchesse, brought the unhappy Italian to the ball, where Mademoiselle de Watteville placed in her hand all Albert's letters, with that written to Léopold Hannequin by the Vicar-General, and the notary's reply, and even that in which she had written her own confession to the Abbé de Grancey.

"I do not choose to be the only sufferer," she said to her rival, "for one has been as ruthless as the other."

After enjoying the dismay stamped on the Duchesse's beautiful face, Rosalie went away; she went out no more, and returned to Besançon with her mother.

Mademoiselle de Watteville, who lived alone on her estate of Les Rouxey, riding, hunting, refusing two or three offers a year, going to Besançon four or five times in the course of the winter, and busying herself with improving her land, was regarded as a very eccentric personage. She was one of the celebrities of the eastern provinces.

Madame de Soulas has two children, a boy and a girl, and she has grown younger, but young Monsieur de Soulas has aged a good deal.

"My fortune has cost me dear," said he to young Chavoncourt. "To really know a pious woman, it is unfortunately necessary to marry her!"

Mademoiselle de Watteville behaves in the most extraordinary manner. *She has vagaries*, people say. Every year she goes to gaze at the walls of the Grande Chartreuse. Perhaps she dreams of imitating her grand uncle by forcing the walls of the monastery to find a husband, as Watteville broke through those of his monastery to recover his liberty.

She left Besançon in 1841, intending, it was said, to get married, but the real reason of this expedition is still unknown, for she returned home in a state which forbids her ever appearing in society again. By one of those chances of which the Abbé de Grancey had spoken, she happened to be on the Loire in a steamboat of which the boiler burst. Mademoiselle de Watteville was so severely injured that she lost her right arm and her left leg; her face is marked with fearful scars, which have bereft her of her beauty; her health, cruelly upset, leaves her few days free from suffering. In short, she now never leaves the Chartreuse of Les Rouxey, where she leads a life wholly devoted to religious practices.

Paris, May 1842

The following personages appear or are mentioned
in other volumes of *The Human Comedy*.

Beauséant, Vicomtesse de (born Claire de Bourgogne)
V: *The Deserted Woman*
VIII: *Old Goriot*

Genovese
XXXV: *Massimilla Doni*

Hannequin, Léopold
VI: *Beatrix*
XXI: *Cousin Bette*
XXII: *Cousin Pons*

Jeanrenaud
IX: *The Interdiction*

Nueil, Gaston de
V: *The Deserted Woman*

Rhétoré, Duc Alphonse de
I: *Letters of Two Brides*
XIII: *The Rabouilleuse*
XVI: *Lost Illusions*
XIX: *The Splendours and Miseries of Courtesans*
XXVIII: *The Deputy for Arcis*

Savaron de Savarus (the family)
XXXVI: *The Quest of the Absolute*

Savarus, Albert Savaron de
XXXVI: *The Quest of the Absolute*

The Vendetta
January 1830

Dedicated to Puttinati, Sculptor at Milan*

GINEVRA DI PIOMBO

Elle prit une feuille de papier et se mit à croquer à la sépia
la tête du pauvre reclus.

LA VENDETTA.

Plate XVIII

In the year 1800 towards the end of October, a stranger, having with him a woman and a little girl, made his appearance in front of the Tuileries Palace and stood for some time close to the ruins of a house, then recently pulled down, on the spot where the wing which is still unfinished was intended to join Catherine de Medici's Palace to the Louvre built by the Valois. There he stood, his arms folded, his head bent, raising it now and again to look at the consular palace or at his wife, who sat on a stone by his side. Though the stranger seemed to think only of the little girl of nine or ten, whose black hair was a plaything in his fingers, the woman lost none of the glances shot at her by her companion. A common feeling, other than love, united these two beings, and a common thought animated their thoughts and their actions. Misery is perhaps the strongest of all bonds. The man had one of those broad, solemn-looking heads with a mass of hair, of which so many examples have been perpetuated by the Carracci. Among the thick black locks were many white hairs. His features, though fine and proud, had a set hardness which spoiled them. In spite of his powerful and upright frame, he seemed to be more than sixty years of age. His clothes, which were dilapidated, betrayed his foreign origin. The woman's face, formerly handsome, but now faded, bore a stamp of deep melancholy, though, when her husband looked at her, she forced herself to smile and affected a calm expression. The little girl was standing in spite of the fatigue that was written on her small sunburnt face.

She had Italian features: large black eyes under well-arched eyebrows, a native dignity, and genuine grace. More than one passerby was touched by the mere sight of this group, for the persons composing it made no effort to disguise a despair evidently as deep as the expression of it was simple, but the spring of the transient kindliness which distinguishes the Parisian is quickly dried up. As soon as the stranger perceived that he was the object of some idler's attention, he stared at him so fiercely that the most intrepid lounger hastened his step, as though he had trodden on a viper. After remaining there a long time undecided, the tall man suddenly passed his hand across his brow, driving away, so to speak, the thoughts that had furrowed it with wrinkles, and made up his mind no doubt to some desperate determination. Casting a piercing look at his wife and daughter, he drew out of his jerkin a long dagger, held it out to the woman, and said in Italian, "I am going to see whether the Bonapartes remember us." He walked on, with a slow, confident step, towards the entrance to the palace, where, of course, he was checked by a soldier on guard, with whom there could be no long discussion. Seeing that the stranger was obstinate, the sentry pointed his bayonet at him by way of *ultimatum*. As chance would have it at this moment, a squad came round to relieve the guard, and the corporal very civilly informed the stranger where he might find the captain of the guard.

"Let Bonaparte know that Bartholoméo di Piombo wants to see him," said the Italian to the officer.

In vain did the captain explain to Bartholoméo that it was not possible to see the First Consul without having written to him beforehand to request an audience. The stranger insisted that the officer should go to inform Bonaparte. The captain urged the rules of his duty, and formally refused to yield to the demands of this strange petitioner. Bartholoméo knit his brows, looked at the captain with a terrible scowl, and seemed to make him responsible for all the disasters his refusal might occasion; then he remained silent, his arms tightly crossed on his breast, and took his stand under the archway which connects the garden and the courtyard of the Tuileries. People who are thoroughly bent on anything are almost always well served by chance. At the moment when Bartholoméo sat down on one of the kerb stones near the entrance to the palace, a carriage drove up and out of it stepped Lucien Bonaparte, at that time Minister of the Interior.

"Ah! Loucien, good luck for me to have met you!" cried the stranger.

Il resta là, debout, les bras croisés, la tête inclinée.

Plate XIX

These words, spoken in the Corsican dialect, made Lucien stop at the instant when he was rushing into the vestibule; he looked at his fellow countryman and recognised him. At the first word that Bartholoméo said in his ear, he took him with him. Murat, Lannes,* and Rapp were in the First Consul's cabinet. On seeing Lucien come in with so strange a figure as was Piombo, the conversation ceased. Lucien took his brother's hand and led him into a window recess. After exchanging a few words, the First Consul raised his hand with a gesture, which Murat and Lannes obeyed by retiring. Rapp affected not to have seen it and remained. Then, Bonaparte having sharply called him to order, the aide-de-camp went out with a sour face. The First Consul, who heard the sound of Rapp's steps in the neighbouring room, hastily followed him, and saw him close to the wall between the cabinet and the anteroom.

"You refuse to understand me?" said the First Consul. "I wish to be alone with my countryman."

"A Corsican!" retorted the aide-de-camp. "I distrust those creatures too much not to——"

The First Consul could not help smiling, and lightly pushed his faithful officer by the shoulders.

"Well, and what are you doing here, my poor Bartholoméo?" said the First Consul to Piombo.

"I have come to ask for shelter and protection, if you are a true Corsican," replied Bartholoméo in a rough tone.

"What misfortune has driven you from your native land? You were the richest, the most——"

"I have killed all the Porta," replied the Corsican, in a hollow voice, with a frown.

The First Consul drew back a step or two, like a man astonished.

"Are you going to betray me?" cried Bartholoméo, with a gloomy look at Bonaparte. "Do you forget that there are still four of the Piombo in Corsica?"

Lucien took his fellow countryman by the arm and shook him.

"Do you come here to threaten the saviour of France?" he said vehemently.

Bonaparte made a sign to Lucien, who was silent. Then he looked at Piombo, and said, "And why did you kill all the Porta?"

"We had made friends," he replied; "the Barbanti had reconciled us. The day after we had drunk together to drown our quarrel, I left because I had business at Bastia. They stayed at my place and set fire to my vineyard at Longone. They killed my son Gregorio; my daughter Ginevra and my wife escaped; they had taken the Communion that morning; the Virgin protected them. When I got home I could no longer see my house; I searched for it with my feet in the ashes. Suddenly I came across Gregorio's body; I recognised it in the moonlight. 'Oh, the Porta have played this trick!' said I to myself. I went off at once into the *mâquis;** I got together a few men to whom I had done some service—do you hear, Bonaparte?—and we marched down on the Porta's vineyard. We arrived at five in the morning, and by seven they were all in the presence of God. Giacomo declares that Élisa Vanni saved a child, little Luigi, but I tied him to the bed with my own hands before setting the house on fire. Then I quitted the island with my wife and daughter without being able to make sure whether Luigi Porta were still alive."

Bonaparte looked at Bartholoméo with curiosity, but no astonishment.

"How many were they?" asked Lucien.

"Seven," replied Piombo. "They persecuted you in their day," he added. The words aroused no sign of hatred in the two brothers. "Ah! You are no longer Corsicans!" cried Bartholoméo, with a sort of despair. "Good-bye. Formerly I protected you," he went on reproachfully. "But for me your mother would never have reached Marseilles,"* he said, turning to Bonaparte, who stood thoughtfully, his elbow resting on the mantelpiece.

"I cannot in conscience take you under my wing, Piombo," replied Napoléon. "I am the head of a great nation; I govern the Republic; I must see that the laws are carried out."

"Ah! ah!" said Bartholoméo.

"But I can shut my eyes," Bonaparte went on. "The tradition of the *Vendetta* will hinder the reign of law in Corsica for a long time yet," he added, talking to himself. "But it must be stamped out at any cost."

He was silent for a minute, and Lucien signed to Piombo to say nothing. The Corsican shook his head from side to side with a disapproving look.

"Remain here," the First Consul said, addressing Bartholoméo. "We know nothing. I will see that your estates are purchased so as to give you at once the means of living. Then later, some time hence, we will remember you. But no more *Vendetta*. There is no mâquis here. If you play tricks with your dagger, there is no hope for you. Here the law protects everybody, and we do not do justice on our own account."

"He has put himself at the head of a strange people," replied Bartholoméo, taking Lucien's hand and pressing it. "But you recognise me in misfortune; it is a bond between us for life and death, and you may command everyone named Piombo."

As he spoke, his brow cleared, and he looked about with satisfaction.

"You are not badly off here," he said, with a smile, as if he would like to lodge there. "And you are dressed all in red like a cardinal."

"It rests with you to rise and have a palace in Paris," said Bonaparte, looking at him from head to foot. "It will often happen that I may look about me for a devoted friend to whom I can entrust myself."

A sigh of gladness broke from Piombo's deep chest; he held out his hand to the First Consul, saying, "There is something of the Corsican in you still!"

Bonaparte smiled. He gazed in silence at this man, who had brought him as it were a breath of air from his native land, from the island where he had formerly been so miraculously saved from the hatred of the *English Party*, and which he was fated never to see again. He made a sign to his brother, who led away Bartholoméo di Piombo. Lucien inquired with interest as to the pecuniary position of the man who had once protected his family. Piombo led the Minister of the Interior to a window and showed him his wife and Ginevra, both seated on a heap of stones.

"We have come from Fontainebleau on foot," said he, "and we have not a sou."

Lucien gave his fellow countryman his purse and desired him to come again next morning to consult as to the means of providing for his family. The income from all Piombo's possessions in Corsica could hardly suffice to maintain him respectably in Paris.

Fifteen years elapsed between the arrival of the Piombo family in Paris and the following incidents, which, without the story of this event, would have been less intelligible.

Servin, one of our most distinguished artists, was the first to conceive the idea of opening a studio for young ladies who may wish to take lessons in painting. He was a man of over forty, of blameless habits, and wholly given up to his art; he had married for love the daughter of a general without any fortune. At first mothers brought their daughters themselves to the professor's studio, but when they understood his high principles and appreciated the care by which he strove to deserve such confidence, they ended by sending the girls alone. It was part of the painter's scheme to take as pupils only young ladies of rich or highly respectable family, that no difficulties might arise as to the society in his studio; he had even refused to take young girls who intended to become artists, and who must necessarily have had certain kinds of training without which no mastery is possible. By degrees his prudence, the superior method by which he initiated his pupils into the secrets of his art, as well as the security their mothers felt in knowing that their daughters were in the company of well-bred girls, and in the artist's character, manners, and marriage, won him a high reputation in the world of fashion. As soon as a young girl showed any desire to learn drawing or painting, and her mother asked advice, "Send her to Servin," was always the answer. Thus Servin had a specialty for teaching ladies art, as Herbault had for bonnets, Leroy for dresses, and Chevet for dainties.* It was acknowledged that a young woman who had taken lessons of Servin could pronounce definitively on the pictures in the Louvre, paint a portrait in a superior manner, copy an old picture, and produce her own painting of genre. Thus this artist sufficed for all the requirements of the aristocracy. Notwithstanding his connection with all the best houses in Paris, he was independent and patriotic, preserving with all alike the light and witty tone, sometimes ironical, and the freedom of opinion which characterise painters. He had carried his scrupulous precautions into the arrangement of the place where his scholars worked. The outer entrance to the loft above his dwelling rooms had been walled up to get into this retreat, as sacred as a harem, the way was up a staircase in the centre of the house. This studio, which occupied the whole of the top story, was on the vast scale which always surprises inquisitive visitors when, having climbed to sixty feet above the ground, they expect to find an artist lodged in the gutter. It was a kind of gallery, abundantly lighted by immense skylights screened with the large green blinds which artists use to distribute the light. A quantity of caricatures, heads sketched in outline with a brush or the point of a palette knife, all over the dark grey walls, proved that, allowing for a difference in the expression, fine young ladies have as much whimsicality in their brain as men can have. A small stove, with a huge pipe that made amazing zigzags before reaching the upper region of the roof, was the inevitable decoration of this studio. There was a shelf all round the room supporting plaster casts which lay there in confusion, most of them under a coating of whitish dust. Below this shelf, here and there, a head of Niobe hanging on a nail showed its pathetic bend, a Venus smiled, and a hand was unexpectedly thrust out before your eyes like a beggar's asking alms; then there were anatomical écorchés, yellow with smoke, and looking like limbs snatched from coffins; pictures, drawings, lay figures, frames without canvas, and canvasses without frames completed the effect, giving the room the characteristic aspect of a studio, a singular mixture of ornamentation and bareness, of poverty and splendour, of care and neglect. This huge sort of hold in which everything, even man, looks small, has a behind-the-scenes flavour: here are to be seen old linen, gilt armour, odds and ends of stuffs, and some machinery. But there is something about it as grand as thought: genius and death are there, Diana and Apollo side by side with a skull or a skeleton; there is beauty and disorder, poetry and reality, gorgeous colouring in shadow, and often a whole drama, but motionless and silent. What a symbol for the mind of an artist!

At the moment when this story begins, the bright sun of July lighted up the studio, and two beams of sunshine shot across its depths: broad bands of diaphanous gold in which the dust motes glistened. A dozen easels raised their pointed spars, looking like the masts of vessels in a harbour. Several young girls enlivened the scene by the variety of their countenances, attitudes, and by the difference in their dress. The strong shadows cast by the green baize blinds, arranged to suit the position of each easel, produced a multitude of contrasts and fascinating effects of chiaroscuro. This group of girls formed the most attractive picture in the gallery. A fair-haired girl, simply dressed, stood at some distance from her companions, working perseveringly and seeming to foresee misfortune; no one looked at her nor spoke to her; she was the prettiest, the most modest, and the least rich. Two principal groups, divided by a little space, represented two classes of society, two spirits, even in this studio, where rank and fortune ought to have been forgotten. These young things, sitting or standing, surrounded by their paintboxes, playing with their brushes or getting them ready, handling their bright-tinted palettes, painting, chattering, laughing, singing, given up to their natural impulses and revealing their true characters, made up a drama unknown to men: this one proud, haughty, capricious, with black hair and beautiful hands, flashed the fire of her eyes at random; that one, lighthearted and heedless, a smile on her lips, her hair chestnut, with delicate white hands, virginal and French, a light nature without a thought of evil, living from hour to hour; another, dreamy, melancholy, pale, her head drooping like a falling blossom; her neighbour, on the contrary, tall, indolent, with oriental manners, and long, black, melting eyes, speaking little, but lost in thought, and stealing a look at the head of Antinous. In the midst, like the *jocoso* of a Spanish comedy, a girl, full of wit and sparkling sallies, stood watching them all with a single glance and making them laugh, raising a face so full of life that it could not but be pretty. She was the leader of the first group of pupils, consisting of the daughters of bankers, lawyers, and merchants—all rich, but exposed to all the minute but stinging disdains freely poured out upon them by the other young girls who belonged to the aristocracy. These were governed by the daughter of a gentleman-usher to the King's private chamber, a vain little thing, as silly as she was vain, and proud of her father's *having an office* at court. She aimed at seeming to understand the master's remarks at the first word, and appearing to work by inspired grace; she used an eyeglass, came very much dressed, very late, and begged her companions not to talk loud. Among this second group might be observed some exquisite shapes and distinguished-looking faces, but their looks expressed but little simplicity. Though their attitudes were elegant and their movements graceful, their faces were lacking in candour, and it was easy to perceive that they belonged to a world where politeness forms the character at an early age, and the abuse of social pleasures kills the feelings and develops selfishness. When the whole party of girl students was complete, there were to be seen among them childlike heads, virgin heads of enchanting purity, faces where the parted lips showed virgin teeth, and where a virgin smile came and went. Then the studio suggested not a seraglio, but a group of angels sitting on a cloud in heaven.

It was near noon; Servin had not yet made his appearance. For some days past, he had spent most of his time at a studio he had elsewhere, finishing a picture he had there for the exhibition. Suddenly Mademoiselle Amélie Thirion, the head of the aristocrats in this little assembly, spoke at some length to her neighbour; there was profound silence among the patrician group; the banker faction were equally silent from astonishment, and tried to guess the subject of such a conference. But the secret of the young Ultras* was soon known. Amélie rose, took an easel that stood near her, and moved it to some distance from the "nobility," close to a clumsy partition which divided the studio from a dark closet where broken casts were kept, paintings that the professor had condemned, and, in winter, the firewood. Amélie's proceedings gave rise to a murmur of surprise which did not hinder her from completing the removal by wheeling up to the easel a stool and paintbox, in fact, everything, even a picture by Prudhon, of which a pupil, who had not yet come, was making a copy. After this coup d'état the Party of the Right painted on in silence, but the Left talked it over at great length.

"What will Mademoiselle Piombo say?" asked one of the girls of Mademoiselle Mathilde Roguin, the oracle of mischief of her group.

"She is not a girl to say much," was the reply. "But fifty years hence she will remember this insult as if she had experienced it the day before, and will find some cruel means of revenge. She is a person I should not like to be at war with."

"The proscription to which those ladies have condemned her is all the more unjust," said another young girl, "because Mademoiselle Ginevra was very sad the day before yesterday; her father, they say, has just given up his appointment. This will add to her troubles, as she was very good to those young ladies during the Hundred Days.* Did she ever say a word that could hurt them? On the contrary, she avoided talking politics. But our Ultras seem to be prompted by jealousy rather than by party spirit."

"I have a great mind to fetch Mademoiselle Piombo's easel and place it by mine," said Mathilde Roguin. She rose, but on second thoughts she sat down again. "With a spirit like Mademoiselle Ginevra's," said she, "it is impossible to know how she would take our civility. Let us wait and see."

"*Eccola!*"* said the black-eyed girl languidly.

In fact, the sound of footsteps coming upstairs was heard in the studio. The words, "Here she comes!" passed from mouth to mouth, and then perfect silence fell.

To understand the full importance of the ostracism carried into effect by Amélie Thirion, it must be told that this scene took place towards the end of the month of July 1815. The second return of the Bourbons broke up many friendships which had weathered the turmoil of the first. At this time families, almost always divided among themselves, renewed many of the most deplorable scenes which tarnish the history of all countries at periods of civil or religious struggles. Children, young girls, old men, had caught the monarchical fever from which the government was suffering. Discord flew in under the domestic roof, and suspicion dyed in gloomy hues the most intimate conversations and actions. Ginevra di Piombo idolised Napoléon; indeed, how could she have hated him? The Emperor was her fellow countryman and her father's benefactor. Baron di Piombo was one of Napoléon's followers who had most efficiently worked to bring him back from Elba. Incapable of renouncing his political faith, nay, eager to proclaim it, Piombo had remained in Paris in the midst of enemies. Hence Ginevra di Piombo was ranked with the "suspicious characters," all the more so because she made no secret of the regret her family felt at the second Restoration. The only tears she had perhaps ever shed in her life were wrung from her by the twofold tidings of Bonaparte's surrender on board the *Bellerophon* and the arrest of Labédoyère.*

The young ladies forming the aristocratic party in the studio belonged to the most enthusiastically Royalist families of Paris. It would be difficult to give any idea of the exaggerated feelings of the time, and of the horror felt towards Bonapartists. However mean and trivial Amélie Thirion's conduct may seem today, it was then a very natural demonstration of hatred. Ginevra di Piombo, one of Servin's earliest pupils, had occupied the place of which they wished to deprive her ever since the first day she had come to the studio. The aristocratic group had gradually settled round her, and to turn her out of a place, which in a certain sense belonged to her, was not merely to insult her, but to cause her some pain, for all artists have a predilection for the spot where they work. However, political hostility had perhaps not much to do with the conduct of this little studio Party of the Right. Ginevra di Piombo, the most accomplished of Servin's pupils, was an object of the deepest jealousy: the master professed an equal admiration for the talents and the character of this favourite pupil, who served as the standard of all his comparisons, and indeed, while it was impossible to explain the ascendancy this young girl exercised over all who were about her, she enjoyed in this small world an influence resembling that of Bonaparte over his soldiers. The aristocratic clique had, some days since, resolved on the overthrow of this queen, but as no one had been bold enough to repulse the Bonapartist, Mademoiselle Thirion had just struck the decisive blow so as to make her companions the accomplices of her hatred. Though Ginevra was sincerely liked by two or three of the Royalists, who at home were abundantly lectured on politics, with the tact peculiar to women, they judged it best not to interfere in the quarrel. On entering, Ginevra was received in perfect silence. Of all the girls who had yet appeared at Servin's studio, she was the handsomest, the tallest, and the most finely made. Her gait had a stamp of dignity and grace which commanded respect. Her face, full of intelligence, seemed radiant, it was so transfused with the animation peculiar to Corsicans, which does not exclude calmness. Her abundant hair, her eyes, and their black lashes told of passion. Though the corners of her mouth were softly drawn and her lips a little too thick, they had the kindly expression which strong people derive from the consciousness of strength. By a singular caprice of nature, the charm of her features was somewhat belied by a marble forehead stamped with an almost savage pride where breathed the traditional manners of Corsica. That was the only bond between her and her native land; in every other detail of her person the simplicity and freedom of Lombard beauties were so bewitching, that only in her absence could anyone bear to cause her the smallest pain. She was, indeed, so attractive that her old father, out of prudence, never allowed her to walk alone to the studio. The only fault of this truly poetic creature came from the very power of such fully developed beauty. She had refused to marry out of affection for her father and mother, feeling herself necessary to them in their old age. Her taste for painting had taken the place of the passions which commonly agitate women.

"You are all very silent today," she said, after coming forward a step or two. "Good morning, my little Laure," she added in a gentle, caressing tone as she went up to the young girl who was painting apart from the rest. "That head is very good. The flesh is a little too pink, but it is all capitally drawn."

Laure raised her head, looked at Ginevra much touched, and their faces brightened with an expression of mutual affection. A faint smile gave life to the Italian's lips, but she seemed pensive and went slowly to her place, carelessly glancing at the drawings and pictures, and saying good morning to each of the girls of the first group, without observing the unusual curiosity excited by her presence. She might have been a queen amid her court. She did not observe the deep silence that reigned among the aristocrats, and passed their camp without saying a word. Her absence of mind was so complete that she went to her easel, opened her paintbox, took out her brushes, slipped on her brown linen cuffs, tied her apron, examined her palette, all without thinking, as it seemed, of what she was doing. All the heads of the humbler group were turned to look at her. And if the young ladies of the Thirion faction were less frankly impatient than their companions, their side glances were nevertheless directed to Ginevra.

"She notices nothing," said Mademoiselle Roguin.

At this moment Ginevra, roused from the meditative attitude in which she had gazed at her canvas, turned her head towards the aristocratic party. With one glance she measured the distance that lay between them, and held her peace.

"It has not occurred to her that they meant to insult her," said Mathilde. "She has neither coloured nor turned pale. How provoked those young ladies will be if she likes her new place better than the old one! You are quite apart there, Mademoiselle," she added, addressing Ginevra in a loud voice.

The Italian girl affected not to hear, or perhaps she did not hear; she hastily rose, walked rather slowly along the partition which divided the dark closet from the studio, seeming to examine the skylight from which the light fell, and to this she ascribed so much importance that she got upon a chair to fasten the green baize a good deal higher, as it interfered with the light. At this elevation, she was on a level with a small crack in the boarding, the real object of her efforts, for the look she cast through it can only be compared with that of a miser discovering Aladdin's treasure. She quickly descended, came back to her place, arranged her picture, affected still to be dissatisfied with the light, pushed a table close to the partition, and placed a chair on it; then she nimbly mounted this scaffolding, and again peeped through the crack. She gave but one look into the closet, which was lit by a window at the top of the partition, but what she saw impressed her so vividly that she started.

"You will fall, Mademoiselle Ginevra!" cried Laure.

All the girls turned to look at their imprudent companion, who was tottering. The fear of seeing them gather round her gave her courage; she recovered her strength and her balance, and dancing on the chair, she turned to Laure and said with some agitation—"Bah! It is at any rate safer than a throne!" She quickly arranged the baize, came down, pushed the table and the chair far from the partition, returned to her easel, and made a few more attempts, seeming to try for an effect of light that suited her. Her picture did not really trouble her at all; her aim was to get close to the dark closet by which she placed herself, as she wished, at the end near the door. Then she prepared to set her palette, still in perfect silence. Where she now was, she soon heard more distinctly a slight noise which, on the day before, had greatly stirred her curiosity and sent her young imagination wandering over a wide field of conjecture. She easily recognised it as the deep, regular breathing of the sleeping man whom she had just now seen. Her curiosity was satisfied, but she found herself burdened with an immense responsibility. Through the crack she had caught sight of the Imperial Eagle,* and on a camp bed, in the dim light, had seen the figure of an officer of the guard. She guessed it all. Servin was sheltering a refugee. She now trembled lest one of her companions should come to examine her picture and should hear the unfortunate man breathe, or heave too deep a sigh, such as had fallen on her ear during yesterday's lesson. She resolved to remain near the door and trust to her wits to cheat the tricks of fate.

"I had better remain here," thought she, "to prevent some disaster, rather than leave the poor prisoner at the mercy of some giddy prank." This was the secret of Ginevra's apparent indifference when she found her easel transplanted; she was secretly delighted since she had been able to satisfy her curiosity in a natural manner, and besides, she was too much absorbed at this moment to inquire into the reason of her exclusion. Nothing is more mortifying to young girls, or indeed to anyone, than to see a practical joke, an insult, or a witticism fail of its effect in consequence of the victim's contempt. It would seem that our hatred of an enemy is increased by the height to which he can rise above us. Ginevra's conduct remained a riddle to all her companions. Her friends and her foes were alike surprised, for she was allowed to have every good quality excepting forgiveness of injuries. Though the opportunities for showing this vice of temper had rarely been offered to Ginevra by the incidents of studio life, the instances she had happened to give of her vindictive spirit and determination had nonetheless made a deep impression on her companions' minds. After many guesses, Mademoiselle Roguin finally regarded the Italian's silence as evidence of a magnanimity above all praise, and her party, inspired by her, conceived a plan to humiliate the aristocrats of the studio. They achieved their purpose by a fire of sarcasms directed at the pride and airs of the Party of the Right. Madame Servin's arrival put an end to this contest of self-assertiveness. Amélie, with the shrewdness which is always coupled with malice, had remarked, watched, and wondered at the excessive absence of mind which hindered Ginevra from hearing the keenly polite dispute of which she was the subject. The revenge which Mademoiselle Roguin and her followers were wreaking on Mademoiselle Thirion and her party had thus the fatal effect of setting the young Ultras to discover the cause of Ginevra's absorbed silence. The beautiful Italian became the centre of observation, and was watched by her friends as much as by her enemies. It is very difficult to hide the slightest excitement, the most trifling feeling, from fifteen idle and inquisitive girls whose mischief and wits crave only for secrets to guess, and intrigues to plot or to baffle, and who can ascribe to a gesture, to a glance, to a word, so many meanings, that they can hardly fail to discover the true one. Thus Ginevra di Piombo's secret was in great peril of being found out.

At this moment Madame Servin's presence produced a diversion in the drama that was being obscurely played at the bottom of these young hearts, and its sentiments, its ideas, and its development were expressed by almost allegorical words, by significant looks, by gestures, and even by silence, often more emphatic than speech. The moment Madame Servin came into the studio her eyes turned to the door by which Ginevra was standing. Under the present circumstances this look was not lost. If at first none of the maidens observed it, Mademoiselle Thirion remembered it afterwards, and accounted for the suspiciousness, the alarm, and mystery which gave a hunted expression to Madame Servin's eyes.

"Mesdemoiselles," she said, "Monsieur Servin cannot come today." Then she paid some little compliment to each pupil, all of them welcoming her in the girlish, caressing way which lies as much in the voice and eyes as in actions. She immediately went to Ginevra under an impulse of uneasiness, which she vainly tried to conceal. The Italian and the painter's wife exchanged friendly nods, and then stood in silence, one painting, the other watching her paint. The officer's breathing was easily audible, but Madame Servin could take no notice of it, and her dissimulation was so complete that Ginevra was tempted to accuse her of willful deafness. At this moment the stranger turned on the bed. The Italian girl looked Madame Servin steadily in the face, and, without betraying the smallest agitation, the lady said, "Your copy is as fine as the original. If I had to choose, I should really be puzzled."

"Monsieur Servin has not let his wife into the secret of this mystery," thought Ginevra, who, after answering the young wife with a gentle smile of incredulity, sang a snatch of some national *canzonetta** to cover any sounds the prisoner might make.

It was so unusual to hear the studious Italian sing, that all the girls looked at her in surprise. Later this incident served as evidence to the charitable suppositions of hatred. Madame Servin soon went away, and the hours of study ended without further event. Ginevra let all her companions leave, affecting to work on, but she unconsciously betrayed her wish to be alone, for as

341

the pupils made ready to go she looked at them with ill-disguised impatience. Mademoiselle Thirion, who within these few hours had become a cruel foe to the young girl, who was her superior in everything, guessed by the instinct of hatred that her rival's affected industry covered a mystery. She had been struck more than once by the attention with which Ginevra seemed to be listening to a sound no one else could hear. The expression she now read in the Italian's eyes was as a flash of illumination. She was the last to leave, and went in on her way down to see Madame Servin, with whom she stayed a few minutes. Then, pretending that she had forgotten her bag, she very softly went upstairs again to the studio and discovered Ginevra at the top of a hastily constructed scaffolding, so lost in contemplation of the unknown soldier that she did not hear the light sound of her companion's footsteps. It is true that Amélie walked on eggs—to use a phrase of Walter Scott's; she retired to the door and coughed. Ginevra started, turned her head, saw her enemy, and coloured; then she quickly untied the blind, to mislead her as to her purpose, and came down. After putting away her paintbox, she left the studio, carrying stamped upon her heart the image of a man's head as charming as the *Endymion*, Girodet's masterpiece,* which she had copied a few days previously.

"Such a young man to be proscribed! Who can he be? It is certainly not Marshal Ney."

These few sentences are the simplest expression of all the ideas which Ginevra turned over in her mind during the next two days. After that, notwithstanding her hurry to be first at the painting gallery, she found that Mademoiselle Thirion had already come in a carriage. Ginevra and her enemy watched each other for some time, but each kept her countenance impenetrable to the other. Amélie had seen the stranger's handsome face, but happily, and at the same time unhappily, the eagles and the uniform were not within the range of her eye through the crack. She lost herself in conjecture. Suddenly Servin came in, much earlier than usual.

"Mademoiselle Ginevra," said he, after casting an eye round the gallery, "why have you placed yourself there? The light is bad. Come nearer to these young ladies and lower your blind a little."

Then he sat down by Laure, whose work deserved his most lenient criticism.

"Well done!" he exclaimed, "this head is capitally done. You will be a second Ginevra."

The master went from easel to easel, blaming, flattering, jesting, and making himself, as usual, more feared for his jests than for his reproofs. The Italian had not obeyed his wishes; she remained at her post with the firm intention of staying there. She took out a sheet of paper and began to sketch in sepia the head of the unhappy refugee. A work conceived of with passion always bears a particular stamp. The faculty of giving truth to a rendering of nature or of a thought constitutes genius, and passion can often take its place. Thus in the circumstances in which Ginevra found herself, either the intuition she owed to her memory, which had been deeply struck, or perhaps necessity, the mother of greatness, lent her a supernatural flash of talent. The officer's head was thrown down on the paper with an inward trembling that she ascribed to fear, and which a physiologist would have recognised as the fever of inspiration. From time to time she stole a furtive glance at her companions, so as to be able to hide the sketch in case of any indiscretion on their part. But in spite of her sharp lookout, there was a moment when she failed to perceive that her relentless enemy, under the shelter of a huge portfolio, had turned her eyeglass on the mysterious drawing. Mademoiselle Thirion, recognising the refugee's features, raised her head suddenly, and Ginevra slipped away the sheet of paper.

"Why do you stay there in spite of my opinion, Mademoiselle?" the professor gravely asked Ginevra.

The girl hastily turned her easel so that no one could see her sketch, and said, in an agitated voice, as she showed it to her master—"Don't you think with me that this is a better light? May I not stay where I am?"

Servin turned pale. As nothing can escape the keen eyes of hatred, Mademoiselle Thirion threw herself, so to speak, into the excited feelings that agitated the professor and his pupil.

"You are right," said Servin. "But you will soon know more than I do," he added, with a forced laugh. There was a silence, during which the master looked at the head of the officer. "This is a masterpiece, worthy of Salvator Rosa!" he exclaimed, with an artist's vehemence.

At this exclamation, all the young people rose, and Mademoiselle Thirion came forward with the swiftness of a tiger springing on its prey. At this instant the prisoner, roused by the turmoil, woke up. Ginevra overset her stool, spoke a few incoherent sentences, and began to laugh, but she had folded the portrait in half and thrown it into a portfolio before her terrible enemy could see it. The girls crowded round the easel; Servin enlarged in a loud voice on the beauties of the copy on which his favourite pupil was just now engaged, and all the party were cheated by this stratagem, excepting Amélie, who placed herself behind her companions and tried to open the portfolio into which she had seen the sketch put. Ginevra seized it and set it in front of her without a word, and the two girls gazed at each other in silence.

"Come, Mesdemoiselles, to your places!" said Servin. "If you want to know as much as Mademoiselle di Piombo, you must not be always talking of fashions and balls, and trifling so much."

When the girls had all returned to their easels, the master sat down by Ginevra.

"Was it not better that this mystery should be discovered by me than by anyone else?" said the Italian girl in a low tone.

"Yes," answered the painter. "You are patriotic, but even if you had not been, you are still the person to whom I should entrust it."

The master and pupil understood each other, and Ginevra was not now afraid to ask, "Who is he?"

"An intimate friend of Labédoyère's; the man who, next to the unfortunate Colonel, did most to effect a junction between the 7th and the Grenadiers of Elba. He was a major in the guards, and has just come back from Waterloo."

"Why have you not burnt his uniform and shako, and put him into civilian dress?" asked Ginevra vehemently.

"Some clothes are to be brought for him this evening."

"You should have shut up the studio for a few days."

"He is going away."

"Does he wish to die?" said the girl. "Let him stay with you during these first days of the storm. Paris is the only place in France where a man may be safely hidden. Is he a friend of yours?" she added.

"No. He has no claim to my regard but his misfortunes. This is how he fell into my hands: my father-in-law, who had rejoined his regiment during this campaign, met the poor young man and saved him very cleverly from those who have arrested Labédoyère. He wanted to defend him, like a madman!"

"And do you call him so!" cried Ginevra, with a glance of surprise at the painter, who did not speak for a moment.

"My father-in-law is too closely watched to be able to keep anyone in his house," he went on. "He brought him here by night last week. I hoped to hide him from every eye by keeping him in this corner, the only place in the house where he can be safe."

"If I can be of any use, command me," said Ginevra. "I know Marshal Feltre."*

"Well, we shall see," replied the painter.

This conversation had lasted too long not to be noticed by all the other pupils. Servin left Ginevra, came back to each easel, and gave such long lessons that he was still upstairs when the clock struck the hour at which his pupils usually left.

"You have forgotten your bag, Mademoiselle Thirion," cried the professor, running after the young lady, who condescended to act the spy to gratify her hatred.

The inquisitive pupil came back for the bag, expressing some surprise at her own carelessness, but Servin's attention was to her additional proof of the existence of a mystery which was undoubtedly a serious one. She had already planned what should follow, and could say, like the Abbé Vertot: *I have laid my siege.** She ran downstairs noisily and violently slammed the door leading to Servin's rooms so that it might be supposed she had gone out, but she softly went upstairs again and hid behind the door of the studio. When the painter and Ginevra supposed themselves alone, he tapped in a particular manner at the door of the attic, which at once opened on its rusty, creaking hinges. The Italian girl saw a tall and well-built youth, whose Imperial uniform set her heart beating. The officer carried his arm in a sling, and his pale face told of acute suffering. He started at seeing her, a stranger. Amélie, who could see nothing, was afraid to stay any longer, but she had heard the creaking of the door, and that was enough. She silently stole away.

"Fear nothing," said the painter. "Mademoiselle is the daughter of the Emperor's most faithful friend, the Baron di Piombo."

The young officer felt no doubt of Ginevra's loyalty when once he had looked at her.

"You are wounded?" she said.

"Oh, it is nothing, Mademoiselle; the cut is healing."

At this moment the shrill and piercing tones of men

in the street came up to the studio, crying out, "This is the sentence which condemns to death——" All three shuddered. The soldier was the first to hear a name at which he turned pale.

"Labédoyère!" he exclaimed, dropping on to a stool.

They looked at each other in silence. Drops of sweat gathered on the young man's livid brow; with a gesture of despair he clutched the black curls of his hair, resting his elbow on Ginevra's easel.

"After all," said he, starting to his feet, "Labédoyère and I knew what we were doing. We knew the fate that awaited us if we triumphed or if we failed. He is dying for the cause, while I am in hiding——"

He hurried towards the studio door, but Ginevra, more nimble than he, rushed forward and stopped the way.

"Can you restore the Emperor?" she said. "Do you think you can raise the giant again when he could not keep his feet?"

"What then is to become of me?" said the refugee, addressing the two friends whom chance had sent him. "I have not a relation in the world; Labédoyère was my friend and protector, I am now alone; tomorrow I shall be exiled or condemned; I have never had any fortune but my pay; I spent my last crown piece to come and snatch Labédoyère from death and get him away. Death is an obvious necessity to me. When a man is determined to die, he must know how to sell his head to the executioner. I was thinking just now that an honest man's life is well worth that of two traitors, and that a dagger thrust, judiciously placed, may give one immortality."

This passion of despair frightened the painter, and even Ginevra, who fully understood the young man. The Italian admired the beautiful head and the delightful voice, of which the accents of rage scarcely disguised the sweetness; then she suddenly dropped balm on all the hapless man's wounds.

"Monsieur," said she, "as to your pecuniary difficulties, allow me to offer you the money I myself have saved. My father is rich; I am his only child; he loves me, and I am quite sure he will not blame me. Have no scruples in accepting it; our wealth comes from the Emperor, and we have nothing which is not the bounty of his munificence. Is it not gratitude to help one of his faithful soldiers? So take this money with as little ceremony as I make about offering it. It is only money," she added in a scornful tone. "Then, as to friends—you will find friends!" And she proudly raised her head, while her eyes shone with unwonted brilliancy. "The head which must fall tomorrow—the mark of a dozen guns—saves yours," she went on. "Wait till this storm is over, and you can take service in a foreign land if you are not forgotten, or in the French army if you are."

In the comfort offered by a woman there is a delicacy of feeling which always has a touch of something motherly, something far-seeing and complete, but when such words of peace and hope are seconded by grace of gesture, and the eloquence which comes from the heart, above all, when the comforter is beautiful, it is hard for a young man to resist. The young Colonel inhaled love by every sense. A faint flush tinged his white cheeks, and his eyes lost a little of the melancholy that dimmed them as he said, in a strange tone of voice, "You are an angel of goodness! But, Labédoyère!" he added, "Labédoyère!"

At this cry they all three looked at each other, speechless, and understood each other. They were friends, not of twenty minutes, but of twenty years.

"My dear fellow," said Servin, "can you save him?"

"I can avenge him."

Ginevra was thrilled. Though the stranger was handsome, his appearance had not moved her. The gentle pity that women find in their heart for suffering which is not ignoble had, in Ginevra, stifled every other emotion;

but to hear a cry of revenge, to find in this fugitive an Italian soul and Corsican magnanimity! This was too much for her; she gazed at the officer with respectful emotion, which powerfully stirred her heart. It was the first time a man had ever made her feel so strongly. Like all women, it pleased her to imagine that the soul of this stranger must be in harmony with the remarkable beauty of his features and the fine proportions of his figure, which she admired as an artist. Led by chance curiosity to pity, from pity to eager interest, she now from interest had reached sensations so strong and deep that she thought it rash to remain there any longer.

"Till tomorrow," she said, leaving her sweetest smile with the officer, to console him.

As he saw that smile, which threw a new light, as it were, on Ginevra's face, the stranger for a moment forgot all else.

"Tomorrow," he repeated with great sadness, "Tomorrow, Labédoyère——"

Ginevra turned to him and laid a finger on her lips, looking at him as though she would say, "Be calm, be prudent."

Then the young man exclaimed: "*O Dio! Chi non vorrei vivere dopo averla veduta!*"*

The peculiar accent with which he spoke the words startled Ginevra.

"You are a Corsican!" she exclaimed, coming back to him, her heart beating with gladness.

"I was born in Corsica," he replied, "but I was taken to Genoa when very young, and, as soon as I was of an age to enter the army, I enlisted."

The stranger's handsome person, the transcendent charm he derived from his attachment to the Emperor, his wound, his misfortunes, even his danger, all vanished before Ginevra's eyes, or rather all were fused in one new and exquisite sentiment. This refugee was a son of Corsica, and spoke its beloved tongue. In a minute the girl stood motionless, spellbound by a magical sensation. She saw before her eyes a living picture to which a combination of human feeling and chance lent dazzling hues. At Servin's invitation, the officer had taken his seat on an ottoman, the painter had untied the string which supported his guest's arm, and was now undoing the bandages in order to dress the wound. Ginevra shuddered as she saw the long wide gash, made by a sabre cut, on the young man's forearm, and gave a little groan. The stranger looked up at her and began to smile. There was something very touching that went to the soul in Servin's attentive care as he removed the lint and touched the tender flesh, while the wounded man's face, though pale and sickly, expressed pleasure rather than suffering as he looked at the young girl. An artist could not help admiring the antithesis of sentiments and the contrast of colour between the whiteness of the linen and the bare arm and the officer's blue and red coat. Soft dusk had now fallen on the studio, but a last sunbeam shone in on the spot where the refugee was sitting in such a way that his pale, noble face, his black hair, his uniform were all flooded with light. This simple effect the superstitious Italian took for an omen of good luck. The stranger seemed to her a celestial messenger who had spoken to her in the language of her native land and put her under the spell of childish memories, while in her heart arose a feeling as fresh and as pure as her first age of innocence. In a very short instant she stood pensive, lost in infinite thought; then she blushed to have betrayed her absence of mind, exchanged a swift, sweet look with the officer, and made her escape, seeing him still.

The next day there was no painting lesson; Ginevra came to the studio so that the prisoner could be with his fellow countrywoman. Servin, who had a sketch to finish, allowed the officer to sit there while he played guardian to the two young people who frequently spoke in Corsican. The poor soldier told of his sufferings during the retreat from Moscow, for, at the age of nineteen, he had found himself at the passage of the Berezina,* alone of all his regiment, having lost in his comrades the only men who could care for him, an orphan. He described, in words of fire, the great disaster of Waterloo. His voice was music to the Italian girl. Brought up in Corsican ways, Ginevra was, to some extent, a child of nature; falsehood was unknown to her, and she gave herself up without disguise to her impressions, owning them, or rather letting them be seen without the trickery, the mean and calculating vanity of the Parisian girl.

During this day she remained more than once, her palette in one hand, a brush in the other, while the brush was undipped in the colours on the palette; her eyes fixed on the officer's face, her lips slightly parted, she sat listening, ready to lay on the touch which was not given. She was not surprised to find such sweetness in the young man's eyes, for she felt her own soften in spite of her determination to keep them severe and cold. Thus, for hours, she painted with resolute attention, not raising her head because he was there watching her work. The first time he sat down to gaze at her in silence, she said to him in an agitated voice, after a long pause, "Does it amuse you, then, to look on at painting?"

That day she learnt that his name was Luigi. Before they parted it was agreed that if any important political events should occur on the days when the studio was open, Ginevra was to inform him by singing in an undertone certain Italian airs.

On the following day Mademoiselle Thirion informed all her companions, as a great secret, that Ginevra di Piombo had a lover—a young man who came during the hours devoted to lessons to hide in the dark closet of the studio.

"You, who take her part," said she to Mademoiselle Roguin, "watch her well, and you will see how she spends her time."

So Ginevra was watched with diabolical vigilance. Her songs were listened to, her glances spied. At moments when she believed that no one saw her, a dozen eyes were incessantly centred on her. And being forewarned, the girls interpreted in their true sense the agitations which passed across the Italian's radiant face, and her snatches of song, and the attention with which she listened to the muffled sounds which she alone could hear through the partition. By the end of a week, only Laure, of the fifteen students, had resisted the temptation to scrutinise Louis through the crack in the panel, or, by an instinct of weakness, still defended the beautiful Corsican girl. Mademoiselle Roguin wanted to make her wait on the stairs at the hour when they all left, to prove to her the intimacy between Ginevra and the handsome young man by finding them together, but she refused to condescend to an espionage which curiosity could not justify, and thus became an object of general reprobation.

Ere long the daughter of the gentleman-usher thought it unbecoming in her to work in the studio of a painter whose opinions were tainted with patriotism or Bonapartism—which at that time were regarded as one and the same thing, so she came no more to Servin's. Though Amélie forgot Ginevra, the evil she had sown bore fruit. Insensibly, by chance, for gossip, or out of prudery, the other damsels informed their mothers of the strange adventure in progress at the studio. One day Mathilde Roguin did not come; the next time another was absent; at last the three or four pupils, who had still remained, came no more. Ginevra and her little friend, Mademoiselle Laure, were for two or three days the sole occupants of the deserted studio. The Italian did not observe the isolation in which she was left, and did not even wonder at the cause of her companions' absence. Having devised the means of communicating with Louis, she lived in the studio as in a delightful retreat, secluded in the midst of the world, thinking only of the officer, and of the dangers which threatened him. This young creature, though sincerely admiring those noble characters who would not be false to their political faith, urged Louis to submit at once to royal authority in order to keep him in France, but Louis would not come out of hiding. If, indeed, passions only have their birth and grow up under the influence of romantic causes, never had so many circumstances concurred to link two beings by one feeling. Ginevra's regard for Louis, and his for her, thus made greater progress in a month than a fashionable friendship can make in ten years in a drawing room. Is not adversity the touchstone of character? Hence Ginevra could really appreciate Louis, and know him, and they soon felt a reciprocal esteem. Ginevra, who was older than Louis, found it sweet to be courted by a young man already so great, so tried by fortune, who united the experience of a man with the graces of youth. Louis, on his part, felt unspeakable delight in allowing himself to be apparently protected by a girl of twenty-five. Was it not a proof of love? The union in Ginevra of pride and sweetness, of strength and weakness, had an irresistible charm; Louis was indeed completely her slave. In short, they were already so deeply in love that they felt no need either to deny it to themselves, nor to tell it.

One day, towards evening, Ginevra heard the signal agreed on—Louis tapped on the woodwork with a pin, so gently as to make no more noise than a spider attaching its thread—thus asking if he might come out. She glanced round the studio, did not see little Laure, and answered the summons; but as the door was opened, Louis caught sight of the girl, and hastily retreated. Ginevra, much surprised, looked about her, saw Laure, and going up to her easel, said, "You are staying very late, dear. And that head seems to me finished; there is only a reflected light to put in on that lock of hair."

"It would be very kind of you," said Laure, in a tremulous voice, "if you would correct this copy for me; I should have something of your doing to keep."

"Of course I will," said Ginevra, sure of thus dismissing her. "I thought," she added, as she put in a few light touches, "that you had a long way to go home from the studio."

"Oh! Ginevra, I am going away for good," cried the girl, sadly.

"You are leaving Monsieur Servin?" asked the Italian, not seeming affected by her words, as she would have been a month since.

"Have you not noticed, Ginevra, that for some time there has been nobody here but you and me?"

"It is true," replied Ginevra, suddenly struck as by a reminiscence. "Are they ill, or going to be married, or are all their fathers employed now at the palace?"

"They have all left Monsieur Servin," said Laure.

"And why?"

"On your account, Ginevra."

"Mine!" repeated the Corsican, rising, with a threatening brow and a proud sparkle in her eyes.

"Oh, do not be angry, dear Ginevra," Laure piteously exclaimed. "But my mother wishes that I should leave too. All the young ladies said that you had an intrigue, that Monsieur Servin had lent himself to allowing a young man who loves you to stay in the dark closet; I never believed these calumnies, and did not tell my mother. Last evening Madame Roguin met my mother at a ball, and asked her whether she still sent me here. When Mama said yes, she repeated all those girls' tales. Mama scolded me well; she declared I must have known it all, and that I had failed in the confidence of a daughter in her mother by not telling her. Oh, my dear Ginevra, I, who always took you for my model, how grieved I am not to be allowed to stay on with you——"

"We shall meet again in the world; young women get married," said Ginevra.

"When they are rich," replied Laure.

"Come to see me, my father has wealth——"

"Ginevra," Laure went on, much moved, "Madame Roguin and my mother are coming tomorrow to see Monsieur Servin and complain of his conduct. At least let him be prepared."

A thunderbolt falling at her feet would have astonished Ginevra less than this announcement.

"What could it matter to them?" she innocently asked.

"Everyone thinks it very wrong. Mama says it is quite improper."

"And you, Laure, what do you think about it?"

The girl looked at Ginevra, and their hearts met. Laure could no longer restrain her tears; she threw herself on her friend's neck and kissed her. At this moment Servin came in.

"Mademoiselle Ginevra," he said, enthusiastically, "I have finished my picture, it is being varnished. But what is the matter? All the young ladies are making holiday, it would seem, or are gone into the country."

Laure wiped away her tears, took leave of Servin, and went away.

"The studio has been deserted for some days," said Ginevra, "and those young ladies will return no more."

"Bah!"

"Nay, do not laugh," said Ginevra, "listen to me. I am the involuntary cause of your loss of repute."

The artist smiled, and said, interrupting his pupil, "My repute? But in a few days my picture will be exhibited."

"It is not your talent that is in question," said the Italian girl; "but your morality. The young ladies have spread a report that Louis is shut up here, and that you . . . lent yourself to our lovemaking."

"There is some truth in that, Mademoiselle," replied the professor. "The girls' mothers are airified prudes," he went on. "If they had but come to me, everything would have been explained. But what do I care for such things? Life is too short!"

And the painter snapped his fingers in the air. Louis, who had heard part of the conversation, came out of his cupboard.

"You are losing all your pupils," he cried, "and I shall have been your ruin!"

The artist took his hand and Ginevra's, and joined them. "Will you marry each other, my children?" he asked, with touching bluntness. They both looked down, and their silence was their first mutual confession of love. "Well," said Servin, "and you will be happy, will you not? Can anything purchase such happiness as that of two beings like you?"

"I am rich," said Ginevra, "if you will allow me to indemnify you——"

"Indemnify!" Servin broke in. "Why, as soon as it is known that I have been the victim of a few little fools, and that I have sheltered a fugitive, all the liberals in Paris will send me their daughters! Perhaps I shall be in your debt then."

Louis grasped his protector's hand, unable to speak a word, but at last he said, in a broken voice, "To you I shall owe all my happiness."

"Be happy; I unite you," said the painter with comic unction, laying his hands on the heads of the lovers.

This pleasantry put an end to their emotional mood. They looked at each other, and all three laughed. The Italian girl wrung Louis's hand with a passionate grasp, and with a simple impulse worthy of her Corsican traditions.

"Ah, but, my dear children," said Servin, "you fancy

that now everything will go on so wonderfully? Well, you are mistaken."

They looked at him in amazement.

"Do not be alarmed; I am the only person inconvenienced by your giddy behaviour. But Madame Servin is the *pink of propriety*, and I really do not know how we shall settle matters with her."

"Heavens! I had forgotten. Tomorrow Madame Roguin and Laure's mother are coming to you——"

"I understand!" said the painter, interrupting her.

"But you can justify yourself," said the girl, with a toss of her head of emphatic pride. "Monsieur Louis," and she turned to him with an arch look, "has surely no longer an antipathy for the King's Government? Well, then," she went on, after seeing him smile, "tomorrow morning I shall address a petition to one of the most influential persons at the Ministry of War, a man who can refuse the Baron di Piombo's daughter nothing. We will obtain a tacit pardon for Captain Louis—for *they* will not recognise your grade as colonel. And you," she added, speaking to Servin, "may confound the mothers of my charitable young companions by simply telling them the truth."

"You are an angel!" said Servin.

While this scene was going on at the studio, Ginevra's father and mother were impatiently expecting her return.

"It is six o'clock, and Ginevra is not yet home," said Bartholoméo.

"She was never so late before," replied his wife.

The old people looked at each other with all the signs of very unusual anxiety. Bartholoméo, too much excited to sit still, rose and paced the room twice, briskly enough for a man of seventy-seven. Thanks to a strong constitution, he had changed but little since the day of his arrival at Paris, and tall as he was, he was still upright. His hair, thin and white now, had left his head

bald: a broad and prominent skull which gave token of
great strength and firmness. His face, deeply furrowed,
had grown full and wide with the pale complexion that
inspires veneration. The fire of a passionate nature still
lurked in the unearthly glow of his eyes, and the brows,
which were not quite white, preserved their terrible mo-
bility. The aspect of the man was severe, but it could
be seen that Bartholoméo had the right to be so. His
kindness and gentleness were known only to his wife
and daughter. In his official position, or before strangers, he never set aside the majesty which time had lent
to his appearance, and his habit of knitting those thick
brows, of setting every line in his face, and assuming
a Napoleonic fixity of gaze, made him seem as cold as
marble. In the course of his political life he had been so
generally feared that he was thought unsociable, but
it is not difficult to find the causes of such a reputation. Piombo's life, habits, and fidelity were a censure
on most of the courtiers. Notwithstanding the secret
missions entrusted to his discretion, which to any other man would have proved lucrative, he had not more
than thirty thousand francs a year in government se-
curities. And when we consider the low price of stock
under the Empire, and Napoléon's liberality to those
of his faithful adherents who knew how to ask, it is
easy to perceive that the Baron di Piombo was a man
of stern honesty; he owed his baron's plumage only to
the necessity of bearing a title when sent by Napoléon
to a foreign court. Bartholoméo had always professed
implacable hatred of the traitors whom Napoléon had
gathered about him, believing he could win them over
by his victories. It was he—so it was said—who took
three steps towards the door of the Emperor's room, after advising him to get rid of three men then in France,
on the day before he set out on his famous and brilliant campaign of 1814. Since the second return of the
Bourbons, Bartholoméo had ceased to wear the ribbon

of the Legion of Honour.* No man ever offered a finer image of the old Republicans, the incorruptible supporters of the Empire, who survived as the living derelicts of the two most vigorous governments the world has perhaps ever seen. If Baron di Piombo had displeased some courtiers, Daru, Drouot,* and Carnot were his friends. And, indeed, since Waterloo, he cared no more about other political figures than for the puffs of smoke he blew from his cigar.

With the moderate sum which MADAME, Napoléon's mother, had paid him for his estates in Corsica, Bartholoméo di Piombo had acquired the old Hôtel de Portenduère, in which he made no alterations. Living almost always in official residences at the cost of the government, he had resided in this mansion only since the catastrophe of Fontainebleau.* Like all simple folks of lofty character, the Baron and his wife cared nothing for external splendour; they still used the old furniture they had found in the house. The reception rooms of this dwelling—lofty, gloomy, and bare, the huge mirrors set in old gilt frames almost black with age, the furniture from the time of Louis XIV—were in keeping with Bartholoméo and his wife, figures worthy of antiquity. Under the Empire, and during the Hundred Days, while holding offices that brought handsome salaries, the old Corsican had kept house in grand style, but rather to do honour to his position than with a view to display. His life, and that of his wife and daughter, were so frugal, so quiet, that their modest fortune sufficed for their needs. To them their child Ginevra outweighed all the riches on earth. And when, in May 1814, Baron di Piombo resigned his place, dismissed his household, and locked his stable doors, Ginevra, as simple and unpretentious as her parents, had not a regret. Like all great souls, she found luxury in strength of feeling, as she sought happiness in solitude and work. And these three loved each other too much for the externals of life to have any value in their eyes. Often—and especially since Napoléon's second and fearful fall—Bartholoméo and his wife spent evenings of pure delight in listening to Ginevra as she played the piano or sang. To them there was an immense mystery of pleasure in their daughter's presence, in her lightest word; they followed her with their eyes with tender solicitude; they heard her step in the courtyard, however lightly she trod. Like lovers, they would all three sit silent for hours, hearing, better than in words, the eloquence of each other's soul. This deep feeling, the very life of the two old people, filled all their thoughts. Not three lives were here, but one, which, like the flame on a hearth, burnt up in three tongues of fire. Though now and then memories of Napoléon's bounty and misfortunes, or the politics of the day, took the place of their constant preoccupation, they could talk of them without breaking their community of thought. For did not Ginevra share their political passions? What could be more natural than the eagerness with which they withdrew into the heart of their only child? Until now the business of public life had absorbed Baron di Piombo's energies; but in resigning office the Corsican felt the need of throwing his energy into the last feeling that was left to him, and, besides the tie that bound a father and mother to their daughter, there was perhaps, unknown to these three despotic spirits, a powerful reason in the fanaticism of their reciprocal devotion; their love was undivided; Ginevra's whole heart was given to her father, as Piombo's was to her, and certainly, if it is true that we are more closely attached to one another by our faults than by our good qualities, Ginevra responded wonderfully to all her father's passions. Herein lay the single defect of this threefold existence. Ginevra was wholly given over to her vindictive impulses, carried away by them, as Bartholoméo had been in his youth. The Corsican delighted in encouraging these savage emotions in his daughter's heart, exactly as a lion teaches his whelps to spring on their prey. But as this apprenticeship to revenge could only be carried out under the parental roof, Ginevra never forgave her father anything; he always had to succumb. Piombo regarded these factitious quarrels as mere childishness, but the child thus acquired a habit of domineering over her parents. In the midst of these tempests which Bartholoméo loved to raise, a tender word, a look, was enough to soothe their angry spirits, and they were never so near kissing as when threatening wrath. However, from the age of about five, Ginevra, growing wiser than her father, constantly avoided these scenes. Her faithful nature, her devotion, the affection which governed all her thoughts, and her admirable good sense, had got the better of her rages; still, a great evil had resulted: Ginevra lived with her father and mother on a footing of equality which is always disastrous. To complete the picture of all the changes that had happened to these three persons since their arrival in Paris, Piombo and his wife, people of no education, had allowed Ginevra to study as she would. Following her girlish fancy, she had tried and given up everything, returning to each idea, and abandoning each in turn, until painting had become her ruling passion; she would have been perfect if her mother had been capable of directing her studies, of enlightening and harmonising her natural gifts. Her faults were the outcome of the pernicious training that the old Corsican had delighted to give her.

After making the floor creak for some minutes under his feet, the old man rang the bell. A servant appeared.

"Go to meet Mademoiselle Ginevra," said the master.

"I have always been sorry that we have no longer a carriage for her," said the Baronne.

"She would not have one," replied Piombo, looking at his wife, and she, accustomed for twenty years to obedience as her part, cast down her eyes.

Already in her seventies, tall, dry, pale and wrinkled, the Baronne looked just like the old women whom Schnetz introduces into the Italian scenes of his genre pictures; she commonly sat so silent that she might have been taken for a second Mrs. Shandy,* but a word, a look, or a gesture would betray that her feelings had all the vigour and freshness of youth. Her dress, devoid of smartness, was often devoid of taste. She usually remained passive, sunk in an armchair, like a sultana *valideh** waiting for, or admiring Ginevra—her pride and life. Her daughter's beauty, dress, and grace seemed to have become her own. All was well with her if Ginevra were content. Her hair had turned white, and a few locks were visible above her furrowed brow and at the side of her withered cheeks.

"For about a fortnight now," said she, "Ginevra has been coming in late."

"Pietro will not go fast enough," cried the impatient old man, crossing over the breast of his blue coat; he snatched up his hat, crammed it on to his head, and was off.

"You will not get far," his wife called after him.

In fact, the outer gate opened and shut, and the old mother heard Ginevra's steps in the courtyard. Bartholoméo suddenly reappeared, carrying his daughter in triumph, while she struggled in his arms.

"Here she is! *La Ginevra, la Ginevrettina, la Ginevrina, la Ginevrola, la Ginevretta, la Ginevra bella!*"

"Father! You are hurting me!"

Ginevra was immediately set down with a sort of respect. She nodded her head with a graceful gesture to reassure her mother, who was alarmed, and to convey that it had been only an excuse. Then the Baronne's pale, dull face regained a little colour, and even a kind of cheerfulness. Piombo rubbed his hands together extremely hard—the most certain symptom of gladness; he had acquired the habit at court when seeing

Napoléon in a rage with any of his generals or ministers who served him ill, or who had committed some blunder. When once the muscles of his face were relaxed, the smallest line in his forehead expressed benevolence. These two old folks at this moment were exactly like drooping plants, which are restored to life by a little water after a long drought.

"Dinner, dinner!" cried the Baron, holding out his hand to Ginevra, whom he addressed as Signora Piombellina, another token of good spirits, to which his daughter replied with a smile.

"By the way," said Piombo, as they rose from table, "do you know that your mother has remarked that for a month past you have stayed at the studio much later than usual? Painting before parents, it would seem."

"Oh, dear Father——"

"Ginevra is preparing some surprise for us, no doubt," said the mother.

"You are going to bring me a picture of your painting?" cried the Corsican, clapping his hands.

"Yes; I am very busy at the studio," she replied.

"What ails you, Ginevra? You are so pale," asked her mother.

"No!" exclaimed the girl, with a resolute gesture. "No! It shall never be said that Ginevra Piombo ever told a lie in her life."

On hearing this strange exclamation, Piombo and his wife looked at their daughter with surprise.

"I love a young man," she added, in a broken voice.

Then, not daring to look at her parents, her heavy eyelids drooped as if to veil the fire in her eyes.

"Is he a prince?" asked her father ironically, but his tone of voice made both the mother and daughter tremble.

"No, Father," she modestly replied, "he is a young man of no fortune——"

"Then he is quite handsome?"

"He is unfortunate."

"What is he?"

"As a comrade of Labédoyère's he was outlawed, homeless; Servin hid him, and——"

"Servin is a good fellow, and did well," cried Piombo. "But you, daughter, have done ill to love any man but your father——"

"Love is not within my control," said Ginevra gently.

"I had flattered myself," said her father, "that my Ginevra would be faithful to me till my death, that my care and her mother's would be all she would have known, that our tenderness would never meet with a rival affection in her heart, that——"

"Did I ever reproach you for your fanatical devotion to Napoléon?" said Ginevra. "Have you never loved anyone but me? Have you not been away at embassies for months at a time? Have I not borne your absence bravely? Life has necessities to which we must yield."

"Ginevra!"

"No, you do not love me for my own sake, and your reproaches show intolerable selfishness."

"And you accuse your father's love!" cried Piombo with flaming looks.

"Father, I will never accuse you," replied Ginevra, more gently than her trembling mother expected. "You have right on the side of your egoism, as I have right on the side of my love. Heaven is my witness that no daughter ever better fulfilled her duty to her parents. I have never known anything but love and happiness in what many daughters regard as obligations. Now, for fifteen years, I have never been anywhere but under your protecting wing, and it has been a very sweet delight to me to charm your lives. But am I then ungrateful in giving myself up to the joy of loving, and in wishing for a husband to protect me after you?"

"So you balance accounts with your father, Ginevra!" said the old man in ominous tones.

There was a frightful pause; no one dared to speak. Finally, Bartholoméo broke the silence by exclaiming in a heartrending voice: "Oh, stay with us; stay with your old father! I could not bear to see you love a man. Ginevra, you will not have long to wait for your liberty——"

"But, my dear Father, consider; we shall not leave you, we shall be two to love you; you will know the man to whose care you will bequeath me. You will be doubly loved by me and by him—by him, being part of me, and by me who am wholly he."

"Oh, Ginevra, Ginevra!" cried the Corsican, clenching his fists, "why were you not married when Napoléon had accustomed me to the idea and introduced dukes and counts as your suitors?"

"They only loved me to order," said the young girl. "Besides, I did not wish to leave you, and they would have taken me away with them."

"You do not wish to leave us alone," said Piombo, "but if you marry you isolate us. I know you, my child, you will love us no more. Élisa," he added, turning to his wife, who sat motionless and, as it were, stupefied; "we no longer have a daughter; she wants to be married."

The old man sat down after raising his hands in the air as though to invoke God; then he remained bent, crushed by his grief. Ginevra saw her father's agitation, and the moderation of his wrath pierced her to the heart; she had expected a scene and furies; she had not steeled her soul against his gentleness.

"My dear Father," she said in an appealing voice, "no, you shall never be abandoned by your Ginevra. But love me too a little for myself. If only you knew how *he* loves me! Ah, he could never bear to cause me pain!"

"What, comparisons already!" cried Piombo in a terrible voice. "No," he went on, "I cannot endure the idea. If he were to love you as you deserve, he would kill me, and if he were not to love you, I should stab him!"

Piombo's hands were trembling, his lips trembled, his whole frame trembled, and his eyes flashed lightnings; Ginevra alone could meet his gaze, for then her eyes too flashed fire, and the daughter was worthy of the father.

"To love you! What man is worthy of such a life?" he went on. "To love you as a father even—is it not to live in Paradise? Who then could be worthy to be your husband?"

"He," said Ginevra. "He of whom I feel myself unworthy."

"He," echoed Piombo mechanically. "Who? *He?*"

"The man I love."

"Can he know you well enough already to adore you?"

"But, Father," said Ginevra, feeling a surge of impatience, "even if he did not love me—so long as I love him——"

"You do love him then?" cried Piombo. Ginevra gently bowed her head. "You love him more than you love me?"

"The two feelings cannot be compared," she replied.

"One is stronger than the other?" said Piombo.

"Yes, I think so," said Ginevra.

"You shall not marry him!" cried the Corsican in a voice that made the windows rattle.

"I will marry him," replied Ginevra calmly.

"*Mon Dieu!*" cried the mother, "how will this quarrel end? *Santa Virgina* come between them!"

The Baron, who was striding up and down the room, came and seated himself. An icy sternness darkened his face; he looked steadfastly at his daughter, and said in a gentle and affectionate voice, "Nay, Ginevra—you will not marry him. Oh, do not say you will, this evening. Let me believe that you will not. Do you wish to see your father on his knees before you and his white hairs humbled? I will beseech you——"

"Ginevra Piombo is not accustomed to promise and not to keep her word," said she; "I am your child."

"She is right," said the Baronne, "we come into the world to marry."

"And so you encourage her in disobedience," said the Baron to his wife, who, stricken by the reproof, froze into a statue.

"It is not disobedience to refuse to yield to an unjust command," replied Ginevra.

"It cannot be unjust when it emanates from your father's lips, my child. Why do you rise in judgment on me? Is not the repugnance I feel a counsel from on high? I am perhaps saving you from some misfortune."

"The misfortune would be that he should not love me."

"Always he!"

"Yes, always," she said. "He is my life, my joy, my thought. Even if I obeyed you, he would be always in my heart. If you forbid me to marry him, will it not make me hate you?"

"You love us no longer!" cried Piombo.

"Oh!" said Ginevra, shaking her head.

"Well, then, forget him. Be faithful to us. After us . . . you understand . . ."

"Father, would you make me wish that you were dead?" cried Ginevra.

"I shall outlive you; children who do not honour their parents die early," cried her father at the utmost pitch of exasperation.

"All the more reason for marrying soon and being happy," said she.

This coolness, this force of argument, brought Piombo's agitation to a crisis; the blood rushed violently to his head, his face turned purple. Ginevra shuddered; she flew like a bird on to her father's knees, threw her arms round his neck, stroked his hair, and exclaimed, quite overcome—"Oh, yes, let me die first! I could not survive you, my dear, kind Father."

"Oh, my Ginevra, my foolish Ginevretta!" answered Piombo, whose rage melted under this caress as an icicle melts in the sunshine.

"It was time you should put an end to the matter," said the Baronne in a broken voice.

"Poor Mother!"

"Ah, Ginevretta, *mia Ginevra bella!*"

And the father played with his daughter as if she were a child of six; he amused himself with undoing the waving tresses of her hair and dancing her on his knee; there was dotage in his demonstrations of tenderness. Presently his daughter scolded him as she kissed him, and tried, half in jest, to get leave to bring Louis to the house, but, jesting too, her father refused. She sulked, and recovered herself, and sulked again; then, at the end of the evening, she was only too glad to have impressed on her father the ideas of her love for Louis and of a marriage ere long. Next day she said no more about it; she went later to the studio and returned early; she was more affectionate to her father than she had ever been and showed herself grateful, as if to thank him for the consent to her marriage he seemed to give by silence. In the evening she played and sang for a long time, and exclaimed now and then, "This nocturne requires a man's voice!" She was an Italian, and that says everything. A week later her mother beckoned her; Ginevra went, and then in her ear she whispered, "I have persuaded your father to receive him."

"Oh, Mother! You make me very happy."

So that afternoon, Ginevra had the joy of coming home to her father's house leaning on Louis's arm. The poor officer came out of his hiding place for the second time. Ginevra's active intervention addressed to the Duc de Feltre, then Minister of War, had been crowned with perfect success. Louis had just been reinstated as an officer on the reserve list. This was a very long step towards a prosperous future. Informed by Ginevra of all the difficulties he would meet with in the Baron, the young officer dared not confess his dread of failing to please him. This man, so brave in adversity, so bold on the field of battle, quaked as he thought of entering the Piombos' drawing room. Ginevra felt him tremble, and this emotion, of which their happiness was the first cause, was to her a fresh proof of his love.

"How pale you are!" said she, as they reached the gate of the hotel.

"Oh, Ginevra! If my life alone were at stake——"

Though Bartholoméo had been informed by his wife of this official introduction of his daughter's lover, he did not rise to meet him, but remained in the armchair he usually occupied, and the severity of his countenance was icy.

"Father," said Ginevra, "I have brought you a gentleman whom you will no doubt be pleased to see. Monsieur Louis, a soldier who fought quite close to the Emperor at Mont-Saint-Jean——"*

The Baron rose, cast a furtive glance at Louis, and said in a sardonic tone—"Monsieur wears no orders?"

"I no longer wear the Legion of Honour," replied Louis bashfully, and he humbly remained standing.

Ginevra, hurt by her father's rudeness, brought forward a chair. The officer's reply satisfied the old servant of Napoléon. Madame Piombo, seeing that her husband's brows were recovering their natural shape, said, to revive the conversation, "Monsieur is wonderfully like Nina Porta. Do not you think that he has quite the face of a Porta?"

"Nothing can be more natural," replied the young man, on whom Piombo's flaming eyes were fixed. "Nina was my sister."

"You are Luigi Porta?" asked the old man.

"Yes."

Bartholoméo di Piombo rose, tottered, was obliged to lean on a chair, and looked at his wife. Élisa Piombo came up to him; then the two old folks silently left the room, arm in arm, with a look of horror at their daughter. Luigi Porta, quite bewildered, gazed at Ginevra, who turned as white as a marble statue, and remained with her eyes fixed on the door where her father and mother had disappeared. There was something so solemn in her silence and their retreat, that, for the first time in his life perhaps, a feeling of fear came over him. She clasped her hands tightly together, and said in a voice so choked that it would have been inaudible to anyone but a lover, "How much woe in one word!"

"In the name of our love, what have I said?" asked Luigi Porta.

"My father has never told me our deplorable history," she replied. "And when we left Corsica I was too young to know anything about it."

"Is it a *vendetta?*" asked Luigi, trembling.

"Yes. By questioning my mother I learnt that the Porta had killed my brothers and burnt down our house. My father then massacred all your family. How did you survive, you whom he thought he had tied to the posts of a bed before setting fire to the house?"

"I do not know," replied Luigi. "When I was six I was taken to Genoa, to an old man named Colonna. No account of my family was ever given to me; I only knew that I was an orphan, and penniless. Colonna was like a father to me; I bore his name till I entered the army; then, as I needed papers to prove my identity, old Colonna told me that, helpless as I was, and hardly more than a child, I had enemies. He made me promise to take the name of Luigi only, to evade them."

"Fly, fly, Luigi," cried Ginevra. "Yet, stay; I must go with you. So long as you are in my father's house you are safe. As soon as you quit it, take care of yourself. You will go from one danger to another. My father has two Corsicans in his service, and if he does not threaten your life they will."

"Ginevra," he said, "must this hatred exist between us?"

She smiled sadly and bowed her head. But she soon raised it again with a sort of pride, and said, "Oh, Luigi, our feelings must be very pure and true that I should have the strength to walk in the path I am entering on. But it is for the sake of happiness which will last as long as life, is it not?"

Luigi answered only with a smile, and pressed her hand. The girl understood that only a great love could at such a moment scorn mere protestations. This calm and conscientious expression of Luigi's feelings seemed to speak for their strength and permanence. The fate of the couple was thus sealed. Ginevra foresaw many painful contests to be fought out, but the idea of deserting Louis—an idea which had perhaps floated before her mind—at once vanished. His, henceforth and forever, she suddenly dragged him away and out of the house with a sort of violence, and did not quit him till they reached the house where Servin had taken a humble lodging for him. When she returned to her father's house, she had assumed the serenity which comes of a strong resolve. No change of manner revealed any uneasiness. She found her parents ready to sit down to dinner, and she looked at them with eyes devoid of defiance and full of sweetness. She saw that her old mother had been weeping; at the sight of her red eyelids for a moment her heart failed her, but she hid her emotion. Piombo seemed to be a prey to anguish too keen, too concentrated to be shown by ordinary means of expression. The servants waited on a meal which no one ate. A horror of food is one of the symptoms indicative of a great crisis of the soul. All three rose without any one of them having spoken a word. When Ginevra was seated in the great, solemn drawing room between her father and mother, Piombo tried to speak, but he found no voice; he tried to walk about, but found no strength; he sat down again and rang the bell.

"Pietro," said he to the servant at last, "light the fire, I am cold."

Ginevra was shocked, and looked anxiously at her father. The struggle he was going through must be frightful; his face looked quite changed. Ginevra knew the extent of the danger that threatened her, but she did not tremble, while the glances that Bartholoméo cast at his daughter seemed to proclaim that he was at this moment in fear of the character whose violence was his own work. Between these two everything must be in excess. And the certainty of the possible change of feeling between the father and daughter filled the Baronne's face with an expression of terror.

"Ginevra, you love the enemy of your family," said Piombo at last, not daring to look at his daughter.

"That is true," she replied.

"You must choose between him and us. Our *vendetta* is part of ourselves. If you do not espouse my cause, you are not of my family."

"My choice is made," said Ginevra, in a steady voice.

His daughter's calmness misled Bartholoméo.

"Oh, my dear daughter!" cried the old man, whose eyelids were moist with tears, the first, the only tears he ever shed in his life.

"I shall be his wife," she said abruptly.

Bartholoméo could not see for a moment, but he recovered himself and replied, "This marriage shall never be so long as I live. I will never consent." Ginevra kept silence. "But, do you understand," the Baron went on, "that Luigi is the son of the man who killed your brothers?"

"He was six years old when the crime was committed; he must be innocent of it," she answered.

"A Porta!" cried Bartholoméo.

"But how could I share this hatred," said the girl eagerly. "Did you bring me up in the belief that a Porta was a monster? Could I imagine that even one was left of those you had killed? Is it not in nature that you should make your *vendetta* give way to my feelings?"

"A Porta!" repeated Piombo. "If his father had found you then in your bed, you would not be alive now. He would have dealt you a hundred deaths."

"Possibly," she said. "But his son has given me more than life. To see Luigi is a happiness without which I cannot live. Luigi has revealed to me the world of feeling. I have, perhaps, seen even handsomer faces than his, but none ever charmed me so much. I have, perhaps, heard voices—no, no, never one so musical! Luigi loves me. He shall be my husband."

"Never!" said Piombo. "Ginevra, I would sooner see you in your coffin!" The old Corsican rose and paced the room with hurried strides, uttering fierce words with pauses between that betrayed all his indignation. "You think, perhaps, that you can bend my will? Undeceive yourself. I will not have a Porta for my son-in-law. That is my decision. Never speak of the matter again. I am Bartholoméo di Piombo, do you hear, Ginevra?"

"Do you attach any mysterious meaning to the words?" she coldly asked.

"They mean that I have a dagger, and that I do not fear the justice of men. We Corsicans settle such matters with God."

"Well," said the girl, "I am Ginevra di Piombo, and I declare that in six months I will be Luigi Porta's wife. You are a tyrant, Father," she added, after an ominous pause.

Bartholoméo clenched his fists and struck the marble chimney shelf. "Ah! We are in Paris!" he muttered.

He said no more, but folded his arms and bowed his head on his breast, nor did he say another word the whole evening. Having asserted her will, the girl affected the most complete indifference; she sat down to the piano, sang, played the most charming music with a grace and feeling that proclaimed her perfect freedom of mind, triumphing over her father, whose brow showed no relenting. The old man deeply felt this tacit insult, and at that moment gathered the bitter fruits of the education he had given his daughter. Respect is a barrier which protects the parents and the children alike, sparing the former much sorrow, and the latter remorse. The next day, as Ginevra was going out at the hour when she usually went to the studio, she found the door of the house closed upon her; but she soon devised means for informing Luigi Porta of her father's severity. A waiting woman, who could not read, carried to the young officer a letter written by Ginevra. For five days the lovers contrived to correspond, thanks to the plots that young people of twenty can always contrive. The father and daughter rarely spoke to each other. Both had in the bottom of their hearts an element of hatred; they suffered, but in pride and silence. Knowing well how strong were the bonds of love that tied them to each other, they tried to wrench them asunder, but without success. No sweet emotion ever came, as it had been wont, to give light to Bartholoméo's severe features when he gazed at his Ginevra, and there was something savage in her expression when she looked at her father. Reproach sat on her innocent brow; she gave herself up, indeed, to thoughts of happiness, but remorse sometimes dimmed her eyes. It was not, indeed, difficult to divine that she would never enjoy in peace a felicity which made her parents unhappy. In Bartholoméo, as in his daughter, all the irresolution arising from their native goodness of heart was doomed to shipwreck on their fierce pride and the revengeful spirit peculiar to Corsicans. They encouraged each other in their wrath, and shut their eyes to the future. Perhaps, too, each fancied that the other would yield.

On Ginevra's birthday, her mother, heartbroken at this disunion, which was assuming a serious aspect, planned to reconcile the father and daughter by an appeal to the memories of this anniversary. They were all three sitting in Bartholoméo's room. Ginevra guessed her mother's purpose from the hesitation written in her face, and she smiled sadly. At this instant a servant announced two lawyers, accompanied by several witnesses, who all came into the room. Bartholoméo stared at the men, whose cold, set faces were in themselves an insult to souls so fevered as those of the three principal actors in this scene. The old man turned uneasily to his daughter, and saw on her face a smile of triumph which led him to suspect some catastrophe, but he affected, as savages do, to preserve a deceitful rigidity as he looked at the two lawyers with a sort of apathetic curiosity. At a gesture of invitation from the old man the visitors took seats.

"Monsieur is no doubt Baron di Piombo?" said the elder of the two lawyers.

Bartholoméo bowed. The lawyer gave his head a little jerk and looked at Ginevra with the sly expression of a bailiff nabbing a debtor; then he took out his snuff box, opened it, and, taking a pinch of snuff, absorbed it in little sniffs while considering the opening words of his discourse, and while pronouncing them he made constant pauses (an oratorical effect which the symbol "—" represents very imperfectly).

"Monsieur," said he, "I am Monsieur Roguin, notary to Mademoiselle, your daughter, and we are here —my colleague and I—to carry out the requirements of the law, and—to put an end to the divisions which —as it would seem—have arisen—between you and Mademoiselle, your daughter—on the question—of— her—marriage with Monsieur Luigi Porta."

This speech, made in a pedantic style, seemed, no doubt, to Monsieur Roguin much too fine to be understood all in a moment, and he stopped, while looking at Bartholoméo with an expression peculiar to men of business, and which is halfway between servility and

familiarity. Lawyers are so much used to feigning interest in the persons to whom they speak that their features
at last assume a grimace which they can put on and off
with their official *pallium*. This caricature of friendli-
ness, so mechanical as to be easily detected, irritated
Bartholoméo to such a pitch that it took all his self-con-
trol not to throw Monsieur Roguin out of the window; a
look of fury emphasised his wrinkles, and on seeing this
the notary said to himself: "I am making an effect."

"But," he went on in a honeyed voice, "Monsieur
le Baron, on such occasions as these, our intervention
must always, at first, be essentially conciliatory.— Have
the kindness to listen to me.—It is in evidence that
Mademoiselle Ginevra Piombo—has today—attained
the age at which, after a 'respectful summons,' she
may proceed to the solemnisation of her marriage—
notwithstanding that her parents refuse their consent.
Now—it is customary in families—which enjoy a
certain consideration—which move in society—and
preserve their dignity—people, in short, to whom
it is important not to let the public into the secret of
their differences—and who also do not wish to do
themselves an injury by blighting the future lives of a
young husband and wife—for that is doing themselves
an injury.—It is the custom, I was saying—in such
highly respectable families—not to allow the serving
of such a summons—which must be—which always is
a record of a dispute—which at last ceases to exist.—For
as soon, Monsieur, as a young lady has recourse to a
'respectful summons,' she proclaims a determination
so obstinate—that her father—and her mother—" he
added, turning to the Baronne, "can have no further hope
of seeing her follow their advice.—Hence the parental
prohibition being nullified—in the first place by this
fact—and also by the decision of the law—it is always
the case that a wise father, after finally remonstrating
with his child, allows her the liberty——"

Monsieur Roguin paused, perceiving that he might talk on for two hours without extracting an answer; he also felt a peculiar agitation as he looked at the man he was trying to convince. An extraordinary change had come over Bartholoméo's countenance. All its lines were set, giving him an expression of indescribable cruelty, and he glared at the lawyer like a tiger. The Baronne sat mute and passive. Ginevra, calm and resolute, was waiting; she knew that the notary's voice was stronger than hers, and she seemed to have made up her mind to keep silence. At the moment when Roguin ceased speaking, the scene was so terrible that the witnesses, as strangers, trembled; never, perhaps, had such a silence weighed on them. The lawyers looked at each other as if in consultation, then they rose and went to the window.

"Did you ever come across clients made to this pattern?" asked Roguin of his colleague.

"There is nothing to be got out of him," said the younger man. "In your place I should read the summons and nothing more. The old man is no joke; he is choleric, and you will gain nothing by trying to *discuss* matters with him."

Monsieur Roguin therefore read aloud from a sheet of stamped paper a summons ready drawn up, and coldly asked Bartholoméo what his reply was.

"Are there laws in France then that upset a father's authority?" asked the Corsican.

"Monsieur——" said Roguin, smoothly.

"That snatch a child from her father?"

"Monsieur——"

"That rob an old man of his last consolation?"

"Monsieur, your daughter belongs to you only so long——"

"That kill her?"

"Monsieur, allow me."

There is nothing more hideous than the cold-blooded and close reasoning of a lawyer in the midst of such scenes of passion as they are usually mixed up with. The faces which Piombo saw seemed to him to have escaped from Hell; his cold and concentrated rage knew no bounds at the moment when his little opponent's calm and almost piping voice uttered that fatal *"allow me."* He sprang at a long dagger which hung from a nail over the chimney piece and rushed at his daughter. The younger of the two lawyers and one of the witnesses threw themselves between him and Ginevra, but Bartholoméo brutally knocked them over, showing them a face of fire and glowing eyes which seemed more terrible than the flash of the dagger. When Ginevra found herself face to face with her father, she looked at him steadily with a glance of triumph, went slowly towards him, and knelt down.

"No, no! I cannot!" he exclaimed, flinging away the weapon with such force that it stuck fast in the wainscot.

"Mercy, then, mercy!" said she. "You hesitate to kill me, but you refuse me life. Oh, Father, I never loved you so well—but give me Luigi. I ask your consent on my knees; a daughter may humble herself to her father. My Luigi, or I must die!"

The violent excitement that choked her prevented her saying more; she found no voice; her convulsive efforts plainly showed that she was between life and death. Bartholoméo roughly pushed her away.

"Go," he said, "the wife of Luigi Porta cannot be a Piombo. I no longer have a daughter! I cannot bring myself to curse you, but I give you up. You have now no father. My Ginevra Piombo is buried then!" he exclaimed in a deep tone, as he clutched at his heart. "Go, I say, wretched girl," he went on after a moment's silence. "Go, and never let me see you again." He took Ginevra by the arm, and in silence led her out of the house.

"Luigi!" cried Ginevra, as she went into the humble room where the officer was lodged, "my Luigi, we have no fortune but our love."

"We are richer than all the kings of the earth," he replied.

"My father and mother have cast me out," said she with deep melancholy.

"I will love you for them."

"Shall we be very happy?" she cried, with a gaiety that had something terrible in it.

"Forever!" he answered, clasping her to his heart.

On the day following that on which Ginevra had quitted her father's house, she went to beg Madame Servin

Il sauta sur un long poignard .... et s'élança sur sa fille.

Plate XX

to grant her protection and shelter till the time, fixed by law, when she could be married to Luigi. There began her apprenticeship to the troubles which the world strews in the way of those who do not obey its rules. Madame Servin, who was greatly distressed at the injury that Ginevra's adventure had done the painter, received the fugitive coldly, and explained to her with circumspect politeness that she was not to count on her support. Too proud to insist, but amazed at such selfishness, to which she was unaccustomed, the young Corsican went to lodge in a furnished house as near as possible to Luigi's. The son of the Portas spent all his days at the feet of his beloved; his youthful love and the purity of his mind dispersed the clouds which her father's reprobation had settled on the banished daughter's brow, and he painted the future as so fair that she ended by smiling, though she could not forget her parents' severity.

One morning the maid of the house brought up to her several trunks containing dress stuffs, linen, and a quantity of things needful for a young woman settling for the first time. In this she recognised the foreseeing kindness of a mother, for as she examined these gifts she found a purse into which the Baronne had put some money belonging to Ginevra, adding all her own savings. With the money was a letter, in which she implored her daughter to give up her fatal purpose of marrying, if there were yet time. She had been obliged, she said, to take unheard-of precautions to get this small assistance conveyed to Ginevra; she begged her not to accuse her of hardness if henceforth she left her neglected; she feared she could do no more for her; she blessed her, hoped she might find happiness in this fatal marriage if she persisted, and assured her that her one thought was of her beloved daughter. At this point tears had blotted out many words of the letter.

"Oh, Mother!" cried Ginevra, quite overcome. She felt a longing to throw herself at her mother's feet, to see her, to breathe the blessed air of home; she was on the point of rushing off when Luigi came in. She looked at him and her filial affection vanished; her tears were dried; she could not find it in her to leave the unhappy and loving youth. To be the sole hope of a noble soul, to love and to desert it—such a sacrifice is treason of which no young heart is capable. Ginevra had the generosity to bury her grief at the bottom of her soul.

At last the day of their wedding came. Ginevra found no one near her. Luigi took advantage of the moment when she was dressing to go in search of the necessary witnesses to their marriage act. These were very good people. One of them, an old quartermaster of hussars, had, when in the army, found himself under such obligations to Luigi as an honest man never forgets; he had become a job master, and had several hackney carriages. The other, a builder, was the proprietor of the house where the young couple were to lodge. Each of these brought a friend, and all four came with Luigi to fetch the bride. Unaccustomed as they were to social grimacing, seeing nothing extraordinary in the service they were doing to Luigi, these men were decently but quite plainly dressed, and there was nothing to proclaim the gay escort of a wedding. Ginevra herself was very simply clad, to be in keeping with her fortune, but, nevertheless, there was something so noble and impressive in her beauty that at the sight of her the words died on the lips of the good folks who had been prepared to pay her some compliment; they bowed respectfully, and she bowed in return; they looked at her in silence, and could only admire her. Joy can only express itself among equals. So, as fate would have it, all was gloomy and serious around the lovers; there was nothing to reflect their happiness. The church and the town hall were not far away. The two Corsicans, followed by the four witnesses required by law, decided to go on foot with a simplicity which robbed this great event of social life of all parade. In the courtyard of the town hall they found a crowd of carriages which announced a numerous party within. They went upstairs and entered a large room, where the couples who were to be made happy on this particular day were awaiting the mayor of that quarter of Paris with considerable impatience. Ginevra sat down by Luigi on the end of a long bench, and their witnesses remained standing for lack of seats. Two brides, pompously arrayed in white, loaded with ribbons and lace and pearls, and crowned with bunches of orange blossom of which the sheeny buds quivered under their veils, were surrounded by their families and accompanied by their mothers, to whom they turned with looks at once timid and satisfied; every eye reflected their happiness, and every face seemed to exhale benedictions. Fathers, witnesses, brothers, and sisters were coming and going like a swarm of insects playing in a sunbeam which soon must vanish. Everyone seemed to understand the preciousness of this brief hour in life when the heart stands poised between two hopes—the wishes of the past, the promise of the future. At this sight Ginevra felt her heart swell, and she pressed Luigi's arm. He gave her a look, and a tear rose to the young man's eye; he never saw more clearly than at that moment all that his Ginevra had sacrificed for him. That rare tear made the young girl forget the forlorn position in which she stood. Love poured treasures of light between the lovers, who from that moment saw nothing but each other in the midst of the confusion. Their witnesses, indifferent to the ceremonial, were quietly discussing business matters.

"Oats are very dear," said the quartermaster to the mason.

"They have not yet gone up so high as plaster in proportion," said the builder.

And they walked round the large room.

"What a lot of time we are losing here!" exclaimed

the mason, putting a huge silver watch back into his pocket.

Luigi and Ginevra, clinging to each other, seemed to be but one person. A poet would certainly have admired these two heads, full of the same feeling, alike in colouring, melancholy and silent in the presence of the two buzzing wedding parties, of four excited families sparkling with diamonds and flowers, and full of gaiety which seemed a mere effervescence. All the joys of which these loud and gorgeous groups made a display, Luigi and Ginevra kept buried at the bottom of their hearts. On one side was the coarse clamour of pleasure; on the other the delicate silence of happy souls: earth and heaven. But Ginevra trembled, and could not altogether shake off her woman's weakness. Superstitious, as Italians are, she regarded this contrast as an omen, and in the depths of her heart she harboured a feeling of dread as unconquerable as her love itself.

Suddenly an official in livery threw open the double doors; silence fell, and his voice sounded like a yelp as he called out the names of Monsieur Luigi Porta and Mademoiselle Ginevra Piombo. This incident caused the pair some embarrassment. The celebrity of the name of Piombo attracted attention; the spectators looked about them for a wedding party which must surely be a splendid one. Ginevra rose; her eyes, thunderous with pride, subdued the crowd. She took Luigi's arm and went forward with a firm step, followed by the witnesses. A murmur of astonishment which rapidly grew louder, and whispering on all sides, reminded Ginevra that the world was calling her to account for her parents' absence. Her father's curse seemed to be pursuing her.

"Wait for the families of the bride and bridegroom," said the mayor to the clerk, who at once began to read the contracts.

"The father and mother enter a protest," said the clerk indifferently.

"On both sides?" asked the mayor.

"The man is an orphan."

"Where are the witnesses?"

"They are here," said the clerk, pointing to the four motionless and silent men who stood like statues, with their arms crossed.

"But if the parents protest——?" said the mayor.

"The 'respectful summons' has been presented in due form," replied the man, rising to place the various documents in the functionary's hands.

This discussion in an office seemed to brand them, and in a few words told a whole history. The hatred of the Porta and the Piombo, all these terrible passions, were thus recorded on a page of a register, as the annals of a nation may be inscribed on a tombstone in a few lines, nay, even in a single name: Robespierre or Napoléon. Ginevra was trembling. Like the dove crossing the waters, which had no rest for her foot but in the ark, her eyes could take refuge only in Luigi's, for all else was cold and sad. The mayor had a stern, disapproving look, and his clerk stared at the couple with ill-natured curiosity. Nothing ever had less the appearance of a festivity. Like all the other events of human life when they are stripped of their accessories, it was a simple thing in itself, immense in its idea. After some questions, to which they replied, the mayor muttered a few words, and then, having signed their names in the register, Luigi and Ginevra were man and wife. The young Corsicans, whose union had all the poetry which genius has consecrated in Romeo and Juliet, went away between two lines of jubilant relations to whom they did not belong, and who were out of patience at the delay caused by a marriage apparently so forlorn. When the girl found herself in the courtyard and under the open sky, a deep sigh broke from her very heart.

"Oh, will a whole life of love and devotion suffice to repay my Ginevra for her courage and tenderness?" said Luigi.

At these words, spoken with tears of joy, the bride forgot all her suffering, for she had suffered in showing herself to the world claiming a happiness which her parents refused to sanction.

"Why do men try to come between us?" she said, with a simplicity of feeling that enchanted Luigi.

Gladness made them more lighthearted. They saw neither the sky, nor the earth, nor the houses, and flew on wings to the church. At last they found themselves in a small, dark chapel, and in front of a humble altar where an old priest married them. There, as at the town hall, they were pursued by the two weddings that persecuted them with their splendour. The church, filled with friends and relations, rang with the noise made by carriages, beadles, porters, and priests. Altars glittered with ecclesiastical magnificence; the crowns of orange blossom that decked the statues of the Virgin seemed quite new. Nothing was to be seen but flowers, with perfumes, gleaming tapers, and velvet cushions embroidered with gold. God seemed to have a share in this rapture of a day. When the symbol of eternal union was to be held above the heads of Luigi and Ginevra—the yoke of white satin which for some is so soft, so bright, so light, and for the greater number is made of lead—the priest looked round in vain for two young boys to fill the happy office; two of the witnesses took their place. The priest gave the couple a hasty discourse on the dangers of life, and on the duties they must one day inculcate in their children, and he here took occasion to insinuate a reflection on the absence of Ginevra's parents; then having united them in the presence of God, as the mayor had united them in the presence of the Law, he ended the Mass and left them.

"God bless them," said Vergniaud to the mason at the church door. "Never were two creatures better made for each other. That girl's parents are wretches. I know no braver soldier than Colonel Luigi! If all the world had behaved as he did, *l'autre** would still be with us."

The soldier's blessing, the only one breathed for them this day, fell like balm on Ginevra's heart.

They all parted with shaking of hands, and Luigi cordially thanked his landlord.

"*Adieu, mon brave*," said Luigi to the quartermaster. "And thank you."

"At your service, Colonel, soul and body, horses and chaises—all that is mine is yours."

"How well he loves you!" said Ginevra.

Luigi eagerly led his wife home to the house they were to live in; they soon reached the modest apartment, and there, when the door was closed, Luigi took her in his arms, exclaiming, "Oh, my Ginevra—for you are mine now—here is our real festival! Here," he went on, "all will smile on us."

Together they went through the three rooms which composed their dwelling. The entrance hall served as drawing room and dining room. To the right was a bedroom, to the left a sort of large closet which Luigi had arranged for his beloved wife, where she found easels, her paintbox, some casts, models, lay figures, pictures, portfolios—in short, all the apparatus of an artist.

"Here I shall work," said she, with childlike glee. She looked for a long time at the paper and the furniture, constantly turning to Luigi to thank him, for there was a kind of magnificence in this humble retreat; a bookcase contained Ginevra's favourite books, and there was a piano. She sat down on an ottoman, drew Luigi to her side, and clasping his hand, "You have such good taste," said she, in a caressing tone.

"Your words make me very happy," he replied.

"But, come, let us see everything," said Ginevra, from whom Luigi had kept the secret of this little home.

They went into a bridal chamber that was as fresh and white as a maiden.

"Oh! come away," said Luigi, laughing.

"But I must see everything," and Ginevra imperiously

went on, examining all the furniture with the curiosity of an antiquary studying a medal. She touched the
silk stuff and scrutinised everything with the childlike
delight of a bride turning over the treasures of the wedding gifts brought her by her husband. "We have begun
by ruining ourselves," she said in a half-glad, half-re-
gretful tone.

"It is true; all my arrears of pay are there," replied
Luigi. "I sold it to a good fellow named Gigonnet."

"Why?" she asked, in a reproachful voice, which betrayed, however, a secret satisfaction. "Do you think I
should be less happy under a bare roof? Still," she went
on, "it is all very pretty, and it is ours!" Luigi looked at
her with such enthusiasm that she cast down her eyes
and said, "Let us see the rest."

Above these three rooms, in the attics, were a workroom for Luigi, a kitchen, and a servant's room. Ginevra
was content with her little domain, though the view was
limited by the high wall of a neighbouring house, and
the courtyard on which the rooms looked was gloomy.
But the lovers were so glad of heart, hope so beautified
the future, that they would see nothing but enchant-
ment in their mysterious dwelling. They were buried
in this huge house, lost in the immensity of Paris, like
two pearls in their shell, in the bosom of the deep sea.
For anyone else it would have been a prison; to them it
was a paradise. The first days of their married life were
given to love; it was too difficult for them to devote
themselves at once to work, and they could not resist the
fascination of their mutual passion. Luigi would recline
for hours at his wife's feet, admiring the colour of her
hair, the shape of her forehead, the exquisite setting of
her eyes, the purity and whiteness of the arched brow
beneath which they slowly rose or fell, expressing the
happiness of satisfied love. Ginevra stroked her Luigi's
locks, never tiring of gazing at what she called, in one
of her own phrases, the *beltà folgorante* of the young

man, and his delicately cut features; always fascinated by the dignity of his manners, while always charming him by the grace of her own. They played like children with the merest trifles, these trifles always brought them back to their passion, and they ceased playing only to lapse into the daydreams of *far niente*.* An air sung by Ginevra would reproduce for them the exquisite hues of their love. Or, matching their steps as they had matched their souls, they wandered about the country, finding their love in everything, in the flowers, in the sky, in the heart of the fiery glow of the setting sun; they read it even in the changing clouds that were tossed on the winds. No day was ever like the last, their love continued to grow because it was true. In a very few days they had proved each other, and had instinctively perceived that their souls were of such a temper that their inexhaustible riches seemed to promise ever new joys for the future. This was love in all its fresh candour, with its endless prattle, its unfinished sentences, its long silences, its oriental restfulness and ardour. Luigi and Ginevra had wholly understood love. Is not love like the sea, which, seen superficially or in haste, is accused of monotony by vulgar minds, while certain privileged beings can spend all their life admiring it and finding in it changeful phenomena which delight them?

One day, however, prudence dragged the young couple from their Garden of Eden; they must work for their living. Ginevra, who had a remarkable talent for copying pictures, set to work to produce copies, and formed a connection among dealers. Luigi, too, eagerly sought some occupation, but it was difficult for a young officer, whose talents were limited to a thorough knowledge of tactics, to find any employment in Paris. At last, one day when, weary of his vain efforts, he felt despair in his soul at seeing that the whole burden of providing for their existence rested on Ginevra, it occurred to him that he might earn something by his handwriting, which was beautiful. With a perseverance of which his wife had set the example, he went to ask work of the attorneys, the notaries, and the pleaders of Paris. The frankness of his manners and his painful situation greatly interested people in his favour, and he got enough copying to be obliged to employ youths under him. Presently he took work on a larger scale. The income derived from this office work and the price of Ginevra's paintings put the young household on a footing of comfort, which they were proud of as the fruit of their own industry. This was the sunniest period of their life. The days glided swiftly by between work and the happiness of love. In the evening, after working hard, they found themselves happy in Ginevra's cell. Music then consoled them for their fatigues. No shade of melancholy ever clouded the young wife's features, and she never allowed herself to utter a lament. She could always appear to her Luigi with a smile on her lips and a light in her eyes. Each cherished a ruling thought which would have made them take pleasure in the hardest toil: Ginevra told herself she was working for Luigi, and Luigi for Ginevra. Sometimes, in her husband's absence, the young wife would think of the perfect joy it would have been if this life of love might have been spent in the sight of her father and mother; then she would sink into deep melancholy, and feel all the pangs of remorse; dark pictures would pass like shadows before her fancy; she would see her old father alone, or her mother weeping in the evenings, and hiding her tears from the inexorable Piombo. Those two grave, white heads would suddenly rise up before her, and she fancied she would never see them again but in the fantastical light of memory. This idea haunted her like a presentiment. She kept the anniversary of their wedding by giving her husband a portrait he had often wished for—that of his Ginevra. The young artist had never executed so remarkable a work. Apart from the likeness, which was perfect, the brilliancy of her beauty, the purity of her feelings, the happiness of love, were rendered with a kind of magic. The masterpiece was hung up with due ceremony. They spent another year in the midst of comfort. The history of their life can be told in these words: *they were happy*. No event occurred deserving to be related.

At the beginning of the winter of 1819, the picture dealers advised Ginevra to bring them something else than copies, as, in consequence of the great competition, they could no longer sell them to advantage. Madame Porta acknowledged the mistake she had made in not busying herself with genre pictures which would have won her a name; she undertook to paint portraits, but she had to contend against a crowd of artists even poorer than herself. However, as Luigi and Ginevra had saved some money, they did not despair of the future. At the end of this same winter, Luigi was working without ceasing. He, too, had to compete with rivals; the price of copying had fallen so low that he could no longer employ assistants, and was compelled to give up more time to his labour to earn the same amount. His wife had painted several pictures which were not devoid of merit, but dealers were scarcely buying even those of artists of repute. Ginevra offered them for almost nothing, but could not sell them. The situation of the household was something terrible; the souls of the husband and wife floated in happiness, love loaded them with its treasures; Poverty rose up like a skeleton in the midst of this harvest of joys, and they hid their alarms from each other. When Ginevra felt herself on the verge of tears as she saw Luigi suffering, she heaped caresses on him; Luigi, in the same way, hid the blackest care in his heart, while expressing the fondest devotion to Ginevra. They sought some compensation for their woes in the enthusiasm of their feelings, and their words, their joys, their playfulness, were marked by a kind of frenzy. They were alarmed at the future. What sentiment is there to compare in strength with a passion which must end tomorrow—killed by death or necessity? When they spoke of their poverty, they felt the need of deluding each other, and snatched at the smallest hope with equal eagerness. One night Ginevra sought in vain for Luigi at her side, and got up quite frightened. A pale gleam reflected from the dingy wall of the little courtyard led her to guess that her husband sat up to work at night. Luigi waited till his wife was asleep to go up to his workroom. The clock struck four. Ginevra went back to bed and feigned sleep; Luigi came back, overwhelmed by fatigue and want of sleep, and Ginevra gazed sadly at the handsome face on which labour and anxiety had already traced some lines.

Il avait le désespoir dans l'âme.

Plate XXI

"And it is for me that he spends the night in writing," she thought, and she wept.

An idea came to dry her tears: she would imitate Luigi. That same day she went to a rich print seller, and by the help of a letter of recommendation to him that she had obtained from Élie Magus, a picture dealer, she got some work in colouring prints. All day she painted and attended to her household cares, then at night she coloured prints. These two beings, so tenderly in love, got into bed only to get out of it again. Each pretended to sleep, and out of devotion to the other stole away as soon as one had deceived the other. One night Luigi, knocked over by a sort of fever caused by work, of which the burden was beginning to crush him, threw open the window of his workroom to inhale the fresh morning air, and shake off his pain, when, happening to look down, he saw the light thrown on the wall by Ginevra's lamp; the unhappy man guessed the truth; he went downstairs, walking softly, and discovered his wife in her studio colouring prints.

"Oh, Ginevra," he exclaimed.

She started convulsively in her chair, and turned scarlet.

"Could I sleep while you were wearing yourself out with work?" said she.

"But I alone have a right to work so hard."

"And can I sit idle?" replied the young wife, whose eyes filled with tears, "when I know that every morsel of bread almost costs us a drop of your blood? I should die if I did not add my efforts to yours. Ought we not to have everything in common, pleasures and pains?"

"She is cold!" cried Luigi, in despair. "Wrap your shawl closer over your chest, my Ginevra, the night is damp and chilly."

They went to the window, the young wife leaning her head on her beloved husband's shoulder, he with his arm round her, sunk in deep silence, and watching the sky which dawn was slowly lighting up. Grey clouds swept across in quick succession, and the east grew brighter by degrees.

"See," said Ginevra, "it is a promise—we shall be happy."

"Yes, in Heaven!" replied Luigi, with a bitter smile. "Oh, Ginevra! You who deserved all the riches of earth . . ."

"I have your heart!" said she in a glad tone.

"Ah, and I do not complain," he went on, clasping her closely to him. And he covered the delicate face with kisses; it was already beginning to lose the freshness of youth, but the expression was so tender and sweet that he could never look at it without feeling comforted.

"How still!" said Ginevra. "I enjoy sitting late, my dearest. The majesty of night is really contagious; it is impressive, inspiring; there is something strangely solemn in the thought: all sleeps, but I am awake,"

"Oh, my Ginevra, I feel, not for the first time, the refined grace of your soul—but, see, this is daybreak, come and sleep."

"Yes," said she, "if I am not the only one to sleep. I was miserable indeed the night when I discovered that my Luigi was awake and at work without me."

The valour with which the young people defied misfortune for some time found a reward. But the event which usually crowns the joys of a household was destined to be fatal to them. Ginevra gave birth to a boy who, to use a common phrase, was *as beautiful as the day*. The feeling of motherhood doubled the young creature's strength. Luigi borrowed money to defray the expenses of her confinement. Thus, just at first, she did not feel all the painfulness of their situation, and the young parents gave themselves up to the joy of rearing a child. This was their last gleam of happiness. Like two swimmers who unite their forces to stem a current, the Corsicans at first struggled bravely, but sometimes they

gave themselves up to an apathy resembling the tor-
por that precedes death, and they soon were obliged to
sell their little treasures. Poverty suddenly stood before
them, not hideous, but humbly attired, almost pleasant
to endure; there was nothing appalling in her voice;
she did not bring despair with her, nor spectres, nor
squalor, but she made them forget the traditions and
the habit of comfort; she broke the mainsprings of pride.
Then came Misery in all its horror, reckless of her rags,
and trampling every human feeling under foot. Seven
or eight months after the birth of little Bartholoméo, it
would have been difficult to recognise the original of
the beautiful portrait, the sole adornment of their bare
room, in the mother who was suckling a sickly baby.
Without any fire in bitter winter weather, Ginevra saw
the soft outlines of her face gradually disappear, her
cheeks became as white as porcelain, her eyes colourless, as though the springs of life were drying up in
her. And watching her starved and pallid infant, she
suffered only in his young misery, while Luigi had not
the heart even to smile at his boy.

"I have scoured Paris," he said in a hollow voice. "I
know no one, and how can I dare beg of strangers?
Vergniaud, the horse breeder, my old comrade in Egypt,
is implicated in some conspiracy, and has been sent to
prison; besides, he had lent me all he had to lend. As to
the landlord, he has not asked me for any rent for more
than a year."

"But we do not want for anything," Ginevra gently
answered, with an affectation of calmness.

"Each day brings some fresh difficulty," replied Luigi,
with terror.

Luigi took all Ginevra's paintings, the portrait, some
furniture which they yet could dispense with, and sold
them all for a mere trifle; the money thus obtained prolonged their sufferings for a little while. During these
dreadful days, Ginevra showed the sublime heights of

her character and the extent of her resignation. She bore the inroads of suffering with stoical firmness. Her vigorous soul upheld her under all ills; with a weak hand she worked on by her dying child, fulfilled her household duties with miraculous activity, and was equal to everything. She was even happy when she saw on Luigi's lips a smile of surprise at the look of neatness she contrived to give to the one room to which they had been reduced.

"I have kept you a piece of bread, dear," she said one evening when he came in tired.

"And you?"

"I have dined, dear Luigi; I want nothing."

And the sweet expression of her face, even more than her words, urged him to accept the food of which she had deprived herself. Luigi embraced her with one of the despairing kisses which friends gave each other in 1793* as they mounted the scaffold together. In such moments as these, two human creatures see each other heart to heart. Thus the unhappy Luigi, understanding at once that his wife was fasting, felt the fever that was undermining her; he shivered, and went out on the pretext of pressing business, for he would rather have taken the most insidious poison than escape death by eating the last morsel of bread in the house. He wandered about Paris among the smart carriages, in the midst of the insulting luxury that is everywhere flaunted; he hurried past the shops of the moneychangers where gold glitters in the window; finally, he determined to sell himself, to offer himself as a substitute for the conscription, hoping by this sacrifice to save Ginevra, and that during his absence she might be taken into favour again by Bartholoméo. So he went in search of one of the men who deal in these white slaves, and felt a gleam of happiness at recognising in him an old officer of the Imperial Guard.

"For two days I have eaten nothing," he said, in a slow, weak voice. "My wife is dying of hunger and never utters a complaint; she will die, I believe, with a smile on her lips. For pity's sake, old comrade," he added, with a forlorn smile, "pay for me in advance; I am strong, I have left the service, and I——"

The officer gave Luigi something on account of the sum he promised to get for him. The unhappy man laughed convulsively when he grasped a handful of gold pieces, and ran home as fast as he could go, panting, and exclaiming as he went, "Oh, my Ginevra—Ginevra!" It was growing dark by the time he reached home. He went in softly, fearing to overexcite his wife, whom he had left so weak; the last pale rays of sunshine, coming in at the dormer window, fell on Ginevra's face. She was asleep in her chair with her baby at her breast.

"Wake up, my darling," said he, without noticing the attitude of the child, which seemed at this moment to have a supernatural glory.

On hearing his voice, the poor mother opened her eyes, met Luigi's look, and smiled; but Luigi gave a cry of horror. He hardly recognised his half-crazed wife, to whom he showed the gold, with a gesture of savage vehemence.

Ginevra began to laugh mechanically, but suddenly she cried in a terrible voice, "Louis, the child is cold!"

She looked at the infant and fainted. Little Bartholoméo was dead. Luigi took his wife in his arms without depriving her of the child, which she clutched to her with incomprehensible strength, and after laying her on the bed he went out to call for help.

"*O mon Dieu!*" he exclaimed to his landlord, whom he met on the stairs, "I have money, and my child is dead of hunger, and my wife is dying. Help us!"

In despair he went back to his wife, leaving the worthy builder and various neighbours to procure whatever might relieve the misery of which till now they had known nothing, so carefully had the Corsicans concealed it out of a feeling of pride. Luigi had tossed the gold pieces on the floor, and was kneeling by the bed where his wife lay.

"Father, take charge of my son, who bears your name!" cried Ginevra in her delirium.

"Oh, my angel, be calm," said Luigi, kissing her, "better days await us!"

His voice and embrace restored her to some composure.

"Oh, my Louis," she went on, looking at him with extraordinary fixity, "listen to me. I feel that I am dying. My death is quite natural. I have been suffering too much, and then happiness so great as mine had to be paid for. Yes, my Luigi, be comforted. I have been so happy that if I had to begin life again, I would again accept our lot. I am a bad mother; I weep for you even more than for my child. My child!" she repeated in a full, deep voice. Two tears dropped from her dying eyes, and she suddenly clasped yet closer the little body she could not warm. "Give my hair to my father in memory of his Ginevra," she added. "Tell him that I never, never, accused him——" Her head fell back on her husband's arm.

"No, no, you cannot die!" cried Luigi. "A doctor is coming. We have food. Your father will receive you into favour. Prosperity is dawning on us. Stay with us, angel of beauty!"

But that faithful and loving heart was growing cold. Ginevra instinctively turned her eyes on the man she adored, though she was no longer conscious of anything; confused images rose before her mind, fast losing all memories of earth. She knew that Luigi was there, for she clung more and more tightly to his ice-cold hand, as if to hold herself up above a gulf into which she feared to fall.

"You are cold, dear," she said presently; "I will warm you."

She tried to lay her husband's hand over her heart, but she was dead. Two doctors, a priest, and some neighbours came in at this moment, bringing every-thing that was needful to save the lives of the young couple and to soothe their despair. At first these intrud-ers made a good deal of noise, but when they were all in the room an appalling silence fell.

While this scene was taking place, Bartholoméo and his wife were sitting in their old armchairs, each at one corner of the immense fireplace that warmed the great drawing room of their mansion. The clock marked mid-night. It was long since the old couple had slept well. At this moment they were silent, like two old folks in their second childhood, who look at everything and see noth-ing. The deserted room, to them full of memories, was feebly lighted by a single lamp fast dying out. But for the dancing flames on the hearth they would have been in total darkness. One of their friends had just left them, and the chair on which he had sat during his visit stood between the old people. Piombo had already cast more than one glance at this chair, and these glances, fraught with thoughts, followed each other like pangs of re-morse, for the empty chair was Ginevra's. Élisa Piombo watched the expressions that passed across her hus-band's pale face. Though she was accustomed to guess the Corsican's feelings from the violent changes in his features, they were tonight by turns so threatening and so sad that she failed to read this inscrutable soul.

Was Bartholoméo yielding to the overwhelming mem-ories aroused by that chair? Was he pained at perceiving that it had been used by a stranger for the first time since his daughter's departure? Had the hour of mercy, the hour so long and vainly hoped for, struck at last?

These reflections agitated the heart of Élisa Piombo. For a moment her husband's face was so terrible that she quaked at having ventured on so innocent a device to give her an opportunity of speaking of Ginevra. At this instant a northerly blast flung the snowflakes against the shutters with such violence that the old people could hear their soft pelting. Ginevra's mother bent her head to hide her tears from her husband. Suddenly a sigh broke from the old man's heart; his wife looked at him; he was downcast. For the second time in three years she ventured to speak to him of his daughter.

"Supposing Ginevra were cold!" she exclaimed in an undertone. "Or perhaps she is hungry," she went on. The Corsican shed a tear. "She has a child, and cannot suckle it—her milk is dried up," the mother added vehemently, with an accent of despair.

"Let her come, oh, let her come!" cried Piombo. "Oh, my darling child, you have conquered me."

The mother rose, as if to go to fetch her daughter. At this instant the door was flung open, and a man, whose face had lost all semblance of humanity, suddenly stood before them.

"*Dead!* Our families were doomed to exterminate each other, for this is all that remains of her," he said, laying on the table Ginevra's long, black hair.

The two old people started as though they had been struck by a thunderbolt; they could not see Luigi.

"He has spared us a pistol shot, for he is dead," said Bartholoméo deliberately, as he looked at the ground.

Paris, January 1830

The following personages appear or are mentioned
in other volumes of *The Human Comedy*

Bidault (known as Gigonnet)
IV: *A Daughter of Eve*
VII: *Gobseck*
XVIII: *César Birotteau, The Firm of Nucingen*
XXIV: *The Bureaucrats*

Bonaparte, Napoléon
IV: *Domestic Peace*
VII: *A Woman of Thirty*
IX: *Colonel Chabert*
XXVI: *The Brotherhood of Consolation*
XXVII: *A Shadowy Affair*

Bonaparte, Lucien
XXVII: *A Shadowy Affair*

Camusot de Marville, Madame (Amélie Thirion)
XV: *Jealousies of a Country Town*
XVIII: *César Birotteau*
XIX: *The Splendours and Miseries of Courtesans*
XXII: *Cousin Pons*

Magus, Élie
XIII: *The Rabouilleuse*
IX: *The Marriage Contract*
XX: *Pierre Grassou*
XXII: *Cousin Pons*

Murat, Joachim, Prince
IV: *Domestic Peace*
IX: *Colonel Chabert*
XXVII: *A Shadowy Affair*
XXXI: *The Country Doctor*

Appendix I:
Journey by *Coucou*
(*Le voyage en coucou*)
by Laure Surville, née Balzac
1854

Translated from the French by R.J. Allinson

I

The *Coucou*

One fine morning in September 1825, Thierry, a coach driver from Claye, a village located six leagues from Paris,* arrived at about eleven o'clock in the courtyard of the inn at Petit-Saint-Martin driving a cabriolet with room for six passengers, drawn by two white horses of unequal stature. This coach abandoned itself to all the imperfections of the road, and the rumblings it made as it rolled along were so singular that one could distinguish them even in the midst of all the noises of Paris. Thanks to this peculiarity, one could predict Thierry's arrival at the inn just as an astronomer predicts a comet shortly before its appearance.

Thierry paid the innkeeper to look after his coach and horses at the hotel, and to take charge of the desk where passengers came to buy tickets during the four hours he spent in Paris every day.

Thierry was a big lad, ruddy and jovial, lacking neither in intelligence nor shrewdness.

"This coach isn't so bad when she's loaded up," he would say to the traveller frightened by its appearance, "and if she were a bit less old and a bit less heavy, I'd never want another. But as it is, she tires the horses and makes them grow thin in no time at all."

A few turns of its wheels quickly disabused the traveller of the alleged soundness of the vehicle, but Thierry, who kept a close eye on things, was always there to provide reassurance.

"If she was completely loaded up you wouldn't feel a single jolt, and we'd still get there just the same." What is seven leagues in four hours? In those days one could only do seven leagues in four hours.

Thierry managed to bait and then console his passengers well enough that, year in, year out, the horses and their master were more or less able to feed themselves.

On that September day, when he had finished unloading the packages belonging to his last passengers, he went into the office to see if there was any chance of more work that evening. He came out again suddenly, and shouted at Lorau, the stable-boy who was in charge of unhitching the horses:

"What luck! Comte Maurice reserved a seat today; tomorrow he'll ride in my coach for the first time!"

"Ah, tomorrow then?" Lorau said mockingly, thinking how, for as long as he could remember, Thierry would try to introduce his magnificent coach into the imaginations of his potential customers.

"That's right, my boy; tomorrow we'll have fifteen passengers instead of nine."

"Bah! A coach with four wheels—that *always* excites the travelers," retorted Lorau. "Comte Maurice is a gentleman from Claye then, isn't he?"

"Idiot, a Comte is more than just a gentleman! You want to be a driver, and that's all the smarts you have? You must know your world; that's what gets you a good tip."

"Well, no offense, Monsieur Thierry, but why would this Comte want to go in your coach?"

"Perhaps he wants to surprise his steward, Monsieur Renaud," replied Thierry, making an excuse for why the Comte would want to go in his coach. "Yesterday I brought back the farmer—they're in the process of redoing the lease—and it looks to me like he's giving a handsome bribe to Monsieur Renaud. Of course it's the Comte who'll pay dearly for all that! That Renaud—always so uppity around the poor—and who is he? Nobody at all! Where would he be without his master? But anyway, it's no concern of mine."

Four hours after this exchange, we find Thierry and Lorau hitching up the horses and arranging the baggage on the roof of the coach, which would otherwise shake convulsively if it carried less weight.

"Do you have a full load today?"

"Well, there are only five including the Comte and one *lapin*."* And at that, Thierry went off sadly to smoke his pipe at the door of the inn where he would wait for his passengers and try to drum up some more business.

No sooner had he leaned against the doorpost than he was approached by a lady followed by a young man carrying a small suitcase. The lady wore a black silk dress, a shawl of dove-gray wool, and a silk hat the color of currants; an umbrella with a royal-blue cane and a straw basket completed her outfit. She spoke at length to Thierry: she was undoubtedly commending her young traveller to him while explaining the exact place where he was to be deposited. Thierry nodded so many times in agreement that it became evident to the lady that he understood and that she need not say anything further. She then made her way into the courtyard towards the coach, found the number of the seat she had reserved, made the young man place his suitcase under the bench he was to occupy, and began giving a series of instructions which had the unfortunate effect of making all those nearby fully aware of matters between mother and son. Lorau smiled from time to time while listening to them, much to the embarrassment of the young man, who was feeling as humiliated by Lorau's smiles as by his mother's words.

"Now, don't buy anything en route, Joseph, you have only enough for Monsieur Renaud's servant and your return trip. Behave yourself at your godfather's, don't eat too much, and take care of your clothes; I cannot always continue to dress you. Above all, no idle chatter, and do not stay more than two weeks."

"But what if they insist on it, Mama?"

"Come home all the same. We must not impose upon our benefactors."

The young man, already bothered by Lorau's smile, shuddered at the sight of two handsome young men who, fortunately for him, also went over to chat with Thierry.

"If they hear my mother, I am done for!" he thought. "They will make fun of me all the way to Villeparisis."*

With more skill than his naive face and clumsy manner would have suggested, he then made a heroic effort to make his mother leave.

"You are standing in a draft, Mama; your arthritis will return if you stay here much longer. It is time for us to leave; I must say goodbye now and get in the coach."

He kissed his mother and took his seat.

The newcomers casually entered the courtyard, and, upon seeing Joseph's mother, they nudged each other, and their faces seemed to say: "*Take a look at her!*"

"Good thing they didn't hear us!" thought Joseph, as he anxiously followed his mother's footsteps, fearing that some forgotten instructions might make her return. He breathed more freely when he saw her disappear behind the door.

"It is this *vinaigrette* that you plan to embark, Alfred?" said one of the young men, indicating the *coucou*.

"*Vinaigrette* is colorful; I am going to be tossed about inside it like a salad—at least I will not be lacking for a little bit of seasoning," said Alfred as he regarded Joseph.

"He is so small that I almost didn't see him!" exclaimed the other.

"Bah! I have nothing against children when travelling, as long as they keep out of the way."

Joseph, too concerned with his appearance and that of his future travelling companion, either did not hear or pretended not to hear these unpleasant remarks. From the Rue des Nonandières, where he lived, all the way to the Rue Saint-Martin,* he had been pleased to have had no unpleasant encounters, but now a single comparison with young men of fashion made him understand how ridiculous he must have seemed to them. He thought of his own face, round and pink, further exaggerated by a head of ruthlessly cropped hair, and involuntarily compared it to the pale face of his future travelling companion, which was framed by light brown curls. Alfred was one of those men whom only commoners and children admire as a model of handsomeness, but who leave physiognomists unimpressed. He was dressed at the height of fashion by his local Staub,* and as a result displayed an imperturbable coolness, while Joseph, coddled, inexperienced, and left to his own devices, now had a sense of his own lack of elegance: everything from his socks to his vest and coat betrayed a paternal inheritance that had been altered to fit him with more good will than success.

These young men had reached the age where one prefers, without hesitation, misfortune to a ridiculous appearance, and where the smallest trifles are the cause of the greatest joys or the greatest pains.

"It's a good thing I thought of hiding myself at the back of the coach," thought Joseph, "if I had been walking ahead of them in the middle of the courtyard, in broad daylight . . . let us hope that this Alfred disembarks before I do!"

These thoughts, which might otherwise take too long to describe, went through his head in just a few seconds.

The two friends continued strolling along, all the while whispering and sniggering at Joseph's expense. The latter, at last having regained a little composure, tried to repay their impertinence by humming a song that was quite popular at the time: "*C'est la faute de Voltaire, c'est la faute de Rousseau,*"* affecting to take no notice of them.

A third traveller now arrived, followed by a small boy, and was announced by Thierry: this traveller, after having a word with the driver, crossed the court, quickly boarded the coach, and sat down next to Joseph. As he bowed, the *lapin* who had come with him climbed onto the roof like a cat where he placed the two buckets, filled with bottles, that he had been carrying with him.

"So, you are already famous here, *Monsieur Dubois!*" cried the boy to the newcomer.

Monsieur Dubois was young and blond, tall and slender, with fine features, luminous eyes, and a distinguished bearing. His dress, quite plain (he wore a shirt of gray cloth and a cap), contrasted so completely with his natural appearance, that he was taken for an artist just starting out on his journeys. Shortly after his arrival, Alfred's friend, who was remaining in Paris, took leave of him. Alfred then went to complain to Thierry, and asked him when he planned on leaving.

"Damnation! My friend, when you have an old contraption like this one, shouldn't you, at the very least, be somewhat punctual? These old nags don't look like the sort that can make up for lost time!"

Thierry, instead of replying, seemed not to understand that he was the one to whom this speech had been addressed, and called out to the boy, who was still on the roof:

"Hey up there! Take my whip and see if you can shoo away the fly that's bothering the horses—there, that's good."

The boy, proud to have been of service, immediately went over to start a conversation with Thierry, who listened to him for a moment, and then told him to go and bother the impatient Alfred.

Alfred, who either believed Thierry to be beneath contempt, or that an altercation with a robust fellow like him would not suit him, made up his mind, without complaining further, to get into the "old contraption," as he called it, limiting himself to muttering the words *lout* and *peasant* under his breath. He sat down on the front bench and, with an air of importance, placed a large portfolio into one of the coach's wall pockets.

"You weren't very polite to that gentleman," whispered Lorau to Thierry.

"Him? Bah! Can't you see that he is just a greenhorn—a nobody?"

Alfred was greeted by a smile from the two young men in the coach, and Joseph, hoping to take his revenge soon, thanked him mockingly for having hastened their departure.

"It is indeed unpleasant to wait," added Jules Dubois.

A tall, wiry man with a pale and austere face appeared and caused a momentary distraction.

Thierry greeted him respectfully and helped him to climb into the cab with a degree of care that the young men noticed with some astonishment, for nothing about the stranger's appearance seemed to indicate any sort of rank to their inexperienced eyes: his hat, pulled down over his eyes, hid an admirable forehead, his gloves prevented them from seeing his pale, delicate hands, and his buttoned frock coat covered his fine clothes. The latecomer took a space on the front bench beside Alfred. Neither Joseph nor the young blond man offered him a place at the back of the coach; they were apparently not aware that one of the best signs of a good education consists of showing respect for one's elders.

"If Monsieur le Comte wishes," said Thierry, "one of these young gentlemen could surely move to the front."

"Why should I give up the seat that belongs to me?" said Joseph curtly.

Monsieur Dubois offered his.

"Thank you, Monsieur, I try never to disturb anyone," replied the Comte.

Thierry had evidently been waiting for this traveler, for as soon as the Comte took his place he climbed up to his seat, adjusted the reins, took up his whip, and they were off.

In response to the delay that the latecomer had caused him, Alfred looked over at his two young companions and said:

"If one wishes to leave on time, one must take a private carriage; that is surely better than having to wait for all the passengers in a public one."

"Or else one should reserve all the places," added Joseph, determined to elevate himself to the same level as the object of his envy.

Joseph's manner, and the idea of him being bounced around the *coucou* all by himself, made the Comte smile, but he said nothing. Alfred was let down for a second time.

The horses continued along at a slow trot; arriving at the Faubourg Saint-Martin,* they managed to ascend it better than one might have expected. Thierry, it is true, gave them a courage born of despair as he ceaselessly lashed them from head to tail; the boy sitting next to him watched with admiration the play of the whip, always skillfully finding its target.

Silence reigned in the interior of the *coucou*; the Comte studied the faces of his three companions as though he were focused on solving some problem. Joseph looked upon the houses of the faubourg with the avidity of a tourist forming the first impressions of his travels. Jules Dubois seemed to be buried in a deep reverie. And Alfred watched for an opportunity to elevate himself in the eyes of his travelling companions.

II

The Route

The horses trotted peacefully along in yellowish clouds of dust. Silence still reigned in the interior of the *coucou*; on his bench, the boy chattered with Thierry, who was amused by his good cheer and his sallies. An exclamation from Joseph as they were approaching the mounds of Chaumont and Romainville* gave the young Alfred, much to his great satisfaction, an opportunity to speak.

"What beautiful scenery!" Joseph had said.

"My young friend," responded Alfred immediately in a benevolent tone, "when you have roamed the world as I have, you will no longer admire miserable bunches of weeds sprouting from molehills . . ."

"Presumably at your age I will also be as experienced as you, for my father intends for me to take a tour of Europe as soon as my education is finished," replied Joseph, piqued by Alfred's patronizing tone.

"This tour of Europe strikes me as being the journey of some famous traveller, my young friend," said Alfred with a laugh; "but do not count on it—how often we end up thwarting our parent's plans! My father wanted me to stay close to him so that he could teach me to be a great landowner, a profession he had practised with some success, but a folly of youth, to which he perhaps responded too severely, threw me into uniform."

"You are a soldier?" exclaimed Joseph and Jules Dubois enviously.

"I attained the rank of captain after giving as well as receiving a few blows of the sword."

"In which war, Monsieur?" asked the Comte.

"I participated only in limited engagements at first, Monsieur, for I am not overly committed by nature, and then in the Spanish War,* from whence I have just returned."

"You have come from Spain?" cried Jules, "a splendidly beautiful country, is it not?"

"The plants grow there as in fairy tales; it was there that I saw aloes all along the roadside grow and blossom in only a few hours . . ."

"And the women there—are they quite beautiful?" asked Joseph, blushing almost to the roots of his hair.

"Their eyes are bigger than their feet and can cast flames that could melt bronze! I even committed murder twice for them!"

"You are a lucky man!" said Jules with a sigh.

"Too lucky: if that weren't enough, one of them even drew me into a very heated duel!"

And the captain, seeing the gullibility of his young listeners, decided to risk the description of a knife fight that made them turn pale.

"Monsieur is from the south, then?" asked the Comte while the duellist was catching his breath.

"I am from a country where one is always ready to face whatever lies ahead," replied Alfred proudly.

"Who would dare to doubt your words, Monsieur?"

"How long have you served, captain?" asked Joseph, who did not wish to see the conversation dropped.

"Long enough to be well-versed in the art of war, at least that is the opinion of my Colonel."

"How old are you then?" asked Jules.

"Thirty on the 29th of this month," replied Alfred with aplomb.

"The military profession certainly keeps men young," remarked the Comte, "one might think you to be less than twenty."

"There is nothing terribly surprising about it. Without that miserable Spanish War, I would know only the life of the garrison, and parades never tire an officer . . ."

"The Spanish sun has certainly spared your complexion."

"It is my family's complexion; nothing can alter it."

"But this feature works against you as a soldier; you must surely envy the tanned and toughened faces of your comrades?"

"Ah, do not tell me!" he replied with feigned affability; "it is because of my fair complexion that I was given the nickname *Mademoiselle Alfred* by the regiment, and I am forced to play the role of leading lady in our camp plays, which, by the way, I usually manage to pull off rather well."

"I do not doubt it," said the Comte with imperturbable seriousness, "if one can pull through a knife fight, one can pull through just about anything."

"But, as you have just returned from Spain, you have no doubt witnessed the taking of Trocadéro?"* asked Jules.

"Bah! A trivial affair," said Alfred with a shrug. "Nevertheless, I displayed enough spirit there to receive both a wound and a cross."

"You were wounded! It must be painful," cried Joseph.

"Where where you wounded?" inquired Jules.

"My left foot. Trocadéro also cost me the tip of my little finger."

"Then why do you not wear a decoration?" asked the Comte, who was visibly amused by the captain's bragging; "you should be proud of your service."

"I am going to a château where it is necessary to hide it," Alfred replied mysteriously, "the lord of the manor is wary of soldiers . . ."

"I understand," said the Comte, "I certainly would not want to be in the place of that man! Especially since he shall be fooled, for your incognito could not be better guarded."

"Really? My martial bearing does not come through a little from beneath my silk shirt?" replied Alfred, apparently quite pleased.

"Not in the least," Joseph assured him. "I am certain you could tell us about your many exciting adventures?" he added with curiosity.

"What would your mother say, my young friend, if I forgot to respect your innocence?"

"My mother?" said Joseph, turning red, "my mother is dead, captain, and as to my innocence . . ."

"What? The lady who accompanied you to the coach is not your mother?"

"That woman is our housekeeper!" replied Joseph brazenly.

While listening to him proudly pretend to be the son of a great family, his three listeners at once let escape great bursts of laughter as they exchanged glances which seemed to say: 'He lies, this little rascal!'

To deny his mother, what a crime!

"As you place so little value on your innocence, I see that I can speak freely," resumed Alfred. When he had regained his composure, he immediately began telling a series of gallant military tales which left all of Ariosto's heroes far behind him.

Jules and Joseph eagerly devoured his lies. The Comte, who from Alfred's first word had guessed him to be a braggart, took care not to interrupt, curious to know just how far the captain would go. He was therefore quite pleased at the effect he had produced by the time they arrived at Bondy.* Thierry gave the horses a rest. Alfred descended briskly from the coach, and tapping the driver on the shoulder said to him:

"I must beg your pardon, my good man, your horses really do keep up a good pace."

"You see then that they'd blanch under the harness if forced to gallop," replied Thierry calmly and accepted a small glass that Alfred offered him.

"At least he's a friendly greenhorn," thought Thierry as he wiped his mouth on the back of his sleeve.

Alfred came back from the inn with a cigar in his mouth, and came over to offer some cakes to Joseph, whom he now referred to only as "the orphan." The latter, enraged, refused them while trying to come up with something he could say to overcome the incredulity of his companions.

Thierry, no doubt spurred on by the promises of a good tip, had them stay only a short time at Bondy. Alfred tossed away his half-smoked cigar.

"He is rich, that sly devil," thought Joseph upon seeing such extravagance.

The coach began rolling again, now moving on to Livry.* The conversation began anew right away. Alfred resumed his fabulous stories. When at last he had finished, he turned to Jules Dubois:

"You are an artist, are you not? We in the military can quickly tell a man's profession by his face."

"Well guessed, Captain, I am indeed a painter," replied Jules. "It is a fine profession that also quite appeals to women."

Here, the Comte, who had understood Alfred and Joseph and had sought to discover what sort Jules might be, assumed the air of a man relieved of doubt.

"I have just competed for the Grand Prix de Rome,"* added Jules, blushing, and looking to see whether the boy could hear him.

"You have a forehead made to wear crowns! Let us shake on it, we are brothers," said Alfred as he extended his hand, "the brush is as good as the sword; both are equally covered with laurels! And you, my intriguing young orphan, after your tour of Europe, what does your father intend for you? Will we one day meet again on the path of glory that we are on today in this very *coucou*? Unless I am much mistaken, your father intends you to work in a small business of some sort?"

"Your powers of divination have failed you this time," responded Joseph, pale with anger. "My father intends for me to become a diplomat."

At the violent outbursts of laughter that followed this declaration, the two horses, already quite touchy, broke into a gallop. Thierry became alarmed, and looked to see if there was anything wrong with their harnesses. Joseph, now as angry as he was embarrassed, swore to his companions that it was all true.

When they had regained some degree of seriousness, Comte Maurice congratulated himself on the good fortune of such a meeting.

"I see that I am travelling with three future celebrities!"

"I will owe my rank of general to the patronage of our future ambassador," said Alfred, as he bowed to young Joseph, "for you must have friends in high places!"

"It is true that I have no connections in Spain as you do, but I can name all the chateaus that I plan to visit and the names of the people I am going to see there," replied Joseph with exasperation.

"I would be interested to know these names, my intriguing young orphan," said Alfred.

"They are not difficult to name. I am going to see Comte Maurice, with whom my father is intimately connected."

"You are going to see Comte Maurice?" said Alfred, stupefied despite his self-assurance.

"You are going to see Comte Maurice?" repeated Jules, aghast.

"My young friend, are you quite sure of what you say?" said the Comte in turn.

"As sure as I can see you right now. I am going to spend the rest of my vacation with his two sons, Paul and Sosthène, with whom I attend school."

"Think now, my young friend; is your father truly a friend of the Comte?"

"So much so that I can tell you anything that you may wish to know about him."

"I truly have need of his protection, and I would like to know how I might approach him successfully."

"Mention all of his titles in your first sentence," said Joseph, regaining his composure, "and you will have half-won your case. He is a deputy, an academician, and a Councillor of State."

"He is quite vain, then?" inquired the Comte.

"Parvenus always are," said Alfred.

"That is so true," responded Joseph, "but despite his miserliness, he would give a quarter of his fortune to keep it from being known that it was earned by his parents in trade."

"Perhaps he is jealous of your father's nobility!" said the Captain with a laugh.

"If what you say is true, he has quite a severe judge for a friend," said the Comte.

"But how can a man who has attained such a high rank without the protection of a great family be so small-minded?" asked Jules.

"There are people who have too much good fortune," replied the Captain.

"Good fortune only accounts for half of one's success; it takes great talent to support it," said Jules.

"The Comte's talents are doubtless beyond the reach of our future diplomat?" replied the Comte, smiling.

"Despite the miserliness that you reproach him for, I know, for my part, that he does much to train his workers," added Jules.

"I stand by what the young man says," said the Captain, "he has audacity, he will go far. So, the Comte's humble beginnings show through his many titles; does he put on airs?"

"In the commonest way imaginable."

"Messieurs, our orphan here must undoubtedly be a virtuoso in these airs!" retorted Alfred, quite pleased with his bad pun.

"So," Jules resumed indignantly, addressing himself to young Joseph, "you now want to prove to us that your father is no friend of the Comte?"

"Do you not see that this child is only repeating comments made by some lackey?" said Comte Maurice.

"A lackey? Monsieur!" cried Joseph, raising his voice.

"All you need now is to call an old man a liar," the Comte replied sharply. Then he called out to Thierry: "*I will get off here.*"

"Here?" said Thierry with surprise. The Comte put a finger to his lips.

"Understood," murmured Thierry as he helped the Comte to climb down. As he presented the driver with a generous tip, the Comte whispered in his ear: "Go slowly as far as the village," and with that, the Comte started off down a path that led to one of the small entrances to the château.

Back up in his seat, Thierry started up again from the side of the road.

"There will be trouble over there, for sure," he muttered, and began whistling the tune *Partant pour la Syrie*,* which he always did when he was preoccupied with something of great importance.

The horses, left by their master to their own devices, were having great difficulty dragging the heavy carriage through the sand, and seemed to be falling asleep while dreaming of lazing around the stables.

"Captain, you know something of physiognomy—were you able to guess the profession of the man who just left us?"

"He must be a justice of the peace or a notary. I am inclined to think the former, because I was surprised by his air of dignity, which is consistent with that level of the judiciary."

"It will be quite easy to find out; the driver seems to know him."

"My friend," said Alfred, "who exactly was that Monsieur *Lecomte* who just got off?"

"He is the mayor of the village over there."

"Ah! Did I not say he was exercising some authority?" replied Alfred.

"He has a distinguished face, and his eyes seem to guess your thoughts," said Jules.

"He does not speak too badly for a village mayor," added Joseph, who wanted to get a word in. "What is this beautiful château we see here?" he asked Thierry.

"That is the château of Comte Maurice."

"What! You do not recognize the home of your father's friend?" said Jules and Alfred together as though relieved of their worries.

"There is a good reason for this; this is the first time I have come here."

Arriving in front of an avenue, Thierry turned the coach and entered it.

"Why are you taking us this way?" asked the three young men.

"Since all three of you get off here, I'm going up to the gate. I wouldn't bother doing this for a single traveller, you know." The faces of the three travellers went through several successive degrees of astonishment. Thierry, who was watching them, said: "Is it my gallantry that's upsetting you by any chance? You didn't know that you were all going to the same place? What's so upsetting about that? What's wrong with everyone going to the same place, since you've all become acquainted?"

"I'm just glad I don't have to carry my buckets all the way down the street," said the *lapin*.

"But we are going to Claye!" cried Jules.

"What are you thinking, Monsieur Dubois? What would Comte Maurice say? He is expecting us to paint the marble in his dining room."

Jules, embarrassed, tried in vain to meet the eyes of his assistant in the hopes of silencing him.

"Why do you trouble yourself, Monsieur Dubois?" asked Alfred, "I see clearly that each of us has a mask to remove at the gate, but it is certainly permissible to have a bit of fun while travelling, is it not?"

The steward, Monsieur Renaud, had just arrived from the château.

"You have brought my godson, little Porriquet, have you not?" he asked Thierry.

"I'll hand him right over to you, him and his little suitcase. He comes highly recommended to me from his mother."

"There is a name that resounds rather nicely in the realm of diplomacy! A mask falls again!" exclaimed Alfred.

Joseph, crushed, said nothing.

Now certain that Joseph had disavowed his mother, Jules instinctively moved away from him with a look of contempt—to deny your own mother, Monsieur, you have no heart!

"Your mother is not flattering to the eye, it is true, but even so it was surely not right of you to disavow her." said Alfred.

"My mother wears calico dresses and bonnets, and I am proud of her wherever she may be," added Jules.

"Why did you make fun of me then?"

"Your behavior is inexcusable, Monsieur; one's vanity should not tarnish such sentiments," Jules responded.

When they reached the gate, Thierry sprang nimbly to the ground, rang the bell, and called out as though announcing a king. "I ring for three, Madame Henry," he said to the care-taker, who was clearly surprised.

Joseph rushed from the coach, and nearly fell to the ground head first.

"There, there, little Porriquet," said Alfred, "there is no need to break your neck over a few bad jokes; after all, there are some much cleverer than you who have done the same." To Jules he said, "So you paint on stone rather than on canvas, eh, Monsieur Dubois? There is no shame in that. But mum's the word on my title. I am here only as a notary's clerk; here, this is my passport," he said, displaying the wallet he took from the carriage's pocket.

Recovering his boldness, he entered the château, flipping back his hair as he did so. In the meantime Jules Dubois helped his assistant bring down the buckets.

As all this was going on, Madame Henry whispered to Thierry, "Good! Good! Tomorrow at seven o'clock at the end of the avenue."

The others, more or less distracted, paid no attention to their exchange, which, however, would have been of inter-est to them, though they did not suspect it. Thierry set off again at a trot.

III
The Château

After speaking with Thierry, Madame Henry said to Monsieur Renaud:

"Monsieur le Comte is waiting for you and your godson."

"Comte Maurice is here now? Since when? Did he come with his horses? How did he know I was waiting for Joseph?"

"You ask more than I know. He came in through the back door with Monsieur Claudin."

Could he have come in Thierry's coach? Did he not sign the lease? These thoughts, quick as lightning, flashed through the steward's head and filled him with worry.

"Was there a pale and thin old gentleman in the coach with you?"

"Yes," said Joseph, trembling from head to toe, for he now realized that the old gentleman was none other than Comte Maurice. Remembering what he had said, he felt the blood rush to his head and the sound of a bell ringing in his ears.

During this exchange between godfather and godson, the gardener welcomed Alfred and the two painters, and Madame Henry asked about their trip.

"Come with me, my children," she said, "I've been ordered to give you supper and lodging—you will want for nothing! It's the Comte's wishes." To Alfred she said, "Monsieur is the notary's envoy? The Comte awaits you; I will take you to him."

Jules entered the caretaker's house with his assistant, pleased to be free from Alfred's remarks for the evening. He promised himself that he would go to bed right after supper, thinking all the while to his chagrin that the very next day he would be painting the dining room under Alfred's gaze, probably as the clerk was sitting next to Comte Maurice at the table.

Alfred, Joseph, the caretaker, and the steward all went in to the Comte's study. The Comte had his back turned to the door and was speaking pointedly to Monsieur Claudin.

"Here is the notary's envoy, Monsieur le Comte," said the caretaker to her master.

"Fine," replied the Comte, without turning his head and taking no notice of either Joseph or the steward, who signalled to his godson to stay put and keep quiet; he undoubtedly wanted to hear the words exchanged between his master and the farmer.

The ex-captain was about to salute when he recognized the master of the house, the traveler that he had treated with such a cavalier attitude during their journey, and became quite flabbergasted at his discovery.

"He knew who I was! It was I who was duped, not him!" The braggart's realization had greatly unsettled him, for it was the only sort of defeat that could have any effect on him.

"Compose yourself, Monsieur," said the lord of the manor, "Captain Alfred can do no wrong to Comte Maurice. After all, he is widowed and has only sons. Your *name*, Monsieur?"

"I am here only as a clerk employed by Monsieur N——, and did not mean to commit any indiscretion that might be detrimental to my patron or his client," said Alfred, quickly regaining his composure.

"You are quite right, Monsieur," replied the Comte with dignity, "you have done wrong to no one but yourself today. But with such exploits, you may not always be so lucky."

"Monsieur?" said Alfred, raising his voice.

"There will be no more bragging, Monsieur; the Captain is no longer here, and you have done nothing to make me take you seriously. Now hand me the lease and sit down."

Alfred, a man of heart, had been deeply humiliated by these words. He obeyed the Comte without a word, opened his portfolio, searched around for the lease, and presented it to his patron's client.

"I say again, Monsieur Claudin, this lease does not have all the clauses I require for me to agree to not increase the annual rent; I will not sign it. Let us discuss this matter together. Monsieur will take my dictation, but before we begin, I must speak with my steward." He was about to ring, but as he turned his head he saw him there with Joseph. The latter, who had witnessed the Captain's execution carried out so decisively, realized with terror that his turn had now come.

"Why did you not show yourself upon entering, Monsieur?" the Comte asked the steward in a stern voice; then, without waiting for an answer, he added: "How long have you known this young man?"

Monsieur Renaud, troubled by the Comte's first question, breathed more freely at the second, and not suspecting any danger in answering, he replied "This child is my godson, Monsieur le Comte; his father is a friend of mine."

"Is it because of you, then, that he was able to reel off such slander about me on the way to my house? Tonight, Monsieur, you will prepare your accounts; I shall expect you tomorrow morning at five o'clock to review and sign them. The boy's place in Thierry's coach will be retained for him for tomorrow."

"But Monsieur le Comte, one does not base a man's dismissal on the words of a child," the steward ventured boldly, thinking that the Comte, like many masters, would shrink from the grave consequences that might result from an attack against a servant's integrity.

The Comte looked at the steward in a manner that made him tremble.

"Your conscience must tell you, Monsieur, that for my part I am showing you generosity by basing your dismissal on a matter other than the one that is truly important, and you must recognize that it is this child who has given me the pretext. Moreover, a man's ingratitude is a fault great enough to drown out all his other faults."

The steward tried to speak.

"My decision is final. The lease, a document written in your own hand, which you wanted to trick me into signing and which would damage my interests, proves that they are not the same as yours. I will give a deposition—this very minute if necessary—proving the justness of my decision. Go now, prepare for your departure; I have nothing further to say to you."

"You wretch! Just what did you say?" yelled Monsieur Renaud at Joseph when they had left the presence of his master.

"It seems that what I said has rendered you a service, godfather, did you not hear what the Comte said?" Joseph said brazenly.

"You shall pay dearly for this 'service;' I will tell your mother and father what you have done, you miserable little gossip! To go and repeat in public what I've said in private! To abuse my trust!" No sooner had the steward uttered these words than he began to regret them.

"I can see that no good will come of this," Joseph replied somewhat audaciously. "My poor godfather . . ."

It was in this extraordinary circumstance that Joseph suddenly discovered in himself a degree of cunning that until now he had perhaps been unaware of. Without guessing the full import of the Comte's words, which would be explained later on, he nevertheless understood enough to make use of them as a weapon that would put his godfather at his mercy.

"You little snake!" shouted the steward, suspecting Joseph's treachery.

Faults always have fatal consequences; in this case they shamed the protector before the protégé, the man before the boy! Instead of speaking to Joseph, Monsieur Renaud bid him to keep quiet.

While the young Porriquet was turning the tables with a finesse that would one day be fatal, Alfred, who had just handed in the lease, was on his way to dinner. "That young man's words will cost him dearly," he said to himself as he feasted on partridge, "and it must be admitted that he will be quite deserving of the punishment he will get from his mother and father. His 'diplomacy' was amusing, but the rest was worthless. To slander the living, for heavens sake! One either invents things, or makes the dead speak; that's how it should be done! Ah, but he is only in primary school; the boy is not strong, and is in need of some guidance. Since we are travelling together again tomorrow, I will give him some. As for the Comte, he is quite clever, and if he wanted to jest, he would certainly be famous!"

The three young travellers, whom chance had brought together in the same coach and under the same roof, would never forget their meeting, for the hours they spent together would decide their fates! Unlike most young men their age, the three of them slept little. Joseph was imagining the *pleasant surprise* that awaited him the following day with his mother and father, and the welcome he would receive if his godfather spoke of his indiscretions; he also sought, with the cunning of a Machiavelli, what he might tell his godfather to persuade him to explain his return without calling it into question.

In recapitulating his exploits from the previous day, Alfred admitted to himself some of his faults. "The works of the imagination do have their pitfalls," he thought to himself, "and it is much better to make use of them in the Parisian ocean than in a village pond. The ocean swallows everything whole, but a pond cannot even drown an eggshell! So the joke is sweet to the *coucou* who flies to Paris, but bitter when she returns to her nest! Most travellers, it is true, will not ordinarily be thrown together at the same château gate, but from this coincidence one should conclude that, before making up stories, one should inquire carefully as to where one's fellow travellers are from." Such were the mistakes that the braggart reproached himself for, and the moral that he took away from the whole affair.

As for young Jules Dubois, displeased with himself and ashamed of having yielded to foolish pride, he was wondering how he could make amends for his lie, the gravity of which had been exaggerated by his sensitive nature. At daybreak he set resolutely to work. While his assistant merrily whistled his favorite tune and prepared the colors, Jules cast an occasional anxious glance out the windows, thinking that he might see the figure of Alfred or Joseph make an appearance. He had decided nevertheless that he was going to nobly make amends for his mistake. But he saw only the concierge's family, young and old alike running about busily. The concierge was crossing the courtyard pulling a small cart full of boxes and parcels. Joseph was pushing the cart from behind, either to give himself something to do, or else to obey the orders of his godfather. Alfred, with his head held high and his portfolio under his arm, walked beside him, perhaps already starting in with the advice he had thought of giving him. The steward was nowhere to be found; he surely would not dare show himself at the château's front gate, and would instead meet up with the others by the avenue.

Jules watched them happily, as though relieved of a great burden.

"You're watching for the departure of our steward?" said the concierge, who was setting the table; "there goes a man who's acted foolishly. Dismissed from the house of a master who's been so good to him! Monsieur le Comte taught him everything he knew, and would have always looked after him."

"Does everyone know why he was dismissed?"

"I think the farmer might say something, perhaps Monsieur le Comte will too; what's important is that justice has been done, and the master wants us all to keep quiet about it."

"What kind of man is your master?" asked the young man.

"He is good man, and fair too; but I sure wouldn't want to take a single flower from his greenhouse behind his back! He counts every one of them."

"Lunch is ready, Mother; shall I tell Monsieur le Comte?" asked the concierge's little girl from the window.

"Yes, go." she replied.

Shortly thereafter, Jules heard the master coming down the stairs, and, looking up as he entered, had the same look of amazement that Alfred and Joseph had had the day before when the Comte's identity had been revealed.

The Comte could not repress a smile, but his smile was so kind and benevolent, that the young man, setting aside his brushes and palette, went over to him.

"You must have a bad opinion of me, Monsieur le Comte, and this troubles me deeply. I paint marble to support my mother, who is a poor widow; my father's death put a stop to my career, and I have never competed for the Grand Prix de Rome. I believed and hoped that my vocation would be greater than that, but the lie I have told has now decided the course of my life. I will work for my mother and for my future, and if one day you hear someone speak of the works of Jules Dubois, remember him as a man of heart and courage, not as the person you met yesterday. I will try to work hard and suffer so that people know my name."

"I did not take you for the same sort as your fellow travellers yesterday, my young friend. Why don't you sit down there, and we can lunch together and talk."

At the end of the meal, during which the Comte had asked Jules many questions, the great benefactor came to a decision about the young man, and said to him:

"I wish to provide assistance to you and help you succeed; I will do this by helping you to avoid the struggles that can exhaust one's energies and talents."

"Monsieur le Comte," replied Jules, moved to tears, "how can I be sure enough of myself to accept your generous offer? How shall I ever know if I will be able to repay my debt to you? It takes years to make a painter, even though God has granted me a great talent."

"I can wait," said the Comte, "calm your scruples. Some day, a single one of your paintings will fulfill your obligations to me, and perhaps it is I who will one day be in your debt."

The young man's joy that followed surpassed the limits of what can be described in this little narrative.

IV
Conclusion

Six years after the journey related here, Jules Dubois had realized the predictions made by Comte Maurice, and the great benefactor unveiled with much fanfare, in the same château where he had dined and spoken with the future painter, the painting which fulfilled the obligations the young man had towards him.

The Comte had chosen the day of the village feast for the unveiling. He presented the artist to his many friends, members of the elite who, while admiring the work of the young painter, were also lining up to purchase one of his paintings.

Under the powerful protection of the Comte, who had become his friend, Jules Dubois had seen fortune and celebrity smile on him early in his career. He was quite pleased by this, since so many geniuses, due to unfavorable circumstances, die poor without ever having enjoyed the glory that was their due.

The village feast was celebrated every year beneath the great trees by the avenue of the château on Ascension Day.

Comte Maurice, followed by his guests, went, as he did every year, to attend the celebration. He took the arm of the young painter, whose elegant figure and handsome face, reminiscent of Van Dyck, were admired by all.

Passing by the shooting gallery, they stopped for a moment to watch the competitors try their luck. Jules recognized among them the proud Captain from the *coucou* whom he had not seen or heard from since his memorable journey.

With his hands on his hips, and a grey hat tipped to the side, Monsieur Alfred was made conspicuous among his rivals by the extravagant knot of his cravat, which was of such a bright blue that it could not fail to catch one's eye. He wore a colorful shirt on which was a printed a pattern of men and women dancing in a frenzied waltz, a waistcoat with all sorts of shimmering colors, and a frock coat at the *height of style* for which the goddess of fashion had designed a cut that was clever enough to conceal the premature stoutness of the young lion from the Grande Chaumière.* Such was the getup of the Captain of Braggarts.

When his turn came, he advanced like a graceful Lovelace of the faubourgs,* slid his hat back, and took aim. A better idea of his offhand manner can be given merely by saying that he was trying to imitate the pose of the Apollo Belvedere.

"We have lost," said one of the discouraged competitors to his neighbor, without waiting for Alfred to take his shot.

"Do you know the fat one over there?"

"I've seen him at all the local festivals win every trophy in place of the villagers at the point of his rifle. He must spend all his time practising . . ."

"Bull's-eye!" everyone cried out.

"Pure luck, my friends," said Alfred.

"Braggart," grumbled one of the other shooters.

Alfred then caught sight of Jules, whom he recognized, and walked over to him.

"Well, well!" said Alfred, assuming the bearing of a dancing master taking the first position, "just as I had predicted: the laurels have sprung up from under our brushes! We have committed ourselves to doing fine work. That picture of yours has the feel of a marble statue to it; no doubt we will have a bust ready for the next exhibition?"

"And you, Captain, just what have you *committed* since last we met?" Jules responded coldly.

"I left the military just as I departed from our *coucou*, as you may know, but young Porriquet's famous tour of Europe sounded tempting to me, and so I gave up my notary's office for the profession of travelling salesman. I sell books, retail and wholesale, in Switzerland, Germany, and other places. If painters could make use of us as booksellers, I would be at your service, Monsieur Dubois."

"*Thrown into the fine arts, I think I know some of its ins and outs.*"

As he spoke these words, the former Captain and ex-clerk, discouraged by the coldness of his former friend, bowed to the Comte, who had returned to the young man's side.

"Monsieur le Comte surely does not recognize me?" said Alfred.

"One always recognizes those who never change, Monsieur," said the Comte, nodding solemnly in return as he led Jules away.

"That man there must live by his wits," said one of the nearby shooters, unhappy about losing the prize, "he's probably first-rate at billiards too."

"And that is all he will ever be," said Comte Maurice to Jules upon hearing those words; "he is like one of those dandies one finds in taverns who swindles gamblers, but must share what he has stolen with the owner."

Just a few paces from where the Comte and the painter had stopped for a moment, two men were hiding behind some trees: none other than the old steward and Joseph Porriquet, who had become his partner and accomplice in many dubious speculations. They were supposedly in the seed trade, and had come to settle up with Farmer Claudin for his last supply of feed. Had they involved themselves in some shady dealings? Had they lost the trust of their customers? The fact remains that they were poor and obliged to hide there, just as they had to everywhere else.

These divine words: *He will reward each according to his works,** are as true in this world as they are in the next, for one almost always carries the burden of the fatal consequences of his sins.

To all braggarts alive or as yet unborn: even if your lies bring only smiles and are excused by your youth, they will cause you to lose the respect of others, and by their very nature will do harm to your character. Every man who measures his words, however, deserves the esteem of all regardless of the rank which God has given him.

Appendix II:
Mateo Falcone
by Prosper Mérimée
(1829)

Translated from the French by Emily Mary Waller
& Mary Helena Dey

Plate XXII

Coming out of Porto-Vecchio,* and turning northwest toward the centre of the island, the ground is seen to rise very rapidly, and, after three hours' walk by tortuous paths, blocked by large boulders of rocks, and sometimes cut by ravines, the traveller finds himself on the edge of a very broad *mâquis*, or open plateau. These plateaus are the home of the Corsican shepherds, and the resort of those who have come in conflict with the law. The Corsican peasant sets fire to a certain stretch of forest to spare himself the trouble of manuring his lands: so much the worse if the flames spread further than is needed. Whatever happens, he is sure to have a good harvest by sowing upon this ground, fertilised by the ashes of the trees which grew on it.

When the corn is gathered, they leave the straw because it is too much trouble to gather. The roots, which remain in the earth without being consumed, sprout, in the following spring, into very thick shoots, which, in a few years, reach to a height of seven or eight feet. It is this kind of underwood which is called *mâquis*. It is composed of different kinds of trees and shrubs mixed up and entangled as in a wild state of nature. It is only with hatchet in hand that man can open a way through, and there are *mâquis* so dense and so thick that not even the wild sheep can penetrate them. If you have killed a man, go into the *mâquis* of Porto-Vecchio, with a good gun and powder and shot, and you will live there in safety. Do not forget to take a brown cloak, furnished with a hood, which will serve as a coverlet and mattress. The shepherds will give you milk, cheese, chestnuts, and you will have nothing to fear from the hand of the law, nor from the relatives of the dead, except when you go down into the town to renew your stock of ammunition.

When I was in Corsica in 18— Mateo Falcone's house was half a league from this *mâquis*. He was a comparatively rich man for that country, living handsomely, that is to say, without doing anything, from the produce of his herds, which the shepherds, a sort of nomadic people, led to pasture here and there over the mountains. When I saw him, two years after the event that I am about to tell, he seemed about fifty years of age at the most. Imagine a small, but robust man, with jet-black, curly hair, an aquiline nose, thin lips, large and piercing eyes, and a deeply tanned complexion. His skill in shooting passed for extraordinary, even in his country, where there are so many crack shots. For example, Mateo would never fire on a sheep with swanshot, but, at one hundred and twenty paces, he would strike it with a bullet in its head or shoulders as he chose. He could use his gun at night as easily as by day, and I was told the following example of his adroitness, which will seem almost incredible to those who have not travelled in Corsica. A lighted candle was placed behind a transparent piece of paper, as large as a plate, at eighty paces off. He put himself into position, then the candle was extinguished, and in a minute's time, in complete darkness, he shot and pierced the paper three times out of four.

With this conspicuous talent Mateo Falcone had earned a great reputation. He was said to be a loyal friend, but a dangerous enemy; in other respects he was obliging and gave alms, and he lived at peace with everybody in the district of Porto-Vecchio. But it is told of him that when at Corte,* where he had found his wife, he had very quickly freed himself of a rival reputed to be equally formidable in love as in war; at any rate, people attributed to Mateo a certain gunshot which surprised his rival while in the act of shaving before a small mirror hung in his window. After the affair had been hushed up, Mateo married. His wife Giuseppa at first presented him with three daughters, which enraged him, but finally a son came whom he named Fortunato; he was the hope of the family, the inheritor of its name. The girls were well married; their father could reckon in case of need upon the poniards and rifles of his sons-in-law. The son was only ten years old, but he had already shown signs of a promising disposition.

One autumn day Mateo and his wife set out early to visit

one of their flocks in a clearing of the *mâquis*. Little Fortunato wanted to go with them, but the clearing was too far off; besides, it was necessary that someone should stay and mind the house, so his father refused. We shall soon see that he had occasion to repent of this. He had been gone several hours and little Fortunato was quietly lying out in the sunshine, looking at the blue mountains, and thinking that on the following Sunday he would be going to town to have dinner at his uncle's, the corporal,* when his meditations were suddenly interrupted by the firing of a gun. He got up and turned toward that side of the plain from which the sound had proceeded.

Other shots followed, fired at irregular intervals, and each time they came nearer and nearer until he saw a man on the path which led from the plain to Mateo's house. He wore a pointed cap like a mountaineer, he was bearded, and clothed in rags, and he dragged himself along with difficulty, leaning on his gun. He had just received a gunshot in the thigh.

This man was a *bandit* (Corsican for one who is proscribed) who, having set out at night to get some powder from the town, had fallen on the way into an ambush of Corsican soldiers.*

After a vigorous defence he had succeeded in escaping, but they gave chase hotly, firing at him from rock to rock. He was only a little in advance of the soldiers, and his wound made it out of the question for him to reach the *mâquis* before being overtaken.

He came up to Fortunato and said—

"Are you the son of Mateo Falcone?"

"Yes."

"I am Gianetto Sanpiero. I am pursued by the yellow-collars. Hide me, for I can not go any further."

"But what will my father say if I hide you without his permission?"

"He will say that you did right."

"How do you know?"

"Hide me quickly; they are coming."

"Wait till my father returns."

"Good Lord! How can I wait? They will be here in five minutes. Come, hide me, or I will kill you."

435

Fortunato replied with the utmost coolness—

"Your gun is unloaded, and there are no more cartridges in your *carchera*."*

"I have my stiletto."

"But could you run as fast as I can? "

With a bound he put himself out of reach.

"You are no son of Mateo Falcone! Will you let me be taken in front of his house?"

The child seemed moved.

"What will you give me if I hide you?" he said, drawing nearer.

The bandit felt in the leather pocket that hung from his side and took out a five franc piece, which he had put aside, no doubt, for powder.

Fortunato smiled at the sight of the piece of silver, and, seizing hold of it, he said to Gianetto—

"Don't be afraid."

He quickly made a large hole in a haystack which stood close by the house. Gianetto crouched down in it, and the child covered him up so as to leave a little breathing space, and yet in such a way as to make it impossible for anyone to suspect that the hay concealed a man. He acted, further, with the ingenious cunning of the savage. He fetched a cat and her kittens and put them on the top of the haystack to make believe that it had not been touched for a long time.

Then he carefully covered over with dust the bloodstains which he had noticed on the path near the house, and, this done, he lay down again in the sun with the utmost sangfroid.

Some minutes later six men in brown uniforms with yellow collars, commanded by an adjutant, stood before Mateo's door. This adjutant was a distant relative of the Falcones. (It is said that further degrees of relationship are recognised in Corsica than anywhere else.) His name was Tiodoro Gamba; he was an energetic man, greatly feared by the *banditti*, and had already hunted out many of them.

"Good day, youngster," he said, coming up to Fortunato. "How you have grown! Did you see a man pass just now?"

"Oh, I am not yet so tall as you, cousin," the child replied, with a foolish look.

"You soon will be. But, tell me, have you not seen a man pass by?"

"Have I seen a man pass by?"

"Yes, a man with a pointed black velvet cap and a waistcoat embroidered in red and yellow."

"A man with a pointed cap and a waistcoat embroidered in scarlet and yellow?"

"Yes; answer sharply and don't repeat my questions."

"The priest passed our door this morning on his horse Piero. He asked me how Papa was, and I replied——"

"You are making game of me, you rascal. Tell me at once which way Gianetto went, for it is he we are after; I am certain he took this path."

"How do you know that?"

"How do I know that? I know you have seen him."

"How can one see passersby when one is asleep?"

"You were not asleep, you little demon: the gunshots would wake you."

"You think, then, cousin, that your guns make noise enough? My father's rifle makes much more noise."

"May the devil take you, you young scamp. I am absolutely certain you have seen Gianetto. Perhaps you have even hidden him. Here, you fellows, go into the house, and see if our man is not there. He could only walk on one foot, and he has too much common sense, the villain, to have tried to reach the *mâquis* limping. Besides, the traces of blood stop here."

"Whatever will Papa say?" Fortunato asked, with a chuckle. "What will he say when he finds out that his house has been searched during his absence?"

"Do you know that I can make you change your tune, you scamp?" cried the adjutant Gamba, seizing him by the ear. "Perhaps you will speak when you have had a thrashing with the flat of a sword." Fortunato kept on laughing derisively.

"My father is Mateo Falcone," he said significantly.

"Do you know, you young scamp, that I can take you away to Corte or to Bastia? I shall put you in a dungeon, on a bed of straw, with your feet in irons, and I shall guillotine you if you do not tell me where Gianetto Sanpiero is." The child burst out laughing at this ridiculous menace. "My father is Mateo Falcone," he repeated.

"Adjutant, do not let us embroil ourselves with Mateo," one of the soldiers whispered.

Gamba was evidently embarrassed. He talked in a low voice with his soldiers, who had already been all over the house. It was not a lengthy operation, for a Corsican hut only consists of a single square room. The furniture comprises a table, benches, boxes and utensils for cooking and hunting. All this time little Fortunato caressed his cat, and seemed, maliciously, to enjoy the confusion of his cousin and the soldiers.

One soldier came up to the haycock. He looked at the cat and carelessly stirred the hay with his bayonet, shrugging his shoulders as though he thought the precaution ridiculous. Nothing moved, and the face of the child did not betray the least agitation.

The adjutant and his band were in despair; they looked solemnly out over the plain, half inclined to return the way they had come; but their chief, convinced that threats would produce no effect upon the son of Falcone, thought he would make one last effort by trying the effect of favours and presents.

"My boy," he said, "you are a wide-awake young dog, I can see. You will get on. But you play a dangerous game with me, and, if I did not want to give pain to my cousin Mateo, devil take it! I would carry you off with me."

"Bah!"

"But, when my cousin returns I shall tell him all about it, and he will give you the whip till he draws blood for having told me lies."

"How do you know that?"

"You will see. But, look here, be a good lad and I will give you something."

"You had better go and look for Gianetto in the *mâquis*, cousin, for if you stay any longer it will take a cleverer fellow than you to catch him."

The adjutant drew a watch out of his pocket, a silver watch worth quite ten crowns. He watched how little Fortunato's eyes sparkled as he looked at it, and he held out the watch at the end of its steel chain.

"You rogue," he said, "you would like to have such a watch as this hung round your neck, and to go and walk up and down the streets of Porto-Vecchio as proud as a peacock; people would ask you the time, and you would reply, 'Look at my watch!'"

"When I am grown up, my uncle the corporal will give me a watch."

"Yes, but your uncle's son has one already—not such a fine one as this, however—for he is younger than you." The boy sighed.

"Well, would you like this watch, little cousin?" Fortunato ogled the watch out of the corner of his eyes, just as a cat does when a whole chicken is given to it. It dares not pounce upon the prey, because it is afraid a joke is being played on it, but it turns its eyes away now and then, to avoid succumbing to the temptation, licking its lips all the time as though to say to its master, "What a cruel joke you are playing on me!" The adjutant Gamba, however, seemed really willing to give the watch. Fortunato did not hold out his hand, but he said to him with a bitter smile—

"Why do you make fun of me?"

"I swear I am not joking. Only tell me where Gianetto is, and this watch is yours." Fortunato smiled incredulously, and fixed his black eyes on those of the adjutant. He tried to find in them the faith he would fain have in his words.

"May I lose my epaulettes," cried the adjutant, " if I do not give you the watch upon that condition! I call my men to witness, and then I can not retract."

As he spoke, he held the watch nearer and nearer until it almost touched the child's pale cheeks.

His face plainly expressed the conflict going on in his mind between covetousness and the claims of hospitality. His bare breast heaved violently almost to suffocation. All the time the watch dangled and twisted and even hit the tip of his nose.

By degrees he raised his right hand toward the watch, his finger ends touched it, and its whole weight rested on his palm although the adjutant still held the end of the chain loosely . . . the watch face was blue . . . the case was newly polished . . . it seemed blazing in the sun like fire . . . the temptation was too strong.

Fortunato raised his left hand at the same time, and pointed with his thumb over his shoulder to the haycock against which he was leaning. The adjutant understood him immediately, and let go the end of the chain. Fortunato felt himself sole possessor of the watch. He jumped up with the agility of a deer, and stood ten paces distant from the haycock, which the soldiers at once began to upset. It was not long before they saw the hay move, and a bleeding man came out, poniard in hand; when, however, he tried to rise to his feet his stiffening wound prevented him from standing. He fell down. The adjutant threw himself upon him and snatched away his dagger. He was speedily and strongly bound, in spite of his resistance.

Gianetto was bound and laid on the ground like a bundle of fagots. He turned his head toward Fortunato, who had come up to him.

"Son of——," he said to him more in contempt than in anger.

The boy threw to him the silver piece that he had received from him, feeling conscious that he no longer deserved it, but the outlaw took no notice of the action. He merely said in a cool voice to the adjutant—

"My dear Gamba, I can not walk; you will be obliged to carry me to the town."

"You could run as fast as a kid just now," his captor retorted brutally. "But don't be anxious, I am glad enough to have caught you: I would carry you for a league on my own back and not feel tired. All the same, my friend, we will make a litter for you out of the branches and your cloak. The farm at Crespoli will provide us with horses,"

"All right," said the prisoner; "I hope you will put a little straw on your litter to make it easier for me." While the soldiers were busy, some making a rough stretcher out of chestnut boughs and others dressing Gianetto's wound, Mateo Falcone and his wife suddenly appeared in a turning of the path from the *mâquis*. The wife came in bending laboriously under the weight of a huge sack of chestnuts, while her husband jaunted up carrying his gun in one hand, and a second gun slung in his shoulder belt. It is considered undignified for a man to carry any other burden but his weapons.

When he saw the soldiers, Mateo's first thought was that they had come to arrest him.

But he had no ground for this fear, he had never quarrelled with the law. On the contrary he bore a good reputation. He was, as the saying is, particularly well thought of. But he was a Corsican, and mountain bred, and there are but few Corsican mountaineers who, if they search their memories sufficiently, cannot recall some little peccadillo, some gunshot, or dagger thrust, or such-like bagatelle. Mateo's conscience was clearer than most, for it was fully ten years since he had pointed his gun at any man; yet at the same time he was cautious, and he prepared to make a brave defence if needs be.

"Wife, put down your sack," he said, "and keep yourself in readiness." She obeyed immediately. He gave her the gun which was slung over his shoulder, as it was likely to be the one that would inconvenience him the most. He held the other gun in readiness, and proceeded leisurely toward the house by the side of the trees which bordered the path, ready to throw himself behind the largest trunk for cover, and to fire at the least sign of hostility. His wife walked close behind him holding her reloaded gun and her cartridges. It was the duty of a good housewife, in case of a conflict, to reload her husband's arms.

On his side, the adjutant was very uneasy at the sight of Mateo advancing thus upon them with measured steps, his gun pointed and finger on trigger.

"If it happens that Gianetto is related to Mateo," thought he, "or he is his friend, and he means to protect him, two of his bullets will be put into two of us as sure as a letter goes to the post, and he will aim at me in spite of our kinship!" In this perplexity, he put on a bold face and went forward alone toward Mateo to tell him what had happened, greeting him like an old acquaintance. But the brief interval which separated him from Mateo seemed to him of terribly long duration.

"Hullo! Ah! My old comrade," he called out. "How are you, old fellow? I am your cousin Gamba." Mateo did not say a word, but stood still, and while the other was speaking, he softly raised the muzzle of his rifle in such a manner that by the time the adjutant came up to him it was pointing skyward.

"Good day, brother," said the adjutant, holding out his hand. "It is a very long time since I saw you."

"Good day, brother."*

"I just called in when passing to say 'good day' to you and cousin Pepa. We have done a long tramp today, but we must not complain of fatigue, for we have taken a fine catch. We have got hold of Gianetto Sanpiero."

"Thank Heaven!" exclaimed Giuseppa. "He stole one of our milch goats last week."

Gamba rejoiced at these words.

"Poor devil!" said Mateo, "he was hungry."

"The fellow fought like a lion," continued the adjutant, slightly nettled. "He killed one of the men, and, not content to stop there, he broke Corporal Chardon's arm; but that is not of much consequence, for he is only a Frenchman . . . then he hid himself so cleverly that the devil could not have found him. If it had not been for my little cousin Fortunato, I should never have discovered him."

"Fortunato?" cried Mateo.

"Fortunato?" repeated Giuseppa.

"Yes; Gianetto was concealed in your haycock there, but my little cousin showed me his trick. I will speak of him to his uncle the corporal, who will send him a nice present as a reward. And both his name and yours will be in the report which I shall send to the superintendent."

"Curse you!" cried Mateo under his breath.

By this time they had rejoined the company. Gianetto was already laid on his litter, and they were ready to set out. When he saw Mateo in Gamba's company he smiled a strange smile; then, turning toward the door of the house, he spat on the threshold.

"It is the house of a traitor!" he exclaimed.

No man but one willing to die would have dared to utter the word "traitor" in connection with Falcone.

A quick stroke from a dagger, without need for a second, would have immediately wiped out the insult. But Mateo made no other movement beyond putting his hand to his head like a dazed man.

Fortunato went into the house when he saw his father come up. He reappeared shortly carrying a jug of milk, which he offered with downcast eyes to Gianetto.

"Keep off me!" roared the outlaw.

Then, turning to one of the soldiers, he said—

"Comrade, give me a drink of water."

The soldier placed the flask in his hands, and the bandit drank the water given him by a man with whom he had but now exchanged gunshots. He then asked that his hands might be tied crossed over his breast instead of behind his back.

"I prefer," he said, "to lie down comfortably." They granted him his request. Then, at a sign from the adjutant, they set out, first bidding adieu to Mateo, who answered never a word, and descended at a quick pace toward the plain.

Well-nigh ten minutes elapsed before Mateo opened his mouth. The child looked uneasily first at his mother, then at his father, who leant on his gun, looking at him with an expression of concentrated anger.

"Well, you have made a pretty beginning," said Mateo at last in a voice calm, but terrifying, to those who knew the man.

"Father," the boy cried out, with tears in his eyes, just ready to fall at his knees.

"Out of my sight!" shouted Mateo. The child stopped motionless a few steps off his father, and began to sob. Giuseppa came near him. She had just seen the end of the watch chain hanging from out his shirt.

"Who gave you that watch?" she asked severely.

"My cousin the adjutant." Falcone seized the watch, and threw it against a stone with such force that it broke into a thousand pieces.

"Woman," he said, "is this my child?" Giuseppa's brown cheeks flamed brick-red.

"What are you saying, Mateo? Do you know to whom you are speaking?"

"Yes, very well. This child is the first traitor of his race."

Fortunato's sobs and hiccoughs redoubled, and Falcone kept his lynx eyes steadily fixed on him. At length he struck the ground with the butt end of his gun; then he flung it across his shoulder, retook the way to the *mâquis*, and ordered Fortunato to follow him. The child obeyed.

Giuseppa ran after Mateo, and seized him by the arm.

"He is your son," she said in a trembling voice, fixing her black eyes on those of her husband, as though to read all that was passing in his mind.

"Leave go," replied Mateo; "I am his father." Giuseppa kissed her son, and went back crying into the hut. She threw herself on her knees before an image of the Virgin, and prayed fervently. When Falcone had walked about two hundred yards along the path he stopped at a little ravine and went down into it. He sounded the ground with the butt end of his gun, and found it soft and easy to dig. The spot seemed suitable to his purpose.

"Fortunato, go near to that large rock." The boy did as he was told, then knelt down.

"Say your prayers."

"Father, Father, do not kill me!"

"Say your prayers!" repeated Mateo in a terrible voice.

The child repeated the Lord's Prayer and the Creed, stammering and sobbing. The father said "Amen!" in a firm voice at the close of each prayer.

"Are those all the prayers you know?"

"I know also the Ave Maria and Litany, that my aunt taught me, Father."

"It is long, but never mind." The child finished the Litany in a faint voice.

"Have you finished?"

"Oh, Father, forgive me! Forgive me! I will never do it again. I will beg my cousin the corporal with all my might to pardon Gianetto!"

He went on imploring. Mateo loaded his rifle and took aim.

"May God forgive you!" he said. The boy made a frantic effort to get up and clasp his father's knees, but he had no time. Mateo fired, and Fortunato fell stone dead.

Without throwing a single glance at the body, Mateo went back to his house to fetch a spade with which to bury his son. He had only returned a little way along the path when he met Giuseppa, who had run out alarmed by the sound of firing.

"What have you done?" she cried.

"Justice!"

"Where is he?"

"In the ravine; I am going to bury him. He died a Christian. I shall have a mass sung for him. Let someone tell my son-in-law Tiodoro Bianchi to come and live with us."

*
Endnotes

References that can be found in an unabridged English dictionary, or are otherwise self-explanatory, are not included here unless they bear some special relevance to the author or the text.

A Start in Life

The inspiration for this novel, which would ultimately become the sixth work of the *Comédie*, came from Balzac's sister and eventual biographer, Laure Surville (1800-1871), to whom the work is dedicated. Often in need of ideas or plotlines to spark his writing, he asked her to come up with "a story for young people." Because she was accustomed to writing stories for children (some of which were published in children's literary magazines under the pen name "Lelio"), she had little difficulty in producing "*Le Voyage en Coucou*" (see Appendix I), a cautionary tale that reveals the consequences of loose talk and braggadocio while in public.

In Balzac's hands, the story went through several versions and was transformed from a simple morality tale into more of a *bildungsroman*, as its hapless protagonist Oscar slowly manages to find his true calling in life after learning two hard lessons. It began in 1841 as a piece intended for *Le Musée des familles*, an illustrated bi-annual magazine, meant to be no longer than 3000 lines. The work, which would either have retained Laure's original title or be called "*Les Jeunes Gens*" ("*The Young People*"), quickly outgrew the magazine's guidelines and was rejected for publication. By 1842, the story had expanded to a novel of fourteen chapters and was serialized in the weekly *La Législature*, beginning with its July 26th issue, as *Le Danger des mystifications*. The serialized chapters, essentially unchanged, were assembled and published in two volumes (along with *La Fausse Maîtresse*) under the final title, *Un début dans la vie*, by Dumont in June 1844. For the Furne edition of 1845, Balzac removed the chapter divisions, made a few corrections, and gave Mistigris a number of additional quips. At this point it was the twenty-fourth work in the sequence, following *Honorine*, before being moved to its final position as the sixth work, as it appears in the definitive Pléiade edition.

3   *the Place de la Concorde . . . the Cours-la-Reine*: the Place de la Concorde is Paris's largest public square, located in what is today the city's 8th arrondissement on the Right Bank of the Seine. It was originally known as the Place Louis XV; during the French Revolution, the equestrian statue of the King, for which it was named, was torn down and the square became known as La Place de la Révolution. It was under this name that the square witnessed the executions of Louis XVI, Marie Antoinette, Charlotte Corday, Danton, Lavoisier, and eventually even Robespierre himself, along with hundreds of others. During the period of the Directory, it was given the name by which it is still known today as an act of reconciliation.

The Cours-la-Reine is a tree-lined promenade and public garden built at the direction of Queen Marie de Médicis in 1616. Located along the Seine, it begins at the Place de la Concorde and ends at the Place du Canada, about a third of a mile away.

the Rue du Faubourg Saint-Denis: a long street in what is now Paris's 10th arrondissement, located on the Right Bank; it is an extension of the Rue Saint-Denis (see note to page 11), a road which leads to the Basilique Saint-Denis, for which it is named.

4   *the Rue Montmartre . . . Cuvier's researches . . . in the lime quarries of Montmartre*: the Rue Montmartre is street that runs north from what is now Paris's 1st arrondissement to the 2nd on the Right Bank. At the beginning of *Ferragus*, the first novel of *The Thirteen*, a trilogy which appears later in the *Comédie*, Balzac writes: "*Quelques rues, ainsi que la rue Montmartre, ont une belle tête et finissent en queue de poisson*" ("Some streets, like the Rue Montmartre, have a charming head and end in a fish's tail").

As a young man, Balzac attended at least one of Cuvier's lectures at the Natural History Museum in Paris and was so impressed after hearing him speak that, along with Napoléon and Irish politician Daniel O'Connell, he considered the naturalist to be one of the three greatest men who had ever lived (Balzac himself hoped to become the fourth). Cuvier is mentioned frequently throughout the *Comédie*.

5   *Beaumont-sur-Oise*: French commune that lies between the Oise River valley and the forest of Carnelle, 18 miles to the north of Paris.

towns like Saint-Denis and Saint-Brice . . . a string of villages as Pierrefitte, Groslay, Écouen . . . Moisselles, Baillet, Montsoult, Maffliers, Franconville, Presles, Nointel, Nerville . . . Chambly: Saint-Denis and Pierrefitte-sur-Seine are communes of the Seine-Saint-Denis département in Paris's northern suburbs; Saint-Brice-sous-Forêt, Groslay, Écouen, Moisselles, Baillet-en-France, Montsoult, Maffliers, Franconville, Presles, Nointel, and Nerville-la-Forêt are communes of the Val-d'Oise département, all less than twenty miles to the north of Paris. Chambly is a commune of the Oise département located in the Picardie region of north central France.

La Cave: The Cellar; at that time an actual coaching inn located in Presles.

the little town of L'Isle-Adam . . . the Princes of Bourbon-Conti: L'Isle-Adam is a commune of the Val d'Oise département, located in the north-central Île-de-France region; the aforementioned communes of Montsoult and Maffliers lie on the edge of the forest of L'Isle-Adam. Balzac likely owes his detailed knowledge of this area to his friendship with the Mayor of L'Isle-Adam and the time he spent with him there.

The Princes of Bourbon-Conti lived for seven generations at the Château de L'Isle-Adam. The title was assumed by a lineage descended from a younger son of the noble house of Bourbon-Condé.

5   *two large hamlets, that of Nogent and that of Parmain*: Nogent, an ancient village, is now a neighborhood of L'Isle-Adam. Parmain is a commune to the west of L'Isle-Adam, on the opposite bank of the Oise.

   Cassan, Stors . . . Persan: Cassan and Stors are estates in L'Isle-Adam; Persan is a commune in the Val-d'Oise département.

6   *the valley of Montmorency . . . Saint-Leu-Taverny*: Montmorency, Val-d'Oise, is a commune located in Paris's northern suburbs.
   Saint-Leu-Taverny was a commune of the Val-d'Oise département which in present times has split into two communes: Saint-Leu-la-Forêt and Taverny.

   Mours, Prérolles: Mours is a commune in the Val-d'Oise département; Prerolles was a fief which is now part of the commune of Presles.

   the Rue d'Enghien . . . the Lion-d'Argent: The Rue d'Enghien is a Parisian street located in what is now the 10th arrondissement. Formerly known as the Rue Mably, it was renamed in 1814 in honor of Louis Antoine Henri de Bourbon-Condé, Duc d'Enghien (1772-1804), who had been mistakenly linked to a Royalist conspiracy by the French police and was summarily executed on Napoléon's orders. This act outraged the courts of Europe, and definitively turned aristocratic opinion against the First Consul.
   the Lion-d'Argent: The Silver Lion.

9   lapins*: rabbits.*

10   *These passengers in the* poulailler: chicken coop.

11   *the Rue Saint-Denis*: one of the city's oldest streets dating back to the 1st century AD, the Rue Saint-Denis is located in what is today the 1st arrondissement. Much of the action of *At the Sign of the Cat and Racket*, the first work of the *Comédie*, takes place in a draper's shop on this street.

12   *the* Café de l'Échiquier *at the corner of the street of that name*: the Rue de l'Échiquier, a Parisian street located in what is now the 10th arrondissement, named after a trading house that formerly did business there. *Échiquier* can also mean "chessboard," and at one point the café was a meeting place for the Paris Chess Club.

13   *the sturdy Auvergnat*: a denizen of Auvergne, a former province located in south central France.

       the Porte Saint-Denis: a triumphal arch located in what is today the 10th arrondissement of Paris at the junction of the Rue Saint-Denis, the Rue du Faubourg Saint-Denis, the Boulevard Bonne-Nouvelle, and the Boulevard Saint-Denis. It was built in 1672 by François Blondel (1618-1686) to honor Louis XIV's military victories in Holland. The monument bears the inscription LUDOVICO MAGNO (To Louis the Great).

15   *the road by the Orge valley*: the Orge River, a tributary of the Seine.

17   *the Chaussée-d'Antin*: the Rue de la Chaussée-d'Antin, a Parisian street located in the city's 9th arrondissement on the Right Bank. The street was named for Louis Antoine de Pardaillan de Gondrin, the 1st Duc d'Antin (1665-1736). During the Revolution, in 1791, it was renamed the Rue de Mirabeau to honor the French politician who died there, and then changed again to the Rue du Mont-Blanc two years later after it was discovered that he had had a secret association with the King. Its original name was restored in 1815.

       In his *Histoire et Physiologie des Boulevards de Paris* (1846), Balzac wrote "the heart of present-day Paris . . .

Plate XXIII: The Comte de Sérisy's Coat of Arms

Plate XXIV: *Le Massacre des Mamelouks
de la Citadelle du Caire* (1819) by Horace Vernet

beats between the Rue de la Chaussée-d'Antin and the Rue du Faubourg-Montmartre."

17   *A Peer of France*: the *Pairie de France*, as it existed in the time of the Bourbon Restoration, was a rank of hereditary nobility established by a provision of the Charter of 1814 and granted by the King. It was similar to the British Upper House of Lords, and was considered to be the very highest honor that a member of the French nobility could attain. Inherited peerages were later changed to lifetime appointments after the July Revolution of 1830, and after the revolution of 1848 the Chamber of Peers was permanently dissolved.

18   party per pale or and sable, an orle and two lozenges counterchanged . . . I, SEMPER MELIUS ERIS: the Comte de Sérisy's arms described using the terminology of heraldry known as blazon. In simpler terms, they are a shield divided vertically between gold and black fields with an inner border and two diamonds of the color opposite to their half (see Plate XXIII). The motto is "always be better."

a Premier President of Parlement . . . Councillor of State in the Grand Council in 1787: prior to the Revolution, parlements were regional judicial bodies that formed part of the sovereign courts and also performed legislative and administrative functions. *Président à mortier* was the name given to the most experienced magistrates of the parlements, who were distinguished by the black velvet caps they wore. The most senior of these judges was the *Premier Président*, who was appointed directly by the King.

A *Conseiller d'État* or State Councillor, under the pre-Revolutionary *Ancien Régime*, was a powerful government official charged with advising the King on matters of his choosing. Promotions to *Conseiller d'État* were given by the King, and the position conferred nobility on its holder; the *Grand Conseil* was a special court of justice charged with handling religious matters or conflicts of interest that were beyond the purview of the parlements.

18   *Arpajon*: commune located about twenty miles south of Paris.

19   *the Council of Five Hundred . . . the eighteenth Brumaire*: the *Conseil des Cinq-Cents* was the lower legislative house of the Directory that existed from 22 August 1795 to 9 November 1799 alongside the *Conseil des Anciens* or Council of Elders.

The eighteenth Brumaire was a date of the French Revolutionary Calendar in the year VIII (9 November 1799) on which Napoléon staged a coup against the Directory and supplanted it with the French Consulate.

when the Bourbons came back: the Restoration of Louis XVIII of the Bourbon dynasty to the French throne after the Revolution and the Napoleonic Wars.

20   *On the 20th March, Monsieur de Sérisy did not follow the King to Ghent . . . the Emperor's second fall*: a reference to *Les Cent Jours* or the Hundred Days (actually 111 days in total) when Napoléon returned to Paris from exile in an attempt to reclaim power on 20 March 1815. Louis XVIII subsequently fled to the city of Ghent in what was then the United Kingdom of the Netherlands. The Emperor was defeated by the combined armies of the Seventh Coalition at Waterloo on 28 June and finally surrendered on 15 July. The King was restored to the throne of France for a second time on 8 July bringing the period of the Hundred Days to an end.

the Privy Council . . . Vice President of the Council of State: During the Restoration, the *Conseil privé* was an advisory council created by the order of the King; it rarely met, and had considerably less power than the *Conseil privé* of the *Ancien Régime*, which served a primarily judicial function.

The *Conseil d'État*, which dates from the time of the Consulate, was created by a provision of the

Constitution of the Year VIII, and under the direction of the Consuls was "responsible for drafting bills and regulations of public administration, and [resolving] difficulties that arise in administrative matters." The institution was preserved under the Restoration as an administrative court, but had significantly less prominence.

the Grand Cross of the Legion of Honour . . . the Orders of the Golden Fleece, of Saint Andrew of Russia, of the Prussian Eagle: the *Ordre national de la Légion d'honneur*, founded by Napoléon in May 1802, was a decoration that could be awarded to soldiers and civilians based on their merits and service to France, and did not require the wearer to be a member of the nobility. The Order is divided into five degrees: Chevalier (or Knight), Officer, Commander, Grand Officer, and Grand Cross; its motto is *Honneur et Patrie* (Honor and Fatherland). Louis XVIII decided to keep the order, but changed the design of the medals so that images of Napoléon were no longer displayed; those loyal to the Emperor felt that it was awarded rather freely by the King, thus diminishing its importance. The award has gone through a number of subtle changes over the years, but to this day remains the highest honor France can grant to an individual.

The Order of the Golden Fleece and the Order of St. Andrew the Apostle the First-Called were chivalric orders founded by Philip III of Burgundy in 1430 and Peter the Great in 1698, respectively; the Prussian Eagle is either the Order of the Red Eagle or the Order of the Black Eagle, the latter being the more prestigious of the two; both are chivalric orders awarded for civil or military distinction.

23   *the party of Danton*: a group of moderates known as the Indulgents, who were arrested and executed for their opposition to the extreme policies of the Committee of Public Safety led by Robespierre.

25   *Saint-Lô*: commune of northwestern France located in
       Normandy's Manche département.

26   *the Collège Henri IV*: a highly competitive and presti-
       gious secondary school, today known as the Lycée
       Henri-IV, that was built on the site of a Benedictine
       monastery in 1796. It is situated on the Rue Clovis
       in Paris's 5th arrondissement on the Left Bank of the
       Seine. Guy de Maupassant, Prosper Mérimée, Alfred
       de Musset, and Alfred de Vigny are among its many
       famous alumni.

       the tiers consolidé: according to Cobbett's French
       and English dictionary: "the third part to which the
       public debt was reduced at the beginning of the first
       revolution."

30   *the* Courrier Français: the name of at least three differ-
       ent French periodicals; during the time in which the
       story takes place, the *Courrier* was a liberal newspaper
       that began in 1820 and continued to be published until
       1851.

       a noble family of the Messin country: the area centered
       around the city of Metz in northeastern France.

32   *No. 7 Rue de la Cerisaie, near the Arsenal:* a street between
       the Boulevard Bourdon and the Rue du Petit Musc lo-
       cated in what is now Paris's 4th arrondissement on the
       Right Bank. It was named for the line of cherry trees in
       the garden of the Hôtel Saint-Pol (what Balzac refers to
       as "the Hôtel Saint-Paul"), a residence built by Charles
       V in the late 14th century, which subsequently fell into
       ruin.
           The Paris Arsenal, bounded by the Seine, the Rue
       du Petit Musc, and the Wall of Charles V, was built by
       François I in 1533. The rooms that made up the resi-
       dence of the Grand Master of Artillery were made into
       a library in 1757, and the writer Charles Nodier (1780-
       1844), one of Balzac's literary acquaintances, became

the librarian in 1824. The Bibliothèque de l'Arsenal is now part of the Bibliothèque nationale.

33   *the site of the Palais des Tournelles*: the *Hôtel* des Tournelles is probably what is meant: a group of buildings dating to the 14th century, used as a residence by Henry II and his wife Catherine de Médicis. After Henry II's death, Catherine ended her residence there and later had the buildings demolished over a period of time starting in 1563. The site subsequently became a square called the Place Royale, now known as the Place des Vosges.

Rue Beautreillis, Rue des Lions, etc.: Parisian streets of what is today the 4th arrondissement. The Rue Beau-treillis, formerly known as the Rue du Pistolet, was so named for the vines that grew against the garden walls of the aforementioned Hôtel Saint-Pol; in 1836 it was ex-tended by the annexation of the Rue Gérard-Beauquet. The Rue des Lions-Saint-Paul takes its name from the menagerie of animals kept in the area by Charles V.

35   *one of the five kings of the day*: a reference to *Le Directoire* or the French Directory, an executive body that held power from 1795 to 1799 composed of five directors selected from a list presented to the *Conseil des Anciens* by the *Conseil des Cinq-Cents*. Over the course of its ex-istence, thirteen men held the posts of Director, and every year one of them, chosen at random, was re-quired to step down and be replaced.

36   MADAME, *the Emperor's mother*: Maria Letizia Bonaparte, née Ramolino (1750-1836), who by decree was given the title of *Madame Mère de l'Empereur*, usually short-ened to *Madame Mère*.

38   *Belleville*: a former French commune to the east of Paris that was later absorbed by the city in 1860.

42   *the* Ambigu Comique: the Théâtre de l'Ambigu-Comique, a Parisian theater founded in 1769 by Nicolas-Médard

Audinot (1732-1801), an actor, playwright, and puppeteer. In its first incarnation, the Ambigu-Comique was located on the Boulevard du Temple in today's 11th arrondissement on the Right Bank. It was destroyed by fire in 1827 and rebuilt in the same year on the Boulevard Saint-Martin in the 10th arrondissement, where it became increasingly popular for its vaudevilles and crime melodramas.

43 *Did not Rousseau of Geneva envy Venture and Bâcle:* the (possibly fictitious) man known as Venture de Villeneuve, mentioned by Rousseau in his *Confessions,* was a travelling confidence man posing as a singer and musician who was envied by the author for his ability to enchant his audiences despite his apparent lack of musical training; at one point Rousseau even decided to adopt a persona similar to that of the mysterious Venture, calling himself Vaussore de Villeneuve.

Pierre (perhaps Étienne) Bâcle (1714-1731) had served as an apprentice engraver with Rousseau in Geneva under a tyrannical master by the name of Abel Ducommun (1705-1771). In his youth Rousseau admired Bâcle for his lively behavior and "clownish jests," but soon became bored with him and shifted his attention to Venture.

a song then in fashion among the Liberals, "C'est la faute à Voltaire, c'est la faute à Rousseau": "It is all the fault of Voltaire and Rousseau."

45 *the bantering wit of a Figaro*: the devious Spanish barber and ex-servant who appears in three plays by Beaumarchais, and perhaps most famously in operas by Mozart and Rossini.

47 *known in French studio slang as a* rapin: a derogatory term for an apprentice or unskilled painter—a bohemian. A critic by the name of J. Chaudes-Aigues wrote of three possibilities for the origin of this name: that it derives from the French verb *rapiner,* which means to

pillage; that it is a contraction of "*rat qui peint*," a "rat who paints;" or that it comes from the word *râpé*, which means "worn" or "threadbare." Chaudes-Aigues's article on the subject appears in an illustrated collection of essays by various authors entitled *Français peints par eux-mêmes* (*Pictures of the French*, 1840), which describes a number of Parisian social types of the day. The collection includes two essays by Balzac, "The Parisian Lady" and "The Grocer."

Mistigris: a wild card, either a blank or a joker, in a variation of Poker of the same name. It can also mean "pussycat."

49   *And is it you who are known as old Léger*: *léger* is French for "light" as in "lightweight."

    Yo, heave ho: 'Haoup! là! ahé! hisse!' in the original.

50   time is a great plaster: "*le temps est un grand maigre*" ("time is a great faster") in the original, a play on "*le temps est un grand maître*" ("time is a great master").

    Paris was not gilt in a play: "*Paris n'a pas été bâti dans un four*" ("Paris was not built in an oven") in the original, *four* in this case being substituted for *jour* (day).

    Short counts make tall friends: "*Les bons comtes font les bons tamis*" ("good counts make good sieves") in the original, a play on "*Les bons comptes font les bons amis*," which translates roughly as "short reckonings make long friends" or "square accounts make square friends."

51   Manners take the van: "*les voyages déforment la jeunesse*" ("travelling deforms youth") in the original, a play on "*les voyages qui forment la jeunesse*" ("travel makes one's youth" or "travelling keeps one young").

51   Tarts are the end of man: *"Les Arts sont l'ami de l'homme"*
       ("The Arts are the friend of man") in the original, a
       play on *"Les Arts sont **la mie** de l'homme"* ("The Arts are
       the bread of man").

53   *the Rue de la Fidélité*: Parisian street located in what is
       now the city's 10th arrondissement.

54   *All men are equal in the eye of the* coucou . . . *as all
       Frenchmen are in the eye of the Charter*: the Charter of
       1814, a constitution required by the Congress of Vienna
       as a precondition for Louis XVIII's restoration to the
       throne. It guaranteed equality before the law and free-
       dom of religion for all Frenchmen, but it also made
       Catholicism the country's official faith.

       La Chapelle is a village close to the Barrière Saint-Denis:
       La Chapelle Saint-Denis is a commune which did not
       become a part of Paris until 1960. The Barrière Saint-
       Denis, now known as the Barrière de la Chapelle, is a
       gate located at the end of the Rue du Faubourg Saint-
       Denis.

55   *shall I pass myself off as Étienne, or as Béranger*:
       Charles-Guillaume Étienne (1778-1845) was a French
       playwright, journalist, and member of the Académie
       française whose best known work is the comedy *Les
       Deux Gendres* (*The Two Genders*, 1810), which he may
       have plagiarized. He is said to have coined the phrase
       "On n'est jamais si bien servi que par soi-même" (usually
       translated as "if you want something done right, do it
       yourself").
           Pierre-Jean de Béranger (1780-1857) was a French
       writer of popular songs.

       One of Marshal Ney's sons: "the bravest of the brave," as
       he was called by Napoléon, Ney had four sons: Joseph,
       Michel, Eugène, and Edgar; two were princes and one
       was a duke.

the government colony in America: the *Champ d'asile* or "Field of Asylum" was a Bonapartist colony founded in Texas by General Charles Lallemand in 1818, but relinquished less than a year later after protestations by the Spanish Bourbons. The character of Philippe Bridau, who will appear later in the *Comédie*, is briefly involved with Lallemand and the *Champ d'asile* in *The Rabouilleuse*.

Ali, the Pasha of Janina: Ali Pasha of Tepelena (sometimes of Yannina, 1750-1822) was the Ottoman governor of a region of southeastern Europe known as Rumelia, which is today shared by Greece and Albania.

56 *In the East . . .* In the least: "*Dans le Levant . . . Dans le vent*" ("In the Levant . . . In the wind") in the original.

57 *the battle of Hanau . . . Montereau*: the first was a minor engagement of the German Campaign in the War of the Sixth Coalition (an alliance of Austria, Portugal, Prussia, Russia, Sardinia, Sicily, Spain, Sweden, the United Kingdom, and others fighting against the French Empire and her allies) that took place on the last two days of October 1813 between retreating Napoleonic forces and an alliance of Austrians and Bavarians led by Field Marshal Carl Philipp von Wrede (1767-1838). A French victory allowed Napoléon to retreat and regroup after his defeat at Leipzig earlier that month.

Montereau was another battle in the War of the Sixth Coalition. The engagement at Montereau (Seine-et-Marne département) was fought on 18 February 1814 between the French and the Austrian Empire, resulting in a victory for Napoléon.

the Order of the Annunciada of Sardinia: the Supreme Order of the Most Holy Annunciation, an award founded in 1362 conferring knighthood for distinguished service to the Kingdom of Italy.

58   *the campaign of 1815 . . . Mont Saint-Jean*: a reference to
the Hundred Days (see note to page 20, *On the 20th
March*); Mont Saint-Jean is a Belgian hamlet located to
the south of Waterloo, the famous site of Napoléon's
final defeat. In France the Battle of Waterloo is sometimes referred to as the Battle of Mont-Saint-Jean.

*Selves, Besson, and some more—who are in Egypt to this day
in the service of Mohammed Pasha*: Joseph Anthelme Sève
(sometimes written Sèves or Selves, 1788-1860) was a
colonel in Napoléon's Grande Armée. He converted to
Islam after a trip to Egypt in 1816, where he was given
the task of modernizing the country's army, and took
the name Suleiman Pasha. He was inducted into the
Legion of Honor as a Grand Officer by Louis-Philippe
in 1845.

Besson was a French engineer in the service of
Muhammad Ali (also known as Mehmet Ali Pasha,
1769-1849: the Egyptian viceroy best remembered for
his military and economic reforms) responsible for
the arming of newly-built Egyptian ships and training
sailors. Interestingly, in the accounts of the rebuild-
ing of Mohammed Pasha's fleet, there is mention of a
"Monsieur de Cerisy," a naval architect who worked
with Besson in the modernization of the Egyptian
navy.

Horace Vernet's picture of the Massacre of the Mamelukes:
see Plate XXIV.

59   *Vechabites*: another name for the Wahhabis, followers of
the Islamic reformer Muhammad ibn Abd al-Wahhab
(1703-1792).

that famous Czerni-Georges who made war on the Porte:
Czerni-Georges is another name by which Serbian
statesman and military leader Karađorđe Petrović
(1768-1817), the father of modern Serbia, is known.
"Black George," as he was also called, led the first
Serbian uprising against the Sublime Porte of the

Ottoman Empire (one name by which the Ottoman government was known), resulting in the first independent Serbian state, which existed from 1804-1813.

60   *Were you a Pasha with many tails*: pashas indicated their rank and importance by the number of horse tails attached to their standards.

the Chaumière *at Mont-Parnasse*: a beer garden and dance hall, popular with students, located on the Boulevard Montparnasse in Paris's 6th arrondissement on the Left Bank.

61   *a glass of Alicante*: a wine of the Alicante province of eastern Spain.

How Marais, Place Royale, and Île Saint-Louis: the Marais is a historic Parisian district located near the Place Royale, the former name of the Place des Vosges (see note to page 33), and the Île Saint-Louis is an island of the Seine. All are located in the 4th arrondissement (the Marais also extends to parts of the 3rd arrondissement), and were, at the time, the site of highly fashionable aristocratic residences.

62   *Bercy*: former commune to the southeast of Paris that was later incorporated into the city; it is now a neighborhood of the 12th arrondissement, located on the Right Bank.

I have a grey horse already: *gris*, French for "gray," also means "tipsy."

Chosrew Pasha . . . Chaureff you call him here, but in Turkey they call him Cosserev: around 1820, the aforementioned Ali Pasha was involved in a power struggle with the Ottoman Sultan Mahmud II. Hurşid Ahmed Pasha (whom Georges refers to as Chosrew), the former Grand Vizier, was dispatched to quell Ali Pasha's revolt and ultimately had the rebel pasha's severed head sent as a gift to the Sultan.

63   *a little Arnaute maid*: Arnaut, the Turkish name for the Albanians.

64   *Monsieur de Rivière, the ambassador*: Charles François de Riffardeau, Marquis de Rivière (1763-1828), was appointed ambassador to the Ottoman Empire by Louis XVIII, and served in that capacity from 1815-1821. He is perhaps best remembered for his purchase of the Venus de Milo after it was discovered by a peasant on the Aegean island of Milos in 1820.

    The Padishah Mohammed: Mahmud II is meant.

65   *I went straight to Mina . . . I fought for the constitutionalists, etc.*: Francisco Espoz y Mina (1781-1836) was a Spanish general who supported the liberal Spanish Constitution of 1812. He fought against the French when they sought to reinstate the unpopular King Ferdinand VII after he was imprisoned as a result of the 1820 revolution.

66   *The Pasha of Egypt*: Muhammad Ali, the viceroy of Egypt, who ruled from 1805-1848.

67   a burnt rat dreads the mire: "*chaque échaudé craint l'eau froide*" ("everyone who is burned fears cold water") in the original, a play on "***chat** échaudé craint l'eau froide*" ("a burned cat fears cold water"), a close equivalent to the English "once burned, twice shy."

    Corpo di Bacco: Italian, literally "by the body of Bacchus!"

68   *the Civil List*: generally, the money allocated to the royal family by the government.

    there is safety in grumblers: "*abondance de chiens ne nuit pas*" ("an abundance of dogs does no harm") in the original, a play on "*abondance de **biens** ne nuit pas*" ("an abundance of wealth does no harm").

69   *And it becomes you* like a pig in dress boots: "*Et ça vous
     va comme un notaire sur une jambe de bois*" ("and it be-
     comes you like a lawyer with a wooden leg") in the
     original, a play on "*ça vous va comme un **cautère** sur
     une jambe de bois*" ("it becomes you like a cautery on a
     wooden leg:" something that serves no purpose).

     I had learned to box in our French fashion: savate, a style
     of French boxing.

70   No thong, no crupper: "*pas d'argent, pas de suif*" ("no
     money, no tallow") in the original, a play on "*pas
     d'argent, pas de **Suisse***" ("no money, no Swiss"), the
     latter being a reference to Swiss mercenaries. A story
     attached to this proverb tells of a group of these mer-
     cenaries who had been hired to fight by the French; on
     an occasion when they were not paid, they were en-
     couraged to live by pillage instead. When they refused
     to stay and instead headed home, an unknown French
     general is supposed to have coined the above phrase.

     Uscoques: the Uskoks, Hapsburg Croatian pirates that
     operated in the Adriatic Sea during the 16th and 17th
     centuries, and fought primarily against the Ottoman
     Turks.

71   *Zara*: the Italian name for Zadar, a city in modern-day
     Croatia on the Adriatic coast, where marasca cherries,
     the main ingredient in maraschino, are grown.

     do in Turkey as the Turkeys do: "*Il faut ourler avec les
     loups*" ("one must hem with the wolves") in the origi-
     nal, a play on "*Il faut **hurler** avec les loups*" ("one must
     howl with the wolves:" one must follow the pack).

72   Drive nature out with a pitchfork and it comes back in
     a paintbox: "*chassez le naturel, il revient au jabot*" ("drive
     nature out, and it returns in frills") in the original, a
     play on "*chassez le naturel, il revient au **galop***" ("drive
     nature out and it returns at a gallop").

72   *I questioned my Diafoirus*: a reference to Monsieur Diafoirus, a doctor in Molière's final comedy *Le Malade imaginaire* (*The Imaginary Invalid*, 1673).

      the worthy hero of a cock-and-bull story: "*Enfin un de ces gaillards qui n'attachent pas leurs chiens avec des Cent-Suisses*" ("Finally, one of those fellows who do not tether their dogs with the Swiss Guard") in the original, meant as a play on "*ne pas attacher son chien avec des* **saucisses**" ("never tether your dog with sausages").

75   Happiness, *they say*, does not dwell under gilt hoofs: "*le bonheur, comme on dit, n'habite pas sous des nombrils dorés*" ("happiness, as they say, does not dwell in gilded navels") in the original, a play on "*le bonheur se trouve rarement sous les lambris dorés*" ("happiness is seldom found under gilded roofs").

76   Those who live last live longest: "*Plus on est debout, plus on rit*" ("the longer one remains standing, the merrier") in the original, a play on "*Plus on est **de fous**, plus on rit*" ("the madder, the merrier" or "the more the merrier").

78   little dishes make long bills: "*Les petits poissons font les grandes rivières*" ("little fish make big rivers") in the original, a play on "*Les petits **ruisseaux** font les grandes rivières*" ("little streams make big rivers").

79   *Our understandings are twins, if not our soles . . .* But a baker's children are always worst bread: "*Nous sommes confrères en bas . . . mais les cordonniers sont toujours les plus mal chauffés*" ("down there we are brothers . . . but cobblers are always the worst heated") in the original, a play on "*les cordonniers sont toujours les plus mal **chausses***" ("cobblers are always the worst shod").

82   *the belfry of Le Mesnil*: Le Mesnil-Aubry, a commune in the Val d'Oise département, site of L'Église de la Nativité-de-la-Vierge, an early Renaissance church.

extremes bleat: *"les extrêmes se bouchent"* ("extremes become clogged") in the original, a play on *"les extrêmes se **touchent**"* ("extremes meet").

84   All is not told that titters: *"tout ce qui reluit n'est pas fort"* ("all that glitters is not strong"), a play on what Oscar has just said: *"tout ce qui reluit n'est pas **or**"* ("all that glitters is not gold").

the Poule Noire: the Black Hen.

Monsieur Andrieux of the Academy, or Monsieur Royer-Collard: François Andrieux (1759-1833) was a French lawyer, poet, playwright, one of the Council of Five Hundred (see note to page 19), and a member of the French Academy. His best known play is the comedy *Les Étourdis* (*The Scatterbrains*, 1787). He remained politically moderate through the Revolution, the Napoleonic Era, and the Restoration, and is famous for saying to the First Consul: "Citizen Consul . . . you know that we can rely only on that which resists!" when the future Emperor accused him of being antagonistic towards the proposed *Code civil des français*—what would become known as the Code Napoléon. Andrieux was asked to review the manuscript of Balzac's first play *Cromwell* (1819), on which the elder man of letters wrote: "The author should do anything he likes, but not literature."

Pierre Paul Royer-Collard (1763-1845) was a French politician, philosopher, and leader of the Doctrinaires, a party active during the Restoration that endeavored to harmonize the liberties gained under the Revolution with royal power in the form of a constitutional monarchy.

St. Sulpice: the Église Saint-Sulpice is a 17th century Parisian church, second in size only to Notre-Dame, located in what is today the city's 6th arrondissement.

84   for the fountain—of learning—brought forth a mouse: "*l'Ennui naquit un jour de l'Université*" ("one day ennui was born from the University") in the original, a play on "*L'ennui naquit un jour de **l'uniformité**"* ("One day ennui was born from uniformity"), a quote attributed to Antoine Houdar de La Motte (1672-1731), a French playwright.

     the Abbé Frayssinous: Denis-Antoine-Luc, Comte de Frayssinous (1765-1841), was a French bishop, politician, writer, and member of the *Académie française*. He played an important part in restoring France to Catholicism after the Revolution; his *Défense du christianisme* (1825), a collection of his lectures on religion and theology, is his best known work.

85   Kings have been known to harry beggar maids: "*On a vu des rois épousseter des bergères*" ("Kings have been known to dust shepherdesses"—"*épousseter un cheval*," "to groom a horse," is another manner in which the verb is used, possibly referring to Oscar's claim that he often rides with the Comte's son), a play on "*On a vu des rois **épouser** des bergères*" ("Kings have been known to marry shepherdesses").

     Doctor Alibert: Jean-Louis Alibert (1768-1837) was a French doctor specializing in the treatment of skin diseases. He served as royal physician for Louis XVIII and Charles X, and was the founder of the French school of dermatology. He devised his own pictorial system of classifying skin ailments known as *l'Arbre des dermatoses* ("the Tree of dermatosis").

86   *Then the lady keeps her husband in hot water*: "*Cette femme a donc un mari à la coque?*" ("then the lady keeps her husband soft-boiled?") in the original.

     exactly like Arnolphe in Molière's play: a character from *L'école des femmes* (*The School for Wives*, 1662), Arnolphe is a middle-aged gentleman who carefully arranges to have his young ward Agnès brought up in such a way that she will be incapable of being unfaithful to him as a wife and mistress.

killing two-thirds with one bone: "*faire d'une pierre deux sous*" ("to strike two cents with one stone") in the original, a play on "*faire d'une pierre deux **coups***" ("to strike two blows with one stone").

87   *God, Honour, and the Ladies! I saw a melodrama of that name*: *Dieu, l'honneur et les dames* (1815), a three-act play by Jean-Guillaume-Antoine Cuvelier de Trie (1766-1824) based on a novel of the same name by Théodore d'Hargeville.

I know the Keeper of the Seals: the *Grand Sceau de France*, used to affix wax seals to official documents. The image embossed upon the seal varied, as did the high official into whose charge it was given, depending on the period in which it was used. French Kings of the Ancien Régime each had their own unique seal that bore their likeness; during the Revolution the royal seal was destroyed and replaced with one that depicted the goddess of Liberty.

88   *That is what I call* a great lie and little wool: "*Voila qui s'appelle faire plus de fruit que de besogne*" ("That is called making more fruit than work") in the original—"fruit" in this case meaning "effect" or "result"—a play on "*faire plus de **bruit** que besogne*" ("to make more noise than work").

The mother of mischief is no more than a midge's sting: "*Chacun pèche pour son serin*" ("Everyone sins for their canary") in the original, a play on "*Chacun **prêche** pour son serin*" ("Everyone preaches to their canary").

the wood of Carreau: an area of the forest of L'Isle-Adam.

88   *the great forest of Saint-Martin*: most likely the Forest of
       Carnelle, a massive wooded area extending east from
       Presles that lies adjacent to the town of Saint-Martin-
       du-Tertre to the south.

89   When you take to your heels you can't take too much:
       "*Quand on prend du talon on n'en saurait trop prendre*"
       ("When one takes the heel one cannot take too much"),
       a play on "*Quand on prend du **galon** on n'en saurait trop
       prendre*" ("When one takes the braid"—or "when one
       gets promoted"—"one cannot take too much," ren-
       dered more familiarly in English as "One can never
       have too much of a good thing").

90   play a dog a bad game and slang him: "*qui veut noyer
       son chien l'accuse de la nage*" ("whoever wishes to drown
       his dog accuses him of swimming") in the original,
       a play on "*qui veut noyer son chien l'accuse de la **rage**"
       ("whoever wishes to drown his dog accuses him of
       having rabies").

92   Never throw the candle after the shade: "*il ne faut ja-
       mais jeter la manche après la poignée*" ("one should never
       throw the handle after the handful") in the original,
       a play on "*il ne faut jamais jeter le manche après la **cog-
       née**" ("one should never throw the handle after the
       hatchet").

93   *the Louis XV style . . . like those on the colonnades of the
       Place Louis XV*: square of Paris's 8th arrondissement
       adorned with many fountains and statues, built in
       honor of the monarch whose name it bears. Today it
       is more commonly known as the Place de la Concorde
       (see note to page 3).

95   *Chauvry*: commune of the Val-d'Oise département.

103   *a future diplomat must surely have* a seat—to his trousers:
       "*un futur diplomate doit être en fonds . . . de culotte*" in the
       original. To be "*en fonds*" usually means to be "in the

money," but it can also mean "in bottoms," in this case the seat of Oscar's *culotte* or trousers.

A coat to dine saves wine: "*Deux habits valent mieux qu'un*" ("Two outfits are worth more than one"), a play on "*deux **avis** valent mieux qu'un*" ("two opinions are worth more than one"—"two heads are better than one").

106   *the Rue Saint-Martin*: Parisian street that runs through what are today the 3rd and 4th arrondissements, named for Saint-Martin-des-Champs, a Priory which was converted into the National Conservatory of Arts and Crafts during the Revolution.

111   An empty stomach knows no peers: "*Ventre affamé n'a pas d'orteils*" ("an empty stomach has no toes") in the original, a play on "*ventre affamé n'a pas **d'oreilles***" ("an empty stomach has no ears)".

113   A trouncing for a bouncing: "*Schlague pour blague*" ("a blow for a jest") in the original.

119   *In the eyes of the commoner sort, bringing home prizes from school is positive proof of future success in life . . . the fourth accessit*: it is perhaps not surprising that the author would take the opportunity presented by this dialogue to comment on school prizes, considering how poorly he fared as a student. At the Collège de Vendôme, the young Balzac was often sent to a place of punishment known as "the alcove" for not completing his lessons. Though he spent many long hours there by himself, he made good use of his time by reading books acquired from the school's extensive library, and perused works on chemistry, physics, history, religion, and philosophy. Significantly, the young captive also showed an especial interest in dictionaries. A fictionalized account of this experience appears much later in the *Comédie* in the novel *Louis Lambert*.

the fourth accessit: honorable mention.

123   *Rue des Bourdonnais*: Parisian street of the 1st arrondissement.

     the Cocon d'Or: the Golden Cocoon.

124   *And now the Camusots are* Ultras: short for Ultra-royalist, the Ultras were a faction unsatisfied with the constitutional monarchy of Louis XVIII, and wanted France to return to the pre-Revolutionary order.

     in 1793 when its owners were ruined by the maximum: in April 1793 during the Reign of Terror, the Committee of Public Safety instituted a law whereby a maximum price was set on goods; as a result, the maximum price was always charged. The existence of a thriving black market also served to undermine the law, and it was abandoned some eight months later.

125   *one of the first houses just above La Courtille . . . the Barrière de La Courtille*: La Courtille was an area near Belleville known for its taverns and dance halls. Because the upper area of La Courtille was located outside the Mur des Fermiers généraux, a wall built for the collection of tolls on goods entering Paris, the establishments there were exempt from having to pay the taxes. *The Barrière de La Courtille*, also known as the Barrière de Belleville, was the nearby gate in the Mur des Fermiers généraux, located at the intersection of the Boulevard de Belleville and the Rue du Faubourg-du-Temple. It was located in what is now the 11th arrondissement of Paris, but like most of the wall, it is no longer standing.

     one of the race of frisky Gérontes *. . . who played the part of Turcaret*: Géronte is the name given to a stock character in French theater that has its origins in the Italian Commedia dell'arte. He is generally a wealthy but miserly old fool and father figure. Turcaret, a greedy financier, is the eponymous character of a 1709 satirical play by Alain-René Lesage (1668-1747), a French novelist and playwright.

126   *the Gaîté theatre*: the Théâtre de la Gaîté was a Paris theater established by French actor and director Jean-Baptiste Nicolet (1728-1796) in 1759 on the Boulevard du Temple, which specialized in vaudevilles and circus performances. It began as the Théâtre de Nicolet, but after performing for Louis XV the company became known as *Grands-Danseurs du Roi*. The advent of the Revolution saw its name changed to the Gaîté for political reasons. The theater building itself was rebuilt a number of times before being obliged to move to the Rue Papin in 1862 due to the city-wide renovation of Paris by Baron Haussmann.

the Constitutionnel . . . *the refusal of rights of burial*: Le *Constitutionnel* was a liberal daily newspaper that promoted Bonapartism and anticlericalism. It began as *L'Indépendant* in 1815 under Joseph Fouché, 1st Duc d'Otrante (1759-1820), a French politician and Minister of Police. The periodical was banned for its views on at least five separate occasions, but each time was quickly revived under a different name. In addition to politics, the paper also focused on literary matters, and with *Revue de Paris* founder Louis Véron (1798-1867) as editor, published works in serial form by Balzac (including *Cousin Bette, Cousin Pons, Colonel Chabert*, and others), George Sand, Eugène Sue, and other illustrious writers of the day.

Anticlerical sentiment unleashed by the Revolution did not disappear with the Restoration of the monarchy and the full reinstatement of Catholicism as the official state religion of France. A growing number of Frenchmen had begun to request secular burials, much to the displeasure of the Catholic Church, which had traditionally controlled sanctified burial grounds and had refused to bury non-Catholics there.

Piron . . . Collé: Alexis Piron (1689-1773) was a French playwright and rival of Voltaire; his best known work is the five act comedy *La Métromanie, ou le Poète* (1738) about the young bourgeois Damis who is seized with

La mère Godichon.

Plate XXV

the urge to write verse (hence the title), and flees Paris for the countryside, where he hopes to be able to follow his muse without interference.

Charles Collé (1709-1783) was a French comedic playwright whose best known works are *La Vérité dans le vin* (*Truth in Wine*, 1747) and *La Partie de chasse de Henri IV* (*The Hunting Party of Henry IV*, 1763).

126   *the high priest of the religion of Lisette*: an imaginary female character that appears in a number of the aforementioned Béranger's songs.

La Mère Godichon: a French folk character of uncertain origin whose name could perhaps be translated as "Little Mother Nincompoop," as *godichon* is a diminutive of *godiche*, a word used to describe someone who is foolish or clumsy. She appears to be the subject of a number of bawdy songs by different authors, so in the absence of further information, the exact song Monsieur Cardot is singing is unclear. See Plate XXV.

127   the *Cadran-bleu*: the Blue Dial.

132   *the Faubourg du Roule*: the Quartier du Faubourg-du-Roule, a neighborhood of what is now the 8th arrondissement, home to the famous Champs-Élysées as well as the Rue Fortunée where Balzac lived (beyond his means) in a grand house at No.18 with his wife Ewelina Hańska (1805-1882). The newly married couple were together there less than a year when Balzac, plagued with multiple ailments, died on 18 August 1850. The street became the Rue Balzac shortly thereafter, and the author's widow stayed at the residence until her death.

133   *the Rue de Béthisy* (sometimes written Béthizy): former Parisian street that ceased to exist in 1852 after the expansion of the Rue de Rivoli, which is today located in the 1st and 4th arrondissements. It is remembered as the scene of two assassination attempts, the second

one successful, against Huguenot leader Gaspard II de Coligny.

134   *see that he learns the Code*: the Code Napoléon.

141   *Attorney to the Châtelet*: prosecutor at the Grand Châtelet, a castle that contained a court of justice and numerous prison cells, located on the Right Bank near the northern bridge to the Île de la Cité. It was demolished after the Revolution.

the parish church of Saint-Séverin: the Église Saint-Séverin is a Catholic Church of Paris's 5th arrondissement in the Quartier Latin, located on the Left Bank, named for the 6th century hermit Séverin de Paris.

142   *the fatal year 1792*: the year that saw the first use of the guillotine, the storming of the Tuileries Palace, the arrest of Louis XVI, the September Massacre of Catholic bishops and priests, and the beginning of the French First Republic.

the Kingdom of Basoche: a derisive nickname for the legal profession or "legal fraternity" of pre-Revolutionary France. The word *"basoche"* can be traced to the Latin word "basilica," where lawyers traditionally practiced.

the Church of Saint Etienne-du-Mont: the Église Saint-Étienne-du-Mont, a Parisian church constructed in sections between 1494 and 1624. It is located in the 5th arrondissement on the Montagne Sainte-Geneviève, a hill on the Left Bank. Marat, Pascal, and Racine are buried in the church's cemetery.

143   *Rolland's, a restaurant in the Rue du Hasard*: the Rue du Hasard ("the street of chance," named for the well-known betting house there) was a street of the 1st arrondissement that ceased to be when it became an extension of the nearby Rue Thérèse in 1880; Roland's

appears to have been an actual restaurant on the Rue du Hasard at No. 6, possibly established on the site of the former gambling den.

from the singing of laudes *in clerkly modes*: Latin, praises.

Talma in Britannicus *at the Théâtre Français*: François-Joseph Talma (1763-1826) was a celebrated French actor, famous for his portrayals of Nero in Racine's *Britannicus* (1669), Augustus in Corneille's *Cinna* (1639), and many others. As a close personal friend of Napoléon's, there was some speculation that Talma had given the First Consul some lessons in public speaking and had shown him how to comport himself in a commanding and imperial manner.

Known variously as the Théâtre-Nautique, the Théâtre de la République, La maison de Molière, and most commonly as the Comédie-Française, the Théâtre Français was founded by Louis XIV in 1680. Since 1799 it has been housed in the Salle Richelieu, a hall in the Palais Royal in the 1st arrondissement.

inter pocula: Latin, "during a drinking bout" or "between cups."

144   *the* Dive Bouteille: the Divine or Holy Bottle, the name given to the oracle that Panurge seeks to consult on the subject of marriage in Rabelais's *Gargantua and Pantagruel*.

the Cheval Rouge on the Quai Saint-Bernard: the *Cheval Rouge* or the Red Horse was the name of an unimpressive eatery located on the Quai Saint-Bernard, a road of the 5th arrondissement that follows the Seine by its Left Bank. The restaurant was used as the meeting place for a secret literary society devised by Balzac, primarily for the purpose of promoting his own work with the help of literary journalists Théophile Gautier, Jules Sandeau, Léon Gozlan, and others; the members were supposed to meet upon receiving a card emblazoned with a red

horse. Gautier fondly recalled this rather comical experience with the *Société du Cheval Rouge* (which only
ended up meeting five or six times) in his study of
Balzac published in 1858.

144   *pies* au jus romanum . . . *a toast* Agaricibus: food that
is served "au jus" means "in its own juices" or "with
gravy;" "*ius romanum*," or "*jus romanum*" as it is sometimes written, is Latin for "Roman law." "*Agaricibus*"
is the Latin word for "mushroom;" a "toast *Agaricibus*"
is therefore "mushrooms on toast."

145   *the Boulevard du Temple*: Paris boulevard located on the
Right Bank that now forms the boundary between the
3rd and 11th arrondissements.

146   *Themis*: a Greek Titaness, the personification of Law
and Order.

148   *at the Rocher de Cancale*: "the Rock of Cancale," a Parisian
restaurant, at that time located at No. 59 on the Rue
Montorgueil. Founded by the Breton cook and restaurateur Baleine in 1780, it was especially renowned for
its fresh oysters (the commune of Cancale in Brittany
was known for its extensive oyster beds). Many of
Balzac's characters visit this fashionable establishment
throughout the *Comédie*.

Pontins: the Pontine Marshes.

149   *She likes to laugh, she likes to drink, she likes to sing as
we do*: the lyrics are actually from the drinking song
"Fanchon" usually attributed to Antoine-Charles-Louis
de Lasalle (1775-1809), the brilliant and reckless French
cavalry general, though Béranger did make use of the
tune for "*Le Vieux Drapeau*" ("The Old Flag," 1820), a
patriotic song that became the unofficial anthem of the
July Revolution (see first note to page 157).

Coulon's dancing school: Jean-François Coulon (1764-1836), a famous French dancer and instructor.

the Rue Pastourelle . . . the Rue de Crussol: Parisian streets. The former is located in what is now Paris's 3rd arrondissement on the Right Bank; it is named for Roger Pastourel, a 14th century member of parliament. The latter is located in what is now the 11th arrondissement, named for Alexandre-Charles-Emmanuel de Crussol (1743-1815), a deputy to the Estates-General for the nobility and a Peer of France. He died shortly after voting for the execution of the aforementioned Michel Ney at the Marshal's trial for treason.

150   *Old Cardot, with his* ailes de pigeon: "pigeon's wings," the curled earlocks that appear on some styles of powdered wigs.

he placed his protégée under Vestris . . . Les Ruines de Babylone: Auguste Vestris (1760-1842), a French dancer and dance instructor, considered to be the best dancer of his generation, as was his father, Gaétan Vestris (1729-1808); both were known as *"le dieu de la dance"* (the god of dance) in their day.

René Charles Guilbert de Pixérécourt (1773-1844), known as the "Corneille of the boulevards," was a French playwright, theater director, and author of the highly successful *Ruines de Babylone* (1810), an exotic Eastern-themed melodrama.

156   *James II's daughter . . . , etc.*: Mary II of England who, along with her husband William III, deposed her father James II in the Glorious Revolution of 1688.

157   *that overthrow of the nobility of which the bourgeoisie then had visions, to be realised in 1830*: the final years of Louis XVIII's life and the succession of Charles X saw the gradual erosion of liberties gained from the Charter of 1814 (see note to page 54) as well as an attempt to restore the old pre-revolutionary order. The

July Monarchy of Louis-Philippe, the "Citizen King," a more moderate constitutional monarchy than that of Louis XVIII, began with the July Revolution of 1830 and lasted until 1848.

157 *The wine was worthy of Borrel, who had at that time succeeded the illustrious Balaine*: Percet Borrel, French restaurateur, the owner of the aforementioned Rocher de Cancale.

Inter pocula aurea restauranti, qui vulgo dicitur Rupes Cancali: "Between golden cups at the restaurant commonly known as the Rock of Cancale."

158 *as drunk as Pitt and Dundas*: a reference to British Prime Minister William Pitt the Younger and his Home Secretary and close friend Henry Dundas, 1st Viscount Melville (1742-1811), who were both known to attend sessions of the House of Commons while drunk, hence the expression.

the Barrière du Trône . . . the Boulevards to the Rue de Vendôme: the "Barrier of the Throne," also known as the Barrière de Vincennes, was a tollhouse on the Avenue du Trône consisting of two gatehouses topped by tall columns, located in what are today the 11th and 12th arrondissements.

The Rue de Vendôme, known as the Rue Béranger since 1864, was a street of what is today Paris's 3rd arrondissement, named for French general Philippe de Bourbon, the 4th Duc de Vendôme (1655-1727). The first home of Lucien and Coralie de Rubempré, characters in Balzac's *Lost Illusions*, is located on the Rue de Vendôme.

159 *the clerks woke to find themselves in Armida's Palace*: a Muslim sorceress, a character in Tasso's *Gerusalemme liberata* (1581) who falls in love with her enemy, the crusader Rinaldo, and imprisons him for a time in a magical garden.

a melodrama at the Porte-Saint-Martin called La Famille d'Anglade: the *Théâtre de la Port Saint-Martin,* which specialized in the presentation of comedies and ballets, was built in 1781 to accommodate the *Académie Royale de Musique,* whose previous home had been destroyed by fire; French playwright Frédéric Dupetit-Méré's (1785-1827) *La Famille d'Anglade* was first performed there on 11 January 1816.

Balzac's drama *Vautrin* premiered at the Porte-Saint-Martin on 14 March 1840.

162 *Cardot orders everything from Chevet*: Chevet was a florist who was obliged to turn his talents to cooking in the wake of the Revolution, and later went on to become a highly successful chef and restaurateur.

171 *Monsieur Joli-Cœur*: literally "Mister Pretty-Heart," a "smooth talker," or "one who plays at being Romeo."

173 *the École Polytechnique*: to this day considered to be one of the finest schools of its type in the world, the *École Polytechnique* is a French engineering school founded in 1794.

the Church of Saint-Paul: the Église Saint-Paul-Saint-Louis, located on the Rue Saint-Antoine in what is now Paris's 4th arrondissement. The 17th century church was designed and built by Jesuit architects at the behest of Louis XIII; during the Revolution, the church was appropriated by the atheistic Cult of Reason, which was in turn replaced by Robespierre's Cult of the Supreme Being. Catholicism was reinstated in France by the Concordat of 1801.

174 *the Dauphiness*: at that time, Marie Thérèse de France (1778-1851), the daughter of Louis XVI and the wife of Louis Antoine, Duc d'Angoulême (1775-1844), the heir apparent. She and her husband reigned as King and Queen of France for twenty minutes after the abdication of the Duc's father, Charles X, before he

too abdicated and was exiled as a result of the July Revolution of 1830.

175   *the best of all Republics*: a phrase used by Lafayette to describe the July Monarchy of Louis-Phillipe.

the fight at the Macta: the Battle of Macta, which took place on 28 June 1835 in Algeria, where retreating French forces under the command of General Camille Alphonse Trézel (1780-1860) were attacked and put to flight by tribal fighters led by Emir Abd al-Qadir (1808-1883).

177   *one of the victims of Fieschi's machine*: Giuseppe Fieschi (1790-1836) was a Corsican soldier and would-be assassin of King Louis-Philippe. His *"machine infernale"* was composed of twenty or twenty-five gun barrels, attached to a frame, which could be triggered simultaneously. It was fired from the window of a house on the Boulevard du Temple on 28 July 1835, slightly injuring the King and members of his entourage, but killing the eminent Marshal Mortier. Eighteen bystanders were also killed and dozens wounded, including Fieschi himself. He and his accomplices were promptly arrested, tried, and guillotined.

the Hirondelle de l'Oise: "the swallow of the Oise."

180   *this sort of Grey Sister*: les Sœurs de la Charité de l'Hôpital Général de Montréal are a Canadian order of Catholic nuns founded by Marie-Marguerite d'Youville in 1738, so-called not because of the color of their habits, but rather because of the founder's late husband, who was a bootlegger. The women were mocked as *"les sœurs grises"* since *"gris"* in French can mean both "grey" and "tipsy." The name was kept as a sign of humility.

181   *Saint-Laurent*: the Saint-Laurent Enclosure was a site near the Rue du Faubourg-Saint-Denis originally utilized as an outdoor fair and theater, and later repurposed to serve as a marketplace.

183   *the famous centrier*: an archaic and somewhat insulting
       name for a deputy who sits in the middle of a legisla-
       tive body and votes with the ministers.

184   *the Society of L'Espérance*: the Society of Hope, a trust
       company.

Albert Savarus

Balzac had considered entitling this novel *Casimir Savarus* or
De la vie et des opinions de M. Savaron de Savarus (*The Life and
Opinions of Monsieur Savaron de Savarus*) before settling on
simply *Albert Savarus*. The story first saw print as a newspaper serial in *Le Siècle* that ran from 29 May-11 June 1842. It
appeared in book form in the first volume of the 1842 Furne
edition as the tenth work of the *Comédie*. A second version appeared with chapter divisions under the title *Rosalie* alongside
stories by other authors in the multi-volume story collection
Les Mystères de province published by Souverain in 1843. The
definitive Pléiade edition restores the work's original title,
and places it in the seventh position.

Rosalie's character was originally named Philomène after
some remains discovered in the Roman Catacombs of Priscilla
in 1802 that were taken (erroneously) to be those of a virgin
martyr from the early Christian era. Philomena soon came to
be considered a saint, a designation that would be contested
in later years, and news of miracles associated with her rel-
ics spread throughout Italy and France during the 1830s. A
deleted sentence from *Albert Savarus* reveals that Philomène/
Rosalie was born in 1817, prior to the time when the cult of the
saint came into being. Though a minor anachronism, Balzac
decided to change the character's name to Rosalie for the sake
of historical accuracy.

However, there may have been an additional motivation
for Balzac in changing the character's name. Balzac's biog-
raphers have generally seen *Albert Savarus* and *"L'Ambitieux
par amour,"* the *mise en abyme* or story within a story contained within the main narrative, as a disguised account of
Balzac's prolonged and troubled courtship of his eventual
wife, the Polish Countess Ewelina Hańska (1805-1882) (see
plate XXVI). Commentators have noted parallels between

Plate XXVI: *Ewelina Hańska* (1835)
by Ferdinand Georg Waldmüller

Plate XXVII: *Endymion. Effet de lune* (1791)
by Anne-Louis Girodet de Roussy-Trioson

Balzac's and Savarus's appearance, his difficulties in politics, and so forth; additionally, the author is said to have first beheld Madame Hańska at a window just as Rodolphe, Savarus's fictional self, first spies Francesca, who is meant to be the fictional Duchesse d'Argaiolo. Madame Hańska was unhappily married to Polish nobleman Wacław Hański (1782-1841), a man more than twenty years her senior, and in *Albert Savarus* they parallel the Duchesse d'Argaiolo/Princess Francesca Gandolphini and the Duc d'Argaiolo/Prince Émilio Gandolphini, respectively. Hański was actually on friendly terms with Balzac, even though the author had secretly proclaimed undying love to his wife as early as 1833. After the Polish gentleman's death in 1841, Balzac and Hańska hoped to marry, but were met with strong disapproval from her family, who did not want the French commoner to be in a position to inherit her late husband's estate. Though the two were married some nine years later, shortly before Balzac himself died, there was continued resistance from Hańska's family, in particular from her aunt Countess Rozalie Rzewuska, whom Balzac felt had become his "sworn enemy." This biographical detail would seem to link the Countess with Philomène/Rosalie, provide the true reason for the change of name, and may explain the unusually harsh fate Balzac inflicts on the character at the novel's end.

The Real World	*Albert Savarus*	"Ambition for Love's Sake"
Balzac	Albert Savarus	Rodolphe
Ewelina Hańska	Duchesse d'Argaiolo	Francesca Gandolphini
Wacław Hański	Duc d'Argaiolo	Émilio Gandolphini
Rozalie Rzewuska	Philomène/Rosalie	

Albert Savarus, then, can be seen as a roman à clef in which "*L'Ambitieux par amour*" is perhaps not only the plot device by which Philomène/Rosalie learns of her mysterious newcomer's relationship with the Duchesse d'Argaiolo, but also a means by which Balzac gives the reader cause to suspect that, if there is a second layer to the story, that there may be yet another: one that is taking place in the real world.

195   To Madame Émile de Girardin: Delphine de Girardin
       (1804-1855), the daughter of novelist Sophie Gay, was
       a French writer and salonnière, or salon hostess, who
       published under the pen name Charles de Launay. Her
       husband (1806-1881), a French journalist and politi-
       cian, was the founder of the daily newspaper *La Presse*.
       Although Madame de Girardin wrote novels, short
       stories, plays, and poems, she is perhaps best remem-
       bered for her *Lettres Parisiennes*, possibly the earliest
       example of what would come to be known as a "gos-
       sip column," which appeared as a weekly feature in
       La Presse from 1836 to 1839, and were later collected
       in 1843. Her salon was frequented by Dumas (père),
       Gautier (see second note to page 144), Hugo, Liszt,
       Musset, Sand, and many other distinguished artists;
       she was also one of Balzac's closest friends. The French
       poet Lamartine (whom Balzac mercilessly parodied in
       the character of Canalis in his novel *Modeste Mignon*)
       christened her "the Tenth Muse."

197   *under the Restoration*: see second note to page 19.

       the Grand Siècle: in France, the period of 17th century
       is known as "the Grand Century."

       Comté: La Franche-Comté.

       an escutcheon of pretence: in the parlance of heraldry
       known as blazon, an escutcheon of pretence, also called
       an inescutcheon, is a smaller shield placed in front of
       the main shield on a coat of arms.

198   The following is a translation of a sentence deleted by
       Balzac from the end of the second paragraph: "Hence
       the name Philomène which had been imposed on her
       daughter, born in 1817, at a time when the cult of this
       or that saint had become a kind of religious mania in
       Italy and a standard for the Jesuits (for in the beginning
       one could not always know for certain to which sex the
       skeleton belonged)."

Rupt *is obviously derived from* rupes: a Latin word meaning "rock," "cave," or "precipice."

199 *the composition of the Royal Court since 1830; virtually every one of the Legitimists had resigned*: see first note to page 157. In France at the time of the July Monarchy, the Legitimists were a royalist faction that did not accept the rule of "Citizen King" Louis Philippe as he was of the Orléans line, adjunct to the House of Bourbon, and therefore in violation of the traditional rules of succession. However, after the abdication of Charles X and his son in 1830 (see note to page 174), there was disagreement among the Legitimists as to who was the rightful ruler, and divisions within the movement led to its decreasing influence until 1848.

201 God save the King . . . *a tune written by Lulli for the chorus of* Esther *or of* Athalie: the tune of the national anthem of the United Kingdom, while of uncertain authorship, was almost certainly not written by French composer Jean-Baptiste Lully (1632-1687), whom Balzac would appear to be confusing with one of his contemporaries, Jean-Baptiste Moreau (1656-1733). Lully had worked with Racine in composing music for at least one of his plays, but it was with Moreau that the famous dramatist had written music for the tragedies *Esther* (1689) and *Athalie* (1691); both composers were also members of the court of Louis XIV, perhaps adding to the author's confusion.

a Frenchwoman, the notorious Duchess of Portsmouth: Louise de Kérouaille (1649-1734), one of Charles II of England's mistresses, for whom the title was created—there was never a "Duke of Portsmouth"—and which ceased to exist after her death.

Pothier and Brunet in Les Anglaises pour rire: Charles Potier (1774-1838) and Jean-Joseph Mira, known by his stage name Brunet (1766-1853), were French comic actors; *Les Anglaises pour rire* (*English Ladies for a Joke*, 1814) was a vaudeville written by the playwrights

Sewrin (Charles-Augustin Bassompierre, 1771-1853) and Théophile Marion Dumersan (1780-1849) that premiered at the Théâtres des Variétés in Paris on 26 December 1814. The play has Potier and Brunet, both in drag, poking fun at the habits, manners, and dress of the Englishwomen of the day.

201 *The* incroyable, *the* merveilleux, *the* élégant, etc.: these three French words, each of which have their obvious cognates in English, in this case refer to a segment of society that came into existence following Robespierre's execution and the end of the Reign of Terror. In the more relaxed environment that prevailed under the Directory, surviving members of the aristocracy and the middle class began wearing extravagant or risqué clothing, affecting exaggerated mannerisms, and attending wild parties. Gentlemen known as *incroyables*, descended from anti-Jacobin gang members known as *muscadins* (so-called because of the cologne they wore), would typically wear ridiculously high collars, coats with long tails that reached the ground, and tight trousers; their feminine counterparts, the *merveilleux*, would often be seen wearing gauzy, revealing dresses in the Greco-Roman style. In later years, the *incroyables* and *merveilleuses* were succeeded by similar modes such as the *élégants, petits-maîtres, fashionables, gandins, cocodès, petits-crevés*, and so forth. It is likely that the excesses of these various groups were somewhat exaggerated by the press and in retrospect, and none of the various subcultures were ever widespread.

The lionne *is due to the famous song by Alfred de Musset, etc.*: the lines quoted ("In Barcelona have you seen . . . My mistress she, my lioness!") are from a poem entitled "L'Andalouse" ("The Andalusian"), which appears in Musset's *Premières Poésies 1829-1835*.

202 *at the time of the Spanish occupation . . . Cardinal Granvelle*: the eastern Franche-Comté region, where the city of Besançon is located, was Spanish territory before it was

taken by France during the War of Devolution (1667-8); it was subsequently returned to Spain under the treaty of Aix-la-Chapelle, then regained by France as a result of the Franco-Dutch War.

Antoine Perrenot de Granvelle (1517-1586) was a powerful Bisontin (the name given to a native of Besançon) cardinal and politician in the service of Holy Roman Emperor Charles V, also noted for his extensive art collection.

the end of the Rue Neuve: former Besançon street of La Boucle, the city's historical center, later renamed the Rue Charles Nodier (see below).

205 *the Clermont-Mont-Saint-Jean, the Beauffremont, the de Scey, and the Gramont families*: the first is a branch of the House of Clermont-Tonnerre, a noble family from Dauphiné in southeastern France that dates back to the 11th century, whose most well-known member is Jacques de Clermont-Mont-Saint-Jean (1752-1827), a French Major General and deputy for the nobility to the *États généraux* (States-General) in 1789.

The Beauffremonts trace their lineage to the Dukes of Burgundy from the Holy Roman Empire in the early 13th century; the Scey-sur-Saône is a branch of this family that began in the 14th century.

The House of Gramont hails from French Basque country in southwestern France; the family's connection to the area of Besançon probably dates to the 17th century when several of its members were appointed bishop of that diocese.

Nodier: Charles Nodier (1780-1844) was a French writer of fantastic tales (see note to page 32) and member of the Académie française, to whom Balzac dedicated *The Rabouilleuse*. The two are buried near one another in Paris's Père Lachaise Cemetery.

Prince Talleyrand: the "Prince of Diplomats," as he was known, Charles Maurice de Talleyrand-Périgord, 1st

Prince de Bénévent (1754-1838), was a highly skilled French statesman who served in governments before, during, and after the Revolution, despite their widely disparate politics and aims.

206   *the little* Gazette . . . *the great* Gazette, *and the* Patriot, *which frisked in the hands of the Republicans*: *La Gazette*, also known variously as *La Gazette nationale de France*, *Le Peuple français*, *L'Étoile de la France*, and the *Gazette de France*, was France's first weekly periodical founded by French physician and journalist Théophraste Renaudot (c.1586-1653) in 1631 with the backing of Cardinal Richelieu. Largely an instrument of the government, the paper did not report the storming of the Bastille, and in later years served the legitimist cause; its final issue was printed on 30 September 1915.

Le Gazettin, or "little *Gazette,*" was a supplement of the *Gazette de France* that reported on the proceedings of the National Constituent Assembly of 1789.

Le Patriote franc-comtois was, as its name suggests, a liberal paper of the Franche-Comté based in Besançon.

a leading article of the school of the Charivari: *Le Charivari* was a satirical daily paper, founded by French journalist and caricaturist Charles Philipon (1800-1861) in 1832, remembered for its political cartoons that took aim at King Louis-Philippe and the middle classes, often inviting censorship and fines from the government; it ceased publication in 1937.

the *Revue des Deux Mondes*: a monthly literary journal founded in 1829 by French newspaper editor François Buloz (1803-1877), which has continued publication until the present day and is Europe's oldest magazine. Chateaubriand, Dumas, Musset, and Sand are a few of the famous 19th century literary figures whose works have appeared in its pages. Balzac's *L'Enfant maudit* (*The Accursed Child*), a novel that forms a later part of the *Comédie*, appeared in the *Revue*'s January 1831 issue.

208 *geography from Guthrie . . . the four rules*: the book is *New Geographical, Historical and Commercial Grammar* (1770) by Scottish historian William Guthrie (1708-1770); it argues that the superiority of Europe over the rest of the world is due in large part to its beneficial geography and climate. It was translated into French in 1801.

The four rules or *"les quatre règles de l'arithmétique:"* addition, subtraction, multiplication, and division.

the *Lettres édifiantes*: The *Lettres édifiantes et curieuses* (*Curious and Enlightening Letters*, 1702-1776) was a collection of letters written by Jesuit missionaries who were stationed in distant and exotic locations such as China, India, and the Americas.

213 *Saint-Pierre*: the Église Saint-Pierre de Besançon, a church designed by French architect Claude-Joseph-Alexandre Bertrand (1734-1797) that was completed in 1786.

214 *Monsieur Berryer*: Pierre-Antoine Berryer (1790–1868) was a French lawyer, orator, and legitimist politician, the only one to remain a deputy after the July Revolution. He became a member of the Académie française in 1852.

219 *so well shown by Molière in the character of Agnès*: see second note to page 86.

225 the *Revue de l'Est*: *The Eastern Review.*

to Dôle . . . to Salins . . . Bourg, Nantua: Dôle is a commune of the Jura département in eastern France; Salins is the name of several communes, but in this context probably refers to Salins-les-Bains in the Jura département; Bourg is included in the name of many communes, but most likely refers to the Bourg now known as Bourg-en-Bresse, located in the Ain département in eastern France; Nantua is also a commune of the Ain département.

225   *the districts of Le Bugey, La Bresse*: Le Bugey is a histori-
       cal area in the Ain département containing the city
       of Nantua; La Bresse is a French region and former
       province to the west of the Jura, containing the city of
       Bourg-en-Bresse.

227   *Fluelen . . . the Lake of the Four Cantons*: the former, usu-
       ally written as Flüelen, is a Swiss commune located to
       the southeast of Lake Lucerne in the canton of Uri; the
       latter is another name for Lake Lucerne.

228   *the pretty hamlet of Gersau*: Swiss commune located on
       the northern shore of the eastern leg of Lake Lucerne
       in the canton of Schwyz.

231   *Lovelace . . . Richardson has given it to a creation whose
       fame eclipses all others*: a reference to the epistolary nov-
       el *Clarissa* (1748) by Samuel Richardson; the character
       Robert Lovelace is a duplicitous gentleman who seeks
       to undermine the eponymous heroine's virtue.

       *His Excellency Count Borromeo of Isola Bella and Isola
       Madre in the Lago Maggiore*: The House of Borromeo is
       a historically significant aristocratic family from Milan
       that can be traced back to at least the 15th century; its
       most well-known members were both cardinals: Saint
       Carlo Borromeo (1538-1584) and Federico Borromeo
       (1564-1631). The former was canonized by Pope Paul V
       in 1610, the latter appears in Manzoni's *I Promessi Sposi*
       (*The Betrothed*, 1827), where he is portrayed as a deeply
       spiritual and beneficent figure.
           Noted for their palazzos and gardens, Isola Bella and
       Isola Madre are two of the Borromean Islands, owned
       by the family since the 16th century. They lie in the
       western arm of Lago Maggiore, a lake which stretches
       from the canton of Ticino in Switzerland to the town
       of Arona in present-day Italy.
           The Count Borromeo that Balzac mentions in "Am-
       bition for Love's Sake," is perhaps meant to be Count
       Gilberto V Borromeo Arese (1751-1837), under whose

stewardship the islands became a highly desirable destination for important figures from all over Europe.

233 *to Brunnen and to Schwytz*: the former is a Swiss commune located on the eastern edge of Lake Lucerne; the latter, sometimes written as "Schwyz," is the capital of the canton of the same name.

Italian refugees . . . outlaws in fear of the Austrian or Sardinian police: beginning in the 1820s, anyone suspected of harboring nationalistic sentiments for a greater Italy (a country which did not come into being until 1871) would have been arrested by the authorities of those countries opposed to the creation of a new unified state; at that time, Switzerland was frequently used as a refuge by Italian patriots, some of whom belonged to secret societies such as the Adelfia, the Filadelfia, and the Carbonari.

234 *Nel lago con pietra!*: "Into the lake with a stone!"

237 *Zitto!*: "Silence!"

238 *the three revolutions in Naples, Piedmont, and Spain*: in 1820 the Kingdom of the Two Sicilies, sometimes known as the Kingdom of Naples, was the scene of an uprising against Ferdinand I (1751-1825) led by Guglielmo Pepe (1783-1855), an Italian general and Carbonaro; the King was forced to accept a constitution, but a year later the rebellion was quashed by the Austrians and Ferdinand restored to the throne.

In 1821, the Italian patriot Santorre di Santa Rosa (1783-1825) was at the forefront of a revolution in Piedmont, at that time part of the Kingdom of Sardinia, but it, too, was put down by Austrian forces.

Rafael del Riego y Nuñez (1784-1823) was a Spanish general who led a revolt in 1820 against Ferdinand VII in the hopes of restoring the liberal Constitution of 1812. The King was forced to accept the constitution, and a period known as the *Trienio Liberal* or the Three

Liberal Years ensued. However, in 1823 France intervened on the side of the King and Riego was captured, found guilty of treason, and executed.

239 *the Spielberg*: a 13th century fortress located in Brno, Czech Republic, today known as Špilberk Castle. During the time of the Austro-Hungarian Empire it was used as a prison, primarily for enemies of the state. The Italian writer Silvio Pellico (1789-1854), imprisoned for his patriotic views, wrote about his experiences there in *Le mie prigioni* (*My Prisons*, 1832).

242 *Povero mio!*: "Poor me!"

243 *E denaro!*: "and money!"

244 *La cara patria*: beloved country.

I played one in Paris under the Empire, with Bourrienne, Madame Murat, Madame d'Abrantès: Louis Antoine Fauvelet de Bourrienne (1769-1834) was a French diplomat remembered for his *Mémoires* (1829-1831) in which he describes (perhaps in not entirely accurate terms) his friendship with Napoléon; Caroline Bonaparte (1782-1839) was one of Napoléon's younger sisters and wife of Joachim Murat, the King of Naples; Laure Junot, Duchesse d'Abrantès (née Permon), was a French memoirist, wife of General Junot, and one of Balzac's mistresses (see the prefatory note to *The Vendetta*).

245 *Che avete, signor?*: "Is that you, sir?"

247 *Vevay*: Vevey, a Swiss commune located on the north shore of Lake Geneva.

in a house at Eaux-Vives: a district of Geneva and former commune in the canton of the same name.

the Villa Diodati: a manor house in Cologny, a Swiss commune located on the left bank of Lake Geneva, remembered as the site of Mary Shelley's "waking dream" that served as the inspiration for her novel *Frankenstein*.

Geneva is anxious to do nothing to displease the Holy Alliance to which it owes its independence: in the wake of the Napoleonic Wars, the Holy Alliance was formed between Russia, Austria, and Prussia at the Congress of Vienna (1814-1815) for the purpose of countering any further revolutionary activities in Europe; Switzerland, which had endured French occupation under Napoléon, had its territory enlarged, its neutrality recognized, and was returned to its former status as a free confederation by provisions of the Final Act of the Congress of Vienna.

Coppet and Ferney: the former is a Swiss commune located on the western edge of Lake Geneva, home to Madame de Staël and one of her famous literary salons.

Ferney, known as Ferney-Voltaire since the Revolution (it was home to the famous philosopher from 1759 to 1778), is a French commune of the Ain département which lies near the Swiss border, close to Geneva.

the Cercle des Étrangers: the "Circle of Foreigners," a gaming-house in Geneva, perhaps named after a more famous and exclusive establishment in Paris.

250   *the famous quartet*, Mi manca la voce: *mi manca la voce, mi sento morire* ("I miss the voice, I feel like dying"), a composition by Rossini from his opera *Mosè in Egitto* (*Moses in Egypt*, 1818).

Oimè!: Alas!

256   *The Villèle ministry*: Jean-Baptiste de Villèle (1773-1854) was the Ultra-royalist statesman made Prime Minister by Louis XVIII in 1822, a position he held until

1827 when he was succeeded by the more moderate Martignac.

256   *at Naples, where the Prince and Princess had been reinstated in their place and rights on the King's accession*: Balzac is likely referring to Francis I of the Two Sicilies (1777-1830), who inherited the throne from his father upon his death in 1825.

        the storm of July 1830: see first note to page 157.

261   *Belgirate*: northern Italian town located near the Swiss border on the southeastern shore of Lago Maggiore.

263   *They suffer what Napoléon suffered, etc.*: 10 August 1792 was the date that a revolutionary mob attacked the Tuileries Palace where Louis XVI and the royal family had been residing, under surveillance, after being forcibly removed from Versailles. On 13 Vendémiaire (5 October 1795) Napoléon, who had seen the King's Swiss Guards defeated while defending the Tuileries from the mob some three years before, ordered Joachim Murat, then a sub-lieutennant, to muster artillery for the defense of the National Convention, which was under attack by Royalist forces. This being done, Napoléon was able to utilize his cannons well enough to defeat a significantly larger force—the famous "whiff of grapeshot" episode that Carlyle describes in *The French Revolution* (1837).

        the deserted alleys of the Bois de Boulogne: a park located in Paris's 16th arrondissement on the Right Bank of the Seine .

264   *Saint-Merri*: the *Église Saint-Merri* is a small Parisian church of the Rue Saint-Martin that was the site of intense skirmishes between Republicans and supporters of the July Monarchy.

269   *as the words* Mene, Tekel, Upharsin, *did in the eyes of Belshazzar*: the "writing on the wall" from the Book of Daniel (5:25-30) that foretold the death of Belshazzar and the fall of the Babylonian Empire.

271   *Qual pianto*: literally "what tears," perhaps better translated in this context as "how sad."

      the Scala: the *Teatro alla Scala,* a world famous Italian opera house located in Milan.

      Is it the Tedeschi *that you regret?*: the plural form of *Tedesco,* the Italian word for "German."

272   *O mia cara diva*: "Oh my dear diva."

273   *cavaliere servente*: literally an "obliging knight," a swain who is openly in love with a married woman and attends to her every whim.

275   *the matter of the two railways to Versailles*: in 1836, concessions were granted for the building of two railway lines from Paris to Versailles. The line traveling from the Right Bank in Paris, known as the *Rive Droite,* was financed by James Rothschild (1792-1868) and Émile Pereire (1800-1875); it was completed in 1839. The line traveling from the Left Bank in Paris, known as the *Rive Gauche,* was financed by brothers Benoît (1792-1858) and Achille Fould (1800-1867); plagued by financial and construction problems, it opened in 1840. There was not enough traffic between the cities to warrant more than one line, but the two firms were nonetheless intent on competing for passengers at any cost.

277   *the Dent de Vilard*: the Dent du Villard, a mountain of the French Alps.

283   *your Faubourg Saint-Germain*: a traditionally wealthy Paris neighborhood of today's 7th arrondissement, located on the Left Bank of the Seine, in the area

surrounding the Boulevard Saint-Germain; it takes its name from Saint-Germain-des-Prés, a Benedictine abbey built in the 6th century.

286   *the Dauphin and Dauphine*: see note to page 174.

Monsieur de Chavoncourt is a Royalist, of the famous 221: at the time of the Restoration and the July Monarchy, the Chamber of Deputies was the lower house of the French Parliament, a body made up of 402 members who were elected to five-year terms by census suffrage. The *Deux-Cent-Vingt-et-Un*, as they were known, were the number of deputies that formed the Chamber's liberal majority; the Address of the 221, given to Charles X on 18 March 1830, was a response to a speech the King had given on 2 March in which he strongly affirmed his intent to retain the full authority of the crown. In their address, the liberal majority expressed displeasure at the actions Charles X had taken in opposition to the elected majority, specifically his replacement of the moderate Prime Minister Jean Baptiste Gay, Viscount de Martignac (1778-1832), with the Ultra-royalist Prince Jules de Polignac (1780-1847). To say then that the fictional Monsieur de Chavoncourt is both a Royalist *and* a member of the liberal majority would seem to be an error on Balzac's part.

287   *Granvelle*: the Palais Granvelle, a Renaissance palace in Besançon built by Nicolas de Granvelle Perrenot, an advisor to Charles V and the father of Antoine de Granvelle Perrenot.

288   *the Rue de Grenelle*: a Parisian street of the 6th and 7th arrondissements named for the village to which it led.

292   *What a glory for Provence to have found a Mirabeau . . .*, etc.: probably a reference to Adolphe Thiers, the French historian, journalist, lawyer, and statesman who served as Prime Minister during the July Monarchy on two separate occasions.

299   *the elder branch*: the House of Bourbon, senior to the Orléans line to which constitutional monarch Louis Philippe belonged.

      The Duc de Fitz-James is to be nominated at Toulouse: Édouard de Fitz-James, the 5th Duc de Fitz-James (1776-1838), was a French politician who served as aide-de-camp and first gentleman of the chamber to the future Charles X. A former Peer of France (see second note to page 17), he was later elected deputy for Toulouse's 2nd arrondissement in 1835.

308   *like that called the tomb of Héloïse at Père-Lachaise*: *Le cimetière du Père-Lachaise*, located in Paris's 20th arrondissement on the Right Bank, is the city's largest cemetery, where Balzac and numerous other illustrious Frenchmen are buried.

      Primarily as a means of attracting clientele to an otherwise sparsely populated cemetery, the remains purported to be those of Pierre Abélard and Héloïse d'Argenteuil were brought to Père-Lachaise from the museum of French archaeologist Alexandre Lenoir (1761-1839) in 1817 and placed in a Gothic-styled tomb, which to this day receives visitors (lovelorn and otherwise) from around the world.

317   *a ball given annually after 1830 for the benefit of the pensioners on the old Civil List*: see note to page 68.

The Vendetta

The Corsican *Romeo and Juliet* story *La Vendetta* was completed at the beginning of 1830 while Balzac was in Paris assisting his mistress, the Duchesse d'Abrantès (1784-1838), with her *Mémoires de l'Empire*. The novel was originally divided into a prologue and four chapters entitled "The Workshop," "Disobedience," "The Wedding," and "The Punishment." It was first published (at least in part) in an April issue of *La Silhouette*, a weekly illustrated newspaper. Further versions appeared in book form as part of an early two volume *Scenes from Private Life* in 1830, and in an expanded four volume edition in 1832; in both cases it was placed at the beginning of the collection following the preface. Subsequent editions of 1835, 1839, and 1842 dispensed with chapter titles and saw some minor modifications to the story. The Furne edition of 1842 has the story as the fourth work of the *Comédie*, while the definitive French Pléiade makes it the eighth.

Balzac, who was wont to borrow his plots freely from other sources, quite possibly took his inspiration for *La Vendetta* from Prosper Mérimée's "*Mateo Falcone*," a similarly-themed short story set in Corsica, which had been printed in the *Revue de Paris* in 1829 (See Appendix III).

321   *Dedicated to Puttinati, Sculptor at Milan*: Alessandro Puttinati (1801-1872), who carved a marble statuette of the author as a gesture of friendship.

326   *Lannes*: Jean Lannes, 1st Duc de Montebello, 1st Sovereign Prince de Sievers (1769–1809), was one of Napoléon's bravest and most able generals who was made a *Maréchal d'Empire*, the highest military distinction in France. A close friend of the Emperor, Lannes was one of the few men who was allowed to address him in a familiar fashion.

327   *I went off at once into the* mâquis: (usu. written without the circumflex) a word derived from the Italian "*macchia*" ("scrub"), which in this case refers to regions of dense vegetation in Corsica, often on high ground, that have traditionally provided a hiding place for bandits and mercenaries.

328   *But for me your mother would never have reached Marseilles*: Maria Letizia Buonaparte (née Ramolino, 1750-1836), known by the title of *Madame Mère de l'Empereur*, and the other members of the Bonaparte family fled Corsica in 1793 when the insurgent island briefly came under English influence (the *parti anglais* or English Party) as the autonomous Anglo-Corsican Kingdom.

330 *as Herbault had for bonnets, Leroy for dresses, and Chevet for dainties*: Herbault was a fashionable milliner who always insisted on selecting or designing the bonnets for his many customers without their input; Leroy was a dressmaker responsible for much of Empress Joséphine's highly ornate wardrobe, which typically consisted of uncomfortable costumes embellished with much lace and embroidery; see note to page 162 for Chevet.

333 *the secret of the young Ultras*: see note to page 124.

334 *she was very good to those young ladies during the Hundred Days*: see note to page 20.

Eccola: "here she is!"

335 *the arrest of Labédoyère*: Charles Angélique François Huchet de La Bédoyère (1786-1815) was a French General, formerly an aide-de-camp to the aforementioned General Lannes, who as colonel was one of the first officers, along with the forces under his command, the 7th Regiment of the Line, to abandon the army of the recently restored Louis XVIII in support of Napoléon upon his return to Paris from exile on Elba. The Emperor showed his gratitude by making him a *Maréchal de camp* and *General de Brigade*. La Bédoyère distinguished himself at the Battle of Waterloo, but after Napoléon's defeat, he was caught returning to Paris in an attempt to bid farewell to his wife and child before a planned escape to America. He was court-martialed and executed on 19 August 1815 at the age of 29.

339 *the Imperial Eagle*: the standard of Napoléon's *Grande Armée*, a small bronze figure of an eagle attached to the top of the regiment's flagpole. Losing the Eagle in battle brought disgrace to the entire regiment, and its members were expected to fight to the death in its defense.

341   *some national* canzonetta: a popular Italian song similar
       to a madrigal.

342   *as charming as the* Endymion, *Girodet's masterpiece*:
       Anne-Louis Girodet de Roussy-Trioson (1767-1824)
       was a French Romantic painter renowned for his por-
       traits of Napoléon and Chateaubriand; he was Balzac's
       favorite painter, and is mentioned frequently through-
       out the *Comédie* (see Plate XXVII).

345   *I know Marshal Feltre*: Henri-Jacques-Guillaume Clarke,
       1st Count of Hunebourg, 1st Duke of Feltre (1765–
       1818), was a French Major General, politician, and
       Napoléon's Minister of War, a position he also held
       under Louis XVIII until 1817.

346   *the Abbé Vertot*: I have laid my siege: René-Aubert Vertot
       (1655-1735) was a French historian who tended to fa-
       vor dramatic effect over factual information in his
       writings; when offered some additional documenta-
       tion on the siege of the Greek island of Rhodes for
       his *Histoire des chevaliers hospitaliers de Saint-Jean de
       Jérusalem* (*History of the Knights Hospitallers*, 1727) he is
       said to have responded "*Mon siége est fait*," which has
       been interpreted by his successors as a statement of
       disinterest in any information that did not fit into his
       conception of history.

349   O Dio! Chi non vorrei vivere dopo averla veduta!: "O
       God! Who would not live after having seen her!"

351   *the retreat from Moscow . . . the passage of the Berezina*:
       after Napoléon's failed invasion of Russia, his *Grande
       Armée* was forced to retreat across the Berezina River,
       where it took heavy casualties at the hands of pursu-
       ing Russian forces, though the French did manage to
       escape complete destruction. The word *Bérézina* in
       French is sometimes used to describe any undertaking
       that ends in complete disaster.

359   *the ribbon of the Legion of Honour*: see note to page 20.

Daru, Drouot: Pierre-Antoine-Noël-Mathieu Bruno Daru (1767-1829) was a French soldier, statesman, man of letters, and cousin of Stendhal.

Comte Antoine Drouot (1774-1847), nicknamed *"Le sage de la Grande Armée,"* was one of Napoléon's generals specializing in the use of artillery.

the catastrophe of Fontainebleau: the Treaty of Fontainebleau (1814), whereby Napoléon agreed to unconditionally abdicate as Emperor of France after being defeated by the armies of the Sixth Coalition. He was exiled to Elba, given sovereignty over the small Mediterranean island, and allowed to keep his title.

362 *like the old woman whom Schnetz introduces into the Italian scenes of his genre pictures . . . a second Mrs. Shandy*: Jean-Victor Schnetz (1787-1870) was a French academic painter and pupil of David remembered for his historically-themed paintings.

Elizabeth Shandy is the unremarkable mother of the title character in Laurence Sterne's *Tristram Shandy*.

like a sultana valideh: the title given to the mother of the reigning Sultan in the Ottoman Empire.

369 *a soldier who fought quite close to the Emperor at Mont-Saint-Jean*: see note to page 58.

385 *l'autre*: "the other," a reference to Napoléon.

387 *the* beltà folgorante *of the young man . . . the daydreams of* far niente: "dazzling beauty" and "doing nothing," respectively.

395 *the despairing kisses which friends gave each other in 1793*: a reference to the Reign of Terror, a period of mass executions, usually by guillotine, orchestrated by the radical Jacobins against members of French Royalty, the moderate Girondins, and any other perceived enemies of the Revolution.

Appendix I:
Journey by *Coucou*

Laure Surville's short story was not published until 1854 when it appeared in her collection *Le Compagnon du foyer*, some four years after her brother's death (see the above note for *A Start in Life*).

405   *Claye, a village located six leagues from Paris*: Claye-Souilly, a commune of the Seine-et-Marne département in the Île-de-France region, located about 17 miles to the east of Paris.

407   lapin: see note to page 9.

       Villeparisis: commune of the Seine-et-Marne département in the Île-de-France region. Balzac lived in Villeparisis in his youth; a park there is named after him.

408   *the Rue des Nonandières . . . the Rue Saint-Martin*: the Rue des Nonnains-d'Hyères, located in what is today Paris's 4th arrondissement on the Seine's Right Bank, named for the order of Benedictine nuns that used to reside in an abbey there. See note to page 106 for Rue Saint-Martin.

       his local Staub: Jean-Jacques Staub (d.1852) was a highly fashionable Swiss tailor. Balzac mentions him in *Lost Illusions* when Lucien de Rubempré pays him a visit.

408   C'est la faute de Voltaire, c'est la faute de Rousseau: see second note to page 43.

411   *the Faubourg Saint-Martin*: a former Parisian suburb that lies to the north of the Porte Saint-Martin, located on the Right Bank, in what is now the 10th arrondissement.

       the mounds of Chaumont and Romainville: Buttes-Chaumont is an area north of Belleville which was the site of a stone and gypsum quarry. It is now the Parc des

Buttes-Chaumont in Paris. Romainville is a commune to the east of Paris in the Seine-Saint-Denis département at the eastern end of the hill of Belleville.

412   *the Spanish War*: the Franco-Spanish War of 1823, which restored King Ferdinand VII to the throne after a French invasion.

413   *the taking of Trocadéro*: Spanish fort protecting the city of Cadiz, taken by the French in the aforementioned war on 31 August 1823.

414   *Bondy*: commune of the Seine-Saint-Denis département, located in Paris's northeastern suburbs.

415   *Livry*: Livry-Gargan, also of the Seine-Saint-Denis département.

        the Grand Prix de Rome: a highly competitive art scholarship for emerging artists (initially in just painting and sculpture before expanding to include other disciplines) founded by Louis XIV in 1663. Winners would attend the French Academy in Rome for a period of up to five years at the King's expense. Watteau, David, Vernet, and Girodet were some of the more noteworthy painters to win this scholarship.

418   *the tune* Partant pour la Syrie: "Leaving for Syria." The music was composed by Hortense de Beauharnais (1783-1837), Napoléon's stepdaughter, and the lyrics written by Alexandre de Laborde (1773-1842), a French archaeologist and politician. The song tells of the crusader Dunois, who is awarded the hand of the beautiful Isabella for his bravery. The song was inspired by the Egyptian Campaign of 1798-1801, and served as a kind of national anthem during the Second Empire of Napoléon III.

427   *the young lion from the Grande Chaumière*: see second note to page 60.

428   *a graceful Lovelace of the faubourgs*: see note to page
        231.

429   He will reward each according to his works: Matthew
        16:27.

Appendix II:
Mateo Falcone

Prosper Mérimée's short story made its first appearance in
the 3 May 1829 issue of the *Revue de Paris* with the subtitle
"*Mœurs de la Corse*" or "Manners of Corsica." It was collected along with some of the author's other stories in *Mosaïque*
(*The Mosaic*, 1833). Mérimée did not visit Corsica until 1839
and so necessarily relied on secondary sources for information, some of which probably romanticized the customs of
the island, even though the tradition of the vendetta (which
continues to the present day in some areas) was reportedly
responsible for the deaths of as many as two percent of the
Corsican population during the mid-19th century.

Mateo Falcone was the inspiration for a 1907 opera of the
same name by Russian composer César Cui.

433   *Porto-Vecchio*: known as *Portivechju* in Corsican, Porto-
        Vecchio is a French commune (except for a brief period,
        Corsica has been part of France since 1770, see note to
        page 328) located on the island's southeastern shore,
        noted for its fine harbor.

434   *Corte*: French commune located in the north central
        region of Corsica. Corte was the capital of the island
        under Pasquale Paoli (1725-1807), the Corsican patriot
        and statesman.

435   *the corporal*: corporals were formerly the chief officers
        of the Corsican communes after they had rebelled
        against the feudal lords. Later the name was sometimes
        given to a man who, by his property, his connections,
        and his clients exercised influence and a kind of effec-
        tive magistracy over a *pieve*, or canton. By an ancient
        custom Corsicans divide themselves into five castes:

gentlemen (of whom some are of higher, *magnifiques*, some of lower, *signori*, estate), corporals, citizens, plebeians, and foreigners.

an ambush of Corsican soldiers: "*une embuscade de voltigeurs corses*" in the original. Voltigeurs were a body raised by the government which acted in conjunction with the gendarmes in the maintenance of order. The uniform of the voltigeurs was brown with a yellow collar.

436   *there are no more cartridges in your* carchera: a leather belt which served the joint purpose of a cartridge box and pocket for despatches and orders.

442   *Good day, brother*: the ordinary greeting of Corsicans.

Selected Bibliography
and Further Reading

The original uncorrected French texts for the stories in this volume can be found online at the following URLs:

Un début dans la vie (A Start in Life):
http://fr.wikisource.org/wiki/Un_début_dans_la_vie

Albert Savarus:
http://fr.wikisource.org/wiki/Albert_Savarus

La Vendetta
http://fr.wikisource.org/wiki/La_Vendetta

Balzac, Honoré de. *La comédie humaine. Première partie, Études de moeurs. Premier livre, Scènes de la vie privée. Tome I.* Paris: les Bibliophiles de l'originale, 1965.

——————————. *La comédie humaine. Première partie, Études de moeurs. Premier livre, Scènes de la vie privée. Tome IV.* Paris: les Bibliophiles de l'originale, 1965.

——————————. *Oeuvres illustrées de Balzac. Les Deux poètes. Un grand homme de province à Paris. La Femme abandonnée. Ève et David. Facino Cane. Albert Savarus. Le Réquisitionnaire. Le Message. Le Martyr calniste. La Confidence des Ruggieri. Les Deux rêves. Melmoth réconcilié. Séraphita. Le Bal de Sceaux.* Paris: Marescq et Cie, 1852.

——————————. *Oeuvres illustrées de Balzac. Le Médecin de campagne. Adieu. Le Curé de village. La Bourse. Les Chouans. Un drame au bord de la mer. Mémoires de deux jeunes mariées. La Maison du Chat-qui-pelote. Un début dans la vie. Maître Cornélius.* Paris: Marescq et Cie, 1852.

——————————. *Oeuvres illustrées de Balzac. La Peau de chagrin. El Verdugo. Louis Lambert. L'Élixir de longue vie. Massimilla Doni. Gambara. L'Enfant maudit. Les Proscrits. La Femme de trente ans. La Grande Bretêche. Béatrix. La Grenadière. La Vendetta. Une double famille.* Paris: Marescq et Cie, 1852.

——————————. *At the Sign of the Cat and Racket.* London: J.M. Dent and Co., 1895.

511

Balzac, Honoré de. *La Grande Bretêche and Other Stories*. London: J.M. Dent and Co., 1896.

——————————. *A Marriage Settlement and Other Stories*. London: J.M. Dent and Co., 1897.

Diaz, José-Luis. "Un début dans la vie." *Balzac. La Comédie humaine*. Le Groupe International de Recherches Balzac-iennes/La Maison de Balzac/ARTFL. 9 Jan. 2011. <http://www.v1.paris.fr/commun/v2asp/musees/balzac/furne/notices/debut_dans_la_vie.htm>

Floyd, Juanita Helm. *Women in the Life of Balzac*. Austin: Holt, Rinehart & Winston, 1921.

Fournier, Édouard. *Énigmes des Rues de Paris*. Paris: E. Dentu, 1860.

France, Peter. *The New Oxford Companion to Literature in French*. Oxford: Oxford University Press, 1995.

Gerson, Noel B. *The Prodigal Genius: The Life and Times of Honoré de Balzac*. New York: Doubleday, 1972.

Keim, Albert and Louis Lumet. *Honoré de Balzac*. New York: Frederick A. Stokes Company, 1914.

Lawton, Frederick. *Balzac*. New York: Wessels, 1910.

Mérimée, Prosper. *Novels, Tales and Letters, Vol. III: The Mosaic and Other Tales*. New York and Philadelphia: Frank S. Holby, 1906.

Mousnier, Roland. *The Institutions of France Under the Absolute Monarchy, 1598-1789: The organs of state and society*. Chicago: The University of Chicago Press, 1984.

Raser, George B. *Guide to Balzac's Paris: An Analytical Subject Index*. Choisy-le-Roi: Imprimerie de France, 1964.

——————————. *The Heart of Balzac's Paris: A Rationale of Condition.* Choisy-le-Roi: Imprimerie de France, 1970.

Robb, Graham, *Balzac: A Biography.* New York: W.W. Norton & Company, 1994.

Sandars, Mary F. *Honoré de Balzac, His Life and Writings.* London: J. Murray, 1904.

Surville, Laure. *Le Compagnon du Foyer.* Paris: D. Giraud, 1854.

Terrasse-Riou, Florence. "La Vendetta." *Balzac. La Comédie humaine.* Le Groupe International de Recherches Balzaciennes/La Maison de Balzac/ARTFL. 9 Jan. 2011. <http://www.v1.paris.fr/commun/v2asp/musees/balzac/furne/notices/vendetta.htm>

——————————. "Albert Savarus." *Balzac. La Comédie humaine.* Le Groupe International de Recherches Balzaciennes/La Maison de Balzac/ARTFL. 9 Jan. 2011. <www.v1.paris.fr/commun/v2asp/musees/balzac/furne/notices/albert_savarus.htm>

Zweig, Stefan. *Balzac.* New York: The Viking Press, 1946.

CPSIA information can be obtained
at www.ICGtesting.com
Printed in the USA
BVHW082132190619
551452BV00007B/166/P